The Way to Cape May

KIMBERLY BRIGHTON

D1595750

Published in the United States of America by Cape Island Publishers

CapeIslandPublishers.com

Library of Congress Control Number: 2023903589

Paperback ISBN: 979-8-9879070-0-9

Ebook ISBN: 979-8-9879070-1-6

This book is dedicated to my parents, the first true loves of my life. Your love for one another is unlike anything I've witnessed in any romance, real or imagined.

I love you both to Cape May and back!

IT IS WITH GREAT HONOR

Delaney &
Dalton

TOGETHER WITH THEIR FAMILIES

JOYFULLY INVITE YOU TO
THEIR WEDDING

saturday, june seventeenth
6:00 pm
the beach at
Congress Hall Resort

COCKTAIL HOUR AND RECEPTION TO FOLLOW

Wedding Party

Parents of the Bride
FAYE AND JOSEPH

Parents of the Groom
CLAIRE AND GEORGE

Maid of Honor
KATE

(Sister of the Bride)

Best Man
ALEX

(Brother of the Groom)

Bridesmaids
NORA

(Sister of the Groom)

CLEO

(Friend of the Bride)

TORI

(Friend of the Bride)

Groomsmen
RYAN

(Cousin of the Groom)

JORDAN (JJ)

(Brother of the Bride)

SPENCER

(Friend of the Groom)

Flower Girl
MAISIE

Ringbearer
LUKE

Thursday, June 8

COUNTDOWN
TO WEDDING
9 DAYS

Delaney

DELANEY ROSS RUSHED ALONG THE NARROW SIDE streets of Center City Philadelphia toward the Criminal Justice Center, where a judge was about to render a decision in the most important case of her career. The judge was known for berating tardy attorneys, so she had to get there before he emerged from his chambers and ripped her a new one.

The race was on.

She was two blocks away when she suddenly found herself airborne. Her briefcase took off on a flight of its own, slamming into the head of an unsuspecting passerby.

"What the hell!" the man screamed.

Delaney touched down on all fours at the corner of Twelfth and Spruce, while one of her stilettos, stuck between two cobblestones, mocked her from nearly half a block away.

"Son of a bitch," she muttered. She'd walked out of her own shoe. Flown, more like it.

She tried to stand, but the narrow hem of her pencil skirt showed no mercy. Her only hope was to crawl to the nearest sturdy object—in this case, a bus shelter—to hoist herself up. She knew better than to request assistance from any of the day-dwelling city zombies stepping over her as they went about their business. She could have set herself on fire and no one would have flinched.

Except for the obscenity-spewing briefcase victim marching toward her.

"Oh. You," he sneered, looking down at her. "I should have known."

Delaney ignored him as she crawled to the shelter like a newborn giraffe trying to stand.

He continued. "You can beg and crawl all you want, Ross, but I'm not dropping charges, especially after that vicious attack."

Delaney glanced up at the amused expression of her opposing counsel, Assistant District Attorney Wells Abernathy III. Who, mercifully, held out his hand and helped her up.

She hobbled—one leg four inches higher than the other—back to the offending shoe, tugging and freeing it from its mortared grasp. The heel was still affixed but wobbly at best.

Great. She'd have to hopscotch to court on one foot. Could this day get better?

Wells handed her the felonious briefcase and chuckled. "I should keep this weapon as evidence of your wanton disregard for human life."

"Funny, you calling yourself human," Delaney said, wincing at the pain in her left knee.

"I wasn't the one crawling on all fours."

Delaney smoothed her espresso-hued French twist, glared at him, and brushed by without a word.

He fell into step beside her. She hobbled faster. Wells kept pace.

"Is this a race? Don't bother, Ross. You don't have a leg to stand on. Or shall I say shoe?"

"Buzz off, Wells. Aren't there any other women you could be accosting right now?"

"How about your friend Cleo?" he asked, waggling his eyebrows.

"She wouldn't be caught dead with someone like you."

"How can you be so certain?"

"Her frontal cortex is fully intact."

Delaney usually enjoyed their competitive and strictly professional (now, anyway) relationship. She respected him as an attorney and a prosecutor, but not when he'd been instrumental in jamming up her innocent client with a bogus murder rap.

"It's not too late to withdraw your motion," he said.

"Withdraw this." She flipped him the bird.

"No wonder I broke up with you. Way too competitive."

"Have you suffered a recent blow to the head?" She chuckled at her own joke. "Oh, yeah. You did. And it was the other way around."

"Rewrite history if you must. I have to say, though, your hope for a positive outcome on this case is amusing. No way the judge is ruling in your favor."

"We'll see about that."

Delaney picked up speed and the two hobble-raced the rest of the way. They reached the large glass doors of the courthouse in a decided tie and shuffled in with the horde of justice-involved humanity. She was just grateful her heel didn't snap off, or she may have had to hitch a piggyback ride from him.

The courtroom was abuzz with spectators and participants. Delaney juked a byline-hungry reporter who tried to tackle her into an interview, until she finally made it to the court's end zone beyond the rail separating lawyers from the rest of the world.

She found her two interns waiting at counsel table. Marley handed her a notepad while Sam poured water into a glass from a stainless-steel pitcher.

"Please tell me that's prosecco," she joked as she took the glass.

"Well, if anyone can turn water into wine, it's Sam," Marley said.

"How about water into a Band-Aid?" Sam pointed to her knee. "Your leg's bleeding!"

"I'm fine." Delaney waved him off and grabbed a tissue from the box on the table to blot it. "I just bumped into something."

"The side of a bus?" Sam chuckled. "It hurts me just to look at it."

"The judge should be out in a few. Is there anything you need us to do?" Marley asked.

"Pray for a miracle," Delaney said, handing Marley her phone and briefcase. "And, listen, however this turns out, I appreciate all the work you both put into this case."

"Our pleasure, boss. We'll be back here if you need us," Sam said as their client was led to the table by a deputy sheriff.

The interns found seats in the gallery. Delaney began jotting notes in preparation for the decision when Marley returned a few seconds later.

"It's Dalton," she said, handing Delaney her phone.

"I'll call him later."

"He says it's urgent."

Delaney sighed. She knew better than to take a call in a courtroom, but Dalton, unaware she was back in court, would probably keep calling until she answered.

"Sup?"

Cradling the phone between her ear and shoulder, she flipped a page of her notepad.

Dalton's serenading voice flooded her ear as he began singing "Chapel of Love."

Delaney smiled through mounting annoyance. "Dalton—"

"Listen," he said. "I've been calm, cool, and collected, but we need to make a final decision about the menu. Are we going with the charcuterie table or a cheesesteak bar?"

Dalton had been neither calm, cool, nor collected. In fact, he'd embraced his wedding duties with such freewheeling enthusiasm, he'd transitioned from a mild-mannered, non-opinionated groom into a rip-roaring, unbridled Groomzilla. Almost overnight.

She'd had no choice but to get Dalton involved in last-minute details. She'd been working on a major post-conviction relief case through the Innocence Project. Newly discovered evidence suggested her client, who'd been convicted of murder, wasn't the perpetrator. She and her team had presented a motion to the court that morning requesting a new hearing based on the evidence, which, if successful, could ultimately result in the dismissal of charges. With her client's life hanging in the balance, Delaney couldn't focus on anything else, including the wedding.

Enter Dalton, whose only task was simply to tie up a few loose ends. Instead, he unraveled and retied them into big, fancy bows.

First, it was the guest list. What began as an intimate affair became a grandiose gala after he added ten coworkers, twelve frat brothers, and his entire college football offensive line. He also dissed the DJ they'd decided upon, hiring his friend's band instead with a drunkenly scribbled (yet legally enforceable) contract on a cocktail napkin. Then, it was the tuxes. Dalton tried on twenty before he found "the one." Who knew tux selection could single-handedly make or break the entire event? (*Spoiler*: Groomzillas know.)

Now here he was, trying to trump her charcuterie board with cheesesteaks. Enough was enough.

Dalton began singing again about going to the chapel and getting married, when the thick wooden door to the judge's chambers burst open and a looming, black-gowned figure emerged. Dispensing with formalities, Delaney shoved the phone in her lap and ended the call.

Or so she thought.

"All rise!"

Delaney leaped from her seat, forgetting her phone was a projectile waiting to happen. And boy, did it happen. She watched, horrified, as it flung from her lap and skidded across the marble floor. She shot a look at the judge to see if he noticed. He didn't, or so it seemed.

Bullet = dodged.

"Be seated," the tipstaff instructed.

The rustling of sitting bodies subsided, and the room fell silent. The judge cleared his throat and—

From the phone on the floor of Courtroom 1A, the serenading voice of Delaney's betrothed filled the eerily silent room.

Delaney gasped. She hadn't ended the call.

She'd put it on speaker.

Staring straight ahead, she pretended not to hear Dalton's pitch-perfect refrain, or the fact that, for this rendition, he'd added the word "cheesesteaks" to the lyrics. She surreptitiously slid her stilettoed foot forward, hoping to pull the phone closer, but only managed to kick it farther away, and closer to the judge.

Dalton continued crooning.

The judge peeled off his glasses and glared into the gallery.

"Whoever's going to the chapel for cheesesteaks better silence that phone immediately," he barked.

And now, a moral dilemma: fetch the phone and fess up, or freeze and feign ignorance *in re:* ownership of said phone?

Retrieving it would be an absolute admission of guilt and a potential death knell for her case. As an attorney, she was expected to be a zealous advocate for her client, and fessing would fling her client, and their case, under the judicial bus.

Then again (light bulb!) she could swivel dramatically in her chair and cast a Stern Look toward the gallery in an Oscar-worthy performance as Innocent and Mildly Disgusted Attorney. She'd been cast as the lead in her high school musical and felt confident in her acting chops, a necessary skill for any litigator. Surely she could cast convincing blame on another.

But as an attorney, she was considered an officer of the court with an ethical duty to tell the truth, the whole truth, and nothing but the truth—so help her the Supreme Court of Pennsylvania Disciplinary Board.

She opened her mouth and prepared to hurl herself on the mercy of the court.

"I'm sorry, Your Honor," came a voice from behind her.

Delaney swiveled in her chair as Marley breezed through the swinging half door and rushed forward, auburn curls bouncing with determination. "This is my phone," she proclaimed.

Marley swooped down to retrieve the phone and froze when the judge scowled at her. She stared back, emerald eyes wide, as if she were Bambi in the middle of a NASCAR track and had just realized the risk she'd taken. Nonetheless, she held her composure, along with her bowels, and with the confidence of a person thrice her age, said, "With all due respect, Your Honor, I beg the court's forgiveness."

Then she half curtsied like a court jester and hightailed it out of the courtroom—juggling her files, the phone, and the huge set of cojones she'd just earned.

Gratitude coursed through Delaney's veins. Marley Maguire was the best intern an attorney could hope for, and Delaney vowed to pay her back, big time, for throwing herself on the sword of judicial disdain. With a brand spankin' new Beamer. Or something. Maybe just lunch.

The judge spoke. "In the matter of *Commonwealth versus Rupert James*, after consideration of the motion filed by the defendant, the Commonwealth's response and legal arguments of counsel, I hereby find the defendant is entitled to an evidentiary hearing."

"Yes!" Sam exclaimed.

Internally, Delaney shared Sam's enthusiasm but made a mental note to remind him he was on a legal team, not a cheer squad.

"Thank you, Ms. Ross," Rupert said, voice cracking as his eyes filled with tears. Her client shook her hand with vigor. "You've given me hope."

The judge continued. "Due to the serious nature of the

charges and the public scrutiny of this case, I'm scheduling this hearing for my nearest available date, which is..."

The judge flipped through his calendar. "Monday, June twenty-sixth."

Delaney tried to register the date. June what? It was already June, so it was happening soon. Why did that date seem familiar?

"I'm assuming both parties will be ready to go?" the judge asked.

Without missing a beat, the assistant district attorney leaped to his feet and announced with magnanimous aplomb, "Yes, sir. The Commonwealth will be ready."

Wells tried to nail the role of Prosecutor Who Just Won His Case, but failed. While his performance may have fooled most, it didn't Delaney, who caught the flicker of defeat flash across his face. The ruling was a setback for the hotshot prosecutor with aspirations to someday become Philly's top law enforcer.

But why did it also look like he was gloating?

"June twenty-sixth it is." The judge banged his gavel and barked, "Court is hereby dismissed."

"My God," Delaney said, as she looked down at her planner and confirmed her fears.

It was smack dab in the middle of her two-week honeymoon.

The judge rose. "Is there something defense counsel wishes to say?"

She shot a look at Wells, hoping he'd throw her a bone and reconsider his readiness. They were friends, despite being courtroom adversaries (not to mention the *Briefcase v. Wells* incident earlier). He knew she was getting married this month—yes, to the man she broke up with him for, but the statute of limitations for pettiness had run out. Time for bygones.

Delaney widened her eyes at Wells, willing him to say something.

Wells, friend-turned-courtroom-foe, merely shrugged.

"Um…" Delaney tapped her pen on the table.

Should she request a new date, or suck it up and shorten their honeymoon?

"What is it, Ms. Ross?" Rupert asked.

Delaney looked into the tired eyes of her client. She was a steward of his freedom, and he'd spent over a decade in jail for a crime he didn't commit. It would be immoral to prolong his misery just so she could float around the Caribbean for an additional week.

Dalton would understand. He respected her work ethic and wouldn't want her to risk her reputation—more importantly, someone's freedom—by delaying a case in favor of an indulgent two-week honeymoon. They'd still have a week to bask in tropical paradise.

"Yes, your honor. The defense will be ready."

"Good." The judge nodded, then turned to the tipstaff as he pointed to her leg. "Someone get her a Band-Aid."

Back at her office, Delaney found her phone on her desk with a Post-it note from Marley to call Dalton, the word "urgent" underlined three times.

She ignored it. Everything was urgent with Groomzilla these days.

Delaney pulled the clip from her French twist and a river of dark-chocolate hair cascaded down her back. She texted Dalton and suggested they meet for a late dinner, then summoned the interns for a meeting.

She broke the news about the hearing date to Marley, who arrived first.

"Wow," Marley exclaimed. "What are you going to do?"

"I have no choice, I have to come back. And Wells just emailed, requesting a meeting tomorrow. Can you and Sam handle it?"

"Of course. No need to worry about anything, we got it. You just enjoy your wedding and what's left of your honeymoon."

"Speaking of the wedding, who are you bringing?" Delaney asked as she forwarded his email.

"My boyfriend, Rick?"

It sounded more like a question than an answer. She'd forgotten about Marley's boyfriend. "Sorry, bride brain! Who is Sam bringing?"

"I have no idea. Nor does Sam."

Delaney was disappointed Marley and Sam weren't coming together. She wondered if they'd ever considered dating. They'd make a cute couple—she had a little Emma Stone thing going on, and he looked as if he'd just waded in from the pages of *Surfer* magazine.

"Where does Rick live, again?"

"Ohio. He works for an IT start-up in Columbus."

"That's right. Long distance relationships are fun, aren't they?" Delaney asked, smirking. "How's it working?"

"We try to visit on weekends at least once a month. And we do a week at the shore every year, which is where I'll be next week. Speaking of which, are you sure it's okay I take off, with the hearing so soon?"

"Of course, you deserve it. I know how important it is to have that time together. Dalton and I did the long-distance thing when we first got together. Thank God he was able to transfer to his firm's Philly office after we got engaged."

"I don't mind the distance, especially having a year of law school left. It's easier to focus with him not here."

"What happens after you graduate?"

"We're trying to figure that out."

A slight grimace flashed across Marley's face, so subtle

11

most people wouldn't notice. But Delaney had honed the skill of reading people, and something told her all wasn't quiet on the Midwestern front.

Sam entered the room then, flashing a dimpled smile as he settled into a chair and man-crossed his legs. "Congrats, boss, I knew you'd do it."

"*We* did it. We're a team. It's your victory too."

"But the true winner was Dalton and his courtroom serenade," Sam said. "Someone alert *American Idol*."

"Holy crap," Delaney exhaled, cupping her forehead. "I saw my whole career flash before my eyes."

"Marley's too," Sam said. "I was like, girl—are you *trying* not to practice law in the future?"

"I owe you big time, Marley. You really saved my butt."

After replaying the daring court caper and waging bets on Marley's questionable future as an attorney in good standing, they got down to business. Marley pulled her shoulder-length curls into a loose bun and scribbled away on her legal pad as Delaney outlined tasks for the interns to accomplish in her absence.

The meeting concluded just as Jim Howe, one of the firm's founding partners, tapped on the door.

"There's my favorite associate," he said. "Congrats on the win. Just wanted to stop by and tell you to enjoy this time off."

A wave of panic swept through her. It must have shown on her face.

"I mean it. You have a whole team here to help," Jim said. "What's the countdown?"

"Nine days," Delaney said.

Why did she feel so panicked? Everything was set. Except a minor change in honeymoon plans. And the Great Charcuterie Debate.

"Let's just hope this thing doesn't become a hurricane," Jim said as he headed toward the door.

"Wait, what thing?" Delaney shot up from her chair.

Jim turned back slowly. Delaney waited for him to laugh and say he was pulling her leg, but the look on his face told her he wasn't joking.

"Please tell me there's no hurricane," Delaney said.

"I hate to say it, but—"

"There's no hurricane," Marley interrupted Sam and waved the men off as if they were silly toddlers rambling on about monsters under the bed.

"But Mar, the Weather Channel—"

Delaney caught the comment-cutting glare Marley shot Sam.

"Then again," Sam said, shrugging, "it's rare for hurricanes to come this far north in June."

"I hope you're right," she said.

"He's right," Jim said, clearing his throat. "No need to worry."

And then Delaney proceeded to worry, because that's what happens when someone says not to. A hurricane was the last thing she needed. The final head count was in, and Mother Nature wasn't on the guest list.

MARLEY HAD JUST RETURNED TO HER OFFICE AFTER THE meeting with Delaney and Sam when her boyfriend, Rick, called.

"Hey, hon," he mumbled.

"What's up?" she asked. "You sound stressed."

"I am." He sighed. "Our deadline just got pushed up two weeks."

For the last few months, Rick's team had been working overtime to complete a complicated project. "That sucks," Marley said.

"I'm so sorry, but I can't take off next week."

Her heart sank. Between his job and her case, their visits had become sparse. Now this. But Marley knew this project was important to Rick and could tell by his tone he didn't want to let her down.

"It's okay," Marley said, trying to mask her disappointment. She didn't want to make him feel bad about something he had no control over. "We can make it up another time."

"That's why I love you. You're so understanding. I was looking forward to having time with you so we can discuss, you know—"

Marley knew without him saying it.

Their future.

She promised they'd talk soon, relieved for the extra time.

Delaney popped her head back in as Marley was hanging up. "I just sent a list of topics to discuss at your meeting tomorrow."

"Okay. I won't be taking off next week, after all. Rick can't make it."

"Oh, I'm sorry to hear that," Delaney said, pouting as sympathy flooded her steel-blue eyes. "But hey, in that case—my bachelorette party's this weekend. Why don't you join us?"

Why not? Marley was honored to be asked and told her she'd be there.

After Delaney left, Marley headed to Sam's office to tell him about the meeting.

"Knock, knock!" she announced.

"Wait till I get my panties on!" he cried in falsetto as he tapped away on his keyboard.

Marley plopped into a chair, crossed her legs, and waited until he was done typing. She needed his undivided attention.

"Sup, weirdo? Is it quittin' time?" he asked.

"Not yet. We have a new assignment."

He swiveled in his chair to face her, raked a hand through his hair, and laced his fingers behind his head. The rolled-up sleeves of his white Oxford provided a striking contrast to his tan forearms.

It was only June, but Sam already looked as if he'd spent the entire summer at the shore. Marley resented that someone as fair-haired as he could bronze so easily from head to toe. The sun adored Sam, swooning like a long-lost love as he paddled through the waves on his surfboard, warming his glistening skin to golden brown, and sprinkling his sea-soaked hair with kisses of honey.

Meanwhile, the rest of the world (*read*: Marley) remained a pasty winter white no matter how many sun salutations she did. As a fellow weekend shore warrior, she spent an equal amount of time on the beach as Sam, but all the sun did for her was toss a smattering of freckles at her opaque Irish skin like a passive-aggressive afterthought.

Thanks, sun. Thanks, Celtic DNA.

Marley glanced away, abiding the unwritten code of male/ female besties, which, briefly stated, prohibited one from staring, ogling, or otherwise noting the attractive features of one's platonic pal. She was well-versed in ignoring Sam's perfectly sculpted...*um, everything*, but occasionally he'd do something to soften her resolve.

Like dragging her into men's clothing boutiques to try on tailored Armani suits during their lunch breaks. She'd pretend not to notice how the slim cut of the trousers revealed the contours of his thighs and bum. Or when he'd bribe her with dinner at Maggiano's if she'd accompany him to the King of Prussia mall to find Tommy Bahama swim trunks. Which, inevitably, fit as if he were Tommy Bahama himself (assuming Tommy was six feet tall and built like an Adonis).

15

Sam stretched his arms to the side, causing his tailored shirt to pull across his chest.

"Mar, do me a solid—rub my shoulders?" He batted his baby blues. "I'm super sore from last night's workout."

She cocked her head.

"Please? I'll pay you."

"You can't afford me," Marley teased.

Forgetting the friend code for a moment, her eyes were riveted to his toned upper body, noticeable even through his Brooks Brothers button-down.

Noticeable, or summoning her like a beacon?

She got a good gander at Sam on the beach every weekend, so it's not like she didn't know exactly what he was packing. She just couldn't help it. The pecs, the washboard abs, the—

"Take a picture—it lasts longer." Sam's joke broke the spell before her mind went any lower.

"Shut up." Marley laughed to edge the tone of guilt from her voice. "You're an ass."

"I'm not the one staring." Sam ducked to avoid the paper clip she tossed at him. "Hey, you almost took out my eye."

Marley cleared her throat, trying to remember what she had to tell him.

"Oh. I have something for you." She scrolled through emails on her phone, blowing away a copper-brown curl that sprang free from her loose bun.

"Please don't let it be about work," Sam pleaded, his eyes gleaming with the promise of impending imbibement. "Isn't it five o'clock somewhere?"

"It's actually six here."

"Then we have some drinking to catch up on," Sam said.

"Don't end your sentence with a preposition."

"Such a flirt. Do you talk to all the guys this way?"

"You know me, luring them in with grammatical corrections."

Sam smiled. "Is that why you're here, to lure me in?"

"Right," she said dismissively, hoping he couldn't see her cheeks flush.

Sam was a perpetual flirt. If he was talking, he was flirting. Marley had learned long ago, the hard way, it meant nothing.

"I'm sending this to your printer," she said.

"A cease and desist order?"

"Something like that."

As the printer churned out the page, Sam wound up, spun in his chair three times, and grabbed the paper on his final revolution.

"Prosecution's requested a meeting," she said. "That's the list of topics to discuss."

Sam waved the paper around in a grand gesture. Marley looked at him dead-on, unamused, waiting for the theatrics to cease.

"Is Delaney going to meet with him?" he asked after skimming the email.

"No, we are. She's leaving for her wedding tomorrow, remember?"

"Delaney's getting married?" Sam yelled, slamming the paper into his chest. "Why wasn't I told about this?"

Marley gave him a measured look. They'd received their invitations weeks ago.

Despite constant inquiries, she still didn't know who he was taking as his plus-one. Sam, who avoided relationship entanglements like the DMV on a Saturday, wouldn't give her a straight answer.

First, he was going alone. Then he was taking their octogenarian receptionist. When he finally announced he'd asked Catherine Parr, Marley was thrilled, if not a little confused—she didn't know this Catherine. He was elusive when pressed for details, only sharing she was "a little older." Marley consulted the next best source: Google.

Sam's "date," it turned out, was the sixth wife of King Henry VIII.

17

Being as close as they had been for the past six years, Marley and Sam were intimately aware of the details of each other's lives, with this one exception. She wasn't sure why Sam was being so squirrelly. It wasn't like the man couldn't find a date with the snap of his fingers. Perhaps his plan was to fake a day-of illness, a major faux pas if he wanted to work for this firm. They both hoped for postgraduation job offers, and she didn't want Sam to blow his chances, or hers, by dishonoring his RSVP and pissing off their future boss.

Sam folded the email into an airplane and aimed for the trash can. It careened into Marley's head.

"We need that." Marley bent over to retrieve the paper intended for the meeting and smoothed the creases. "Stop ruining the planet."

"Know what I was thinking about the other day?" he asked.

"You should drop out of law school and twirl close-out signs on Delaware Ave?"

"Hey, someone has to alert the world when inventory is being drastically reduced, and that someone is *me*." Sam pointed at his chest with both thumbs. "No, smart-ass, I was thinking about how much you hated me when we first met."

"I didn't hate you." She did. "You were just someone I wouldn't have befriended."

"But you're happy you did. Admit it."

"Except I didn't. You befriended me."

"That's not how I remember it."

"Oh, yeah?" Marley tilted her head. "How'd it go, then?"

"You feigned a gross misunderstanding of the course material in a daring attempt to gain my assistance. Relentlessly, and without shame."

It had gone nothing like that. Quite the opposite.

"Or maybe that was me," he admitted.

It was. They'd met in Criminal Law 101 during their freshman year at Temple University. She was the studious future lawyer with aspirations to attend Villanova Law School; he, the flannel-wearing sloth who couldn't answer a simple question about Miranda rights. As he stumbled over the answer, Marley blurted it out. She couldn't help it—they'd been covering this topic for weeks and she was anxious to move on.

"Thanks for bailing me out. I'm a little hungover," he'd said after class. "I'm Sam Adams. And you're?"

"*Not* named after a beer," Marley said as she flung her backpack over her shoulder and stormed away.

The next day he was called upon by the professor, again unable to answer.

"Someone should inform the founding father the tea party's over," Professor Weinstein said. "Time to focus on this class."

Sam had tried to strike up conversations with her in the following days. The more she ignored him, the harder he tried. She wasn't encouraging him one bit, unlike the gaggle of flirty girls who flocked around him every day after class. Not that she'd noticed.

Then, one day, he scootched his chair closer to hers, leaned his elbows on his knees, and announced he had a question. She braced herself for a fresh round of stupidity as he smiled up at her, nearly sweeping her off her seat with a look she presumed had been practiced until perfected. He was so close she could see flecks of green in his Caribbean-blue eyes. She forgot what his question was, until she realized he hadn't asked it. Why was this guy so maddingly beautiful—objectively, of course—while at the same time so vacuous? She didn't like extremely good-looking guys. Or blondes. She trusted neither, preferring dark-haired, dark-eyed guys. Grounded. Serious. Their looks inconsequential as long as their intellect matched hers. This player was the complete opposite.

He asked her why she hated him.

"I don't hate you," she'd said, her propensity toward

kindness taking over. "I just don't have time for frat boy antics. I'm trying to get into law school."

"I'm not a frat boy. And I'm also going to law school. Villanova."

Marley recoiled as if cockroaches spewed from his mouth. No way was this guy getting into her dream law school. She wasn't even sure how he got into college.

"You do realize you need more than charm to get into law school?"

"I guess I should ask my dad, who's a lawyer himself. In fact, he graduated from 'Nova. If I'm correct, that makes me..." Sam snapped his fingers. "Oh, yeah! A legacy."

Later that week, he invited her to a study group. She was about to decline but thought it might be helpful if other serious students were involved. She reluctantly agreed, hoping it wouldn't just be a bunch of jocks trying to glean her intel.

Marley and Sam were first to arrive for the study session and chatted as they awaited others. She was surprised to learn they shared common interests, despite growing up on opposite sides of the SEPTA tracks. Both loved living in Philly, cheering for the Eagles, and drinking beer. Both hated Styrofoam, the word "moist," and when people say "no offense" right before they offend you.

Sam was a lot smarter than he let on. And funny.

"Oh, and I can't stand that white strip in chicken fingers. Like, what the hell is that, anyway?" Sam asked.

"No offense, but you're crazy not to love that thing."

They'd laughed, and Sam had asked her what her boyfriend was like.

Marley was taken aback by his sudden question. She didn't have a boyfriend at the time but didn't want to disclose that factoid to him. Especially since her dating status, or lack thereof, was an unrelenting theme at family gatherings. Marley felt as picked apart as the turkey on the Thanksgiving table when relatives offered their theories on her inability to snag a man. Painfully shy. Too studious. Doesn't know how to flirt. The Family Maguire considered it strange a woman would choose college over marriage. Before Marley, none had. Instead, they wed after high school and pumped out little Irish tater tots, like generations before them. Marley wondered if they should change the family crest, featuring a knight on a white steed, to include a woman being dragged behind him.

Sam had interjected before Marley could answer. "Let me guess. He's a geeky four-eyed IT type. A dependable guy of substance, not spark."

She'd been stunned at the accuracy with which he described her perfect (nonexistent) boyfriend. She was also surprised when no one else showed up for the study group. They agreed to meet the following week. Again, no one else came. This time they studied and aced the exam. Marley decided it was worth her time to make it a weekly event.

Now here they were, co-interns on a real criminal case, after surviving four years of college, two years of law school, and one humiliating misunderstanding that almost ended their friendship.

Kate

K ATE ROSS HAD JUST RETURNED TO HER OFFICE IN DOWN-town DC when her sister called.

"Hey, bride-to-be!" Kate said, trying to sound cheery.

"What's wrong?" Delaney asked.

"Eh, just another brutal meeting." Kate sighed for effect. "You know, life of a lobbyist—never a dull moment."

It *had* been a brutal meeting, but nothing new in the Land of Political Contention.

In truth, Kate was bracing herself for Delaney's latest round of wedding woes. It seemed her sister was so focused on her case, she couldn't enjoy the wedding prep or appreciate her enthusiastic fiancé helping to pull it all together.

If only Kate had such "problems."

"What's up?" she asked.

"I'll take the Fifth," Delaney said. "A fifth of whiskey, that is. Remarkably, it's not 'Zilla this time."

Delaney rambled on about a hearing scheduled for the middle of her honeymoon.

"Bummer," Kate said. "Can't you change it?"

"No." Delaney said, offering no explanation.

Kate had never understood her sister's desire to put her career ahead of her personal life, especially an event as important as her own wedding. She wanted to say something but wasn't sure she should.

"What's the silence for?" Delaney asked.

Kate hesitated before sharing her thoughts. "You've been so stressed lately. I get you have a lot going on, but you're not enjoying yourself. Instead of always looking forward to the next thing on your to-do list, why not take a breath, look around, be in the moment. This should be a fun time in your life!"

"You're right, I know. I just want everything to be perfect. The case *and* the wedding."

"I can't speak to your case, but I can say the wedding *won't* be perfect. No wedding is. Instead of worrying about the little stuff, focus on the big picture. Which is—you're getting married!"

Kate was proud of herself for coming up with such wisdom. Like she was some sort of relationship guru, when she couldn't even bribe a decent guy to stick around.

Which was why she was considering joining a convent.

"When did my little sister get so smart? I know what you're

saying but it's in my nature, you know," Delaney said.

"Let go and let destiny." It was Kate's favorite mantra. "Everything will work out."

"I disagree, but enough about me." Delaney's tone lightened. "I'm about to make your day. I found you the perfect wedding date. It's Dalton's cousin, Ryan."

"I don't need a date," Kate grumbled, sinking back in her seat. She blew a wayward strand of her wavy blonde bob from her forehead. "I'll be so busy tending to you I won't have time for anyone else."

Joking, of course. There'd be nothing for Kate to do on Delaney's big day besides give a heartfelt speech and feign untethered excitement. Not that she wasn't thrilled Delaney was marrying her childhood sweetheart. She was just a tad envious her sister had found a guy who didn't take off for the promise of something better. Like Kate's had.

"This isn't about Greg, is it?" Delaney asked, as though reading her mind.

"Greg who?"

Delaney chuckled. "My plan is already working."

"Plan for what?"

"For you to move on. Seriously, it's been two years since you guys broke up."

"I have moved on. I'm officially done with men."

"Says the hopeless romantic. I'll believe it when I see it."

Kate certainly believed it. When she and Greg broke up, she was excited by the prospect of meeting someone new, starting fresh. Being with the same person since college had grown old, even if the man-child she'd been dating hadn't.

She took a dive back into the dating pool, hoping to make a splash. Instead, she found herself among bottom dwellers. Cheaters, binge drinkers, gamblers, and catfishers bobbed and banged around her like flotsam in a vat of mediocrity. It was enough to make someone like Greg look like a prize.

Occasionally, she'd meet someone who hid their flaws well, until they couldn't.

"Not open for business," Kate announced, swirling in her chair. "Face it, Delaney. I'm gonna die alone, a shriveled-up spinster surrounded by cats. It's my destiny."

"You have to stop with this destiny shit," Delaney scolded. "You need to make better choices, take control of your life. Starting with this date."

"Nope. Bring on the cats and let them eat me alive. Better than a fix-up, any day."

"It's not an official fix-up," Delaney said, "just someone to chill with at the wedding, since everyone else will be paired off."

"Pass."

"Don't make me sic Groomzilla on you," her sister warned. "He'll be vastly disappointed seeing you sitting by yourself. It may ruin his entire night."

"Better his than mine. What level of repulsiveness are we talking?"

"He's Dalton's cousin. The men in their family couldn't be repulsive if they forced themselves face-first into a meat grinder."

"A vegan, then?" Kate asked.

"Carnivore."

"Serial killer!"

"Total sweetheart," Delaney insisted.

"That's what they say about all the serials. 'He was so nice, we had no idea!'"

"You're a pain in my ass."

"What's his deal, then?" Kate's tone conveyed her suspicion. "If he's so 'hot,' why can't he find his own damn date?"

"He just broke up with someone. Guess what I'm holding right now?"

Before Kate could ask, Delaney blurted it out. "Bride card!"

Dang it. When Delaney got engaged, the sisters had made a deal: Delaney wouldn't insist on something wedding-related unless it was of paramount importance. So far, she hadn't. "Waah," Kate whined. She had zero interest in being fixed up, paired off, or encouraged to "chill" with Ryan or any other guy. Even if he was single and "hot." But she had no choice—there was no outsmarting a bride with a card.

"Why the sudden departure from your otherwise burning desire to meet men?"

"Have you seen what's out there?" Kate scoffed. "No thanks."

"Does it have anything to do with the article? I'm assuming you saw it."

"What article?"

Delaney clucked her tongue. "I guess that means no. I probably shouldn't tell you this, but *Men's Monthly* just did a full spread on Greg."

"*My* Greg?" Kate sat straight up. "Why on God's green earth would a magazine want to do an article on him?"

"It's about—"

"What a loser he is for driving cross-country in a disgusting van to chase a silly pipe dream?" Kate asked. "Don't tell me— on the way to becoming a full-time surfer, he found a cure for cancer." She chuckled at her own humor.

Delaney was silent.

Had he?

"Seriously, what's the article about?" Kate swiveled back toward her desk and tapped her laptop back to life. "Can I find it online?"

"Nah, it's a print-only magazine, apparently."

"Can you read it to me?"

"You should read it for yourself. Get some closure."

Kate had gotten all the closure she needed when Greg decided he'd rather spend his life in the ocean, alone, than on land with her.

"I'm too busy for this right now," she said. "I'll check it out later."

Her ringing desk phone provided the perfect excuse to sign off. Even if it was a robocall.

"Can I tell Ryan you're in?" Delaney asked.

Kate groaned.

"I'll take that as a yes."

"For the wedding only. Nothing else."

"We'll see."

As soon as she ended the call, Kate bolted for the door. Too busy, her ass. There was a newsstand on the corner, and she couldn't wait to read what Greg the Perpetual Toddler had done to land himself in *Men's Monthly*.

Back in her office, Kate flipped through the pages of the magazine until she found it.

A full spread, featuring Greg in all his sun-kissed glory.

On one side, a close-up of his face with the headline "CEO of the Sea" was splayed across the top. Opposite, an image of him on the beach, sunlight dancing off his pecs, wet suit stripped to his waist, holding on to his manhood. Which, in this case, was a surfboard.

Kate's heart roused itself from its two-year slumber as she read about the man she once thought she'd marry. Who had left her, instead, for a cross-country trip to "find himself." According to the article, he'd found himself all right—at the top of the wildly successful surfing franchise he'd created. Impressive for a man who once struggled to make change for a dollar.

Greg's dream was to surf, nothing more. He'd planned to pick up side jobs—work at a surf shop, run a food truck, something, anything—to support himself between wave sets while he figured out what he wanted to do with his life.

Kate, on the other hand, had already known what she wanted to do with her life: land a cushy job in a DC lobbying firm, get married, have babies—in that precise order. She'd already crossed the first item off her list and was focused on the second when he made his announcement.

She tried to talk sense into him. They'd been dating so long, marriage was the next logical step. He tried to convince her to come with him, but she'd just started her new job, which she loved. She wasn't about to trek across the country like some hairy-armpitted vagabond, drinking from streams and plucking berries for sustenance.

After their big fight, she'd bid him farewell and watched him drive off into the sunset in a sputtering, dilapidated VW van, certain he wouldn't make it to the entrance of the Pennsylvania Turnpike.

But make it, he did. According to the article, he'd emerged from the sea, carved a pension from a surfboard, and was now the head of a seven-figure start-up. Making surfboards, of all things. In two years, he'd morphed from a knuckle-dragging simian to an upright, suit-wearing, Manhattan-drinking CEO like a creature on a microbe-to-man evolution chart.

"You son of a bitch," she said, flicking his face with her middle finger. "You coulda told me you were going to make it big."

He was tanner than usual, but that was to be expected of a guy who spent his days bobbing in the Pacific, testing new surfboards. His muscular physique, also new, was likewise expected after all that hanging ten. His expression was a combination of confidence and amusement, as if he, too, was surprised (stoked!) to have found success doing something he loved.

Kate was slammed with a trifecta of emotions. She was jealous, remorseful, pissed. If only she had a pipe dream like

Greg. If only she had gone with him to chase his. If only—

A knock at her door jolted her back to the present.

"Delivery for Ms. Kate." The front desk receptionist entered the room cradling a long white box as if it were a newborn baby.

The kind of long white box roses come in.

Who on earth would be sending her roses? Her last date, over a week ago, was the most likely sender—a guy with a self-proclaimed shoe fetish. Kate had caught him snapping photos of her Jimmy Choos under the table of an upscale sushi place. It was at that precise moment she'd decided to cancel all her dating apps. Not to mention her dating life.

This must be some sort of delayed gesture of apology from stiletto stalker.

Kate accepted the package and closed the door behind the retreating receptionist. She gingerly untied the white silk ribbon and lifted the box lid as if she expected a fake snake to boing out of it. Inside were a dozen long-stemmed—

"Green roses?" Kate mused aloud.

She'd never seen anything like them. What did green stand for? Apology? As in, "Sorry for worshiping the shoes you walk in"? "Sorry to thrust you into a lifelong vow of celibacy"?

An envelope was tucked beneath the stems, featuring handwriting that looked as if a chicken had stepped in ink and walked across the envelope.

Sharp inhale.

Behold, the writing of Greg Fallon, CEO of the Sea. And Duke of Crappy Penmanship.

It had been a long time since she'd seen one of his scribblings. For some ridiculous reason, it made her smile. The envelope contained a copy of Greg's magazine article and a Post-it note:

Hey Kate, Green roses stand for good news and new beginnings. Good news—I made it to California! More good news—I've made a living surfing. Here's to new beginnings!

Kate's heart fluttered, fully awakened from its Rip van Winkle stint. For months after they'd broken up, she had dreams Greg would come back, unshaven and burnt to a crisp, admitting folly as he tried to barrel back into her life. She'd rebuke him each time because she was *so over him* especially after what he'd put her through. All those talks of the future when he meant none of it. All the dreams she'd had of them riding into the sunset when all he dreamed of riding were gnarly waves.

But never in those dreams did he arrive in a Maserati, fanning a stack of C-notes. Hypothetically.

New beginnings, huh? Was he trying to get back together with her? Would she want that?

Maybe...

"I'm not that shallow," she said aloud to his magazine face.

Or was she? Certainly, she could learn to be depthless, at least for a few months. Head west, young woman. Reap the rewards of her ex's oh-so-fabulous lifestyle. Spend days lollygagging by a pool overlooking the Pacific, sipping mimosas, waving to her student loan debt as it swept out to sea.

Becoming a kept woman had a certain allure.

"Yeah, but we broke up for reasons, Greg." She continued talking to his picture as if it was arguing with her. "None of which had to do with your lack of net worth. Lack of motivation and maturity, definitely. Lack of a job, absolutely."

But now that he had all those things, most of all net worth—wait, how much was it?

Kate flipped back to the first page of the article.

Holy fuck. So many zeros.

"Nope," she said, slamming the magazine closed. She tossed

it across the room. It ricocheted off the wall and landed on the floor with a thud.

Open to his article.

A sign?

No.

This was a job for Laura, her college friend, who knew Greg almost as well as Kate did. Laura, who had no tolerance for man-babies of the Greg Fallon sort, encouraged their breakup when he announced he was moving away. She'd be the perfect person to hold her back from the growing urge to wallpaper her office with his (holy shit, so handsome) face.

She texted Laura.

> Help. Me.

> You saw the article?

She knew about it too?

Kate's phone rang.

"Get a hold of yourself, girl," Laura said.

"He sent me roses. Green ones. They symbolize new beginnings."

"Right, to let you know *he* had a new beginning. In California, without you. Don't fill in the blanks and make the story different than it is."

"But the storyline has changed."

"What's changed? He still left you for a surfboard."

"Well, not a board—"

"Surf life, then. The plot twist here is he found a way to make bank playing in the ocean, the fucker. No twist in your plot. You're still here, anchored by a student loan, lobbying to save our planet like a grown-ass adult. Unless you've suddenly turned 'Gidget Goes Surfing' on me."

"No. You're right."

"Stay the course, my friend."

"Okay," Kate agreed. Then, "What if he was my person? What if we were destined to be together and I blew it?"

"We've dissected this ad nauseam. He wasn't your person—not then, not now." Laura huffed. "You and this destiny stuff, I swear."

"But he's rich..." Kate whispered.

"Wealth does not a happy person make. Maybe for some, but that's not who you are. You're not a gold digger."

"I could try..."

"Your person is out there, Kate. You just haven't met him yet."

"And won't, now that I'm off men," she said.

"Ooh-kay. We'll see about that. In the meantime, I gotta bounce."

Kate hung up, her friend's voice of reason ringing in her ears. Laura was right—nothing had changed about their relationship, their breakup, or Kate's current life. The only thing different was that Greg's bronzed face had shown up in a glossy periodical.

And he'd apparently grown up. Started a business, bought a beachfront home in Malibu, and now slept on a bed of Franklins.

But new beginnings...

"I'm not a gold digger," she repeated Laura's words before feeding the article to her shredder. She marched the roses back out to the receptionist.

"For you," she said, handing her the box. "Take these home and enjoy them."

"Oh, that's so sweet," the receptionist said, then crinkled her face. "What's wrong with them?"

"Long story."

Cleo

C LEO DUGGAN HAD JUST STARTED HER PART-TIME BAR-
tending shift at Center City's popular hot spot. Aptly
named the Clink, its proximity to the criminal justice
center made it the perfect location for the legal crowd's
post-work libations.

She scrolled through the email on her phone as her friend,
Tori, looked on. Cleo hoped the manager wouldn't see her
and accuse her of neglecting the patrons, of which there were
a whopping two. The large, ultramodern bar and restaurant
was fairly empty for a Thursday afternoon, but a glance at the
time reminded Cleo court was probably still in session. Before
long, the place would be crawling with lawyers, judges, and
cops, *oh my.*

She and Tori were discussing Important Bridesmaid News.
Although not Cleo's favorite topic, she was happy to spend
some time with her old roommate before the barrage of
booze-thirsty barristers descended upon the place.

"Did you find Nora's email?" Tori asked.

"Still looking for it," Cleo said, scrolling.

Dalton's sister, Nora, was in charge of planning Delaney's
bachelorette party, slated for the upcoming Saturday—a pub
crawl along the shore. Nora sought the input of the bride's
best friends to make sure she'd chosen Delaney's favorite
places to visit.

Ah, there it was. Cleo perused the list and agreed Nora was
spot-on.

Cleo ran a hand through her pixie cut, then snapped a selfie
to make sure it looked okay. Her latest fling, He Who Shall

Not Be Named, was due any moment and she wanted to look her best. She just hoped Tori would be out of there before he arrived. She wasn't ready to have her two worlds collide just yet. Or ever.

She stashed her phone on the shelf under the bar before she got busted. The manager was a class A douche bag, with the undeniable power to make her night a living hell if he caught her with her phone when she was on the clock. But bridesmaid duties called, which meant he could fuck right off.

But then she remembered he was on vacation. Ah, well—he could still fuck off.

"This color's good on you," Tori said, pointing to Cleo's hair. "Very Joan Jett."

"Thanks. You don't think black is too much against my pasty skin?"

"No, you wear it well. Makes your hazel eyes pop," Tori said, making fireworks with her fingers. "I love how you change hair color the way some people change outfits. A true ar-*teest*."

"Black seemed apt, to reflect my state of mourning."

"Mourning over what?"

"The wedding," Cleo said. "I may have to object."

Tori giggled. "On what grounds?"

"Marriage is stupid."

Cleo was only half-joking. She'd seen what it had done to her parents.

"The three of us were having a great time," Cleo moaned, "until Dalton put a ring on it and you sold your soul to the Turd. Y'all left me to fend for myself."

The Turd, so named by Cleo, was Tori's boyfriend. To his constituents, he was known as State Representative Theodore "Ted" Roberts.

Tori looked at her phone. "Speaking of Ted, I gotta run. We're meeting for dinner."

"Tell him I didn't say hi."

To say Cleo didn't like him was an understatement of epic proportions. She pretty much hated the Turd for stealing her friend's soul. Cleo found him to be a boring bag of ego who didn't value Tori the way she deserved.

Tori pulled a compact mirror from her purse and reapplied her lip gloss. Cleo marveled at her friend's beauty. With her straight, naturally blonde hair, doe eyes, and curves, she was a Barbie doll come to life.

"When does our shore rental begin again?" Tori asked, snapping the compact shut.

"Saturday," Cleo said. "Pick you up around ten?"

"Ten, it is."

"Oh, wait," Cleo reconsidered, tapping her black fingernails on the bar. "Make it noon. I'm off Friday night. I spy, with my mind's eye, a massive hangover."

Cleo and Tori taking a vacation together was rare, given the demands of Ted's political event calendar, the tentacles of which were wrapped around Tori's availability like a stranglehold. As Delaney's trusted bridesmaids, it was their duty—no, obligation—to spend the week before her wedding at the shore in case she needed them for wedding duties.

In reality, they just wanted an opportunity to relive their carefree days by the sea.

"Toodles!" Tori said, wiggling her fingers at Cleo as she took off.

Cleo grabbed her phone and pulled up her saved list of New York bars. Now that Delaney was heading into the holy hell of matrimony, and Tori was plastered to the Turd, she needed a plan.

Cleo's dream had always been to make it as an artist. Moving to New York was a newly formed and loosely organized plan, one she worked on whenever she felt lost and needed something to look forward to. So far, the only thing she had was a friend's offer to crash on his Lower East Side couch and a list of potential bartending jobs where she could make enough to get started. She was fearful of change and dreaded the thought of moving, but not as much as she dreaded being left behind. A pain she was all too accustomed to.

Cleo looked up when a familiar figure approached.

"A man walks into a bar..." Cleo joked as he sauntered toward her and slid onto the barstool like a regular. In fact, he was a regular—not only at the Clink, but between her sheets as well.

"...and orders up the finest piece he's ever known," he whispered as he leaned over the bar and kissed her.

"Piece of what, ass?" Cleo asked, amused.

"I was gonna say dime piece."

"Good, 'cause we don't serve ass," she said. "Just assholes."

"Then I've come to the right place," he said, flashing a lopsided grin.

So it was between Cleo and the latest of her flings, Wells Abernathy III. A man who, fully dressed, was the most arrogant asshole she'd ever known. But undressed...well...let's just say he earned the right to act like one. And then some.

He gazed at her with his pale green eyes and Cleo silently congratulated herself on her latest choice of boy toys. His tailored suit, Ivy League haircut, and chiseled features were the exact opposite of what Cleo normally went for. He was Fine with a capital *F*, looking like he'd just stepped off the cover of *GQ*, for fuck's sake. Unlike the dodgy misfits she usually turned to for good old-fashioned fun, he was quick with his comebacks, skilled in the art of flirtatious banter, and had absolutely nothing in common with her. That's what made it all so exhilarating.

Not to mention safe. There was no way she'd fall for him. Or him, her.

"Tough day at the office, dear?" Cleo joked as she served up his usual—a gin martini, extra dirty.

"Tough day in the courtroom," he corrected. "Your room-mate showed no mercy. Beat me to a pulp."

"That's my girl."

Normally, she rooted for Wells to win his cases, but not when he was up against Delaney. Bestie blood ran deeper than gin.

It could have been a weird dynamic between the friends if Delaney knew Cleo was hanging out with Wells, which is precisely why she didn't share that minor detail with her. Delaney didn't give two shits who Wells dated now. But still...

Hold up. Cleo and Wells weren't actually dating. It was a lot less formal than that, at Cleo's insistence. The only thing she sought from the hot prosecutor was fun and games. Jabbing each other with playful insults. The chill, minus the 'Flix. An occasional no-strings hookup. While bestie blood ran deep, Cleo was no fool. If Delaney got wind of it, she'd either throw a ticker-tape parade to encourage a real relationship, or worry the smooth prosecutor would hurt Cleo, forgetting her friend's heart was made of Teflon.

Nope, Delaney didn't need to know about it because there was nothing to know.

"I take it you lost the hearing?" Cleo probed as she swirled a plastic sword around her mouth with her tongue. His eyes glazed over and dropped to her cleavage, artfully compressed between her elbows as she leaned on the bar. She loved the power she had over this man.

"That's putting it mildly," Wells said, his hard swallow not lost on her. "Delaney's good, I have to give her that. So...when do you get off tonight?"

"It depends," Cleo said, tapping on the bar as she turned toward a newly arrived customer, "on when you can get me off."

Cleo delighted in hearing his hearty laugh as she served the patron their drink. She was proud of Delaney for wiping the courtroom with him. Wells deserved it. Most days, his ego could be found at the cruising altitude of a Boeing 737 MAX, so even a major court loss wouldn't ground him. It was part of his allure, his unbreakable confidence-slash-cockiness, his delightfully infuriating hubris. It elevated the thrill of her chase, going after someone so deliciously pompous and unlike her in every way.

He—a "law and order" man, and the next great district attorney of Philadelphia (or so they said).

She—a "rules are suggestions" kinda gal, and the next great homeless artist (once Delaney kicked her ass out of their shared apartment).

Fully clothed, they made as much sense together as oil and water. But au naturel, watch out. *Magnifique!*

Cleo had heard so much about their mutual case from Delaney over the past few months, she could probably try the case herself. But Delaney could keep that shit. Cleo was more interested in the creative side of life, finding oils and watercolors far more fascinating than courtrooms and lawyers.

Except maybe this one.

His gaze swept down the length of her low-cut blouse and miniskirt, the required uniform of the Clink's female bartending staff. After recalling her jerk manager was on vacation this week, Cleo had taken a break of her own by unbuttoning her blouse to one below code and tying its tails just above her bellybutton.

Wells clenched his jaw as his eyes burned into hers; the space between them frizzled. She wished she had her palette to capture his look on canvas. She had no idea what it was about him, or her with him, but she'd never had this effect on a man.

"What happened to make your case go south?" Cleo teased. "Were your briefs too tight?"

"I wasn't wearing any."

"Hung jury, then?"

"Don't know about the jury, but..." Wells hooked an eyebrow and looked down at his lap.

"That's appealing." Cleo followed his gaze and whispered, "But I'll need to see the evidence before I make my ruling."

Wells gave her a half smile. "Come to my chambers, I'll firm up your conviction."

Cleo cracked up, and Wells took a celebratory bow over his victorious punsmanship. It was a game they liked to play, seeing who could make the other laugh first. "I rest my case."

"You can rest it on me anytime, counselor," Cleo said as she turned away, her cheeks (and other body parts) feeling as if they were fully engulfed in flames.

It's what their sexy repartee did to her every time. She had no idea how this guy could get her so charged up. He brought out her wittiest humor, her best comebacks. She was sexy, smart, and invincible with him, something she wasn't with other guys.

"Is that new?" Wells asked, pointing to Cleo's latest painting on the wall.

"Yeah, that's the one I finished last week."

"You're amazing," he said as he gazed at the painting. "I love the colors. So that's—" Wells paused and nodded around the room, counting. "Seven pieces on display here? It's like you have your own gallery."

A combination of pride and gratitude washed over Cleo as she recalled the fortuitous encounter she'd had one day at the Philadelphia Museum of Art. She was copying a painting when a man, who'd been watching her, introduced himself. He was looking for art for his new bar in Center City, and asked if he could see some of her pieces. They arranged to meet a week later. Not only did Cleo sell several pieces, she also scored a part-time bartending job. Mostly because she wanted to be there if anyone inquired about or commented on her work, but also because she was strapped for cash, as the tips at her regular bartending job weren't cutting it.

Cleo was pouring Wells another drink when something caught her attention in the dining room.

The Caesar salad cart.

"First date, table ten," she said, nodding toward the dining area where a waiter rolled up with the cart and presented it to a couple sitting at the table. In addition to the Clink being a hangout for the legal crowd, it had also grown a reputation for being one of Philly's swankiest restaurants, a premier first-date venue. The owner had insisted upon the archaic yet arguably impressive tableside service, for those willing to pay the equivalent of a month's rent for a damn salad.

"Nothing says 'I dig you' on a first date like tableside Caesars," Wells joked.

Another game they liked to play, mocking couples on dates. They'd developed a rating system of sorts, trying to guess which couples would be in it for the long haul. A shared bottle of wine meant a casual hookup. Two bottles meant a second date. Tableside Caesars meant they were headed to the altar.

A thirsty throng swarmed the bar, and Cleo was caught up in a whirlwind of busy. She made sure everyone was served and settled as the acoustic guitarist began his set.

"Hey, Clee," Wells said, sliding his glass nervously between his hands. "I have a question for you."

"I have an answer." She leaned on the bar, taking in the heady ocean scent of his aftershave as she swayed to the guitarist's swoony rendition of "Simply the Best."

He gazed at her with—oh God. What was that look on his face?

Shit.

"I was wondering..."

No, no, no. Don't do it, Wells. Don't go soft on me. Don't—

"Will you have dinner with me tomorrow night?"

Fuck.

"I want to take you out on a proper date. Maybe take it further than...well, you know..."

"Tableside Caesars?" Cleo joked, her voice wry as she raised an eyebrow.

"If you play your cards right," he said, chuckling.

This can't be happening.

She wasn't looking to take this any further, and hadn't thought he was, either.

"I don't know, Dubs," Cleo said, as she looked around to find something to do. Ah, yes—wipe the bar. She grabbed a towel and began wiping away.

"What don't you know?" he asked, cocking his head. "Listen to the song, Clee. You and me. Simply the best."

Horizontally? Abso-fucking-lutely. Vertically? Hell no.

"Um—" Cleo chewed on the inside of her cheek and avoided his gaze. "I have to work."

"I thought you were on vacation?"

She was. *Think fast, Cleo.*

"I just agreed to take on an extra shift at the tavern."

Just about to, that is. It wasn't a complete lie—Cleo's primary bartending gig was at Murphy's Tavern, a dive bar in Northeast Philly. The owner, Murph, had texted to ask if she could work Friday night. She hadn't answered him yet but... *ta-da!* The perfect alibi.

"Let me take you to breakfast then. After your shift."

Dammit.

Two new patrons entered the bar. Delaney's interns. She was never so happy to see them as she was just then.

Cleo slid two bottles of brew their way, tossing the popped caps where she wished she could toss this conversation—right in the trash. She greeted them with uncharacteristic enthusiasm, anything to take her away from Wells until she was able to come up with an excuse. Food poisoning, broken clavicle, an active warrant for her arrest—the possibilities were endless.

There was no way she was turning their nothing into a something. Not her MO, and not his either. He didn't seem the type to go for anything more than a casual fling, but Cleo's intimacy-fearing synapses were firing in rapid succession, telling her that's exactly where it was heading. *Danger, Cleo Duggan! Danger!*

Oh well. Fun while it lasted.

Marley

THE HOUR OF HAPPINESS HAD FINALLY ARRIVED. MARLEY and Sam snagged the last two open seats at the Clink. The bartender, a friend of Delaney's, had their beers uncapped before they sat.

"Good stuff," Sam said, taking a gulp of Philly's famed microbrew. "So. Tell me. Why are you obsessing over my plus-one?"

"Not obsessing, just wanna make sure I approve."

"Can't I go with you and Rick?"

"I don't feel like entertaining your drunk ass all night."

Sam would follow them around like a lost puppy. His constant need for social stimulation, both a curse and a blessing, would commandeer their night.

"When's Rikki-Tikki-Tavi coming?" Sam asked, drumming his fingers on the bar in rhythm to the nickname he'd given Rick long ago.

"Not till next weekend."

"What happened to your week at the shore?" He swigged his beer and eyed her sideways.

"He has too much going on at work. It's for the best, with Delaney gone. You'd probably blow the entire case, left to your own devices."

"What case?" Sam joked.

"Exactly."

"I'm glad you're not going. I'd hate to have to carry the whole workload myself."

"Aw. It's cute you think you actually do work."

"He should make it up to you, take you somewhere really nice. Isn't the shore thing getting old?"

Marley shrugged. "I guess when you're landlocked in Ohio, Jersey's an exotic getaway."

"But Mar, there are so many cool places in this world," Sam said. "Like Cancun. Tahiti. Or the Mall-dives."

"Deeves," Marley corrected. "It's Mal-*deeves*."

"Thanks, Rosetta Stone," Sam said.

"He'll say it's too expensive."

"You're worth the indulgence."

Marley appreciated Sam's support. He was right; it was time for something different.

Like many young Philly professionals, Sam and Marley spent their summer weekends at the southern Jersey Shore. They'd each rented houses with friends—she with girls and he with guys—in Strathmere, a sleepy seaside town nestled between family-oriented Ocean City to the north and singles-scene Sea Isle to the south. While she loved Strathmere, a vacation somewhere else would be fun.

"Do you think it's because he's cheap?" Sam asked.

"Frugal," Marley corrected, not wanting to cast Rick's propensity for cautious spending in a negative light. She appreciated his practicality; it was much like her own.

Sam leaned toward her and narrowed his eyes. "Do I detect a hint of trouble in paradise? A storm on the horizon?"

Marley hesitated. Things weren't bad between them, but

tensions had been growing lately. She rarely discussed her relationship with Sam but needed the advice of her good friend.

"We've been talking about what's gonna happen after I graduate."

"You think you'll still be dating?"

"Not just dating." Marley frowned, confused by Sam's misunderstanding of the seriousness of her relationship. "Engaged. He's been talking about it for a while."

"Wow." Sam turned and faced straight ahead, taking another long swig.

"Right?"

She expected Sam to tell her she was too young for marriage. But he didn't. She could see the muscles in his jaw tightening, suggesting he had an opinion on the subject, but none was offered.

Instead, he seemed more interested in peeling the label off his bottle. Unusual for Sam, always quick with snarky comebacks, especially when it came to matters involving Rick. Marley expected he'd at least say something about how boring her life would be if she married him. But he said nothing.

The truth was, Marley enjoyed the status quo. Distance provided her with the best of both worlds—a comfortable, dependable relationship, balanced by the freedom to concentrate on her studies and hang out with friends. But Rick was settled in his job and ready to move to the next stage, which meant one of them moving—him to Philly, or her to Ohio. She couldn't fathom leaving the city she loved and the state in which she was being groomed for the practice of law. But Rick loved his six-figure job and was starting to look for houses.

Sam finally spoke. "You basically just crawled out of diapers and now you're gonna be someone's wife?"

"Something like that," she said, thankful his snark had returned.

"I guess you guys have been dating for a while. I just thought

Rick was, like, your Mr. Right Now. Not your Mr. Right."

He was wrong. Rick *was* her Mr. Right. He was kind, dependable, motivated. They never fought. He was the only boyfriend she'd ever had, the only guy to ever choose her.

They'd met the summer before their senior year of college at a mock trial competition. He was an IT intern, the spitting image of what Sam had projected to be her "type." When he'd asked for her number, she doubted she'd hear from him. Most guys she gave her number to went missing, as if they'd faked their own deaths or entered the witness protection program. But Rick had called. And, ultimately, he'd shown her what it felt like to be loved. Cherished, even.

That alone was worth more than anything, despite being on different timelines.

Marley was about to ask Sam for advice when he slid off his barstool, announcing he was going to the potty.

She took a sip of her beer and eyed a couple sitting in the booth where she and Sam had sat the night of her twenty-first birthday.

That Night.

The night that almost changed everything.

Sam and Marley had been the first of their friend group to reach legality, Sam two months before her. For her birthday, he'd rented a limo and they hit every entertainment venue Philly had to offer, from tiny Cherry Street Tavern to sprawling waterfront dance clubs. They ended their night at the Clink, sharing one last drink before closing time. Before they went back to her apartment and—

"I'm back," Sam said, interrupting her thoughts. "What'd I miss?"

Oh, just me reminiscing about a night that should never be revisited.

Sam flagged the bartender for another round. He placed his foot on the rung of Marley's stool, his knee brushing

THE WAY TO CAPE MAY

against her thigh and resting there in platonic familiarity.

"I got a text from my friend Rhonda when I was in the loo. Remember Jenna, that girl I dated in high school?"

"If you're referring to *the* Jenna, oft-quoted 'love of your life,' I remember."

"Not oft." Sam held up a finger. "Once. When I was dead-ass drunk. I'm really glad you never forgot that."

"Downplay it if you must, but you always say you'll never let a woman break your heart again. So—if not oft-quoted, at least oft-remembered."

"Whatever."

"What about *Jen-na*?" Marley sang her name.

"She's back from Florida."

"Sam, that's great!" she said, grasping his wrist.

"Why?"

"So you can discover if there's still a flame. If not, you'll know."

And finally move on to someone else. But she didn't say that part.

Marley had been hoping Sam would find a steady girlfriend so they could double-date when Rick visited. It was exhausting watching Sam chase surface-level encounters with women devoid of substance. He had no problem attracting women—his personality and looks served as a powerful magnet for most single straight women in the tristate area.

Marley suspected he just wasn't over Jenna.

She knew the story well. Sam, once a gangly teen, experienced a growth spurt in tenth grade, suddenly filling out and turning heads. Including the one belonging to Jenna, popular girl and cheerleader extraordinaire. They dated a few weeks until he found her making out with his best friend. Her family moved to Florida a week later, never to be seen again.

Whenever Marley challenged Sam to move on and find someone else, he'd refuse, saying he'd never trust another woman. Marley believed it wasn't as much about trust as it was being hung up.

"Have you checked Insta to see what she looks like now?" Marley asked.

"No," he said. "Maybe once or twice."

Probably more than that, Marley guessed. Nobody could resist the urge to look up exes in the age of social media, even after the crushing blow of a thwarted first love.

Marley pretended to search for Jenna's profile. She held up a picture of a toothless woman in a housecoat, holding a mangy-looking cat.

"You've found her, at last!" Sam exclaimed. "I'd know that pussy anywhere."

Marley searched for real, this time revealing a beautiful woman with stunning blue eyes and golden hair—the profile picture of the girl Sam loved.

Marley forced a smile. "I think I just found your plus-one."

Delaney

DELANEY HURRIED ALONG DUSK-CLOAKED CHESTNUT Street, her day finally over. She arrived at her favorite restaurant where, through the softly lit window, one man caught her attention.

Seated alone, he ran a hand through his dark, wavy hair before resting a sculpted arm along the back of the booth. The candlelit gleam of gold on his third finger, left hand, made Delaney smile. Dalton had insisted on wearing a wedding band when they got engaged, reasoning it wasn't fair for her to be branded as "taken" if he wasn't. She loved that about him, a true egalitarian.

He must have seen her looking because he turned, midnight-blue eyes twinkling as he met her gaze.

Delaney loved these rare moments when she caught a glimpse of her fiancé as if seeing him for the first time. She'd known him most of her life and often wondered if she'd find him attractive if she met him now. Her quickened heartbeat was answer enough: yes. A thousand times, yes.

"Hey, beautiful," Dalton rose and pulled her in for a kiss when she joined him inside. As they took their seats, he slid a glass of red wine her way. "A toast to your success."

She took a sip and a deep breath, relaxing for the first time that day. For better or worse, she was finished. She'd spent the afternoon plowing through work, but now she could finally focus on their wedding.

Dalton reached across the table and linked his fingers with hers. The warmth of his grasp underscored the strength of their bond, alleviating any lingering concerns about her honeymoon disclosure. She knew he'd understand.

"What's up?" Delaney asked, wanting to get his urgent news out of the way before sharing hers, figuring it would be trite. Something from the *Book of Groomzilla*, like a perceived emergency in the wedding favor department or an alarming last-minute change in the plated meal garnish. These were the things that whipped her otherwise easygoing groom into a wedding fiasco frenzy.

Dalton suggested they order before getting into it.

As Delaney perused the menu, she could sense his leg bouncing under the table. He seemed nervous about something.

Which reminded her. "Did you hear about this storm? We're gonna need to figure out what to do if it intensifies."

"No worries," Dalton said, without looking up from the menu. "It's rare for hurricanes to come this far north in June."

"That's funny. Sam said the same thing."

She closed her menu. It was useless to look when she

already knew she was getting her favorite—a deep, succulent dish of Jones's signature cheesy mac and cheese. Final fitting be damned.

After they ordered, Dalton handed her a slim black box.

"Is this my wedding gift?"

"Kinda, not really," Dalton said. "Go ahead, open. I'll explain."

Inside the box was a Big Ben bookmark.

"Change in honeymoon plans," Dalton blurted out. "Two weeks in London, baby." He beamed with pride, raised both hands arranged in a hang-ten gesture, and stage-whispered, "The crowd goes wild!"

He quickly explained she needn't do anything; he'd taken care of the details. Delaney listened as he rambled, her mouth gaping in disbelief.

The crowd was about to go wild, all right. Just not the way he'd hoped.

"But Antigua—"

"Forget Antigua," Dalton said, leaning forward and taking her hands. "You deserve London. We've talked about it for years and I figured, with our jobs, who knows when we'll be able to take this much time off again?"

"I can't go to London," Delaney exclaimed. "My hearing's been scheduled for the twenty-sixth. We only have a week."

He sank back in his chair, deflated. "When were you going to tell me?"

"I just found out."

Dalton closed his eyes, dark eyelashes fluttering, which meant he was trying to find a solution. He was a problem solver. Other than occasionally getting revved up about irrelevant wedding details, he wasn't prone to panic.

She hadn't wanted to share her news like this. She'd planned on couching it in softer terms.

He opened his eyes. "Okay. London for a week."

She shook her head. "We'll be returning the day before the hearing. I'll be completely wiped out. I can't do that."

"Then we come back a day or two earlier so you can adjust."

"No!" she insisted. "We discussed going to London for our first anniversary so we could take a couple weeks and travel around Europe. We have to stick with Antigua. For one week."

Dalton didn't say anything.

"I'm sorry." she said, her voice softening. "I appreciate you trying to do this, but I can't right now. A year from now, yes, let's do everything you've planned. When we have time to relax and do it right."

Dalton rubbed his chin and gave her a sheepish look.

"I already paid for it."

"Is it refundable?"

"Of course, I always get the insurance."

"What about Antigua, do we still have our bookings? Our flights, the hotel—"

"I canceled them." he said, shrugging.

"You canceled our honeymoon plans without consulting me?"

"I did it to create a bigger, better honeymoon."

"Why can't you ever be happy with the plans we've made? Since you've been involved, you've tried to change everything."

Dalton looked as if she'd slapped him. "I just wanted to surprise you."

Delaney was too furious to respond. She knew he was only trying to make her happy, based on a set of facts he knew to be true at the time, but her entire career was wrapped up in this case right now. A man's life depended upon her.

Their food came, but Delaney was too upset to eat. Dalton, who could eat in the middle of a rush hour shoot-out on I-95, ate not only his dinner but Delaney's as well. That made her even angrier. She was forever amazed (annoyed) at how much this man could eat and maintain his college quarterback physique while she had to subsist on a diet of cardboard if she wanted to keep her figure.

He finally broke the heavy silence between them on their drive home. "Laney, please don't be mad. I hate it when you're mad."

She turned and faced the window. Dalton cupped her chin, turning her head to face him.

"Oh boy. There's that same look you had when I knocked over your sandcastle."

She suppressed a chuckle. He always knew how to make her laugh.

"I loved that sandcastle," she pouted.

It was how they first met. Delaney's family had just moved into their vacation home in Ocean City, and she'd spent hours creating the perfect drippy castle when a set of feet crashed into it. The feet were attached to a boy around her age, who continued to twist and mangle her masterpiece. He ran off to the water and Delaney chased after him, calling him a *meanie-bo-beanie*—the worst insult her seven-year-old brain could conjure.

She returned to the castle to find an older boy trying to fix it. He introduced himself as Alex and apologized for his brother, explaining he was "kind of a poop head." Delaney agreed.

"It was a good castle," Dalton admitted. "I was jealous. I knew I could never build one that nice. But think about it. If I hadn't done that, we may not have met."

"We were next-door neighbors. I'm pretty sure it was a given we would have met."

"But the adversity made you fall in love with me. You're just lucky I got over you calling me a meanie-bo-beanie."

"But you were! The sandcastle, all the times you made fun of me—"

"Made you laugh."

THE WAY TO CAPE MAY

"True, but only after we became friends."

Dalton took her hand. "I'm sorry. I never thought surprising you with a trip to London would be a bad thing."

"It's not that. I know you were trying to make me happy, and I appreciate it. It just feels like you're always trying to change our plans, like you're kicking my castle again."

"I'm sorry. I just want everything to be perfect."

Delaney turned to face him. "It is perfect. Just the way it is."

"I'll cancel London and rebook Antigua for the week, on one condition."

She knew what was coming.

"Dispense with the charcuterie table and agree to my cheesesteak bar."

Delaney smiled. "Deal."

Cleo

CLEO AND WELLS HEADED TOWARD HIS APARTMENT IN Society Hill after her shift ended. She wasn't sure she should go after he got weird on her, but he seemed to be back to normal after Cleo shot him down with the excuse she had to pack for her vacation. Not entirely out of the realm of possibility, as she was last-minute Charlie on everything, and everyone knew it. He got the message, or so it appeared. Good, because she didn't want anything between them to change. Things were fine just the way they were.

But when they turned onto a cobblestoned side street, he reached for her hand.

Cleo yanked it away. "What are you doing?"

"Trying to hold your hand?"

"Why?"

"Because I want to?"

"Oh." Then, "Are you that drunk?"

Wells chuckled. "Just with glee."

Cleo shot him a look, waiting for him to say he was joking. She'd been the only one serving him, and he hadn't had enough to make him squishy with feels.

Wells had never held her hand before. It's not what they did. She wasn't into PDAs of any sort.

She wished she had pockets to occupy her hands as they walked. Instead, she pointed out the various architectural designs she'd learned about in art school. He seemed fascinated and asked the right questions, until they came upon a park with no buildings. She had no choice but to let her hand dangle, and soon the heat radiating from his hand warmed hers as he loosely linked their fingers.

"This okay?" he asked, looking down at her with a mischievous grin.

"This, meaning your shoddy attempt at abduction?" she said, giving a half-hearted laugh.

"You're onto me. My spaceship's a block away. I'll have you back by midnight."

Despite her misgivings, having his hand wrapped around hers felt—nice. Protective, even though she didn't need protection. Strong, even though she was already strong.

He squeezed her hand, and it took her breath away. She went with it, even though her heart was pounding with anxiety. Heart attack, perhaps? Surely not that other thing they talked about. They, meaning people who did relationships.

"You good?" Wells asked, his tone soft as he tightened his grip.

Another surge of warmth coursed through her body. "What's this all about?" she asked.

"I'm holding your hand, Clee, not stealing your soul."

"Good, because I don't have a soul."

"Then you have nothing to worry about," he said.

"Excellent. As long as you don't say you like me." Oops, did she just say that out loud?

Wells pulled her close, wrapped his arm around her waist. "But I do like you," he whispered.

This wasn't supposed to be happening. Like leads to love which leads to loss, at least in Cleo's life. Sure, she could be adventurous and uninhibited when it came to surface-level physicality, but the mere act of a man holding her hand felt more intimate. Dangerous. As if it would lead to more than what she wanted.

More than she could give.

She wasn't exactly joking when she said she didn't have a soul. At least not one worth giving to someone, only to have them turn around and crush it. As they always did.

They passed Independence Hall and turned onto a cozy tree-lined street flanked by gardens. Wells sat on a stone half wall and pulled her to him, sandwiching her petite frame between his strong thighs.

"Hey," he said, his eyes brimming with emotion. "Hey."

"Totally digging your mastery of the English language," Cleo teased.

"I'm totally digging you, tiny one."

Her synapses began firing their warnings again, but this time they were overruled by a new *sump'm-sump'm* flowing through her veins.

He brushed his lips against hers, parted and teased them. They'd kissed a thousand times before, but this one was different. Soft, sensual. An instinctive moan escaped her as he cupped her face and crushed his lips to hers.

They kissed for a long while, his hands sliding down her hips and pulling her in tightly. Her heart raced and he groaned as she dug her fingers into his thighs. The amount of shits Cleo gave just then about the brazen PDA equaled zero. Why had she ever been against it in the first place?

She wished they could instantly be transported to the California king in his swanky loft so they could disappear, naked, into the soft folds of his plush down comforter.

"Girl, you have no idea what you do to me," he whispered.

Cleo had a pretty good idea, if what she felt straining against her thigh was any indication. She couldn't wait to get to his place and release the Kraken.

But right now, this kiss, she couldn't break away. Wells eventually hopped off the wall and told Cleo to jump on his back. They ran through the streets of Society Hill, cackling like lunatics all the way. She disembarked when they got to his building, and he smushed her up against the wall, kissing her.

She motioned to the door of his building, where his doorman pretended not to watch. "Can we just—"

"Yeah." He grabbed her hand and pulled her past the doorman and into the open elevator. They stood there like Respectable People until the doors closed, and then it was every person for themselves.

She pushed him up against the wall, he grabbed a handful of ass, she wrapped her leg around his. He engulfed her with his kiss as he spun her and they slammed against the other wall of the elevator. Ignited by incontestable chemistry, their frenzy of groping, lips pressing, and tongues teasing ensued until they tumbled into his apartment.

But once in his bedroom, he slammed on the brakes. He moved in slow motion, all urgency giving way to tenderness as he lifted her shirt, his fingertips lightly brushing her skin, sending jolts of electricity through her.

She wanted to rip open his Oxford button-down like they do in the movies, but the vibe he gave off didn't lend itself to such recklessness. Usually, they'd succumb to fevered passion, but this night was different. It was purposeful. Delicious.

He laid her down softly on Egyptian cotton sheets as if she

were some sort of goddess, lightly trailing his fingers down her body and kissing his way back up. He crawled toward her like a wild animal on the prowl. His perfectly sculpted torso glistened in the moonlight pouring in from the balcony's French doors, as if they were in a fucking romance movie.

Day-um, if she wasn't so against intimacy, it would've been... *Stop, Cleo. Keep your wits about you.*

He cradled her head in the crook of his arm and tucked his leg between hers, looking at her with such intensity she nearly burst into flames. He traced his finger down the side of her cheek, tilting her chin as he brushed his lips against hers so tenderly they barely touched, so soft, so teasingly, she couldn't take it anymore.

She'd never had someone touch her, kiss her like that. She should've known right then where it was all headed, but she was drowning in dopamine and couldn't think straight.

After the slowest, sweetest session in the history of mankind (which, she discovered, was even better than the hot, harried variety), he snuggled her head against his chest, his fingertips like feathers as he brushed them up and down her arm.

She'd never felt so peaceful, so relaxed, so fulfilled. She could definitely get used to this.

Until, hours later, Cleo was awakened when his stubbled cheek brushed across hers, his warm breath mingling in her ear.

"Beautiful girl, I think I'm falling for you," he whispered and kissed her on the tip of her nose before rolling over.

Cleo's eyes flew open, and she lay still, staring at the ceiling.

What in the actual fuck just happened?

This wasn't in the contract. Her heart pounded, and she fought every urge to tear out of his apartment. He wasn't falling for her, he had to be drunk. Or delusional.

She waited for his breathing to become regular before she

untangled herself from the sheets (God, were they soft—she was gonna miss them), grabbed her clothing, and tiptoed to the living room.

Her breath came in gasps as she struggled to get dressed, signaling one of her trademark panic attacks. Then she let herself out.

Out of his apartment. Out of his life.

Friday, June 9

COUNTDOWN
TO WEDDING
8 DAYS

Delaney

DELANEY WAS SEATED AT HER BISTRO TABLE, GULPING her coffee as she pored over her to-do list. There were several more things to do before she left for her family's shore house, and she'd better get going if she wanted to beat Friday afternoon shore traffic.

Of all the trips she'd made to Ocean City in her lifetime, this would be the most important—the final leg of her journey toward Cape May, where she'd join her future husband in holy matrimony.

After checking the final item off her list and inspecting her packed bags for the fiftieth time, she closed the door to her condo. She was relieved this stage was over. All the wedding issues had been resolved, including the honeymoon debacle, and it should be smooth sailing from here on out—as long as Mother Nature refrained from bringing her tempestuous plus-one.

As Delaney crossed the bridge from Pennsylvania to New Jersey, regret washed over her. She recalled Kate's words about enjoying this process and wished she had taken a moment before she'd left her condo to appreciate the significance of the morning.

It was the last time she'd sit in singlehood at the little table, overlooking the tree-lined cobblestone streets of her Old City neighborhood. Where she and her roomies dished about their weekends on Sunday mornings. Where she and Dalton had eaten dinner by candlelight the first time she cooked for him, and where she consoled a heartbroken Kate when she broke up with Greg. Where she'd prepared her cases and planned her wedding.

In fact, the little table knew more about Delaney's life than some of her family members.

When she'd closed the door to the condo, she was closing the door to a monumental chapter of her life. She should have let that sink in, and paid homage to Delaney Ross before she became Delaney Brooks. As excited as she was to spend her life with Dalton, being single had meant all her decisions were her own. Now, she'd always have to consider someone else's opinions, goals, and desires.

While she was ready for that, she wished she'd taken more time to be present with her singleness, and less time obsessing over what had to be done.

When Delaney finally climbed the outdoor steps of her family's beachfront house, she gazed at the horizon, where a sparkling sapphire sea met a white-sand beach dotted with colorful umbrellas. She caught a glimpse of the blue-and-white wooden lifeguard stand where she and Dalton had shared their first kiss. It was a nice reminder of what mattered, through all the planning and details.

Inside, she found her parents in the kitchen, making lunch.

"Here comes the bride!" her mom called out, scurrying to hug her oldest daughter. Delaney's dad followed suit. The three gathered on the deck for Delaney's favorite summer lunch—thick slices of juicy Jersey tomatoes on mayo-slathered white bread and sweet tea. A large patio umbrella shaded the glaring sun as they discussed the upcoming festivities.

"I've been keeping an eye on this weather," her dad said. "The track of the storm's unclear at this point, but you should contact the hotel to find out what your options are."

"Already on it," Delaney said. She'd called that morning to discuss contingency plans. "We have the option to reschedule if it turns into a thing. We'll have to decide on Thursday unless it's obvious before then. If it's just rain, we already have plan B."

Plan A was to have the ceremony on the beach at Congress

Hall, Cape May's historic oceanfront resort, with cocktail hour on the lush green lawn and reception in the ballroom. Plan B meant taking it all inside. The only thing she didn't have was a plan C, for things like major hurricanes. How could she have missed that?

"I hope that doesn't happen," Delaney's mom said. "A beach wedding would be so nice."

"Relax, Faye," her dad said. "It's rare for hurricanes to come this far north in June."

Now everyone was a meteorologist—including her dad. Hopefully all these self-proclaimed weathermen were right.

Satisfied the wedding of the century would take place come hell or high flood waters, her mom wasted no time delving into gossip. Particularly, Greg's article.

Delaney shut her mom down a couple seconds later.

"Mom, he broke Kate's heart. I don't think she's fully processed how wrong they were for each other. We shouldn't encourage her to look back. If we do, she could move to the West Coast, and we'll never see her."

"Oh, I didn't think about that."

Next, they moved to the topic of Kate's blind date fix-up. It made perfect sense to Delaney to pair her with Dalton's cousin, the only two members of the bridal party without dates. She wasn't lying when she told Kate it was just for the wedding, but she knew they'd hit it off. As friends for sure, but maybe more.

"What's this Ryan like?" Her mom leaned forward on her elbows.

"The good news is, he's the male version of Kate—smart, successful, and deserving of the right person. The bad news is, he's the male version of Kate—attracts the wrong people and keeps them around too long."

Her mom fired off a series of questions, which Delaney answered dutifully. Political analyst. Lives in Georgetown.

THE WAY TO CAPE MAY

No, not far from Kate. Yes, amazing they're in the same field. Dark hair, blue eyes. Yep, like Dalton—they are cousins. Of course he's nice, and no, not gay. You're right, at the very least he could become a friend.

Even better if he makes her forget about Greg.

Tired of her mom's interrogation, Delaney turned the conversation to her other sibling, her sixteen-year-old brother.

"Where's JJ?" she asked. "Has he started his job on the boardwalk yet?"

"He's there now," her mom said. "He loves it, which is great because he's getting a lot of hours. And making bank."

Delaney laughed at her mom's use of slang.

"Good. Maybe he can help us pay for this wedding," her dad said.

After lunch, Delaney retreated to her childhood bedroom to unpack. She reached into a drawer to put her clothes away when her knuckles brushed against the corner of an object tucked under her old swimsuits. Her childhood diary. She opened the tattered blue cover and turned to the first page.

Dear Diary,

I turned eight today! It's our second summer in our shore house.

I'm happy my best friend, Cleo, is staying with her grandmother at the shore again this summer! My sister Katie is sick with chicken pox. I already had it when I was four. I hate chicken pox!

Today, Cleo and I bought matching Little Mermaid boogie boards, and Alex's going to teach us. He's an expert. I can't wait!

PS: Dalton said girls can't boogie-board but Alex said we can. He's older than Dalton, so he knows. He's not a dork like Dalton.

Delaney smiled at her characterization of the boy who'd soon be her husband. She turned the page.

Dear Diary,

Katie gave her chicken pox to the Brooks kids. Well, Nora and Alex have it. I hope Dalton gets it and turns into a chicken. I'm so happy Cleo doesn't have it. If she gets sick, I won't have anyone to play with. That would make me sad.

PS: Dalton would not be fun to play with. I'm still mad he knocked down my sandcastle last summer.

The Great Chicken Pox Summer. She remembered how it ended but read on.

Dear Diary,

Now Cleo has chicken pox too. I'm so mad at Katie, it's all her fault. Dork Dalton is the only one besides me who's not sick. Today he asked me to go boogie boarding. I told him I'd rather die.

PS: I meant it.

Delaney smiled, recalling what happened next.

Dear Diary,

Well, today I almost did die of boredom, so I went boogie boarding with Dalton. It was fun until I got pulled out to sea. Dalton grabbed my rope, and I thanked him for saving my life. He told me he didn't want to, but his mom would be mad if he didn't.

PS: I hate Dalton.

PPS: Then we made a sandcastle.

PPPS: And then we both knocked it down!

She flipped ahead to a random page.

Dear Diary,

I turned ten yesterday!!! They had a big birthday party for me and Dalton on the beach. His birthday is the day before mine. I hate that I had to share my party with him. He thinks he's better than me 'cause he's older, but I'm smarter. My favorite gift was a Barbie Dreamhouse. Dalton's favorite gift was a set of walkie-talkies.

PS: I don't think walkie-talkies are a good gift.

She continued reading about other events the young version of herself found newsworthy. She'd written about the night, age eleven, when she and Dalton had failed to return home with some other kids after a game of hide-and-seek. Their defense: an impromptu scavenger hunt. They'd found each other hiding under the boardwalk. When both refused to hide elsewhere, Dalton suggested they ditch the game and search for hidden treasures. It was after dark when they returned home with their haul in makeshift T-shirt buckets. They were greeted by their worried parents, who swiftly sent them to their rooms.

Dalton snuck her one of his walkie-talkies.

He told me to use it so we don't shrivel up and die in solitary confinement. He made funny noises and bet me I couldn't guess what they were supposed to be. I won because most of the noises he made were farts. Now he owes me $3. He's kinda funny and he made prison a lot more fun.

PS: He's still a dork.

She flipped ahead to the summer they were thirteen. Delaney and Dalton were on the boardwalk with friends and he threw up on a ride. When their friends teased him, Delaney told them they were jerks and walked him home. He had a stomach bug, it turned out, which he generously shared with her. Walkie-talkies, once again, got them through quarantine.

She hugged the stuffed unicorn on her bed as she read a passage from her fifteenth summer.

Dear Diary,

I hope you're sitting down because I have news! Of course you're sitting down—you're a diary! Remember that cute guy I told you about? He asked me out! He's picking me up at 7 and I can't wait!

PS. He never showed. Katie told Dalton I was stood up. Dalton made fun of me, but then asked if I wanted to go to the boardwalk with him. I didn't want to, but I wasn't about to sit at home and rot to death. I was sad about the date, but Dalton made me laugh. He's funny, even if he's scrawny and like a foot shorter than me. He bought me ice cream and won me a stuffed unicorn.

PPS: Dalton's not so dorkish anymore. He's my friend.

PPPS: But I'd never date him.

PPPPS: He better not ask.

Delaney fast-forwarded to the first day of their seventeenth summer, when she spotted "the cutest" lifeguard. She walked by to check him out while pretending not to notice him at all, a move she and her friends had perfected. The slow-motion, sucked-in-stomach, sunglass-concealed-side-glance walk designed specifically for cute lifeguard–spotting. She was surprised when the guy called her name and even more surprised to find it was Dalton. Not scrawny, and definitely not the awkward boy she'd known for so long. He'd grown tall, developed muscles, and had become the starting quarterback of his high school football team.

They chatted as he swung his lifeguard whistle around his finger, looking cool. She'd never felt nervous talking to her childhood buddy before. He was no longer the annoying kid next door but someone who made her heart thump like it was going to jump out of her chest.

That night, Dalton showed up at Kohr Brothers, the ice cream stand where Delaney worked. They walked home on the beach and sat in the lifeguard stand in front of their houses, where Dalton gave Delaney her very first kiss.

They dated all summer and tried to keep their relationship going throughout the school year, but distance proved challenging. Both in their senior year of high school in different states, they were too busy with friends, activities, and college applications to visit one another. She broke up with him the following summer. She was going to college in the Midwest and he in Boston and she didn't want to be tied down. Grad school landed him in Chicago for an MBA, and she returned to Philly for law school. Their timing seemed doomed, until a chance meeting—years later, on the streets of New York—brought them back together. This time, they didn't let distance keep them apart. They dated long-distance until Dalton transferred to his firm's Philly office after they got engaged.

Delaney continued flipping through the pages of her diary, disappointed to find her high school breakup with Dalton was the last time she recorded her memories. From that point on, the book went from diary to planner, filled with to-do lists crafted in meticulous handwriting. Including her strategic plan for graduating college at the top of her class—a list of action steps, next to which were perfectly drawn squares, containing perfectly drawn check marks. Then there were her post-college goals for getting into law school, each with the same perfect squares and check marks. On the last page, in ornate font, she'd written, *Seek perfection*.

Her heart sank. Her diary-turned-planner proved Kate right. Delaney lived by her to-do list. She was so focused on the next goal, so worried about failing, she didn't allow herself to just be in the moment. Like that morning in her apartment.

If only she could go back and tell her younger self to chill a little—it would all work out, even if not perfectly. *Put down the pen, stop plotting your life, live a little.*

Let go and let destiny...

Kate's motto echoed in her brain. Delaney was envious of her sister's laid-back attitude, which allowed her to settle into imperfection in a way Delaney couldn't. Comfortably nestled in the shadow of an overachieving older sister, Kate didn't stay up all night studying feverishly for exams and stressing over grades. She didn't worry about being the best in her field or winning the approval of those who mattered. She had an unshakable faith everything would work out and didn't get rattled when things went wrong, because something equally spectacular was coming.

Now, seeing her teen years written out as a series of game plans designed to achieve success, Delaney wondered if it was too late to change. For starters, she could try being more like Kate. There had to be a happy medium between their different approaches to life: plan, but embrace the unexpected. Have faith things will work out, even if not in perfectly orchestrated fashion.

Maybe she still had a chance.

ABOUT TO LEAVE FOR OCEAN CITY, KATE WAS LIFTING A suitcase into her trunk when Bianca, another college friend, called.

"Why are you out of breath?" Bianca asked.

"Packing up my car," Kate responded as she began a game of luggage Tetris. She'd packed most of her wardrobe so she'd have plenty to choose from for the extravaganza known as Wedding Week.

"Boo. I thought you'd be halfway across the country by now. Did you see Greg's article?"

"Not you too."

"Amazing, isn't it? Great coverage. California agrees with your ex-beau."

"Since when do you all read *Men's Monthly*?" Kate asked. "Seriously, before yesterday I had no idea it existed. You guys act like it's the *New York Times*."

"It's been all over his Insta."

"You follow him?"

"Hell yeah. It's not every day your college friend ends up living the lifestyle of the rich and suntanned."

Yes, it was kind of a big deal, but not Kate's to be excited about. Except—

"He sent me roses," she blurted out, instantly regretting it as Bianca shrieked. Kate held the phone away from her ear to avoid a shattered eardrum.

"They were green, which stands for new beginnings. Who knew?"

Bianca's voice took on a swoony tone. "That's so romantic! Have you reached out to him?"

"He's no longer of interest to me, no matter how many sports cars he can fit into his garage."

Six, according to the article. He'd filled every bay. Not that Kate cared.

Bianca was silent. Then, "Give me his number. I'll reach out."

Kate laughed. Between Laura and Bianca, it was like having an angel on one shoulder, devil on the other. She just wasn't sure who was who.

"Laura said you'll be joining us in Avalon?" Bianca asked.

Speaking of the devil. (Angel?)

"For a couple days," Kate said, "as long as the bride doesn't need me to run interference on anything."

Kate was splitting the week, spending the first half helping Delaney, then joining her college friends in their Avalon shore house for a couple nights. It had been a minute since they'd all hung out, and Kate was looking forward to the slight respite from all things wedding.

Tetris game complete, she slammed her trunk shut as her phone dinged an incoming message. She looked at the screen to find a Google Photos "On This Day Two Years Ago" message.

Kate gasped. It was a selfie of her and Greg on the beach wearing matching Ocean City hoodies and smiling into the camera lens as fog wafted around them.

It was a chilly day in June when the photo was taken. He'd asked her to go for a walk on the beach to commemorate the fifth anniversary of their first date. She was convinced he was going to propose, but instead he broke the news about his West Coast move. He asked her to come, they fought, and he left the shore in a huff.

"You're not going to believe this," Kate said, and told Bianca about the photo. "I swear to God, these phones know everything."

"Or is it a sign?" Bianca asked.

Kate moaned. "Bee, I'm trying not to think like that."

"Okay, not a sign. Sorry. I just think you guys were good together."

"You're forgetting he left me to go live in a van down by the beach."

"It paid off," she said. "Maybe he's finally ready to settle down?"

"That ship has sailed," Kate said, hoping to convince herself. "Sunk, actually."

Laura's words echoed in her brain. Nothing about Kate's life had changed. That's where she needed to keep her focus because, truth be told, she couldn't get the image of Greg and his gleaming surfer physique out of her mind. She'd worked too hard to get over him to be wiped out by a wave of regret.

"Laura thinks it's too late," Bianca continued. "She's such a downer."

"Sorry, but I'm Team Laura on this one," Kate said.

"Suit yourself. I just have a feeling it isn't the end of your Greg story."

Kate disagreed, yet a shot of hope pierced her heart.

Hope that was swiftly dashed when she remembered she'd agreed to a lousy wedding date with a total stranger. Which meant she couldn't just enjoy her sister's wedding without having to entertain someone. Not that she'd be enjoying the wedding anyway, with this fresh reminder of how her own plans for marriage had been squashed by a nomadic ex-boyfriend with a hankering for nautical adventure.

After they hung up, Kate plugged the address of her family's shore house into Google Maps. Her ETA was illuminated in ominous red, warning of a lengthy delay in her trip. She weighed her options: spend the afternoon in traffic, or wait out the delay with a little retail therapy? It didn't take long to decide, and soon she was strolling Alexandria's King Street, browsing her favorite boutique shops.

The traffic situation provided a great alibi for the truth: Kate wasn't quite ready to face wedding week festivities in light of this news about Greg. She needed time to process, to think. And shop. As maid of honor, she had a leading role in this wedding, and needed the moral support of her favorite fashionistas, Lilly Pulitzer and Trina Turk. She wasn't trying to pull a Pippa and upstage the bride or anything, but there was no harm in looking her absolute best. Perhaps then people would notice her for what she had and not what was missing—her successful ex-boyfriend.

Once Kate was fashionably satiated, financially spent, and fortified with designer shopping bags, she headed for her car.

Two minutes into her trip, she decided she couldn't fathom a four-hour drive without coffee, so she steered into the black hole of time known as a Starbucks drive-through, thereby delaying her trip even longer.

All this dawdling wasn't because she didn't love her sister or think the wedding wasn't the most exciting thing to happen in their lives. She just needed all the strength a cup of joe, a new wardrobe, and a passive-aggressive delay could deliver.

When Kate finally arrived at her shore house, she decided to change into her new swimsuit before joining her family on the beach. She'd spent more on the yellow Billabong string bikini than she normally would, but the splurge was worth it. The tan she got on a recent trip to Bali, combined with her workout sprint these past few months, provided the confidence boost she needed.

She twisted her golden waves into a messy bun and turned to examine her flat abs, compliments of the private trainers at her gym. Kate was fortunate to live a lifestyle that allowed her to dine, shop, and work out among DC's elite. She'd earned it, although not through grueling work like her sister. More by cultivating key contacts, being in the right place at the right time, and having faith in good outcomes. She was lucky that way, at least professionally.

Not so much in her personal life. The long drive had given Kate an opportunity to ponder her existence. Greg's success had Kate thinking about the past, how his departure left a definitive hole in her life. She'd tried to fill it with someone new, until she'd discovered most available men were "Status: Single" for a reason.

Or had she been too picky? What exactly was she looking for in a guy?

For the first time since their breakup, she wondered if she was the problem. Had she been too dismissive when Greg asked her to join him out West? Or was she just now seeing greener grass on the flip side of the country?

Kate finally joined her family on the beach and her dad launched into his typical travel interrogation: the route she took, the price of gas in Virginia, and whether she'd gotten her oil changed before she left. She hadn't, so she adeptly diverted his attention with a dramatic recount of her "brutal" commute, which cost her "hours" due to "ridiculous" Friday summer travel, omitting the minor details of her two-hour shopping excursion and Starbucks drive-through time warp.

The family caught up on the basics of her life until Kate sensed her mother bursting at the seams—either to spill some tea or slurp it up.

"What's with the face?" Kate asked her, unable to ignore it any longer.

"What face?" her mom asked, incredulous, as if she'd just been accused of tax evasion.

"That face. The one that tells me you you're either brimming with gossip or a probing question. I'm guessing it's the latter."

"Yeah, I have to agree with you, Kate," her dad said, laughing, as he turned to his wife. "So, Faye, which is it?"

All eyes focused on her mom.

"Okay!" she burst. "It's about Greg, the article. I'm dying to know if you've seen it."

Delaney grunted and Kate rolled her eyes.

"Yes, I saw it," she said, her voice monotone. Her family couldn't know she hadn't thought of much else.

"Did you see the part about his love life?" her mom asked, in a tone so shrill it indubitably captured the attention of neighboring dogs.

Kate tried to recall the article. In truth, she'd been fixated on his photos more so than the actual article, which had delved into the mechanics of creating a new surfboard design. Blablabla, yaddayaddayadda, seen one surfboard, seen 'em all.

But his smile...

"The interviewer asked if he had anyone special in his life. Here—" She dove her hand into her beach bag. "I have the article, read it for yourself."

"Oh God. Here we go," Delaney muttered as she slunk down in her beach chair and pulled her baseball cap over her eyes.

"Page forty-one," her mom declared.

Kate flipped to page forty-one. She scanned the article, but her mom beat her to the punch.

" 'No one currently, but there's someone from my past I haven't gotten over,' " her mom recited.

"You're incorrigible," Delaney said.

Kate found the passage, and damn if her mom's recitation wasn't spot-on.

She stared at the words, trying to convince her heart not to react.

"It's gotta be you he's talking about, right?" her mom whispered, as if Greg were mere feet away. "I mean, who else?"

"Could be anyone, Mom," Kate said, snapping the magazine closed and handing it back. "He's been out there for two years; I'm guessing he hasn't been celibate this whole time."

"I don't know, Kate," her mom said. "You're not someone who's easy to get over."

"Can we stop talking about this?"

Respecting her wishes, they went on to discuss other topics, but Kate could barely keep her mind on the conversation as Greg's words reverberated in her mind. Maybe her mom was right—he was talking about her. The possibility put a whole new spin on his green rose gesture.

Eventually, her parents headed back to the house, leaving the sisters alone on the beach.

"How ya feeling?" Kate asked, relieved to get out of her own head as she shifted her focus to Delaney. "Are you ready for all the hoopla to begin?"

"Ready as I'll ever be. Funny how the true meaning of a wedding gets lost among the tiny details."

"That's what they tell me."

"Your day will come," Delaney said and then, as if to get her dig in, added, "once you figure out what you're looking for."

"I'm in no rush to get married." Kate gave a cynical half smile as she drew the outline of a heart in the sand with her toe, adding a jagged line through it. "It's super fun to always be a bridesmaid, never a bride."

"Doesn't have to be that way, you know," Delaney said, in condescending older-sister tone. "By the way, I told Ryan you're in. He's excited to meet you."

Ryan Schmyan.

Kate erased the heart drawing with her foot and kicked sand onto it for good measure.

"Smirk now, but you'll be pleasantly surprised," Delaney promised. "He's a good guy."

"People said that about Ted Bundy, and you know how that ended."

Marley

MARLEY STOOD OUTSIDE HER APARTMENT BUILDING ENjoying the cool June breeze. A perfect day to drive to the shore in a drop-top—rare for summertime in Philly, when it was either steaming hot or pouring rain.

Music blasting from car speakers heralded Sam's arrival from a block away.

"Two thirty on the nose!" he yelled.

Marley climbed into his cherry red Jeep. Sam threw it into gear and peeled away as he waved to the doorman storming toward them.

Their summer Friday routine consisted of putting in a few hours at work before heading home to change. Then Sam would pick up Marley at her place, pulling into the no-parking zone in front of her building. She'd hop in and he'd speed away before Felix, her doorman, spotted them. He ran a strict curbside operation, and Sam was a repeat offender of the no-parking rule. Marley had to move fast or suffer one of Felix's lectures when she returned. Their weekly goal was to get over the Ben Franklin Bridge—BFB as it was known colloquially—before snarled traffic kept them bottled in the city.

Marley enjoyed riding in "Big Red," a welcome break from SEPTA, their mode of public transportation during the week.

"Here you go. You can thank me later," Sam said as he tossed a Wawa bag containing their favorite treats—a cream-filled doughnut with chocolate glaze (Sam) and a plain one (Marley).

"Nice hair," she said. He'd somehow gotten a haircut since they left the office. She ruffled his sun-bleached waves.

"Hey." Sam jerked from Marley's reach and whipped his hair back into place.

"This new?" Marley asked, grabbing the sleeve of his Hawaiian shirt.

"Birthday gift from my mom."

New hair, new shirt, freshly ironed Vineyard Vines shorts and Sperrys...what was up with this boy? He usually donned his "Where the hell is Strathmere?" tee, faded swim trunks, and Reef flip-flops for their ride down the shore.

Intriguing outfit aside, it was time for business. She pulled a legal pad from her bag.

"Enough small talk," she announced. She flipped to the notes she'd taken during their earlier meeting.

"This is a no-work zone. The weekend has officially begun," he announced as he grabbed the pad from Marley's hands and flung it into the back seat.

Marley spun around to retrieve the notepad, but it flopped and fluttered before a gust of wind carried it down the 42 Freeway.

"Oh, shit." Sam laughed.

"Sam!" Marley yelled over the whipping wind. "My notes— you have to pull over."

"Sorry, can't." Sam flashed a smile. "Too much traffic, Mar. You'll never make it across one lane alive, let alone four. I prefer my shore friends to get there in one piece, not seventy."

Marley sulked. Sam poked her cheek; she ignored him. He wrapped one of her curls around his finger, tugging slightly. She continued to stare straight ahead. What else was on that legal pad? Notes about their case, previous staff meetings, grocery lists. God knows what else.

Sam tried to stick the end of her curl in her ear. She recoiled and swatted at his hand.

"I'll take my treat now," he said.

She handed him the glazed doughnut. He waved it off and pointed to the plain.

"You always go with glazed," Marley challenged.

"Sometimes plain is nice."

His comment reminded her of one of their early study sessions, before they'd become friends. Sam had brought assorted doughnuts and told her to choose carefully, as her selection would say a lot about her.

She'd selected a plain one. He postulated, correctly, that she was drawn to safe and unassuming things in a desire to blend in.

He'd selected a glazed one. She asked what it said about him.

"It's covered with a glistening glaze, suggesting I'm easily pulled in by shiny objects. But note the bland casing beneath, suggesting a dichotomy, raising inquiry as to whether it's form without substance. Or is it substantive and multidimensional, like self? Reticent, when not confident. Introverted, when not the life of the party. Studious, when not drinking my face off."

Marley had been impressed, using such big words for a boy.

He continued. "Outwardly, I'm adventurous, daring. I like living on the edge. Unlike you, I do not settle for plain and boring. I want excitement, a little uncertainty, and definitely pizzazz. Gotta have pizzazz, or what's the point? Let's find out what's on the inside."

He took a slow, deliberate bite, revealing an oozing blob of chocolate filling. He sucked it from its casing. Marley was annoyed at herself for noticing.

"Mmm...my God." Sam's eyes closed as he relished his treat. "What a delightful surprise, an intensely pleasurable interior. Smooth custard, so creamy and light you're not even sure you're eating it, until you swirl it around with your tongue and it slides down your throat."

Marley swallowed hard, her mouth dry. She had no idea pastries could be so sexy.

"Wanna bite?" he'd asked, bringing it to her lips.

Marley wasn't a tease, but this doughnut was begging for it. She scooped the tiniest bit of dripping custard with the tip of her tongue and closed her lips around the cakey exterior as Sam watched intently.

Two can play at this game.

"Mmm." She sighed, closing her eyes as she sucked on the sugary sweetness.

His breath hitched, voice husky. "Yep, I knew it. You think you want plain, but you really want pizzazz."

Marley prided herself on titillating the smooth-talking Sam Adams. Even if just a little.

Now, riding along in Big Red, Marley licked the glaze from her fingers. He was right, pizzazz tasted pretty good.

Sam asked what her plans were for the night.

"Deauville, as always," Marley answered, referencing the historic waterfront inn within walking distance of their houses. Their favorite place to start the weekend.

"I'm in!" Sam said without waiting for an invitation. "Are boys allowed?"

"*Boys* being the operative word."

"I'm more man than you could handle." He flashed her his trademark sexy grin.

"Then man up and get us there."

Sam put on his "Roar to the Shore" playlist, which consisted mostly of songs from the eighties, a decade with which he was obsessed. Music and movies, mostly, but occasionally fashions. Strange tastes, that Sam.

"Got anything written after the Stone Age?" Marley teased.

"Watch it. Nobody messes with the eighties."

"Sorry, REO Speedwagon. My bad."

Before long, they were crawling along Ocean Drive through Sea Isle. It was already hopping with the usual Friday evening crowd—sandy families coming off the beach, singles weaving in and out of bars, older couples heading to dinner.

Minutes after Sam dropped her off at her house, the first six notes of the *Rocky* theme trumpeted from Marley's phone. It was the signature ringtone he'd plugged into her phone for his contact, so she'd know when he called or texted. He announced that he and his housemates were heading over to Deauville.

Marley and her entourage eventually made their way through the narrow bayside streets of Strathmere and blended into the party-in-progress on Deauville's outdoor deck. She spotted Sam mingling with two dark-haired beauties. She headed to the bar to order a drink before joining him when she saw a woman perched on a barstool, holding the rapt attention of several guys.

Marley instantly recognized her, even though she'd only seen her picture. She appeared as perfect in person as she did in her profile picture.

Jenna. Sam's ex.

Marley did a double take, confirming she was staring into the abyss of Sam's unrequited past. He was still on the other side of the bar, flirting with the brunettes, seemingly unaware his long-lost heartthrob was mere feet away.

Marley caught Sam's attention, her eyes wide as she tipped her head in Jenna's direction. His face lit up and he began making his way over. Marley didn't want her third wheel rolling into their special reunion, so she ducked away to the restroom, taking her time so they could catch up.

They were deep in conversation when she returned.

"Hey, Mar!" Sam waved her over. "This is Jenna, my friend from high school. Jenna, Marley. My good friend."

Did he just emphasize "good friend" more than necessary?

"*I* was a little more than *just* a friend." Jenna smiled, flipping her blonde hair. "We were serious boyfriend and girlfriend."

"Oh, right." Sam chuckled. "For a minute."

"A minute!" Jenna punched him playfully in the arm. "It was, like, a month. He doesn't give himself enough credit."

The self-serving comment wasn't lost on Marley.

"I ordered you Shore Crush, Mar," Sam said.

It was her favorite Deauville drink. She wiggled her fingers in excitement.

He put one hand on Marley's shoulder as he reached for her drink with the other. Jenna eyed his lingering touch, as if trying to determine their true relationship status. Was Marley a girlfriend? Friend with benefits? Or *ding-ding-ding!* Correct answer: platonic friend. Marley recognized the look because she'd seen it on countless women who flirted with Sam while shooting sidelong glances at her, wondering who she was to him.

Marley's phone signaled an incoming text.

"It's Delaney," she said. "She's scheduling a call Monday at ten to discuss our meeting with the prosecutor."

"Why did you meet with a prosecutor?" Jenna asked, wrinkling her nose at Sam.

"We're working a criminal case," he explained.

"Don't tell me you want to practice criminal law!" Jenna said. "Gross."

"I do want to practice criminal law," Sam said with confident defiance. He shot Marley a nervous glance.

"There's no money in that," Jenna announced.

Wow. Don't hold back, Jenna.

"Are you in on a shore house this summer?" Marley asked to change the subject but also because she was curious how Jenna happened to appear in the same bar, on the same night, as Sam.

Jenna snickered. "My parents own a beachfront home, no need to group-rental slum it."

"Slumming's fun. You should give it a try sometime," Marley countered.

Sam shot her a quick look, which she took as a request to get lost. She excused herself and went in search of her housemates.

Marley had always been curious what kind of person had stolen Sam's heart and cured him of relationships forever, but assumed she'd be nicer. She told herself to suspend judgment, as she disliked when Sam was critical of Rick. It was a bummer when your good friend didn't care for your significant other.

She found her housemates doing shots with a group of guys. They handed her one and she threw back the bittersweet liquid, chasing it with her drink.

A second shot was passed around a couple minutes later, and the group toasted the weekend. The seventies cover band started playing, transforming the deck into a dance floor. Marley caught a glimpse of Sam and Jenna, her arms flung around his neck as she gazed at him.

"That didn't take long," Marley said aloud to nobody.

One of the guys handed Marley a third shot as the band played summer's anthem, "Sweet Caroline." He pulled Marley to the center of the dance floor, mere feet from Sam and Jenna. The song built to its crescendo and the crowd chanted the familiar refrains, fists pumping air. Marley saw Jenna peck-kiss Sam on the cheek just before someone danced into her line of vision. Leaning forward to keep her eye on them, she lost her balance.

"Whoa!" Marley's dance partner grabbed her as she fell into him.

Damn shots. She rarely did them. When she did, it was usually just one. Three felt like someone had poured Tito's directly into her cranium.

Her eyes locked with Sam's. He was watching her with an expression of amused confusion as she pulled her partner into a maniacal disco move.

Marley wasn't sure what point she was trying to make, dancing like this with a stranger when she was practically betrothed to another. But something compelled her to make Sam watch.

Jenna kissed him on the cheek again. Marley had enough.

"Let's go get some air," she said as she took the guy's hand, trying to remember his name—Dave, Don, John, whatever— and led him to the railing overlooking the bay.

"Hey, Mar, everything good?"

She pretended not to hear Sam's voice behind her until he tapped her on the shoulder.

"Oh, hey," she said as she spun around. "Yep, I'm good. This is my friend, um—"

"Mark," he said, holding out his hand to shake Sam's.

THE WAY TO CAPE MAY

Sam grabbed his hand firmly but didn't shake. His power move.

"Need another drink?" Sam asked.

"Define need." She giggled, linking her arm with Mark's. "Nah, I'm good."

"I'll take one," Mark said.

Sam ignored him and left.

Before long, the deck felt like it was rocking. She excused herself and headed toward the exit, passing Sam and Jenna, who were now smushed into a corner. She considered asking Sam to walk her home, but that would be rude. He needed to resolve whatever lingering issues he had with his high-school sweetheart so he could learn to trust again. Whether that be Jenna, or someone else.

Hopefully someone else.

As she crossed the Deauville's gravel parking lot, the ocean called to her. Excellent idea, a beach walk, despite it being in the opposite direction of her house.

Her stomach was in knots, as if she was going to be sick, but she knew it was due more to her emotions than anything. She should be happy for Sam, but Jenna didn't seem deserving of his yearslong infatuation.

The sea and its breeze conspired to whisper one word: *Jealous*.

"I'm not jealous," she bellowed.

Her phone bleated the *Rocky* theme.

"Where are you?" Sam yelled over the background din.

"I'm walking home," Marley yelled back.

"Why are you yelling?"

Right. She wasn't the one in a crowded bar.

"You okay?" he asked. "Should I walk you home?"

Back in the city, they always left bars together.

"I wouldn't want to tear you away from *Jessica*."

She purposely snarled the incorrect name. She couldn't help it. Maybe the ocean was right—she was jealous.

"You know her name."

"Right, Henna. I wouldn't want you to tear yourself away from Mount Saint Helens. Oh heavens, I wouldn't want precious *Jen-na* slumming it in a rented shore house!"

Sam gave an annoyed sigh, but she and her four thousand drinks found her behavior to be quite amusing.

"Where are you? You're not right. You shouldn't be walking home by yourself."

"I'm a big girl and—look! Here I am, at my house already."

"Promise?"

"Promise," she lied, mimicking the squeak of her shore house screen door.

"Marley, you just made that sound with your mouth."

"Hey, Gwen, I'm home!" Marley yelled out to her imaginary (but real) housemate.

"Convincing. Except, Gwen's right here with us." Sam sounded unamused. "Seriously, Mar. I saw you doing seventy shots."

Sam's voice was quieter now. He must have stepped outside, away from the band and the crowd chanting the lyrics to "Wildwood Days."

"Lemme at least come check on you, make sure you're okay," he said.

"Why? So I'll come on to you like I did that night?"

Wait. *What?*

Oh. My. God.

Did she just say that? Did she really just bring up the only taboo subject between them? The unresolved subject of That Night?

She stared at her phone, horrified. She could hear silence on Sam's end, then the faint sound of his voice saying they should talk.

She didn't want to talk.

She hung up and burst into tears as the memory of That

Night bubbled to the surface. The night she hadn't thought about for so long, the one she'd willed herself to forget.

Here it was, popping up again, for the second time in two days.

She walked along the water's edge, sobbing into the wind as the fuzzy scenes flashed through her mind like a choppy home video. She tried to fast-forward, beyond That Night and the resulting weeks of humiliation, to where she finally resolved not to feel anymore. Head over heart, mind over emotion, practiced steadily and consistently until it was second nature.

Time was a trusted friend to those who needed to replace feelings with facts, allowing them to look at someone they once crushed on and feel only friendship.

For some reason, though, the button was stuck on replay.

"I'm not jealous," she yelled at the ocean, in case it didn't hear her the first time.

Okay, maybe this was jealousy. The way Sam was with Jenna was what she'd once yearned for. Not anymore, of course, which is what made all these emotions so confusing. She'd witnessed Sam with other women over the years but this one was different.

Probably because it meant something to him.

Ninety-nine bottles of booze down her throat certainly weren't helping her assess the situation clearly, or reel in her emotions.

That's it, I'm never drinking again.

Time to sober up. She climbed into a lifeguard stand and called Rick, her go-to man, always a source of comfort. He answered immediately, the concern in his voice evident as he asked her what was wrong. She never called this late.

"Sam met someone!" Marley wailed, then lowered her tone. "Okay, he didn't just meet her. It's his high school ex, the one who broke his heart."

"Don't we want him to find a girlfriend?"

"She broke his heart, *Rick*." Seriously. Men.

"Maybe she's changed. Don't you want him to be happy?"

"*I. Don't. Like. Her*," Marley hissed.

"You're not the one dating her," Rick reminded her.

"No, but my best friend is. I don't want to see him hurt."

"It's not your job to protect him. He's a big boy. If it doesn't work out, he'll get over it. Just be a friend." Rick paused, then added, "But be *just* a friend."

"What's that supposed to mean?"

Wrong question. She knew what it meant.

When Rick first met Sam, he noted they seemed "oddly close." She assured him that their relationship was platonic. She never told him about That Night because it happened pre-Rick, so it was irrelevant.

Or was it? Would the fact that she and Rick were about to spend their lives together warrant the disclosure of her big secret?

"Make sure the new girlfriend knows you're just friends," Rick clarified. Then, "It's still nothing more than that, right?"

The truth called to Marley like sirens to sailors, hopefully with a less tragic fate. "Maybe once. Kind of. It was before you."

She proceeded to word-vomit into her phone about That Night, sticking to just the facts. She told him how they hit all the bars on their beer bucket list—twelve, to be exact. How she had too much to drink and tried to kiss Sam, even tried to do a striptease. He shut down her performance, saying she wasn't his type.

"That's it?" Rick asked.

"Yes."

SparkNotes version, at least.

"Sorry I didn't tell you sooner. Nothing to worry about, I was just drunk."

Rick laughed.

"Why are you laughing?"

"The visual of your striptease is too funny."

"That's your takeaway?"

She'd deliberated for three years whether she should tell him about That Night, and all he did was laugh?

At least he wasn't freaking out.

One of the things Marley found most attractive about Rick was his even temperament, his confidence. Nothing about him, or their relationship, was dramatic. His was a constant love, consistently administered. Marley never had to worry how he felt about her because he let her know all the time. He let her pick restaurants and movies. He agreed with her about current events. Or didn't have an opinion, which was sometimes annoying.

But every now and then, Marley wished Rick would show passion about something. A differing opinion about where to eat, which might lead them to discover a new restaurant. Debate over current events, which might cause a shift in perspective. Maybe even an argument leading to hot, rip-your-clothes-off makeup sex, evidence of two people passionate about one another. But there was no need for hastily shredded clothing when sex was always planned and executed in neat and orderly fashion, predictable and safe.

It wasn't fair to compare, but Marley got a charge from her friendship with Sam, who brimmed with passion for things big and small. The Innocence Project. The Eagles. Pat's cheesesteaks. He wasn't afraid to challenge her when he thought she was wrong about a point of law or when they disagreed over an Eagles penalty call. He made the mundane fun and was predictably unpredictable, with an unbridled energy that manifested in a variety of ways—through drum solos on the deli counter as he waited for his order, or a sprint across Rittenhouse Square to chase pigeons off a park bench. Strolling down Chestnut Street at lunch, he would stop, pivot, and drag her into a store, all because a shirt in the window spoke to him—whether for him or her. He loved shopping for Marley as much as himself, often acting as her fashion police.

He even spent a Saturday afternoon pulling out stacks of sweatshirts and leggings from her closet, telling her she needed to stop dressing like a toddler going down for a nap.

Sam was, without a doubt, the best friend a woman could ask for. Marley was keenly aware she'd struck gold with these two men: a fun friend, and a steady love. But sometimes she wished she and Rick had a little more—something.

Pizzazz?

Rick's sobering effect made her sleepy. Marley ended the call as two figures appeared on the beach path a block over. They passed through a strip of moonlight and paused for an embrace.

Sam and Jenna.

She scrambled from the lifeguard stand and scurried off the beach before they could see her.

Maybe it had been wrong to purposely omit key details of That Night, but there was no reason to burden Rick with the full truth. Like how unusually affectionate Sam was before she'd done the unthinkable. How his hand lingered longer than necessary on Marley's back as he led her through crowded bars. How he danced seductively with her during slow songs and held her hand at the Clink as they reminisced over funny things they'd experienced together.

The night had culminated with Marley nearly falling out of the limo, and Sam staying to make sure she was okay. Nothing unusual—they often stayed at each other's places.

But that night, Marley and her good friend alcohol had decided to kiss Sam.

He'd bolted upright and told her to stop. That should've been enough, but the booze told her to keep going. She stood and began humming a striptease tune—that part was true—as she tried to pull her shirt over her head. She fell over, laughing.

Sam picked her up and led her back to the bed where she tried to kiss him again. He told her they shouldn't be doing this.

"Whyyynot?" Marley slurred.

"You're drunk."

"Yesssiam. But alcohol is truth, and the truth is I have such a crush on you!" She waved her hands like she was conducting an orchestra. "Suchhaaacrruusshh."

He told her it was the alcohol talking. She insisted they were her true feelings, and she knew he felt the same way.

He told her he didn't want to ruin their friendship. She insisted it wouldn't.

She tried to kiss him a third time, and that's when Sam said something to forever change the trajectory of their friendship.

"I'm sorry, Marley but—you're not my type."

Ah, the lowest blow one could deliver, tantamount to saying, "It's not me, it's you."

"And I'm not yours," he added.

Marley may have agreed in a more sober state. Sam was a player, while Marley wasn't. She sought meaningful relationships while he sought good times. She'd spent years watching Sam pick up women, but never her. Apparently, she wasn't enough for him.

Marley sobbed and he consoled her until she finally fell asleep.

She'd awakened the next morning with a splitting headache and sick feeling in her stomach, but the physical remnants were nothing compared to gut-wrenching humiliation.

Fortunately, Sam was gone before she woke. She successfully avoided his phone calls and texts over the next week, until he left for summer study abroad in China. She was grateful to put three months and seven thousand miles between them, enough time and distance to mend her broken heart.

Two weeks later, she met a nice boy who asked for her phone number. He wasn't encumbered with dashing good looks, but he called when he said he would. He never let Marley think she wasn't his type, because she was. And he, hers.

That boy was Rick.

Cleo

CLEO COULDN'T WAIT UNTIL HER FRIDAY NIGHT SHIFT AT Murphy's Tavern was over, the one she'd picked up to avoid Wells and his Big Stupid Date. Which, of course, was no longer a threat.

Still, Murph needed her, and she was a woman of her word.

And—cha-*ching!* Summer in Philly, with all its Liberty Bell–loving tourists, was when she made bank. She wouldn't rake in as much at the Tavern as she would at the Clink, where the tips were as rich and shiny as the patrons themselves. But Tavern folk were her kinda people—the blue-collar, hard-working, gritty backbone of Philly. They were like family.

Better than family, actually.

Slinging drinks one more night meant lining her pockets with a few extra bucks before heading to the sparkling Jersey Shore. She just had to get through this last shift before she could speed across the BFB, leaving Philly and her sizzling (now-ex) fling in the grimy city dust.

Poor Wells. He never stood a chance in Cleo's court, even if he was the hottest thing she'd ever tried. It was a bummer, dismissing his case before he presented his evidence. She liked him, and over the course of their short-lived, playful, and purely physical thing, the two had become friends of sorts. She didn't want to hurt him, but no thanks on the relationship front.

His text had come hours after she'd left that night.

> Hey! Where'd u go?

She debated letting him down easy, making a lame excuse to avoid the truth, but decided instead to rip off the Band-Aid.

> Can't do relationships, Wells. Sorry.

Cleo had stared at the bubble and three bouncing dots, waiting...and waiting...for his response. Part of her wanted him to just be okay and go happily into the sunset. But another part of her hoped he would—something. Make her feel like she didn't just imagine the whole thing. Or maybe that she was worth fighting for.

But the bubble disappeared. No text followed.

She convinced herself she was right to put an end to it but couldn't help stealing glances at her phone all day. When she didn't hear from him, she convinced herself this was how it had to be. She couldn't risk their casual thing becoming something more, because then he'd know the truth about her.

"So that's the end of that, Gus," Cleo said with a shrug, after summarizing the events of last night.

The man at the corner of the bar narrowed his eyes in apparent disbelief before sliding his glass to her. "I'm gonna need another."

She'd kept her story relatively stripped of spicy details, cutting to the chase where Wells started acting all squishy. "And that's when things went south."

"What do you mean, went south?" Gus asked.

"It all got fucked up," Cleo said, shrugging. "Like it always does."

"If that's what fits your narrative..."

"What, you don't think he meant what he said?" Cleo countered his skepticism with a glare.

"I'm sure he meant it," Gus said. "You just don't want to hear it."

"What does that mean?"

"You know exactly what it means."

"No, I don't, old man," she insisted. "Spill it."

Cleo didn't actually know how old Gus was. He could be fifty; he could be a hundred. He was a man of mystery despite their yearslong friendship. She'd told him everything about her life, including that her parents were raging drunks and she was raised, for the most part, by her grandmother who'd died a year ago after a short battle with cancer. Gus was there with her through that whole ordeal. All Cleo knew about Gus was his drink of choice (Pabst Blue Ribbon, whiskey chaser), his favorite barstool (corner farthest from the door, where he roosted every night between ten and two), and that he was as bitter about life as was Cleo. Over the years, she'd also learned he was once married, it ended badly (or so she assumed, based upon his outward disdain for relationships), and he'd lost his only child, a daughter, to cancer three years ago. Gus often remarked how similar his daughter and Cleo were.

"You don't want to believe someone may actually care about you," he continued.

Cleo snorted and rolled her eyes.

"What's wrong with the lad?" he asked, Irish accent lilting his speech as it did when he drank. "Your face lights up when you speak of him. Why not give him a chance?"

"This from the guy who tells me to avoid relationships at all costs?"

She and Gus had spent years mocking the R-word. He always encouraged her to stay single, live her life, not become someone's property. He should be proud of her reaction to this news, not judgy.

"How did it end?" he asked. "As I'm sure it did, knowing you."

"I left before he woke up. Took off like a bat out of Society Hill."

"Just like that?" an incredulous Gus asked. "You didn't even tell him?"

"I texted him later."

"That was a jerk move."

"Yep, it was," Cleo said, taking the righteous high road. "But whatever."

"What'd you tell him?"

"I can't be in a relationship right now."

"Or ever." Gus squinched up his face.

Cleo sighed as she bit down on her lower lip. "Shame it had to end. I loved those damn sheets."

She waited for Gus to tell her good sheets were no reason to hold on to a man when she could just go buy her own. Instead, he shook his head like a judgmental son of a bitch, took another swig, and scowled at her.

"It didn't have to end, you know."

"Ah, Gus," Cleo said. "Don't you go soft on me too. I need you to be my rock, tell me I did the right thing. I'm not falling in love with anyone. Period. Much less an asshole lawyer."

"But you have no problem sleeping with him."

"No shit. You gotta see this guy, you'd sleep with him too." Gus laughed.

And then, because Cleo never knew when to STFU, she said the thing she hadn't planned on telling Gus just yet.

"I'm not gonna start a relationship right before I move to New York."

And there it was. The news was out, and not in the way she'd hoped. She wanted to grab her words and shove them back into her piehole before they made it to Gus's ears.

Too late, judging by the look on his face.

"You're...what, now?" he said, his sad eyes flooding with fury.

Cleo hesitated. If she chose the right words, maybe she'd be able to lessen their blow. Aside from the women in her life, Gus had been one of her closest friends and trusted confidants. They'd spent four nights of every week together at this bar. He was the grandfather she never had, the one she'd always wished for. She knew, without him ever having to say it—he loved her like his own.

"I'm sorry, Gus. I didn't mean for you to find out that way," she said. "But it's time for me to go and make a career of my art."

"There's no art here in Philly? Have you seen those big steps Rocky ran up? It's called the Art Museum for a reason, Cleo Jane. Nope, you can stay right here and do your art."

Cleo had never seen the old man so fired up.

"Augustus James Rourke, I adore you to the Schuylkill River and back." It was one of their long-standing jokes. "But my friends are moving on with their lives. There's nothing here for me."

Shit, more regretful words. Gus threw back a shot, chased it with the rest of his beer, and slammed down his usual tip, a single dollar bill.

"You have me," he said as he slid off his barstool, "but I guess that's not good enough. Never is, is it, Cleo? The minute you get close to someone, you run away. So—" he saluted with one hand before putting on his tattered Eagles cap with the other "—off you go."

With that, the old man left the bar.

And possibly her life.

Cleo locked the tavern door after the last of the regulars shuffled out. Her eyes burned from holding back the tears that had threatened since Gus left. It was finally hitting her. Everything was changing, everyone was moving on, everyone she cared about was leaving her.

Again.

Waves of loss—profound, yet not unfamiliar—crashed down on her. The carefree life she shared with her roommates. The irreplaceable love of her grandmother. The casual relationship with Wells—the one she thought didn't matter but was now hitting her in a way that suggested it did.

And now Gus.

That was the problem with love. Loss was always waiting in the wings, ready to take it away.

For the first time since she considered moving, Cleo began doubting her plans. Maybe Gus was right. She didn't need to move to New York to be an artist, she just needed to paint. Right where she was. But a move to another city represented an escape, a way of moving forward with her life instead of staying stagnant.

She recalled the advice of her high school art teacher, who'd convinced her to apply for a scholarship to University of the Arts. *You'll never know until you try*, she'd said.

Cleo had followed her advice back then, applied for a scholarship, and got it. She hadn't planned on going to college but figured why not, if someone was willing to pay? Her dysfunctional parents had drunk their money away, so they had no cash to fork over. Her doting grandmother raised her with the belief she could do anything she put her mind to, so she accepted the scholarship to see what she could do with it. And what she did, to her great surprise, was graduate with a Bachelor of Fine Fucking Arts degree.

Since then, she'd been too busy trying to make ends meet and caring for her grandmother to dedicate any time to pursue an art career. But now that her grandmother was gone and her roommates were moving on with their lives, she had a chance to do something different. Put down the bottle, pick up the brush, go to the city that always paints. She didn't know if she'd make a living as an artist. But, like the scholarship, she wouldn't know until she tried.

Outside, the sky let loose as torrents of rain pelted the windows like gunfire. As Cleo turned the tavern sign to Closed, a shriveled face appeared in the window. Eagles cap soaked, water streaming down his face, Gus mouthed for her to let him in.

"Get in here, old fool," Cleo laughed, relieved she'd have a chance to make things right with him.

He thrust a soggy manila envelope at her.

"What's this?"

"Open it," he directed.

Inside the envelope were bundles of bills.

"Bribery will get you everywhere," Cleo joked.

He turned to go.

She grabbed his arm and was shocked at how bony it felt. She looked him over and noticed he was thinner than usual.

"You okay, G?" she asked, her voice flooded with concern. "Taking good care of yourself?"

He muttered something and reached for the door.

"Wait, I'm sorry," she said, remembering the old man didn't like to be questioned about his health. "What'd ya do, rob a bank?"

"It's the tips you earned over the years," he explained.

"You must be losing your mind, old goat," she said. "You've left me a tip every night. Remember?"

"I left you a dollar every night. Not exactly what you deserved."

"Of course not," Cleo agreed, "but you're a stingy old fart, and everyone knows it. Take this stolen money back."

"I did it so you wouldn't leave. I was afraid if you earned enough, you wouldn't have to work here anymore."

"Oh, Gus."

"It's what I should've paid. A thousand, that should do."

Cleo gulped. Gus didn't have this to give her. He barely made ends meet from what she could tell.

"You've already given me all I'm gonna accept," she said,

shoving the envelope back at him. "We're good."

"We're not good, Cleo. I'm sorry for getting my panties in a bunch when you told me about New York. I just wasn't expecting it. I knew you wouldn't stay here forever, but an old man can hope."

Cleo hugged his wilted frame. "It's just New York. I'll be back to visit."

"You better mean it." His sad eyes told her he didn't believe her. "Well, have fun on your vacation this week. Just—promise me you'll give some guy a chance."

"A chance to what?"

He paused. "To love you."

Cleo gave a hearty guffaw, until she saw his serious expression.

"To love you, not lust after you," he clarified.

"Right."

This, coming from the man who cheered her on when she dumped guys, high-fived her when she blew off dates for minor infractions, and convinced her no man would ever be good enough.

"Are you that drunk, Gus?" Cleo teased. "Because up until now you've made a mockery of relationships."

"Only with the wrong people. Maybe you just haven't met the right guy yet, but that doesn't mean you won't ever. You just have to give someone a chance."

"Why?"

"Because right now, it seems I'm the only man in your life you can trust."

"I trust Delaney's dad too. He's been more of a dad to me than mine ever was. Kind of like you're my surrogate grandfather."

"Well, we're not gonna live forever. When I leave this world, I want to know someone's here to take care of you."

"Where you planning on going?"

"Hell's the only place that'll have me."

"What makes you so sure even hell will have you?"

Gus ignored her. "I'm being serious, Cleo. You know, all this stuff you do and say comes from a belief you're not lovable," Gus said.

"Oh, I'm definitely not lovable. Just ask my parents."

"Your parents were pieces of shit," Gus said.

"Don't hold back."

Cleo recalled that night when she was five, crouching on the steps of their apartment while she watched her parents through the spindles of the banister. Empty bottles, illuminated by the flickering kitchen light, littered the table. She heard her father say he was leaving. Cleo thought he meant to the store.

"You're gonna leave me and your daughter, just like that?" her mom asked.

"How do I even know she's mine?" he said, then called her mom names Cleo wouldn't understand until she was much older.

"Oh, she's yours," her mom said, giving a maniacal laugh as she slammed her glass on the table. "How else you think she got that ugly red hair?"

Cleo's eyes welled with tears. She wrapped a strand of hair around her finger and studied it. Up to that moment, she'd loved her hair. The girls in her kindergarten class called her Ariel because she looked like the Little Mermaid. Hearing that, she wished for hair like Cinderella instead.

"I don't have time for a kid, anyway," he added, slamming the door behind him.

"Like I do?" her mom yelled as she threw a bottle and slunk to the floor, crying. Cleo padded to the kitchen and curled up with her, telling her it was going to be okay. At her young age, she still had hope her chaotic, addiction-riddled life was going be okay.

Her mom had hugged her and asked how much she'd heard. Cleo pretended she hadn't heard a thing, but the words were forever etched on her heart.

The next day, Cleo pulled out her Disney paint-by-numbers set and took a swath of yellow paint to Ariel's hair. It was the beginning of her love of painting, seeing how quickly something could change with a little color. It was cathartic. A week later, her mom shipped her off to her grandmother's, where she'd stay for months at a time until Grandma took her in permanently.

Maybe Gus was on to something. No wonder she felt unlovable—the two people in the world who should have loved her the most didn't want anything to do with her. Then, or now.

She was brought back to the present as Gus continued.

"You also think you're not good enough. Truth is, for the right boy, you're more than enough."

"So, after you robbed the bank you—what? Stopped off at UPenn for a psych degree?" Cleo lightened the mood to keep from being sucked into her tragic past.

"What makes you think I don't already have one?" he asked. "Anyway, they say there's a lid for every pot. Time to find yours."

"Don't need a lid."

"You gotta get over these abandonment issues," Gus said.

"I will, as soon as people stop leaving me."

"Your parents were messed up, for sure. But your grandmother didn't abandon you—she died. It's what people do, they die."

"Like how I'm dying to end this conversation?" she deadpanned.

"Keep wisecracking. All these jokes and avoidance tactics stem from fear, you know."

"No shit, Doctor Shrinky Dink. What's your excuse? I thought you hated love."

"That's where you're wrong, my girl," he said. "I don't hate love. I hate loss."

Saturday, June 10

COUNTDOWN
TO WEDDING
7 DAYS

BYRON JAMES
ABC METEOROLOGIST

"Hey, all you beachgoers, make the most of this beautiful Saturday because we're in for unsettled weather next weekend. The National Hurricane Center is keeping an eye on this low-pressure system, which just became the first named storm of the hurricane season. While it may be too soon to predict where Tropical Storm Inez will go, early projections suggest she may be heading for the mid-Atlantic region of the United States. We'll keep you posted as we learn more. For now, get out there and enjoy this perfect beach day."

Delaney

DELANEY SAT IN THE OLD WOODEN LIFEGUARD STAND, recalling her diary entries and conversation with Kate.

Maybe her sister was right. Time to tuck away her inner control freak and let things happen as they may. The wedding was now just a few days away. Aside from weather, what else could possibly go wrong?

"Hey, girl," Dalton's voice was carried by the soft sea breeze. "I thought I'd find you here."

He effortlessly hoisted himself up with one strong pull, like he did as a young lifeguard, and kissed Delaney's cheek.

She lowered her head to his shoulder. "I've been thinking. London would be a really nice place to go on our honeymoon."

He pulled away and looked at her. "You mean that?"

She nodded and smiled. "I do."

"It's no problem switching back to Antigua. I got the insurance on both trips. Hold on—"

Dalton reached into his pocket and pulled out a vibrating phone. His boss's name flashed across the screen before he silenced the call. Delaney may not have thought anything of it, if not for the look on his face, which she couldn't quite name.

"Why is Evelyn calling you on the weekend?" she asked.

"Oh, who knows." Dalton waved her off, his tone dismissive. He twisted his torso one way, then the other, as if to stretch.

"Shouldn't you take it?"

"Nah," he said.

Weird. Dalton always took Evelyn's calls, even on weekends.

He rubbed his hands together. "So, where were we?"

"The honeymoon," Delaney reminded him. "You were saying you could switch it back. I was about to say, let's leave it the way it is."

"London it is, then," Dalton said, and gave her a broad smile. "I know you'll love it."

"Okay, but—no more surprises."

"You got it."

He pulled her in for a slow, soft kiss. It reminded her of their first.

"That's the same move you pulled when we were seventeen," Delaney said, giggling as she recalled the fireworks she felt when her dork-turned-hunk neighbor kissed her for the very first time.

"Man, I was so nervous that night, coming to pick you up at work unannounced. I'd been crushing on you for years, and thought you'd tell me to pound sand. I'm glad you didn't."

"It was the first of many of your surprises. Actually, no—I stand corrected. The first was when I came to the beach that day looking for my scrawny friend Dalton."

"I remember him," he said.

"But I saw that hot lifeguard instead, so I strolled by, hoping he'd notice me."

"Did he?"

"No," she said. "But you did."

Dalton laughed.

"Do you think this is the same lifeguard stand?" Delaney asked.

"There's one way to find out."

They hopped down and crouched to look under the seat. There it was—a carving of a heart with the words "D+D, Summer '05" inside. Next to it was another heart inscribed with the letters "LOL."

"Wait, what's the 'LOL' heart?"

"I added it the next summer, after you broke up with me."

"LOL—as in, so funny it didn't last?"

"No. LOL, as in 'Love of a Lifetime.' I told you I knew it that summer. Even after you broke up with me, I knew it would just be a matter of time."

"Oh, Dalton," she said, as she wrapped her arms around him. "How did I ever get so lucky to have found you?"

"I'm the lucky one," he said, as he kissed her.

It had been twelve years since the carving, but he was right. Theirs was a love of a lifetime, and nothing could pull them apart.

Marley

MARLEY AWAKENED SATURDAY MORNING TO TEN MISSED texts, all from Sam.

And three more variations on her name. Then:

Marley responded.

> 3: none of your business.

"There she is!" Gwen exclaimed as Marley came downstairs. "Where'd ya go last night?"

"I left early."

"Sam was looking for you."

"When that girl wasn't in his face!" one of her housemates added.

"His ex," Marley explained.

"Didn't look like an ex," another chimed in from the next room.

Marley didn't want to hear anymore, so she poured herself a cup of coffee and settled into an Adirondack chair on the deck. She gazed at the horizon, layered in beachy hues. It promised to be a beautiful day. She basked in the plentiful sunshine, enjoying this slice of silent solitude on the empty deck—rare for a summer Saturday morning in a house full of women.

She thought about last night. Rick was probably right—she shouldn't worry about Sam. Jenna may have been nervous, seeing him after all that time, and didn't mean to be a jerk. Or maybe she was a jerk. Time would tell. Sam had given Rick a chance (kinda) and now it was Marley's turn to do the same for her friend.

When she joined her housemates on the beach later, all eyes were focused on a guy striding into the surf with a shrieking female flung over his shoulder.

Yawn. It happened a hundred times a day on the Jersey coast, big deal. But when Gwen cast her a glance, Marley looked closer.

It was Sam and Jenna. He was about to toss her into the Atlantic, allegedly against her will (or so she wanted everyone to think). But instead of catapulting her into the water (which Marley rooted for), he slid her down the front of his body, slowly.

Jenna wrapped her legs around his waist, her arms around his neck. Marley looked away, embarrassed to be watching their intimate moment. She grabbed a book from her beach bag and tried to concentrate, but the words didn't make sense.

"Good book?" one of her housemates asked.

"What?" Marley asked. "Oh, yes, it is."

The group giggled.

She was holding the book upside down.

Jenna broke free from Sam and jogged back to his housemates, who watched with eyes glazed over, as if they'd never seen a woman before.

They must have hooked up last night, or why else was Jenna still there? Marley could understand Sam's physical attraction to Jenna, but her outward beauty didn't seem to extend too far inward. Then again, Sam was a guy, which meant Jenna's looks likely eclipsed her personality. He wasn't normally that shallow, but love can do strange things. Like create the illusion of substance where none exists.

Jealousy, too, can do strange things. (*Shut up, ocean.*) So much for giving Jenna the benefit of the doubt.

Marley plugged in her earphones, turned on her beach playlist, and went for a walk. Half a block later, someone crashed into her from behind.

"What the hell!" she yelled.

A looming figure hoisted her up from the surf.

"Hey, asshole, how about a warning?" She slugged Sam on the arm and walked away.

"Sorry, Mar! Boy doesn't know his own strength."

He bent over and swished his hands in the water, splashed two handfuls on his hair, and whipped his head to the side to swoosh it off. He seemed to move in slow motion as sun-kissed waves of amber hair sprayed cool droplets that sizzled on her hot skin. Beads of water darkened his eyelashes, casting his eyes in hues of Arctic ice.

Something passed between them in that nanosecond. Sam grazed his bottom lip with his teeth. Her heart lurched.

But the moment dissipated as quickly as it appeared.

What was going on here? She was ogling Sam more than usual. Must be that time of month. A full moon. Something.

It wasn't the first time she'd appreciated Sam in his element. She'd spent plenty of early mornings sitting on the beach, knees tucked under her sweatshirt, watching him surf. Seeing him emerge from the ocean, glimmering with saltwater and sunscreen. Or catching a glimpse of his V-line when he'd roll over on his beach towel, half asleep. The line that led to...

Stop. Shake it off.

She loved Rick but found no harm in (secretly) observing Sam, as one would a piece of ass—*art*. Ha! Freudian slip.

When Sam would catch her looking, she'd feign a gag or roll her eyes. Sometimes he'd crack a joke to break the tension. Other times, his mouth would simply slide into a suggestive smile.

He bent again, scooped up some sea, and tossed it at her thighs as if to cool her down. She kicked water at him, relieved for the distraction.

"Where'd ya go last night?" he asked, kicking back. "I was looking for you."

"Sure you were." Marley lightened her tone so he wouldn't suspect it bothered her. "I see why you haven't gotten over Jenna. She's gorgeous."

"Yeah." He smiled. "She's a looker."

"So, you hooked up last night?"

Sam ran toward a wave and kicked it, spun in midair, and nailed the landing like a world-class gymnast.

Marley held up six fingers. "Work on the dismount."

She kept walking, sloshing her feet through the frothy ankle-high waves, Sam trailing behind. She was acutely aware he hadn't answered her question. His silence told her all she needed to know.

"Who'd you leave with?" he asked, catching up to her. "I was texting you all night. I figured you ditched Rick the Dick for Mark the Snark."

Marley snorted with laughter.

"Not that I care if you wanted to jump Mark's bones," he continued, "but Rick might. And I might have to tell him, depending how much your dirty little secret is worth. Unless Rick's willing to pay more for my intelligence."

"Let me know when you get some," Marley quipped.

"Good one," Sam chuckled, giving her props. "When you didn't return my texts, I worried he was taking advantage of you or something."

"What would make you think that?" She squinted up at Sam, shielding her eyes with her hand. "Maybe it was the other way around."

"Nah, he's not your type."

"Of course. No one's ever my type, right?"

The challenge was intentional. A throwing down of the gauntlet, so to speak. Now's your chance, Sam. You've done the math, now show your work.

Too late. A pair of feminine hands snaked from behind his head, covering his eyes.

"Guess who!" cried Jenna.

Marley drew satisfaction from Jenna's slight faux pas. It was one of Sam's biggest pet peeves, but she wouldn't know that unless she'd sat in a coffee shop with him as Marley did, one snowy Tuesday instead of going to class, listing Annoying Things People Do.

In other words, know your audience, Jenna. Newsflash: he found it juvenile.

Except he wasn't acting that way now.

"Who could this possibly be?" he asked, giggling.

Giggling? What on God's green earth was going on? Who abducted Sam and left this goofy, flirty, silly man in his place?

"Surprise!" Jenna sang as she jumped between them, then turned to hug Marley. "Hey, girl!"

Sam ran off to join a kids' football game in progress, uninvited. Jenna seemed nicer today, not as condescending. Maybe she'd realized Marley was Sam's best friend and should stay in her good graces.

"You gotta see this," Jenna whispered, spinning Marley around.

Jogging toward them was the Greek god of lifeguards, with six-pack abs and a perfectly sculpted package. A whistle bounced off his bulging pecs and he held a red rescue buoy as he ran.

They stood, transfixed, basking in the glow of the bronzed hottie.

"Oh—"

"My—"

"GOD!" they exclaimed in unison, finally finding common

ground, unaware the only thing standing between their hero and a drowning boy was them.

"'Scuse me," he yelled as he dodged the squealing women and ran through choppy surf.

Sam returned and dragged his leg through a wave, showering them with a wall of water.

"Sorry to douse your flames, ladies, but he's taken."

"How do you know?" both Marley and Jenna demanded in unison.

"Obvious," he said. "Too good-looking to be single."

"But you're single," Marley said, without thinking.

Sam turned to her. "Thanks, Mar."

"Yeah, I was thinking the same thing," Jenna said, a look of confusion on her face as she glanced between Marley and Sam.

The lifeguard emerged from the water, glistening and muscle-bound, holding the boy.

"Should I ask?" Sam offered.

"No!" It was unanimous.

"Probably for the best, Mar." Sam tousled Marley's hair. "He's not your type, anyway."

Kate

KATE HEADED TO THE STARBUCKS ON ASBURY AVENUE Saturday morning to get some caffeinated sustenance. She placed her drink order and was eyeing up the pastries when the barista called out.

"Greg! Order for Greg is up!"

Kate smirked. Of course, the name would be Greg. But it was too common a name to see it as another sign from the universe.

She stared down one particular doughy delicacy, debating whether it was worth the calories. She was about to give in to her sweet tooth when the barista called out again.

"Greg! Greg—Fallon, is it?"

Kate gasped. Her heart leaped as she shot a look at the barista, who was examining the writing on the side of the cup. "Yes. Greg Fallon, your order's ready."

Greg Fallon! Could it be *her* Greg Fallon?

Kate practically pushed over an elderly woman as she darted through the line to get a better view of the patrons waiting in the pickup area.

"Greg?" Kate called out, forgetting herself for a moment. "Greg!"

The customers eyed her sideways as if she was coocoo for Cocoa Puffs.

"Sorry. I—wouldn't want his drink to get cold," Kate explained sheepishly to the masses.

Holy moly. If destiny had returned Greg to the East Coast and dropped him in this precise Starbucks at this precise moment, that was it. They were meant to reconnect.

Kate peered around the corner where patrons sat. Some stared at laptop screens, others chatted with each other. No Greg in sight, at least not her Greg. Wishful thinking, perhaps.

Disappointed, she made her way back to the pastry section when she heard a man's voice behind her.

"Did you call my name?" he asked, "Greg Fallon? Sorry, I was in the restroom."

Kate's head spun around so fast she was surprised it didn't twist right off her neck and fly across the room.

Dang, not her Greg. This guy looked to be in his sixties. She should have known—no one under thirty gives last names at Starbucks.

"You're not the Greg Fallon in this article, are you?" a woman seated at a nearby table asked as she held up her copy of *Men's Monthly*.

"You're the third person to ask me that today," the man said, chuckling. "I only wish."

"You and me both," Kate said, apparently out loud. The man regarded her oddly.

"Sorry," she sputtered, "I mean, for your sake. Sounds like he's doing quite well for himself."

The barista called Kate's name. She slunk away to retrieve her mocha latte, slipped out the door, and relieved Starbucks of her half-crazed presence.

What in the name of Pete was *that* reaction all about? Greg's full name on the lips of a barista, and suddenly she was an offensive lineman, knocking over fellow patrons to get a gander? The Eagles should consider drafting her. Just tie Greg up on the goalpost and she'd lead them right to the Super Bowl.

Her reaction could only mean one thing.

She wasn't over Greg.

Cleo

THE LAST THING CLEO WANTED TO DO ON HER FIRST night of vacation was attend a bachelorette party, even for her best friend. But it was one of the last times they'd party together at the shore before they went off to their new lives, so she rallied.

She just wasn't down with what this rite of passage represented—the last fling before the ring, as if a woman was prohibited from having fun once the ball and chain were affixed.

While Cleo loved spending time with her girls, she wasn't looking forward to the pitiful looks and unsolicited "advice" her otherwise well-intentioned Velcroed-to-a-man friends doled out like condoms on a college campus. She was amazed how women who were once single themselves suddenly became relationship experts the second a guy called them back. One on one they weren't bad but as a group they were relentless, always trying to fix her up, as if being tied down to one singular soul-sucking guy for the rest of her life was something Cleo wanted.

Delaney had texted the group to let them know her intern, Marley, would be joining them. Cleo didn't know what Marley's deal was, but she was always with that boy Sam at the Clink. She assumed, by the way they looked at one another when the other wasn't looking, there was a whole lot of lustful wishing going on there.

Bartenders don't miss a trick.

Ugh. Thinking about the Clink conjured an image of Wells hovering over her, his hot bod cast in moonlight. A pang of something shot through her. Perhaps this was what missing someone felt like.

Blech. She swept the thought from her mind.

Cleo shoved the bachelorette T-shirts she'd designed into a crumpled Acme bag and, with great wistfulness, regarded the pile of penis-shaped items she'd been stockpiling. They would've been hilarious had Tori not put the kibosh on Cleo's X-rated props. A light-up Willy Bopper headband for Delaney, featuring flashing neon wieners on springs. A hop-along ding-a-ling to set on the bar. Rod ring pops, dong drinking straws, schlong shot glasses. Tori was right—it wasn't Delaney's style—but they were funny as fuck.

Delaney texted to let her know they'd arrived. As Cleo ran her fingers through her hair, her eyes shot to the latest masterpiece she'd designed, the image of her grandmother that she'd had tattooed on her inner forearm.

God, how she missed that woman.

"Tor, they're here," she called out.

"Be right out," Tori responded from the bathroom, where she'd been for eternity. It took Tori longer to paint her face than Michelangelo to paint the Sistine.

"Okay, see you next week."

As Cleo turned to leave, she grabbed the Willy Bopper headband and stuck it on her head. If Gus was right about there being a lid for every pot, Cleo had just found hers.

Sorry, Wells, but a band of bopping boners was the only lid she needed.

Let the reindeer games begin.

Delaney

C LEO AND TORI JOINED DELANEY, KATE, AND MARLEY IN the limo. After a last stop in Stone Harbor to pick up Dalton's sister, Nora, they headed down the coast.

Once everyone was settled in, Cleo poured a round of drinks and offered a toast.

"To Delaney, and her bridesmaids. May we all get drunk and lucky!"

"Except for me," Nora said, her hand on her belly as she waved off her drink and smiled. "I just found out I'm pregnant!"

The women erupted with a chorus of congratulations, followed by a barrage of questions.

"Is this your first?" Marley inquired.

"Third, actually," Nora said. "I have two toddlers at home, so tonight is a welcome break from tantrums and tears."

"Just give us time," Cleo joked.

The driver asked where they were headed, and Nora handed him a list of their stops.

"So, we're on the way to Cape May, huh?" he asked. "You ladies familiar with the song?"

"Of course!" Cleo exclaimed and began singing the lyrics to "On the Way to Cape May." The other women joined in, serenading Delaney with the Jersey-famous song about a couple who, like she and Dalton, met in Ocean City and fell in love on their way to Cape May.

Nora laid out their plans for the evening: a coastal tour of Delaney's favorite watering holes, starting in Cape May and working their way north. Delaney was happy she'd agreed to this outing until Cleo announced she had props.

"Oh no!" Delaney chuckled. Did the others know how risky that was, trusting Wild Child with such a task?

They must. If her blinking penis headband wasn't enough of a clue, they'd all known Cleo for years. The only one who couldn't be charged with aiding and abetting was Marley.

Delaney braced herself for Cleo's trademark raunchiness but was pleasantly surprised when she pulled out custom-designed T-shirts in tangerine for the bridesmaids, turquoise for Delaney.

"Cleo, these are awesome," Kate said. "I love the artwork. Did you design them?"

"I did," Cleo responded.

"What, no penis products?" Nora pouted.

"I decided to keep it classy this time."

"May I?" Nora asked, taking the headband off Cleo's head and placing it on her own. "If I can't get lit tonight, at least I can light up the night with these flashing phalluses."

Before long, the limo arrived at their first stop. Delaney and her entourage walked through the town of Cape May, enjoying a drink at a few different establishments. Nora, still with flashing penises on her head, led them back to the limo after their last bar.

"Thank God one of us is sober," Cleo said. "I have no idea where I'm going."

"I don't know what's more fun, shepherding toddlers or a bunch of drunks," Nora teased. "Wait, I do. At least you guys won't spill your juice boxes and fight over who got more Cheerios."

"The night's still young," Cleo joked.

Back in the limo, they made their way north, stopping in a few towns along the way to visit Delaney's favorite hangouts. As they headed to their final destination, Kate poured glasses of champagne.

"A toast," she announced. "To destiny, for bringing Delaney and Dalton together."

"How did destiny bring you together?" Marley asked.

"It wasn't destiny," Delaney explained. "We met as kids and dated as adults."

"But destiny caused our families to buy neighboring shore houses," Kate suggested.

"They're called realtors, Kate," Delaney said as Cleo clinked her glass with hers.

Ignoring the two nonbelievers, Kate turned to Marley. "They fell in love as teens and never got over each other, even after dating others."

"I knew they'd end up together," Nora said. "Dalton did too. He told me that the night he first kissed you."

"Doesn't that prove Delaney's point?" Cleo interjected. "If he decided at seventeen he was going to marry her, that's choice."

"But if it was all about choice, they probably wouldn't have pursued each other after they broke up," Kate said. "Something had to happen, by chance, to bring them together."

Tori agreed. "She talked about him all the time in college, but when I'd suggest she reach out to him, she'd refuse. Denial with a capital *D*."

Delaney smiled, recalling how hard she'd tried to deny her burning curiosity about her teen crush. Despite being summer neighbors, she and Dalton rarely saw each other during their college years and beyond, thanks to internships, summers abroad, and jobs.

"I'm still not getting the destiny piece," Marley said.

"It was that typical situation where two people like each other but are never available at the same time," Tori explained.

"Until they ran into each other in New York," Kate interrupted. "She was there for a conference; he, for work. Neither knew the other was there. She turned a corner and bumped into him. *Literally*. Destiny brought them together on the same exact corner at the same exact time in the largest metropolitan city in America. I get goose bumps just thinking about it. And now they're getting married. *Boom!*" She dropped an invisible mic.

"I just got goose bumps too," Marley said.

"I thought destiny was predetermined and there's nothing you can do to change it?" Cleo asked. "If so, I know exactly where I'm heading."

"Hell?" Delaney asked.

"Eventually. But first, jail. If there's nothing you can do to change your future, I may as well rob a few banks, do some illicit drugs, run naked through Philly. Why not, if I'm only going to meet the devil in the end?"

"Hold on there, Calamity Jane," Kate said. "You're confusing destiny with fate, an unchangeable finality determined by the cosmos. Destiny is different, malleable. It happens when choice and chance meet."

"Oh, I like that," Tori said.

"Choice and chance, I like that too," Marley said. "So, we choose a path to our future, but our destiny is what happens when opportunity steps in?"

"Exactly," Kate said.

"Example, please," Cleo said, gulping her champagne and waving for another.

"So, my friend Sam got his heart broken by his high school girlfriend and isn't open to relationships as a result," Marley said. "That's his choice, to avoid getting hurt again."

"Wise boy," Cleo chimed in.

"Then, by chance, she appeared at the Deauville last night—same place and time as Sam. Destiny provided an opportunity for them to reconnect, to adjust the trajectory of what their future would have been had that chance meeting not happened."

"You do get it," Kate said, high-fiving Marley. "I have the same thing going on with Greg right now."

"I meant to ask you if you saw his article," Tori said.

Delaney groaned. "Please don't encourage her."

"There've been signs, perhaps even opportunities, suggesting that chapter of my life may not be over," Kate said. "Like yesterday, in Starbucks. They called out his name."

"Greg's a pretty common name," her sister noted.

"His *full name*. The guy's actual name was Greg Fallon."

"Who gives their last name on a Starbucks order?" Cleo asked.

"Baby boomers," Kate answered. "So it wasn't my Greg Fallon, but another person with the same friggin' name. How weird is that?"

"Pretty weird," Tori agreed.

"That's three things now," Kate continued, counting on her fingers. "The article, the photo memory, and now the Starbucks guy. Clearly, the universe is trying to tell me something."

"Yeah, that you're delusional," Delaney offered, "seeing signs and reading meanings in random occurrences, when what you need to do is forget about him, move on. He's old news."

"Then why the signs?" Kate asked. "Maybe it's destiny's way of providing me with an opportunity to change my future."

"Or maybe they're signs it wasn't meant to be," Tori surmised. "If what you say about destiny is true, he was presented with an opportunity to do something cool for himself, which meant moving. If he hadn't grasped it, his success may not have happened."

"You hear what she's saying?" Delaney asked, turning to Kate. "He had an opportunity to put himself first. Time for you to do the same."

"At least be open to it," Tori said, looking at Cleo. "We could all use that advice."

"Not me," Cleo piped in. "Opportunity ain't knocking on this door anytime soon."

"It's that No Trespassing sign you wear," her roommate said, voice dripping with sweet sarcasm. "Maybe if you gave someone a chance once in a while."

The limo driver tapped on the window. "We've arrived at your destination."

"Wow, how did we get here so fast?" Delaney asked.

"Must be destiny!" Cleo exclaimed.

Sunday, June 11

COUNTDOWN
TO WEDDING
6 DAYS

Delaney

DELANEY WOKE UP ON SUNDAY, HAPPY CLEO AND TORI had stayed for a final roomie sleepover after the bachelorette party.

"*Gooood* morning," a sleepy Tori sang as she stirred. She turned to face Delaney. "That was fun last night."

"It was the perfect combination of people, conversation, and booze. I'm not hungover in the least," Delaney said as she stretched and yawned.

"Me either," Tori agreed. "So glad I've outgrown the college drunk fest."

A grunt came from a lump on the air mattress between them. "Speak for yourselves."

"Come on, Cleo," Tori said, bouncing her toe off the air mattress. "I've seen you drink twice as much and get half the amount of sleep we just did."

"I'm old now," Cleo said, her face still in the pillow. "And stop making the room bounce."

"I don't know about you guys, but I'm starving," Tori said, as she threw back her covers and sat up. "Let's brunch!"

Delaney sat up too. "I'm in."

"I'm not," Cleo groaned.

"Rise to the occasion, girl. You're coming with us."

Tori took her lifeless arm and pulled her to a seated position.

"I hate you morning people," Cleo said, as she fell back on her pillow like a rag doll.

A few minutes, a couple threats, and a bribe or two later, the trio headed to the boardwalk, lucky to be seated in their favorite brunch spot without a long wait.

"What looks good?" Tori asked as she perused the menu.

"My bed, until you morning freaks robbed me of sleep."

Delaney turned to Tori. "When's Ted coming? Will he be here for the rehearsal dinner?"

"He's planning to," Tori said.

Cleo shot Delaney a look. Tori's boyfriend had a penchant for canceling plans.

"Why the look?" Tori, who must have seen them, asked.

"Nothing," Cleo said, raising her hands like she was being held up. "I didn't say a thing."

"Not this time, but I know you're thinking it."

"Thinking what?" Delaney asked.

"He's not going to show for the rehearsal," Tori guessed.

"Not just the rehearsal," Cleo said, "the wedding."

Delaney and Cleo had shared their concerns for their friend's relationship, suspecting Ted canceled when he didn't see political gain from attending the function in question. It had been happening more frequently.

"Are things going okay for you guys?" Delaney asked.

"Never better," Tori said, her voice strained despite her smile. "Look, I know you guys don't like Ted."

"It's not that we don't like him. We just love you and want to make sure you're happy. We're here for you, if you ever need to talk," Delaney said.

"I need to talk," Cleo said, slamming down her empty mug and wiping her mouth, "about this orgasmic coffee. Better than any sex I've had, but don't tell him I said that."

"Doesn't say much for the guy," Tori laughed, looking relieved to be off the hot seat.

"Wait, *him*?" Delaney asked. "There's a him, as in a singular man? Have you met someone?"

"I mean, *them*," Cleo tittered. "You know, the guys I've been with in the past." A wave of crimson crossed her face.

Delaney suspected there was more to the story than her

friend was letting on.

"Any-hoo." Cleo sighed as she waved the server over. "This coffee's the bomb. Let's order more."

If Delaney didn't know any better, she'd think Wild Child was hiding something.

Kate

KATE AWAKENED ON SUNDAY AFTERNOON AND FOUND Delaney and her mom at the dining room table.

"There she is!" her mom called out, more enthusiastically than usual.

Kate, who couldn't fathom talking before coffee regardless of the time of day, grunted and made her way to the coffeepot.

"Is it okay if I tell her?" her mom asked.

"Tell me what?"

"Go ahead," Delaney said, sighing. Then, to Kate, "Just— promise not to read into it."

"I make no such promises," Kate said as she leaned against the counter.

"My friend's cousin, who's Greg's parents' neighbor, said Greg's coming home this summer for the reunion."

"What reunion?" Kate asked.

"There's an all-class West Chester University reunion in Sea Isle. Maybe you can reconnect, find out if you're the one he referenced in the article," her mom suggested.

Kate laughed, almost spitting out her coffee, picturing herself tugging on Greg's sleeve to ask if he was still pining away for her.

"I'm not going to a reunion. Five years isn't long enough to want to see those people again."

At least, that's what her head thought. Her heart, however, went, *Hmm. Reunion?*

Stop it, heart.

"When is it?" she asked, yawning for effect. Casual, as if she didn't care, while her heart fluttered away. She hoped it wasn't the weekend of the wedding.

No, hoped it was.

Wasn't.

"The week after the wedding," her mom said. "You have no excuse not to go."

Yay! (Crap.)

"Yes, she does," Delaney insisted.

Kate shot her a look, awaiting an explanation.

Her sister shrugged. "I don't want her to."

"Because of *Ryan*?" Kate's sardonic expression matched her mocking tone.

"No. Because of you," Delaney said.

"What does that mean?"

"You need to move on from Greg."

"I've moved on," Kate insisted.

"Have you?"

"Of course. I've been on hundreds of dates since Greg." Maybe twenty. "And they all sucked," she reminded her.

"Did they? Or were you just choosing the wrong guys for the wrong reasons?"

Kate rolled her eyes.

Delaney continued. "You've had serious back-to-back boyfriends since you were fifteen. You never learned how to be on your own, discover yourself without a guy in your life. Greg's dust cloud hadn't even settled before you were off in search of the next boyfriend."

"I was trying to get over him. Like you're telling me to do now."

"Not by replacing him with someone else equally wrong

for you. Focus on yourself instead, so you can figure out exactly what it is you're looking for. Only then will you know when the right guy comes along."

"But if you're preaching I stay single for a while, get a cat or six, spend Saturday nights on my couch, why are you pushing this Ryan guy on me?"

"I'm not pushing anyone on you. It's a wedding date, for crying out loud. Maybe he'll be a friend, who knows? Or the love of your life. But you won't know that until you discover what truly matters to *you*."

"What if I decide, after all that, Greg is my person?" Kate asked.

"Then by all means, go get him—as long as you know for sure he meets adult-Kate's needs."

She understood what Delaney was saying, even if she didn't want to admit it. She'd been so focused on finding the next boyfriend, she hadn't fully processed what went wrong with Greg. He'd chosen a life that didn't include her, when all she'd wanted was to feel chosen.

Delaney was right. Maybe it was time she chose herself.

Marley

SAM ARRIVED ON SUNDAY EVENING TO PICK UP MARLEY for their ride home. She threw her overnight bag into the back and inspected the interior of the car with exaggerated flair.

"What are you doing, weirdo?" Sam asked.

"Where's Jenna?" she asked, looking under her seat.

"Real funny," he said. "How was the bachelorette party? Pick up any hotties?"

Marley turned and cocked her head. "Why do you always

think I'm trolling for guys? I have a serious boyfriend—"

"Who's never around."

"Who I'm probably going to marry. I'm not a slut like you, you know."

Ouch. Even Marley had to admit her words stung.

"Why do you say such mean things to me?" Sam whined, pretending he was hurt.

"Truth."

"Lies. I haven't picked anyone up for a long time."

Marley raised her eyebrows. "Last night?"

"Wasn't a pickup," he said.

Okay, maybe running into an ex was more reunion than traditional pickup. She tried to remember others but came up short.

"August was the last time," he said.

That's right. Rick was visiting, and they'd gone to Kix bar, where Sam had met someone.

"And I only kissed her."

"Right," Marley said, mocking agreement over the *only kissed* part.

Sam looked at her, expressionless. Maybe he was telling the truth, but she couldn't resist teasing him.

She threw up her hands. "Can someone please tell me how, on God's green earth, single women survived this massive Sam drought?"

"You tell me." Sam gave her an eyebrow flash. "Seriously. You think I'm a player, but I'm not. Apparently I have a reputation to break."

Marley snickered but stopped when Sam shot her a look. He was being serious.

"Okay, good!" She nodded in agreement. "Good."

"Good," Sam said. "I'm glad we agree on this."

Several minutes passed in unusual silence as Marley watched the trees whizzing by on the Garden State Parkway.

Typically they'd share weekend gossip, but the vibe felt different today. Jenna may not have been lurking under the seat, but her virtual presence filled Big Red.

Sam finally broke the silence. "I'm not a bad guy."

"I never said you were."

"But your eyes do. I can see you judging me when I'm flirting with someone."

"How do you know I'm not judging her? Making sure she's good enough for you?"

Sam was silent for a moment. "Never thought about that."

"Listen," Marley said, turning to him. "You don't need to hear this because you already know it, but you're a catch. I wanna make sure they bring as much to the table as you do."

"What, exactly, do I bring to the table?"

"You know," Marley accused, pushing her fingers into his bicep.

This was Sam's cheap way of soliciting flattery. He looked at her expectantly.

She sighed. "You're gonna make me say this, aren't you?"

Sam smiled. "Of course, you brought it up. Go on..."

"You're smart, you're going to be a lawyer, you have money. Which is good, since you're gonna have to pay off the bar examiners."

Sam laughed.

"And beneath all that charm is a guy who's deep and thoughtful. Too bad about your looks, though."

"A wildebeest."

"I'd say gargoyle. Seriously, I don't want to see you get hurt again, which is why I'm a little concerned about this quick—whatever-it-was this weekend. How was it, running into her like that?"

"Nice, unexpectedly."

"I'll say," Marley exclaimed. "I knew she was back in the Philly area, but to end up at the same bar at the same time? Seems like destiny."

Sam's sheepish expression begged forgiveness. "Destiny had nothing to do with it. One of my housemates invited Rhonda and Jenna to come for the weekend."

Gut, meet punch.

"So, you knew on Friday she was—*ooh*, now I get it. New haircut, new shirt..."

Sam flashed her a smile. "Guilty as charged."

Why didn't Sam tell her this on Friday? They were best friends who shared everything. Or so she thought.

"You still like her?" she asked.

"Why? Shouldn't I?"

Part of her wanted to scream, "No!"

She didn't trust Jenna. There was something about her—a fakeness, or something—and she didn't see Sam with someone like her. But friends should tread lightly with each other's romantic choices, so she kept her mouth shut, recalling a time Sam had questioned her choice.

It was the first time Rick had come to visit her in Philly, and she'd invited a group of friends to meet her new boyfriend. When he went to the bathroom, Sam cornered her at the bar and told her he didn't think Rick was her type.

"Oh yeah?" The bar was crowded, and they were inches from one another. She looked up at him, teasingly. "What's my type then? Since it's not you."

It was more flirtatious—more honest—than she'd allowed herself to be since That Night, three months earlier. Having a boyfriend emboldened her.

Before Sam could answer, someone knocked into him from behind. He careened into Marley, spilling his beer on her shirt. Rick returned and grabbed napkins from the bar as Sam apologized and disappeared.

Later, she replayed the scene in her head. Wondering whether she'd imagined, in the split second before Sam doused her, that he'd been pointing to himself with his beer.

Now, as they nudged their way on to the AC Expressway, it

seemed Sam wanted her approval of Jenna. Marley should be supportive, even though she wasn't convinced.

Finally, she relented. "She seems okay."

She leaned her head on the window and pretended to sleep as Sam expertly guided Big Red through typical Sunday evening stop-and-go traffic on the 42 Freeway. She fake-awakened when she sensed they were nearing her building. She couldn't wait to get into the safety of her apartment, where she could sort out her feelings.

"What's wrong?" Sam asked as he turned down her street.

Marley focused rapt attention on her purse, searching for her key.

"Mar, what's the matter?" He placed his hand on her arm.

"Nothing," she said, yanking it away.

"Something is. Are you mad because I didn't tell you about Jenna coming down, or are you just mad about her generally?"

"What's that supposed to mean?" she snapped.

Sam eased Big Red into the no-parking zone. Marley grabbed the handle to let herself out—she didn't want to hash this out right now—but Sam locked the door.

"Seriously, child locks?"

"The child locks will go off when you stop acting like a child," he said. "What's pissing you off so much you pretended to sleep the whole time?"

Busted.

"Are you jealous or something?"

"Please," she exhaled, exasperated. "Jealous? Of her? No, I'm not jealous of Jenna. Jealousy is the last thing on my mind."

"What *is* on your mind?"

"Why didn't you tell me she was coming down this weekend?"

"I don't know. I didn't want you to—"

"What, fling myself out of a moving vehicle?"

"Says the girl who's about to be engaged."

Marley tried the door handle again.

"Wait," Sam said, grabbing her arm. "I'm sorry I didn't say anything. It's just—you seem so obsessed with who I'm dating, always trying to fix me up. I didn't want it to get weird."

"Obsessed?" Marley snapped. "You're so full of yourself! I'm not the slightest bit obsessed with you or your love life."

"Then why're you always asking me who I'm interested in, if there's anyone I want to date, who I'm taking to the wedding?"

"I dunno, Sam—did you ever think I just want you to be happy? Relationships are good things. I've been happily involved in one for three years, and I want you to find someone too. Is that a crime?"

Sam paused, then answered with a soft, "Yes."

Marley's heart skipped a beat. Maybe this conversation *was* long overdue.

"According to the Pennsylvania Crimes Code, it's a misdemeanor of the third degree. Punishable by rat torture," Sam said.

Marley laughed out loud. "Okay, I take it back. I don't want you to be happy."

She appreciated Sam's humor and the way it defused the tension. Felix appeared at her window with a circular motion of his hand, telling them to move on.

Sam put the car in drive. "I'm starving," he said. "They say you should never go home hungry. Or is it angry? I dunno. Let's grab a bite."

Cleo

CLEO AND TORI WERE MEETING UP WITH DELANEY AT THE Deauville for happy hour. They found her waiting at the bar with a round of drinks.

"You're not going to believe who just called," Delaney said, her tone melodic as she handed them drinks.

"Who?" Tori asked.

"Wells Abernathy III, of all people."

Cleo almost spit out her drink.

"Your opposing counsel?" Tori asked. "Why is he calling you on a weekend?"

"I wondered the same thing, myself." Delaney took a sip of her drink and raised her eyebrows. "Any ideas, Cleo?"

"Me?" Cleo sputtered, hand to her chest like she'd been falsely accused of murder. "I dunno, to beg you not to marry Dalton?"

"Nope. Something about the case, which could have waited till I returned."

Cleo stiffened as Delaney locked eyes with her.

"He asked how you were."

Cleo coughed to keep her drink from going down the wrong pipe.

"I didn't know you guys were friends," Delaney continued, her tone light in contrast to the look of interrogation she cast over her margarita. Her eyes were big, nosy. (Knowing?) "At least, not on a 'how's she doing' basis."

Cleo cleared her throat. "Oh, yeah. He's a regular at the Clink." (And other places.)

"I didn't know he hung out there." Delaney continued giving her That Look. "But then I remembered him making a joke about wanting to get with you. At least I thought it was a joke."

Cleo gave a hearty guffaw. "As if I'd let his tightwad ass anywhere near this."

Delaney cocked her head and narrowed her steely eyes.

"What?" Cleo deflected. She tried to keep her mouth from sliding into a smile, recalling the pinkie promise she and Wells had made to keep Delaney from knowing they were "hanging out," as they called it. The pinkie promise morphed into a thumb war, which turned into a wrestling match, which succumbed to—*oh, boy*.

"Why are you acting guilty? And why has your face turned red? Are you guys—" Delaney's eyes grew to the size of grapefruits. "Oh, my God, I'm right! You guys are—"

"In a relationship," Cleo said, nodding, matter-of-fact as shit.

"I knew it!" Delaney jabbed at the air between them, eyes gleaming as if she'd just picked a winning racehorse.

"An attorney-client relationship, that is. What do you mean, you 'knew it'?"

"I *knew* something was going on. I could tell by the way he asked. Wait. Attorney-client relationship? For what?"

"Never mind," Cleo said, wanting to slap herself for not coming up with a better excuse. "What does that even mean, 'by the way he asked'?"

Cleo was aware she was acting like a high schooler, trying to decipher the meaning behind a boy's words, but couldn't help herself. Then again, why should it matter how he sounded? She'd blown the guy off, and now she wanted confirmation he missed her?

Pick a lane, Cleo!

The truth was, she hadn't stopped thinking about Wells since her conversation with Gus.

"I dunno. When he asked about you, he seemed nervous or something."

"In what way?"

Dammit, Cleo. Act your age.

"I'm just curious," she added, trying to save face, "because if he insinuated I hadn't paid him yet, I have. Tenfold."

Oh my God, the lies. *Stop it.*

"So, you hired him as an attorney," Delaney said, as if she were Perry Mason about to fry her lying ass in fierce cross-examination.

"Yes." Even though she had no legal issues. None she was aware of.

"What did you hire him for?"

"Can't say."

"Why not?" Delaney prodded.

"Attorney-client privilege." She thrusted her chin in defiance, proud she remembered this legal term, then flipped the accusations onto Delaney. "You of all people should know that."

"Except you're the client and it's your privilege, which means you can spill it to anyone you want." Delaney hitched an eyebrow. She wasn't messing around. "So spill it. I'm curious to know about this so-called legal issue you're mired in."

"I didn't say mired."

"I know, but as your bestie, I'd think you'd come to me first with your legal issues. It must be pretty bad if you went to Wells. Let's have it."

"Can't. Conflict of interest," Cleo pulled more limited law knowledge from her ass.

The sound of crashing glass and a loud shriek pierced the night. Cleo turned to see Tori, wide-eyed and empty-handed, margarita glass in pieces at her feet. Cleo grabbed napkins and crouched to sop up the spilled drink.

Delaney bent down to pick up shards of glass just as Cleo stood, coming face-to-face with Tori.

"You're welcome," Tori whispered. "But I want details."

Cleo was thankful for her friend's purposeful distraction but didn't want to share information about her tawdry Wells past with Tori any more than she wanted to share it with Delaney.

Because that's exactly where the whole thing with Wells was—in the past, where it belonged. No need for anyone to know more.

Lane = chosen.

Marley

MARLEY AND SAM SAT IN COMFORTABLE SILENCE ON the big steps at Penn's Landing, overlooking the Delaware River, as they ate their hoagies. A barge floated past and a group of teens blasted their music nearby. Sam tapped a drum solo on his thigh.

Marley was relieved the tension between them had subsided. That was the greatest thing about their friendship, how easily they could transition from heated debate to casual discussion.

She finished eating and lay back on the steps, gazing at the sky. Mother Nature had finally lifted her blanket of humidity to reveal a cool June night. The city lights illuminated the sky behind them, while across the river the stars twinkled against a darkened night sky.

Sam lay back too.

This was how it should be between them: at peace, happily coexisting. Eventually the teens moved on, taking their music with them, exposing the sound of lapping waves and the clanging of a metal object against a dock. In the distance, they heard a gunshot.

"How can you want to leave this?" Sam joked.

"Who said I want to leave?"

"Mr. Ohio?"

Marley didn't answer. The subject made her nervous about her future. She never wanted to leave Philly.

"You gonna take the bar in both states?" Sam asked, as if reading her mind.

"I guess."

"Temple's prepared us well for the Pennsylvania bar," he said pensively.

He was right. She had no clue about Ohio law, but she'd have to learn it if she moved there.

Marley rolled to her side and regarded Sam with curiosity. "Do you ever regret going to Temple instead of Villanova?"

"Not for a second," he said without hesitation, turning to look at her.

In an unexpected twist, Samuel Adams—legacy and accepted member of Villanova Law School—had turned down his admission and chosen Temple Law School instead. Sam's father had been livid. He'd practically planned Sam's future at birth—attend Villanova, join the firm founded by Sam's great-great-grandfather, and one day become partner. It was Sam's plan, too, until their criminal law class changed both his major and his outlook. It was a rocky time in Sam's life, that summer between college graduation and 1L. His father finally accepted his choice, but still pressured Sam to join the family firm.

Marley, on the other hand, had been wait-listed at Villanova, despite graduating summa cum laude. She was offered a merit-based scholarship to Temple Law, so the choice was made for her.

Several minutes passed as the two lay in silence. Marley could feel herself drifting off to sleep when Sam whispered in a tone she didn't recognize. Deep, husky. Sultry, almost.

"Hey, Mar…"

"Hmm?" She opened her eyes to see him leaning on his elbow, looming over her, his face mere inches from hers.

"About that night…" He paused, and Marley could feel him catch his breath as he fixed his stare on her.

She blinked and a thousand nights with Sam flashed before her eyes. Studying until morning, hysterical from lack of sleep. Lying next to each other, sharing headphones over a newly dropped release. Netflix and pizza, dancing at parties, closing dive bars, lost in conversation.

He could've been referring to any one of those nights. But she knew which one he wanted to talk about.

He bit his lip and raised his eyebrows.

"Nooo," Marley whined and covered her eyes with her forearm. They hadn't spoken about That Night since it happened, and she didn't want to start now. The memory was still too painful, embarrassing. "Can we not talk about this?"

"We have to." Sam's voice was firm but soft. He lifted her forearm. "I tried like hell to talk to you before I left for China, and you ghosted me. You owe me this."

Marley slowly opened her eyes. His expression was pleading, his minty breath warmed her skin. She wondered when he'd a chance to put in a breath mint.

And why.

"Okay, Sam, let's talk about how sloppy drunk I got. How I danced around like a lunatic trying to get you to sleep with me. You rejected me, I was humiliated, I thought I'd ruined our friendship. That's why I avoided you. Can we move on now?"

"I didn't reject you. I just didn't want to sleep with you."

"Yeah, I got it."

"That night."

"That night, any night. Rejection sucks just the same."

Sam leaned in closer. "Hear me. Please. I didn't want to sleep with you *that night*. Because you were drunk and there was no way you knew what you were doing when we got back to your apartment."

"I was drunk, but unfortunately I remember it pretty well." She cringed, willing away the memories. "You told me I wasn't your type."

"I know, and that's what I wanted to talk to you about. I only said it because you weren't taking no for an answer."

Marley blinked. So...he wasn't repulsed by her, all these years?

"Do you remember what else you said?" he asked, his voice soft.

"I said a lot of stupid shit."

"It wasn't stupid. And it wasn't shit."

Marley refused to answer for fear it would incriminate her.

"Come on," Sam prodded, poking her in the side.

Marley looked away, defeated. She knew she had to play this game. Sam could be relentless when he wanted something.

"That I had a crush on you." She said the words quickly, eyes squinched shut, voice monotone to lessen their impact.

"Yes." His breath hitched. "That."

They couldn't be going there. She had to defuse this with—what? Oh, humor.

"I do remember saying it," she said, "but I thought you were someone else."

"Yeah? Who?"

"Professor Weinstein."

Sam nodded. "Yeah, I can see it—bulbous nose, ear hair..."

Marley smiled, hopeful the shift in tone would end the conversation.

"Sooo...?"

He wasn't giving up. He wrapped the string of Marley's hoodie around his forefinger until it reached her chin, then brushed his fingertip down the middle of her mouth, causing her lower lip to part.

"Sooo...what?" Marley's voice took on a flirtatious tone as she dared herself to look up into Sam's crystal eyes, too close for comfort, but—oh. So. Damn. Fine.

Desire coursed through her veins and her head was spinning, wondering where he was going with this, hoping he wouldn't take it any further. At the same time, hoping he would.

"Was that true?" His voice barely a whisper.

Marley willed herself to keep her counsel, not wanting

to confirm or deny this allegation. Her face remained expressionless, but he must have seen it in her eyes. His gaze strengthened ever so slightly, a nearly imperceptible smile tugged at his lips.

The jig was up.

"I wish you would've talked to me before I left. I wanted to tell you I didn't want to sleep with you...that night." He emphasized the last two words, his stare fixed on hers. "But every other night..." He shook his head and exhaled. "Damn, it's all I thought about."

The breath was sucked out of her as she tried to ignore the tingly sensation rippling through her body. They were about to tread into dangerous territory, and as they stood on the edge of this precipice, she knew she should back away before they did something they'd regret.

"I was drunk," Marley whispered, pleading her case. "I usually don't throw myself at guys."

"I know. That's why I said no. I didn't want to be your mistake."

Would he have been her mistake? Where would they be now if she hadn't avoided him?

"I wanted to know if you felt the same way the next day," he said. "Did you do that because you'd drained all the alcohol from the City of Brotherly Love? Or...was something else there?"

He waited, breathless, for her answer. She debated making another joke but got caught in the intensity of his gaze.

From somewhere deep inside her came an overwhelming conviction that he deserved to know the truth, even if it would forever change things between them.

She took a deep breath and stepped off the ledge she'd been teetering on for so long.

"Something else," she whispered.

Sam exhaled, clenching his jaw again, not taking his eyes off her. "Damn."

"Yeah," Marley said, her voice thickening.

"I wish—"

"But I—"

They laughed as their words tumbled out simultaneously.

He leaned down and touched the tip of her nose with his, as he'd done many times during their friendship—to calm her down when she was freaking out before an exam, or during staring contests when he'd try to make her break. The proximity of his face to hers, his mouth to hers, wasn't new.

But this time, the intent was.

He grasped her hand, slipping his fingers between hers. Their eyes locked on one another's, and all the years of her unspoken desire came to the surface. He gently kissed her hand, then grazed his teeth against her skin. She gasped as an electric jolt surged through her. He pulled her closer, lightly tracing his thumb across the little strip of belly where her hoodie had ridden up.

"Marley..."

She moved closer and they melted into one another, legs intertwining.

"Sam," her own voice was so husky with desire she almost didn't recognize it.

Kiss me! Just kiss me! She was pretty sure she'd never wanted anything as much as she wanted what was about to happen, right here on the steps of Penn's Landing.

He lowered his lips, so close they were almost touching hers, coming in slowly, seductively, teasingly, when—

Damn it. Rick.

Marley could see his face above her, floating over the mighty Delaware, as if he was summoning her.

She closed her eyes and willed Rick's face cloud away so she could finish what she'd tried to start That Night. There must be a grandfather clause somewhere to allow this kiss. Just once. After all, Sam was here first.

But she loved Rick, and she wasn't a cheater. She may not be ready for engagement right now, but it was inevitable. She wasn't supposed to end up with Sam—they were too different. Even if she let this happen, it would only be a matter of time before he'd move on to the next conquest as he'd done so many times with other women. Especially now that Jenna had returned.

Oh, but just this one night, this one chance to experience something she'd thought about for so long. Feed the curiosity, scratch the itch, then go on to married bliss with someone else, forever dousing the flame of *what if*.

She'd often wondered what it would be like to have Sam hovering over her, staring at her like he was now. What it would be like to look up into his beautiful face—his full lips, perfect nose and, oh, those eyes—as he moved, parting her legs with his, the intensity of his unwavering gaze. The way he'd breathe her name.

It was exactly how she envisioned. And it was about to happen.

But they weren't in college anymore.

A friendship was at stake.

Significant others too.

(Still, it was right here for the taking...if only...)

"Can't!" Marley heard herself say, pushing against his chest with her hands. She turned to free herself from his weight, scrambling to sit up.

"I'm sorry," Sam said as he, too, sat up. He ran a hand through his hair and took a deep breath. "Whoa. That wasn't right. Sorry, Mar." Then he looked back at the city and called over his shoulder, "Sorry, Rick!"

Marley, perplexed, looked in the direction Sam yelled.

"You know, he's—west of here."

Marley chuckled. "Thanks, Rand McNally. And don't forget about Jenna."

"Yes. Jenna."

Marley pulled her knees to her chest and hugged them, both to console and convince herself she'd done the right thing.

Sam must have sensed her hesitation.

"You sure?" he asked softly as he bumped his shoulder against hers.

"I'm sure. There are a hundred reasons why this shouldn't happen."

"Name them."

"One, Rick. Two, Jenna. Three, our jobs. Four, our friendship. Five…" Marley's voice trailed off as she tried to come up with a fifth reason.

"That's four," Sam said.

"There are other reasons."

"Ninety-six of them?"

"Yes, to be exact."

"Okay," Sam acquiesced. "It's late. Let's get you and your ninety-six reasons home."

And just like that, the magic was gone. The one thing Marley had secretly thought about over the course of their six-year friendship, even wished for, and that she easily could've clinched that night, evaporated into the evening breeze.

She wasn't sure how to feel—proud of herself for doing the right thing, or disgusted for closing the door on the possibility of what could be lurking beyond that kiss. The what-if part, the what-happens-next part.

Either way, the spell was broken.

They slowly stood and climbed the steps—back to the city, back to reality, back to platonic friendship.

An awkward silence filled the car between them like a thick, heavy fog. Marley was afraid to speak for fear she'd shatter her fragile resolve. A dear friendship was on the line, not to mention a trusting boyfriend five hundred miles away.

Any wrong move now could potentially result in hurt feelings, splintered trust, and worse.

Sam pulled up in front of Marley's building. "I could come in," he offered, giving it one more shot.

"No."

"Once I pull away, the offer's rescinded."

"Okay," she said.

"I'm serious, I won't entertain any last-minute motions."

"Yep."

"No late-night booty calls begging me to come back." He watched her carefully, brows raised.

"Got it." She opened the door and slid out of the Jeep, her knees so weak she was surprised she didn't puddle on the sidewalk.

He leaned across the front seat. "Last chance..."

"Good night, Sam." She closed the door and walked toward the building on shaky legs, willing herself not to turn and jump back in.

A smiling Felix held the door open for her. "You're glowing, Miss Marley," he said. "Must've been a great weekend!"

She sank against the wall of the elevator, breathing for the first time in an hour, it seemed. The doors slid together and were about to close when a hand reached out to stop them.

In that split second, Marley recalled Sam's face above hers, his revelation, the steps, the near kiss, the bachelorette party conversation about destiny.

"Chance..." she whispered.

Someone had stopped the door from closing. Someone was trying to get on. Was destiny opening the door of opportunity? Had Sam decided to come for her?

If this was Sam's hand—if he was indeed coming after her—that was her sign. If he wanted her badly enough to leave his car in a no-parking zone, risking the wrath of Felix and a hefty towing bill, then all bets were off.

Bring it.

The hand, clearly belonging to a man, pried open the door.

Marley held her breath, and her heart pounded. The hand pushed the door open. Followed by an arm. Followed by—

Her middle-aged neighbor.

Marley deflated in disappointment.

This was nothing more than a test of her love for Rick. Or maybe just the test of Sam. His teasing touch, steamy gaze, minty breath...

Stop it, Marley.

His clear, undeniable, and nearly-overpowering attraction to her in that moment.

Seriously.

Something she'd never experienced with another human.

Okay, girl, calm down.

Yet still, she'd passed the test.

She collapsed into bed, wondering what would have happened had she taken Sam's calls after That Night. If they'd explored the possibility of what could be between them, weeks before she met the man she was going to marry.

But she didn't, and now her future was with someone else, *what if* relegated to a pointless question rather than being full of possibility.

All because she was too good a person to ask it.

There was also Sam's disinterest in settling for just one woman. If she'd taken a bite of the forbidden fruit, she'd be left in the wake of his wandering ways. She cared about him too much to risk it, knowing he had the undeniable power to break her heart and shatter their friendship in the process.

She eventually drifted off to sleep.

Or was she on a beach? Sam was there, looking a few years older, splashing in the water with two blonde boys. The happiness radiating from his smile filled her with joy. A woman wearing a wide-brimmed hat approached him, holding a little girl. The woman's face was turned away so Marley couldn't tell who she was. The toddler squirmed out of her embrace and ran to Sam, squealing with delight, her arms outstretched. He lifted her and kissed her little belly. He turned and gazed at the woman with such passion it warmed Marley to the core. This was what she wanted for her friend—someone who illuminated him. In all the times she watched him flirting with girls, those vacuous conquests, she never saw that spark in him.

Marley awakened from the dream before she could confirm what she suspected—the woman in the hat was Jenna.

Marley knew what she had to do. The sanctity of their friendship depended on them being with the right people. She wanted Sam to experience a love like she had with Rick—a steady, calming love that lasts. Crime or not, Marley wanted him to be happy.

Rat torture be damned.

Monday, June 12

COUNTDOWN
TO WEDDING
5 DAYS

Marley

To say things were awkward between Marley and Sam at the office that morning was an understatement. They didn't engage in their typical workday banter and went out of their way to avoid each other.

Until Marley turned a corner and careened into Sam's chest.

He stood aside and bowed with grandeur. "After you."

"Thanks," she muttered and scurried past, eyes downcast.

"Don't forget Delaney's call," he said. "I'll come to your office."

Marley turned, seeing a flicker of something familiar in his eyes. Just as quickly, it was gone.

"Yeah," was all she could muster. She hurried to her office before she could make something of that look.

Rick called a few minutes later, asking about her weekend. She told him about Jenna and Sam hooking up, and how Jenna seemed nicer on Saturday. Rick would be meeting her at the wedding, and Marley didn't want him thinking she was jealous of Sam's date.

"Sorry about this week. I promise I'll make it up to you later this summer."

"How about a long weekend on an island somewhere?" Marley asked, recalling Sam's suggestion. "Tahiti sounds fun."

"It sounds expensive."

"I'm sure we could find a good deal," she continued. "It would be fun to do something different."

"Strathmere's on an island. And it's free."

"Not really, if you consider the summer share I paid," Marley said, annoyance mounting.

"Should I reimburse you a prorated amount?" Rick asked, his voice sarcastic.

"That's not the point. We don't ever do anything romantic. Aren't I worth it?"

He sighed, sounding irritated. "It's not that, Marley. I'm trying to save money."

"That's always your excuse. I just—"

"Sorry, getting called to a meeting," he interrupted. "Talk later?"

As he hung up, Marley growled and slammed her hands on the desk.

"Whoa!" Sam, who'd just entered her office, ducked behind a chair. "Should I have worn protective gear?"

The look on his face cracked her up. "Just—sit down and don't bother me. I'm in a mood."

"You'd never know. Wanna talk about it?"

"Not today, Freud."

After their call with Delaney, which was all business as they discussed the meeting with Wells, Sam turned and leaned up against the side of her doorway on his way out of Marley's office.

"I'm sorry about last night," he said, looking contrite. "It wasn't fair to do that to you."

Marley was thankful he'd broken the ice. "It wasn't just you. There were two of us there."

"Can I make it up to you over lunch?"

Two hours later, it was back to usual as they argued over where to eat. Marley wanted a salad. Sam, a cheesesteak. They agreed on the Reading Terminal Market, where everything from bagels to baba ghanoush could be found.

Sam tore open the wrapper and sank his teeth into his cheesesteak.

"Mmm, better than sex," he said through a mouthful of Cheez Whiz, Philly's iconic cheesesteak topping.

"Doesn't that depend on who you're having it with?" Marley inquired as she tried to stab a grape tomato with her fork.

"With whom you're having it," Sam corrected.

"Screw you."

"You couldn't afford me."

She picked up the uncooperative tomato and flung it at Sam. It hit the guy behind him.

"Sorry, my bad," Sam said, taking the rap when the surprised diner turned around.

The chaotic, familiar atmosphere of the crowded market normalized things between them. Loud chatter, metal chair legs screeching against concrete, and people milling around provided more peace than the day's earlier silence.

"I took your advice and suggested a tropical getaway to Rick," Marley said.

"What did he say?"

" 'Strathmere's an island,' " she said, with a deadpan expression.

"What a dick!" Sam said, laughing. Then, "Oh, did I say that out loud?"

"I get he's busy and wants to save money, but we've never taken an actual vacation other than to the shore, where I go every weekend, so..."

"Jenna's parents have a time-share in Aruba," Sam said. "A bunch of us are talking about going. Would he do that if he only had to pay airfare?"

Marley was distracted by his mention of Jenna's name.

"Planning a vacation together, hmm?" She smiled teasingly. "Must be getting serious."

Sam, focusing on his sandwich, ignored her.

"Listen," she said, as she pushed her salad away and leaned her elbows on the table. "I had a dream last night and it made me realize something. You deserve to be happy."

"Don't make me cue the rats..."

"Seriously. If you like a girl, grow a set. Let her know."

And don't make the same mistake you made with me.

Sam nodded and smiled through his sandwich. "I do like a girl."

"Then tell her."

"What if she shoots me down?"

"That's not the Sam Adams I know," she said. "When are you ever nervous about women? You *must* be serious about her."

Sam paused a moment, sobering. "Very."

"Oh, gosh." Marley bit the side of her lip. "Okay."

A stab of jealousy, followed by relief. Thank God they hadn't taken things further last night when he had such feelings for another. A good reminder of what made Sam dangerous.

"I've never tried to win a girl's heart," Sam announced, as if it were breaking news.

"No shit. Maybe other things, but—"

"Hey, keep it clean," he teased. "So what advice would you have?"

Marley didn't know if she truly wanted to help Sam woo Jenna, but she remembered her dream and how happy he seemed. If Sam got into a serious relationship, perhaps Marley could unstick the replay button of That Night.

And now Penn's Landing.

"What do you know about her?" Marley asked.

Sam leaned back and laced his fingers behind his head.

"She's smart. Funny. Beautiful. Not afraid to make mistakes and doesn't take herself too seriously. She has a wide variety of interests."

"Does she like sports?" she asked.

"Yes. Except for curling. It pisses her off how much those guys get paid."

"Really?"

"Nah," he said, "it just sounded funny."

"Is she romantic?"

"Hopeless."

"What's her favorite flower?" she asked.

"Dunno. Name a good one."

"Roses are too cliché. Carnations—*meh*. But tulips symbolize new life, emerging in spring after a long winter. They'd be perfect because—" She snapped her fingers. "Oh, this is good, 'They symbolize renewal, a reawakening. Just like us.' You can even use that line."

Sam grinned. "Better quit your day job, Walt Whitman."

Marley was fueled by a stream of excellent ideas. "Arrange for a nice dinner. Say something romantic. Here." She pulled a pen from her purse and slid it to him along with a napkin. "Operation Get the Girl, Lesson One. Be honest. Tell her the time you spent with her last weekend was the best you've had in a long time. Write this down!"

Sam obliged.

"You've dated a lot of women," she continued, "but no one makes you feel the way she does. Tell her why she makes you happy, the things you appreciate about her personality. Does she make you laugh? Have quirky traits? Make you a better man? That's it!"

Marley clapped her hands with each word. "She. Brings. Out. The. Best. In. You." Marley slammed her hand on the table. "Damn, am I good!"

Sam smiled as he jotted down her words. "Operation Get the Girl. You crack me up."

"You'll thank me later when OGG is a success. Trust me, I know what women like."

He glanced up through his long lashes and gave her a half smile. Her heart blipped—it was the look of a man in love.

Jenna was a lucky girl. It had been a long time since Rick had looked at her like that.

Delaney

AFTER HER CALL WITH THE INTERNS, DELANEY SAT ON the deck to soak up some sun when the swoosh of the sliding glass door was followed by her dad's voice.

"More weather updates for you, my child."

"If you're here to tell me the storm's intensifying, I already know," she said, her voice grim. "Not looking too good, is it?"

Despite the cloudless day, the latest forecast predicted the storm could intensify into a hurricane within the next twenty-four hours, with a projected course for the eastern seaboard.

"Actually, one of the models has it veering off the coast," he said. "So hang in there—there's hope for your wedding, yet."

Delaney shaded her eyes and looked at her dad, the Energizer Bunny of positivity.

"You are the most optimistic person I've ever known," she said. "If only I had half your hopeful outlook."

"Oh, it's in there. You just don't realize it."

"Tell that to Kate," Delaney laughed. "She thinks I'm too uptight."

"Driven," her dad said. "There's a difference."

"She told me I needed to let things go, not be so focused on the next goal."

"She has a more laid-back approach to life, that's for sure," he agreed. "But you and Kathryn are two different people."

"We are, that's for sure," Delaney said, smiling. "Two sisters, same parents, same upbringing, but obviously two different outlooks."

"You were different from the moment you were born. You just had a tougher go of it, at first."

Delaney was ten when her parents had told her she was adopted. They explained how badly they'd wanted to have a child but weren't able to, despite several in vitro treatments. The day they brought Delaney home was the most wonderful day of their lives, they said, because it was the day they became parents.

Then, fourteen months later, two pink lines emerged on a plastic strip, heralding the arrival of her sister. Kathryn June Ross entered the world with blonde ringlets and sparkly brown eyes, the undeniable combination of her parents, and the exact opposite of her older sister, with her dark hair and blue-gray eyes. Followed, years later, by another surprise—her brother, JJ, who looked just like his sister Kate.

Her parents' timing for telling Delaney she was adopted was perfect. At ten, she was old enough for reason, too young for rebellion. She was already practical in her approach to life, inherently fact-driven, and knew her parents loved her just as much as her natural-born sister and brother.

Now, sitting on the deck with the only dad she'd ever known, Delaney admitted to wondering what traits she got from her birth parents and which ones were a result of her environment.

"That may be something you can find out, with all the DNA kits on the market," he said.

"That's your plan, isn't it? Unload me onto my birth parents before the wedding bills roll in," Delaney teased, poking his leg with her toe. "Sorry to break the bad news. You're stuck with me, Mr. Happy."

"I guess that calls for celebration. How about lunch at Hula Grill?"

She smiled. "You had me at Hula."

She was relieved to change the subject. While she was curious to know more about her origin and heritage, she didn't want to offend her parents or appear ungrateful for the life they'd given her. Someday she may want to learn more, but for now she was happy to enjoy the family she had. Her real family.

The father-daughter duo took off for their favorite lunch spot on the boardwalk, placed their orders, and found a seat at one of the blue metal tables outside.

"So aside from this little weather issue, how's everything else going?" her dad asked.

"It's okay, I guess."

"Are you having second thoughts?"

"No, I'm good," she said. "It's just—I don't know. Maybe it's everything happening at once. The case, the wedding, and now this little weather issue, as you refer to it. It's a lot."

"I know your case is important to you, and I'm proud of your work ethic. Always have been. But you also must learn the delicate art of balance. Life can't be all one big to-do list."

"You sound like Kate," she joked.

"She's not wrong, you know."

"Kate still believes in fairy tales, Dad. Magic and destiny."

"There's nothing wrong with that. You could use a little dose of that kind of thinking, once in a while. That's why I'm glad you're marrying Dalton. He'll fill your lives with surprise, and never let you take life too seriously."

"But life is serious," she insisted. "Especially in my line of work."

"Of course it is. But it's also something to celebrate. I wish someone had told me this when I was your age."

"You've always been a hard worker," Delaney said. "I think that's where I got it from."

"We're alike in that respect," he admitted. "I spent most of my adult years afraid I'd let an opportunity to get ahead pass me by."

"It paid off, right? We wouldn't have our shore house if you'd been less motivated."

"But as you kids have grown, I've come to realize what really matters in life."

"Whiskey?" Delaney teased, knowing it was her dad's favorite.

"No, silly. Time. It has a way of getting away from us if we aren't present."

Delaney liked her answer better.

He continued. "People like you and me, we believe time will stand still because we have a work thing or task we need to address. Meanwhile, life is going on around us but we're too focused on that thing to realize it. And we sometimes miss out on life's greatest moments."

"Did that ever happen to you?"

"Of course," he said. "I wasn't there when Kate got Happy."

Happy was Kate's kitten, a present she'd received for her sixth birthday. It was all she'd ever wanted since the time she could talk. Delaney remembered Kate's reaction when she opened the box, screaming, jumping up and down, and bursting into tears. She'd never seen her sister as happy as she was that day, thus the kitten's name.

"Why weren't you there?" she asked.

"I don't even remember, which is the biggest sin. I guess something was going on at work and I thought I had to stay late. I remember justifying it, knowing I'd see Kate later, thinking that would be enough. In so doing, I robbed myself of the precious moment when your kid's face lights up from pure joy. I regret it."

Her dad was silent. Delaney could tell he was recalling other moments he'd missed.

"The closing night of your last high school musical," he said, nodding. "I didn't realize it would be the last time you'd be performing on a stage. We were in the middle of a merger, and I worked all weekend."

"At least you got to see the video."

"Not the same as being there," he said, shaking his head. "Oh, and I almost missed JJ's birth, because I was doing a presentation when I got the call."

"Now *that* would have been bad," Delaney said. Still, her dad's comments hit home. "That's kind of how I've felt all along about the wedding," she admitted. "I've been so focused on my case, I wasn't present for a lot of the things that had to be done. I turned it over to Dalton and then got mad at him when he made decisions I didn't agree with."

"A groom should be involved," he said. "Nothing wrong with that."

"You know how they say a bride cries when she finds the right dress?"

"That's what your mom says. I know she cried with hers, and with yours."

"Not me," Delaney said, pointing to herself. "Getting the dress was just another to-do thing. The only thought I had was, 'Good, this is done. On to the next thing.' Meanwhile, Mom and Kate were crying so much I thought they'd flood the place."

"You're just a different person than they are," he said. "Just keep in mind what I'm saying. Learn how to be in the moment because this time will never come around again."

"I'll try."

Her dad leaned forward and took her hands in his. "None of us know how long we have on this planet, so it's important to make every moment count. That means being present for people and things you love. Work hard, yes, but take time to enjoy the things that matter. Starting now. Trust me, this wedding will be over before you know it, and I don't want you to regret not being here for it."

Delaney promised her dad she'd take his advice.

When they finished their meal, Delaney headed into town. She was strolling along Asbury Avenue when she spotted someone she recognized all too well.

He was hugging a woman on the sidewalk before helping her into a car. He bent over and spoke with her through the open window before she pulled away. Delaney only caught a brief glimpse of the woman and couldn't place her, but the man was well known to her.

As Dalton.

She froze in place, her world stopped. Why was her fiancé with a woman? More importantly, who was she, and why he was hugging her?

Was he meeting someone today? Her mind came up blank. She ran the woman's features through her mental database of Dalton's family members, trying to recall if she was maybe a cousin or distant relative. Delaney pretty much knew everyone in his family and circle of friends, but this woman was not registering as one of them.

Delaney took a deep breath to infuse reality into the situation. This was Dalton. He wasn't cheating on her, not now before their upcoming wedding, and not ever. It had to be an innocent thing, an old school friend or somebody he'd run into.

Unbunch your little girl panties and put on the big ones.

Squashing her emotional reaction, she flipped the switch in her brain to focus on facts.

Fact: Dalton was crazy about her.

Fact: They were about to get married.

Fact: She knew how to dispose of bodies without anyone knowing.

Kate

KATE WAS ABOUT TO TAKE A BEACH WALK AND WAS searching in her closet for a sweatshirt when something caught her eye. Crumpled on the floor in the back was the Ocean City hoodie from the photo memory. The one she'd worn when Greg had announced his plans to move.

She hadn't seen it since that fateful day.

Against her better judgment, she pulled it over her head, only to discover it was Greg's sweatshirt, not hers. He'd left her shore house in such a huff that day, he must have forgotten to take it with him.

She breathed into the fabric to see if it still smelled like him. His scent was long gone, but a flood of memories washed over her as she reminisced about the good times they'd shared. College parties, walks on the beach, strolling the boardwalk hand in hand.

But then she remembered the disagreements, the frustration. The heartbreak, watching him drive away after he chose a life that didn't include her.

She resisted the urge to attach significance to her finding.

Delaney was right. She needed closure, and it was time to move on. After her walk, she'd go through her closet in search of other Greg remnants to donate to Goodwill.

As she was taking off the hoodie, she felt a hard object in the front pocket. Her fingers curled around a seashell. Greg loved to collect trinkets on their walks, always on the quest for a unique shell or cool piece of sea glass. She pulled it out and observed a perfectly shaped white scallop shell.

Should she keep this one memento?

Nope, moving on. She tossed it onto her bed. As it twirled through the air, Kate noticed a flash of purple inside the shell. She picked it up and turned it over.

And gasped.

Someone had written a message with a purple Sharpie.

Not just someone.

Greg.

And not just a message.

A proposal.

The words, "Kate, will you marry me?" were surrounded by little hand-drawn hearts.

Her eyes instantly flooded with tears, the words blurring. "Oh, my god..."

Kate swiped her eyes with the back of her free, trembling hand. The words reappeared, sharp and certain.

He must have had the shell in his pocket when they took their beach walk that day, the last time he would have worn the sweatshirt.

Thinking back, Greg had seemed nervous when he suggested a beach walk. He hadn't been himself in the days leading up to it—jumpier than usual, uncertain. She'd ask him a question and he'd either give an answer that didn't make sense or claim he didn't hear her, as if he was in his own world. After the breakup, Kate attributed it to nerves over her anticipated reaction to his move announcement. With good reason, it turned out.

Now, his behavior took on new meaning. No wonder he was nervous. He was going to propose to her.

If only he'd led with that, she may have agreed to go.

"Dammit," she whispered, a fresh flood of tears cascading down her face. She'd said such awful things to him that day. After they'd left the beach, they continued fighting back at the house as months of pent-up frustration over his lack of maturity flowed freely. She'd told him what she thought of his plan and how he was ruining hers. He looked heartbroken as she berated him, before he climbed into a van and drove away.

They hadn't spoken to each other since.

Kate ran her fingers over the writing on the smooth underbelly of the shell. Cocooned in the hoodie pocket, protected from light, the words had been perfectly preserved, as vibrant as if he'd just written them yesterday.

Was the sentiment behind them well-preserved too?

There's someone from my past I haven't gotten over, he'd told the interviewer.

It had to be Kate. They'd had a pretty good relationship for most of the time they'd been together, except toward the end when they fought about everything. Her biggest issue had been his inability to commit to a lifetime with her.

Here was physical evidence she'd been dead wrong.

She knew what she had to do. Forgetting her earlier resolve to move on, she pulled out her phone and plugged his still-familiar phone number into a new message field.

And she began typing.

Cleo

"CAN WE PICK A SPOT, ALREADY?" CLEO WHINED AS SHE trudged through thick sand.

Tori held her wide-brimmed straw hat to her head as a hot gust of wind threatened to carry it away. They had their standards when it came to sitting on the beach—far enough from families with kids, but not too far from the water. And, at Cleo's insistence, within reasonable eyeshot of the lifeguards.

"I think this'll do," Tori announced, opening her beach chair.

Before committing to the spot, Cleo pulled a pair of binoculars from her boho bag and focused them on the lifeguard stand. "Yes, this'll do nicely."

Tori got to work on her bridesmaid tan. Cleo trained her binoculars on the guards, hoping to find something interesting, but they looked as if they were still in middle school. (Pass.)

A few hours later, the wind shifted to a land breeze, ushering in biting, green-headed flies. They gathered their belongings and headed to the Point, Sea Isle's tropical-themed beach bar, lucky to find seats at the bar among a crowd of other fly-fleeing, drink-seeking beachgoers.

Cleo watched, mesmerized, as the bartender swaggered over. He wore a tight black T-shirt and jeans. There was something about him that made her want to see him in neither.

"What do you fancy, love?" he asked Cleo.

"You," Cleo said, giving him a once-over.

She wasn't sure if it was the British accent—she was a sucker for that—or the way the sleeves of his black T-shirt outlined his biceps, one of which was tattooed with the word "Mum." Unoriginal, yes, but endearing in an old-school way. Maybe it was the curly onyx hair that tumbled over one eye, giving him the look of a swashbuckling man of mystery. Whatever it was, she fancied the eye candy standing before her.

"Do you have Sex on the Beach?" Cleo asked, raising her eyebrow.

"Only with the right gal."

Good man.

Tori snapped her fingers in Cleo's face. "Down, girl. You're embarrassing him."

Cleo turned to him. "My friend Tori here thinks I've embarrassed you. Have I?"

"Not at all. Nice to meet you, Tori," he said, offering her a handshake before turning to Cleo. "And who are you?"

"I'm called Cleo," she said, just like the Brits do, "but you can call me anytime. And you're..."

"Nigel," he said, flashing her the kind of smile that turns an ordinary face into a charming—hell, make that sexy—one.

Be still, my fluttering girl parts.

"What can I get you ladies?"

"Surprise me," Cleo said after Tori asked for a menu.

He swaggered away and Cleo fell into a trance.

This was precisely why one shouldn't give in to the first Tom, Dick, or Wells who came down the pike, professing undying love. Not that Wells said anything about the L-word, but one could only assume that's where he was headed.

"Oh my God!" Tori exclaimed as her eyes filled with tears.

Her asshole boyfriend must be at it. Again.

"What's the Turd done now?" Cleo asked, bracing herself.

Tori blinked at her phone in disbelief. "He's not coming to the wedding."

Cleo believed it. "What's his lame excuse?"

"Work. He has a—thing. Something about a town hall."

"Bullshit."

Cleo knew the real story. Something better had come up.

Nigel returned, handing Cleo a cocktail. She swirled, sniffed, and sipped like a practiced sommelier.

"Not bad," she said, smacking her lips. "Could use a little more vodka, but it'll do."

"She's a bartender," Tori explained.

Nigel gave Cleo a fist bump. "I knew there was a reason I liked you."

She liked him too, although it had less to do with their shared profession and more the fit of his tight jeans.

"Where do you tend?" he asked.

"Philly, for now, but moving to New York," she said, "eventually."

"I'm heading there, too, when this place closes for the season."

Say what? Maybe destiny was a thing, after all.

"Is bartending the only reason you're heading to the Big Apple? Or do you have a fella there?" he asked.

Cleo gave a hearty guffaw. She'd been accused of a lot of things in her day, but having a boyfriend wasn't one of them.

"Nah. I'm just going there to get drunk people drunker. And paint stuff."

"You're an artist," Nigel said, more a statement than a question. "I could tell."

Cleo took it as a compliment, intended or not.

"What's your story?" Cleo asked. "Why New York and not London? I'm assuming that's where you're originally from."

"Originally from Nottingham, actually," Nigel said. "I lived in London for a couple years but decided it was time to see the rest of the world."

"That sounds exciting, Nigel from Nottingham."

"How about you guys? Are you from here?" he asked.

"Philly, myself," Cleo said, then pointed to Tori. "She's a Jersey girl from Deptford."

Nigel turned to Tori. "What can I get for you, darlin' from Deptford?"

"A date for a wedding."

"Straight up, or on the rocks?" he asked.

"Straight up, since her other situation's already on the rocks," Cleo joked.

"Sorry to hear that."

Nigel didn't look sorry. Eager, maybe. Men flocked to Tori like seagulls to an open bag of chips, and not just for her looks. Tori exuded genuine sweetness, which also caused her to attract fecal matter. Like Ted.

"I have just the cure," he said.

He returned two minutes later with a cloudy white drink. "It's not a date to the wedding, but it is one of my new drinks. I call it—"

"Snog in the Fog?" Cleo guessed.

"You know what—that's exactly what I'm going to call it," he said, laughing. "Brilliant! I like your way of thinking."

He turned to Tori. "Why can't your boyfriend come to this wedding?"

"Work."

"He's full of shit," Cleo said. "He's known for a year our friend's getting married this weekend."

"Yeah, but he can't help that a work situation came up,"

Tori said, always ready to defend the jerk. "As a state representative, he's constantly getting pulled into this and that."

" 'This and that' being better offers." Cleo couldn't help herself.

Tori ignored her, as she often did her friend's disparaging comments. But Cleo kept it up, hoping something would sink in eventually.

"Sounds like rubbish. Who works weekends? Besides you and me." Nigel motioned to Cleo. "How about you, Ms. Mixologist? Do you have a date for this wedding?"

"June seventeenth," Cleo said.

Her stomach flopped. It was the kind of joke she and Wells shared. Why, now, would he pop into mind when she was about to succumb to British Invasion?

"I like the way you roll." Nigel gave her a lopsided grin and turned to wait on others.

She'd be up for a roll. He could be just what she needed to forget about Wells.

Tori scrolled through her phone, presumably searching for a plus-one.

"Just go solo," Cleo suggested. "I would if Delaney hadn't insisted I take a date, which I need like an open, gaping head wound."

Cleo's "date," as she loosely referred to him, was their platonic friend Kirk, a perpetual teenager trapped in a video game world. But still, a date—assuming he could break away from Minecraft for half a second. She only asked him, and he only agreed, because he owed her a favor.

"Oh, my God," Tori whimpered. "You gotta be kidding me."

"What now?"

Tori's look went from pitiful to pissed. She showed Cleo a message from the girlfriend of one of Ted's cronies.

> Hey girl! Looks like the boys are going to Palm Springs to golf this weekend. Let's get together!

"What a fucking moron!" Cleo snapped.

"It was only a matter of time before you realized," Nigel said as he returned to them.

"Not you."

"Whew." He wiped the back of his hand across his forehead in jest. "Although, truth be told, I am a fucking moron."

"Then you should date Tori," she quipped. "That's all she dates."

Tori furiously texted, slammed her phone down and drained her drink in one swallow.

"*Ooh*-kay," Cleo said, taking the empty glass from her. "He's not worth it."

"I told him I know about his golf plans."

"Good girl," Nigel said.

"What am I gonna do?" Tori leaned forward and groaned, covering her eyes with her palms. "I've had enough of his bullshit."

"For starters," Cleo said, "break up with his ass—"

"And the rest of him," Nigel said.

"Then take that trip you've been putting off. Pursue your own dreams."

"What trip have you been putting off, love?"

Tori told him how she'd been working for *Philly Mag* and was planning a trip to Europe to build her photography portfolio when she was assigned to cover Ted's campaign. They began dating soon thereafter..

"The Turd didn't like her working evenings, which were reserved for political events," Cleo explained. "He made her quit the magazine and get a day job."

She turned to Tori. "You need to ditch him, and that job, and go on that trip."

"Life's too short to be tied down to something you don't love," Nigel said.

His words, meant for Tori, had an impact on Cleo. The man had a point. While she liked bartending, it wasn't her passion like art was. Maybe she should heed his advice too.

"But first, I need to find a plus-one."

"I'm available," Nigel said.

He looked like a hungry lion with a rare steak. Of course he'd be interested in her beautiful friend. He was male, after all.

"Aw, that's sweet," Tori said. "It's a date."

Tori and Nigel exchanged numbers, and a flicker of excitement ignited in Cleo, knowing this wouldn't the last time she'd be in the royal presence of Nigel of Nottingham, Lord of Her Lady Parts.

Even if he was escorting her good friend—Tori, Duchess of Deptford.

Delaney

DELANEY AND DALTON HAD PLANNED TO FINISH THEIR separate missions (hers: legit; his: suspicious) and meet up with Cleo and Tori at The Point when they were done.

Delaney arrived before he did and joined the girls. When Dalton finally arrived, he wore a broad smile as he strode across the sand to meet them. Delaney's heart did the same little jig whenever she saw her handsome fiancé. There had to be a plausible explanation for him hugging a random woman on the street.

At least, she hoped so, for his sake. Otherwise, cue the body bag.

Ten minutes into the gathering, Dalton was acting weird, like he was inebriated, talking fast and giggling.

"Are you high on something?" Cleo asked, an eyebrow raised as she backhanded him on the arm.

"Only on life," Dalton said, wrapping his arm around Delaney's waist and pulling her hip into his. "I'm marrying this woman in five days. Can you blame me?"

"Easy there, Romeo," Delaney warned as she licked a trail of margarita from her hand, splashed there by Dalton's boundless affection. Did his euphoria have something to do with his Casablanca moment on Asbury Avenue?

Dalton jolted as his phone lit up his pants pocket. He held up a finger to excuse himself and took his secret agent phone call to the other side of the bar.

Okay. Something was up.

"What's his deal?" Cleo asked, nodding her head in Dalton's direction. "He seems jumpy."

"He *is* jumpy, isn't he?' Delaney asked, standing shoulder to shoulder with Cleo as they both sipped their drinks and watched him. "I think he's cheating on me."

"Now *you're* high," Cleo said. "You know he's crazy about you. Why would you even think that?"

"I saw him hug someone on the street today. I don't know who she was."

"Your wedding is this weekend. I'm sure you can't swing a ring bearer without hitting extended family members. They're probably crawling all over town."

A definite possibility. It was probably nothing nefarious, but she wouldn't be the first to be duped by a cheating fiancé days before their nuptials.

She was getting annoyed. They were supposed to be here with friends, yet there he was, on the other side of the outdoor bar, pacing, gesticulating, and laughing into his phone.

Delaney made WTF arms. He mouthed the word, "meeting."

"Meeting my ass," Cleo said, calling it before Delaney could. "Who has meetings on vacation? Besides you, of course."

"Even I've cut myself off from work." Other than her call with Sam and Marley that morning. "Now look at him, laughing like a hyena," Delaney observed. "Who laughs like that in meetings?"

"Wouldn't know, having never been in one my entire life," Cleo answered. "Perhaps he *is* high."

High on his rendezvous, maybe.

And then it dawned on Delaney: the ignored phone call from Dalton's boss. His lame excuse of a meeting. The mystery woman.

Delaney knew who she was.

His boss, Evelyn.

But why was she here in Ocean City, on a Monday? And why was she calling Dalton now? What was so compelling he had to step away from the group like he was a secret operative for the CIA?

Now she recognized the look on his face that morning on the beach, when he refused to take the call. The unmistakable expression of guilt.

That's it. Time for a showdown.

As soon as they left the bar and got into the car, she went for broke. The lawyer in her wanted to get right to the point. "What's up?" she asked. "Something is, so start talking."

Dalton made a show of looking in the console, avoiding her inquisitive look. "Why do you think something's up?"

"I saw you with a woman on Asbury today." She purposely didn't name the person in case it wasn't his boss.

Dalton stopped what he was doing and looked up. "You mean Evelyn?" he asked, as if it was no big deal. "You saw us?"

"Yes." Delaney said, waiting for him to deny it. "Hugging."

"Why didn't you come over and say hi?" he asked.

"I thought I was catching you in the act," she admitted.

"You purposely didn't come over because you thought I was doing something wrong?"

"Something like that. I work in criminal justice. Guilty until proven innocent."

"I thought it was the other way around?" he said.

"You'd think. Why didn't you take her call this morning?"

"Because I was with you."

"She's also the one who called you in the bar?" Delaney asked.

"Yes."

"Why all the calls when you're on vacation? And why was she here in Ocean City?"

He sighed. "Big changes coming up. I can't say more."

Delany guffawed. "Why, or you'll have to kill me?"

"Possibly," he said, chuckling.

"Do you promise you're not cheating on me?"

"Are you kidding me? Come here," Dalton said as he hugged her. "I'm the luckiest man on the planet. There's nobody else I'd rather be with. Ever."

He'd better be telling her the truth, if he didn't want to end up in a landfill.

IT HAD BEEN SIX HOURS SINCE KATE TEXTED GREG, WITH no response.

Well, not exactly six hours. More like four, as it had taken her two hours to compose the perfect message. She tapped and backspaced, typed and erased what seemed like hundreds of times, trying to strike the perfect balance between casual and formal, aloof and interested. She'd considered sending a photo of the shell but that would be too creepy to start with.

She wasn't sure which approach to take, especially given this newly discovered evidence.

Greg was going to propose to her. And she'd blown it.

But then, she remembered the green roses, his comment about new beginnings. It was time to find out if he meant it.

She finally settled on a message to convey everything she was feeling.

> Hey.

Yep, the perfect way to start a conversation two years overdue. At least it was a start. "Hey," when sent as a text message, could mean a variety of things. It could mean, "Hey...I'm thinking of you." Or "Hey...what's up?" Or, in this case, "Hey...just found out you were going to propose, and now you're rich. Free this weekend?"

Kate consulted her phone for the twentieth time since sending the text, realizing her carefully crafted, one-word message didn't require a response. She sent another.

> Congrats on the article and thanks for the flowers. They're beautiful!

> About that new beginning...

She hit send, then waited. When no reply came through, she went for a run, purposely leaving her phone behind.

The second she returned, she pounced on it.

Still no response.

When Kate finally crawled into bed at two in the morning, she'd lost all hope he was interested in reconnecting. She'd always known Greg to be a conscientious texter. The fact that she hadn't heard back meant he wasn't going to take her bait. She needed to move on.

Unless...

He may have been sick, or traveling, or surfing all day. Perhaps he'd been attacked by a shark or—worse!—swept out to sea.

She'd give it one more day to see if he responded. If he didn't, she'd have her answer: he wasn't interested.

Or, he was bobbing, gashed and helpless, somewhere in the Pacific.

Marley

RICK CALLED THAT EVENING AS MARLEY WAS ABOUT TO leave the office.

"Hey," he said, his tone distracted. "I'm looking at flights for Thursday."

"You sure you can take time off?" Marley asked.

"Not really, but I'm trying to make it up to you since we didn't get our week in. At least it'll give us an extra night."

"Or we could just make it up later," she suggested. "How about Aruba? Sam said—"

"I frankly don't care what Sam has to say about our vacation, Marley. We just can't afford a trip like that."

"Can't...or won't?"

Rick made six figures and lived with his parents. He stashed his paycheck away every week, saving for a house, something she'd admired about him when they first met. But there was more to life than saving for the future. Like enjoying the present.

"Do I have to say it?" he asked. "I'm saving for your ring."

"Shouldn't we talk about that first?"

"Marley." Rick sighed. "I love you and want to marry you. I've made that clear."

"Me too," she said, her voice higher than normal. "But—"

"Is your hesitation related to our conversation Friday night?"

Friday night? Oh, right. Her disclosure about her sordid Sam past.

If only he knew about Sunday.

Marley swallowed hard. Should she come clean about the Incident at Penn's Landing? Think, think, think—

Nope. What (almost) happens in Philly...and so on.

"It's not about Sam, if that's what you're insinuating. It's about us."

"What's wrong with us?"

She recalled the look on Sam's face at lunch when he talked about Jenna. She missed seeing Rick look at her like that, when his chocolate eyes would melt into hers. Letting her know, unequivocally, she had his heart. But lately, something had stripped him of that tender vulnerability. He didn't look at her that way anymore.

Her voice became small. "I feel like we've—lost a spark or something. I want to see if we still have it before we start talking rings."

"We need a tropical island to figure that out?" he demanded. "Grow up, Marley."

She recoiled from his verbal slap. Her gloves came off. "The fuck does that mean?"

"Life isn't all fun and games. I'm over here working my ass off, trying to save for a ring and a house. Meanwhile, you and Sam act like you're still in college. Whenever I bring up the future, you change the subject. When are you going to get serious?"

"I can't talk about the future when we don't have a present. We haven't seen each other for months because of your work, and it feels like you don't care. Like I'm not worth your time and money."

"I'm in the middle of an important job. Sorry you don't know what that's like."

"And I'm helping to defend a man's life," she said. "If that's not important enough, I've got another job for you. It's called fuck off!"

She hurled her phone across the office.

Right into Sam's head as he entered the room.

"Ow!" he screamed, flinging himself backward. He clutched his punctured forehead as a trickle of blood cascaded down the bridge of his nose.

"What in the worldwide fuck was that?" he demanded. "I'm gonna have a black eye!"

Marley handed him a wad of tissues. "You don't get a black eye from being hit on the forehead, fool."

"A concussion then," he whimpered. "Damn, that really hurt."

She hated to admit it, but it was cathartic to displace her anger onto a flying object. She really should consider axe throwing as her next hobby.

"I'll make sure you stay up all night," she offered.

"Promise?"

Marley loosened her scarf, dumped ice from her empty soda cup into it, and lay the makeshift ice pack against his life-threatening wound.

"You're fine," she assured him.

"I'm concussed."

Marley giggled.

"Seriously, why did you throw your phone at me?"

"I wasn't throwing it at you. I didn't know you were coming into my office."

"Why—"

"Don't want to get into it. Let's get out of here."

They headed to the train station with Marley's floral scarf tied around Sam's head like a do-rag. Paired with his tailored suit, he looked like a card-carrying member of a Jos. A. Bank street gang. The wound dressing was at his insistence, lest he bleed out on the streets of Philadelphia.

"I'm taking it you had a fight with Rikki-Tikki-Tavi?" Sam asked as they walked.

Marley stared straight ahead. "Still don't want to talk about it."

She couldn't believe she'd hung up on Rick, a first for her. Or that she told him to fuck off.

"Good enough," Sam relented. "Hey, it's Monday. How about some Chinese with our favorite TV bachelorette?"

"Wow, you do know me."

Chinese food and a houseful of gorgeous hunks, baring chests and souls to win the love of the bachelorette (a fellow attorney), was just what she needed right now. The mindless reality show would keep her mind off Rick and their fight.

"And I could use some more advice about my big date," Sam added.

Right, Operation Get the Girl.

"Then you're buying dinner."

"You got it." He fell in step next to Marley as they approached the platform. "A small price to pay for you helping me win back the 'love of my life.' "

Marley shot him a look.

"Your words, not mine."

They boarded the crowded train and Sam motioned for Marley to take the last seat. He stood over her, his hand holding on to a pole. His man package was directly at her eye level, and it was all she could do to keep from staring. After an unsuccessful attempt at averting her eyes, she looked up to find Sam smiling down at her.

"Take a picture," he mouthed, flashing his eyebrows seductively.

"Don't flatter yourself," she whispered back.

"I don't have to, when you do it for me."

Suddenly the train screeched to a halt and he fell into Marley.

"Sorry to drop in like this."

As she helped push him up, her mind flashed to last night as they lay together, his face so close, their legs intertwined—

"What's that smile about?" he leaned down and whispered.

She nodded at a guy three seats down, slobbering and talking in his sleep. "About how much I want to give that guy a lap dance."

Sam laughed. "Nice work, Mar. You finally found your type."

When they got to her place, Marley changed into her couch-fit, as Sam called it—an oversized crimson Temple sweatshirt and baggy gray pants. She tossed a pair of Rick's sweats and a shirt to Sam.

"Nah," he said, batting them away.

"I thought you'd want to be comfortable."

"I'm fine like this." He took off his tie and rolled up his sleeves. "Besides, I wouldn't want you to mistake me for Rick and cop a feel."

"You saw right through me."

When their food came, they settled on the overstuffed couch, engaging in their usual chitchat, when Sam broke in with a random question.

"What's your true north?" he asked, a grain of rice stuck to his chin.

Marley leaned over to flick it off, but he recoiled and deflected her advancement with his hand.

"Head wound."

Sam still had Marley's scarf tied to his head, insistent upon protecting his (certainly fractured) skull, possibly the only thing holding his cranium together. Only Sam could pull off a look so goofy yet cute at the same time.

When she didn't answer, he clarified. "True north: where your internal compass focuses when the world spirals out of control."

Hmm. The obvious answer was Rick, the one who got her

through Sam's devastating rejection, righted her world, made her feel wanted. Regret over her earlier nasty words nagged at her. She should give him a pass, as it had been completely out of character for him.

"Hey, I just realized something," Sam said, interrupting her thoughts. "If you combined 'true' and 'north,' you'd get 'truth.'"

"Brilliant, Webster. Put it in your dictionary. What's yours?"

"Cheesesteaks. Although this—" he held up his container of kung pao "—is a close second."

"I expected nothing less from you."

When their show was over, Sam asked Marley to check his "head laceration" to make sure he wasn't "gushing blood."

"If it was, you'd be dead by now," Marley assured him.

She gingerly unwrapped the scarf. Not one drop of blood. She decided to have some fun.

"Oh my God!" She gasped.

"What?"

"It's worse than I thought. The blood!"

"Should we go to the ER? I don't want to die tonight. Call 911! I think I'm gonna pass out."

Marley couldn't suppress her laughter any longer. "You're fine. See?" She waved the bloodless scarf around.

He grabbed it and pulled it, and her, toward him. "I'm gonna get you for this."

He squeezed her sides and wiggled his fingers into her ticklish spots. She fell back on the couch, shrieking hysterically, legs flailing. He held her down, his knees straddling her hips as she laugh-screamed for him to stop.

"Okay." He stopped tickling but remained straddling her. "Maybe next time you'll think twice before making fun of someone's blunt force trauma."

"Noted."

Marley raised her arms for him to help her up but he

clasped his fingers with hers instead.

"I'm not letting you up until you answer my question."

She continued to lie flat on her back, panting, looking up at him, fingers entwined. Visions of Penn's Landing danced in her head.

Question? Was there a question?

"Your true north," he reminded her, blinking slowly. "And you can't say Mr. Ohio."

"Why not?"

"My game, my rules," he said. "Besides, he can't be your north when he's out west."

"Okay, Lewis and Clark. I'd say..."

Marley knew what—who—she wanted to say in lieu of Rick, but couldn't bring herself to do it.

So she said the next best thing.

"Tacos."

Sam nodded, a slow smile spreading across his face. "That's my girl."

He stood and pulled her up by her hands. "By the way, I'm off for the next three."

"Next three what?"

"Decades." He looked at her dead-on. "Earth rotations, fool. I'm doing that project for my dad."

Marley had forgotten Sam's father's firm was borrowing him to assist with case prep. She wished him luck and made him promise he wasn't going to jump ship. Not that he'd ever consider it.

It later dawned on Marley they never talked about his upcoming date with Jenna.

Which was just fine by her.

Tuesday, June 13

COUNTDOWN
TO WEDDING
4 DAYS

Cleo

CLEO'S PHONE RANG AT THE UNGODLY HOUR OF O'DARK thirty.

What was wrong with people? Didn't they know she was on vacation? It had only been a couple hours since she and Tori stumbled home after raging into the wee hours with a group of college boys. While fun, she was getting too old for this shit. They should have left when Delaney and Dalton did.

She felt around for her phone and found it wedged between her bed and the wall.

It was Murph, of Murphy's Tavern.

"What do you want?" she croaked, too exhausted to engage in formalities. She'd rather be charged by stampeding buffalo than awakened before noon.

"Gus is in the hospital," he said.

Cleo shot upright in her bed, any remnants of a hangover gone. "What happened?"

"He fell off his barstool last night," he reported.

Cleo hoped his words would be followed by a punch line, a chuckle, or a proclamation of jest. But they weren't—the morose morning hour of his call served as strong indication he wasn't fucking around.

"They think he had a seizure. They're keeping him at Penn for observation."

"I'm on my way."

She threw on a pair of leggings and an old tee, scribbled a note for Tori, and drove to Philly like a fleeing felon.

Cleo found her crumpled friend in a bed four times his size, making him look more like a toddler than a grown-ass man. She pulled up a chair and took Gus's bony hand. His translucent liver-spotted skin revealed a network of bulging blue veins, most likely from—

From what? She had no idea what he'd done for a living. By the time they'd become friends, Gus had already retired. Probably a blue-collar job, something using his hands. She made a mental note to ask him later.

Cleo talked to him even though he was asleep, so he'd know he wasn't alone. She told him about her vacation, including the hot bartender she'd met.

Gus's heart monitor picked up speed.

"You like that, don't you?" she chucked. "Dirty old man. Don't worry, nothing happened. He likes Tori."

Gus's finger twitched.

"You like Tori too, I know. Who doesn't? Anyway, as I was saying..."

She rambled on about all sorts of nonsense until he finally stirred.

"Wow, I guess they'll let anyone in here," he said, his voice groggy.

Cleo tried to hide the smile creeping across her face. "They let you in, didn't they?"

"I'm a card-carrying member," he said.

"Come here often?"

"Whenever I need a hot, fresh meal."

"Ever try a restaurant?" she asked. "Philly does have 'em, you know."

"I've been banned from most."

"Doesn't surprise me." Cleo reached for the cup on his tray table. "Ice chip?"

Gus nodded and waved his IV-clad hand toward his mouth. "I gave this place a great review on Yelp," he said, crunching the ice she fed him.

Cleo was impressed whenever her old pal referenced pop

culture. Especially something to do with the "Inter Nets," as he called it.

"Enough niceties, old man. Give it to me straight. What happened?"

"Captain Morgan chased a Wild Turkey and knocked me off my barstool. But good ol' Jim Beam helped me up."

Cleo leveled a look at him.

He sobered. "Seizure of some sort. Probably from chemo."

"Chemo?" she asked, alarmed. "Since when are you getting chemo?"

"Last week. My first treatment."

"What the hell are you getting chemo for?"

"Shits and giggles," he said. "You should try it."

"This isn't funny. Do you have cancer?"

"It appears I do."

If he'd smacked her in the face with a hospital tray, it would have been less shocking. And less painful. She couldn't lose another person to cancer. Especially Gus.

"Enough about me. How 'bout them Phillies?" he joked.

But Cleo was too stunned to respond.

D ELANEY AWAKENED ON TUESDAY MORNING TO A TEXT from Dalton.

> Need to talk. Beach walk?

> Meet you in ten.

She blinked and stared at the ceiling, wondering what he could want to talk about. It sounded urgent so she dressed quickly.

Outside, the sky was gray and the air moist, a prelude to the major storm brewing off the coast. A gust of wind lifted her hair, and she shivered as she made her way across the boardwalk to their usual meeting spot at the beach steps.

"Hey," Dalton said as he hugged her. She breathed in his familiar scent, his strong arms warming her. Whatever was on his mind, it couldn't be that bad.

"Walk with me," he said, taking her hand.

They trekked across thick sand to where towering waves tumbled over one another in a graceful show of power. Dalton was silent, almost brooding, as they walked along the frothy water's edge. They came upon the jetty, and he leaned up against a large rock, pulling Delaney in close.

His attitude, his actions, the look on his face—all cast a pall of gloom.

"What's wrong?" she asked, concerned.

He was silent for a moment. "I was telling you the truth yesterday. I just—wasn't ready to tell you the whole truth." He kept talking. Delaney tuned him out.

Son of a bitch! Here it comes. It wasn't a meeting yesterday. He was—

"—offered the position in London," he said.

She came up short. "What position in London?"

"You know, the office they're opening. They want me to head it up."

"Wait, you never said anything about a London office," she said. This didn't make any sense. "What does that mean, head it up?"

"It means me, us, living in London while I open the new office. I thought I'd told you—"

"No, you didn't. You mean London, as in, the UK?"

"The same. Red telephone booths, Union Jack, God save the King and shit, London."

"Don't even joke about this."

Dalton sighed. "I'm not joking."

"I'm assuming you said no? Please tell me you said no."

He looked away. His jaw tightened.

"Dalton," she said, her voice wavering. "Everything we care about is in Philly—our careers, our family, our friends..."

Philly was their home. It was where they planned to live, only venturing as far as the suburbs when it was time to raise children. Why would he even consider this?

Dammit, just when she'd decided to relinquish control and let things happen.

"No more surprises. You promised," she whispered, her eyes brimming with tears.

"Don't cry," Dalton said, wiping her cheek as a fat tear broke away. "I know it's not ideal, but it's an incredible opportunity. I'll make a humongous amount more than I do now. To an obscene degree."

"This is about money?"

"No, but that part's pretty nice. It's about a promotion. When I come back, I'll run the Philly office, which means even more money and flexibility."

"So, this is temporary?" she asked, hoping for a silver lining.

"Yes," he reassured her. "Definitely."

She took a deep breath. Don't panic. Get facts.

"How long are we talking?" she asked.

"A year. Tops."

"A year?" Delaney snapped, all resolve to be chill gone. "You expect me to live in London for a *year*? That's not temporary. What about my job? Am I supposed to give that up?"

"Of course not. I thought you could practice over there."

"Dalton, lawyers can't just practice law wherever they want. We have to take the bar exam for each state. God knows what I'd have to do for another country."

"Take a year off, then. Travel around Europe. I'll join you on weekends, like a sabbatical."

"There are no sabbaticals in law!" She clasped her head to keep it from blowing right off her body. Good God, did he even know her? No way she'd leave a career she'd spent a lifetime building.

"You changed our honeymoon because of this, didn't you?"

"I wanted you to fall in love with London, as I know you will. But I won't take the position if you don't want me to. I can tell them you're—I'm—not interested."

"Oh yeah, put it on me. It's not fair to make this my decision. If I say, 'Sure, take the job' I ruin my career, but 'No, don't take the job' means I ruin yours. Either way, one of us starts off our marriage resenting the other."

"It won't ruin my career," he said, but not convincingly. "I'll still keep my Philly position. The promotion will just go to someone else."

"But I'll be keeping you from that!" she cried.

"Then how about I go to London, you stay here, and we'll visit when we can?" He gave a half-hearted chuckle.

"Get married to live in separate countries? Why even bother?"

Despite the fury rising within her, she couldn't believe how calm her next words sounded. "Look, if this really matters to you, maybe we need to postpone the wedding."

"*No.* Forget it. Forget I said anything."

Delaney was relieved. She hadn't really meant it.

A sense of victory coursed through her. Talking nonsense about living in London—what was he thinking?

Her phone dinged. She pulled it from her hoodie just as Dalton's phone also sounded an incoming notification.

"Oh, shit," he said, as Delaney's heart sank.

It was a notification from the National Hurricane Center. Tropical Storm Inez had just become a hurricane.

"What do we do now?" he asked.

"We'll have to contact the hotel and see what their plans

are," Delaney said. "If—I don't know..." She couldn't bring herself to say it.

Perhaps the storm was a sign from the universe, trying to send them an important message: the wedding wasn't meant to be. At least not this weekend.

Kate

KATE CHECKED HER PHONE FIRST THING TUESDAY MORNing to see if Greg had responded.

And...nothing.

She lay in bed, staring at the ceiling. Something must have happened to keep him from responding after he wooed her with roses. While the likelihood of him being swept out to sea was remote, it was an occupational hazard in surfing, so couldn't be ruled out altogether.

Another possibility: she'd misread his gesture, and he wasn't interested in revisiting the past.

After making coffee, Kate went to the deck. She curled up on a lounge chair, looked out over the tumultuous sea, and gave a silent warning to the hurricane brewing off the coast to stay away from her sister's wedding.

Delaney and Dalton emerged from the windswept beach, looking as though they were purposely keeping distance from one another. His hands were shoved in his pockets, and her arms were wrapped around her waist. They both looked upset.

Dalton took off on a slow jog down the boardwalk and Delaney darted toward the house. She looked as if she'd been crying.

"Hey, what's wrong?" Kate asked, scrambling to get up.

Delaney thrust out a hand as if to stop her and went inside.

Kate followed. "Did you guys have a fight?"

She didn't answer. As Delaney ran down the steps to the bedrooms, Kate could hear her soft cries. Maybe they'd decided to postpone the wedding, after all.

Kate gave her space, knowing her sister needed time before she'd share what was going on. But that didn't stop her from alerting the others. She group-texted Cleo and Tori, asking if they knew what was going on with Delaney, explaining she'd come off the beach with Dalton, crying.

Tori responded that she didn't know what was going on and asked if she should come over. Kate told her to hold off—Delaney wasn't ready to talk.

Cleo messaged that Dalton was acting weird yesterday at the bar. She was currently at the hospital with Gus but would FaceTime later.

Tori then responded that she was on her way to the shore house.

Kate knew her sister wouldn't be happy she'd summoned the troops, but a crying bride four days before her wedding called for drastic measures.

When Tori arrived, they knocked on Delaney's bedroom door to ask what was going on. After she let them in, she took a deep breath and told them about Dalton's job.

"I don't know what to do," she said, blotting her lash line with her forefinger to stop another round of tears from breaking loose. "I wasn't expecting this."

"Oh, girl," Tori said. "I'm sorry. What are you going to do?"

"What can I do? He's been given an opportunity, an awesome one for him. But what does it mean for me? For us?"

"Can you practice law in London?" Kate asked.

"I don't know, but probably not. I can't cross the Delaware River and practice in New Jersey without taking their bar exam. Let alone the Atlantic and a different country."

"You've passed every test you've ever taken with flying colors,"

Kate reminded her. "If anyone can make it work, it's you."

"What if I don't go with him?" her sister asked. "The storm just became a hurricane. If we're forced to postpone, maybe we push it off a year. He could go, and I'd stay here."

Kate and Tori exchanged a glance before Tori asked, "Do you really want to do that? It seems, I dunno—"

"Drastic," Kate said. "Is that what Dalton's suggesting?"

"No. It's just—he's really pulling a fast one, dropping this on me four days before our wedding."

"Did he really pull a fast one, or is this just important to him?" Kate asked, her voice hushed.

"A door of opportunity, perhaps?" Tori asked. "A chance for something new. For you both."

Kate's phone buzzed. "Cleo's FaceTiming."

"Hey chicas," Cleo said when she answered. "What'd I miss? Is Delaney still boo-hooing?"

Kate grimaced. "Sorry," she said to her sister. "I called for reinforcements when I saw you crying. I figured you needed your dream team here for you."

Delaney

DELANEY SHOULD HAVE BEEN MAD AT HER SISTER FOR summoning her friends, but she knew Kate meant well.

"Hey, Cleo," she said when Kate held up her phone. Distracted by her background, Delaney asked, "Where are you?"

Cleo told her she was at the hospital with Gus. Delaney asked how he was doing.

"Better than you, apparently. What's with the waterworks?"

She proceeded to fill Cleo in on Dalton's promotion.

"That's pretty fucking cool, if you ask me," her friend said. "You'll get to strut around court in a funny white wig! I'd be all over that shit."

Delaney couldn't help smiling for the first time since her posse arrived. She was grateful they were there for her. "I'm not sure if they still do that."

"There's only one way to find out," Cleo said. "I can't wait to see you Marie Antoinette the place up!"

Delaney laughed. Cleo had a way of finding humor in just about anything.

"Hey, you've encouraged me to take the big leap to NYC," she continued. "If I recall correctly, your words were 'Don't get so comfortable with good that you miss an opportunity for great.' That advice seems to apply here too."

"It does," Kate agreed. "It's as much an opportunity for you as it is for him. How romantic, to start your lives together in a new country. Maybe it's your destiny."

"You *would* think that, Kate." Delaney flopped back on her bed. "But life isn't all wine and roses. I have to be practical."

"Practical about what?" her sister asked. "You've established your career and things are going well. Why not take a little detour from your path, try something new?"

"Because I like the path I'm on. I worked hard to get here."

"Work isn't everything. When I was presented with an opportunity to go with Greg to California, I chose my career instead. Now, I can't find a decent guy to save my life."

"And I did the opposite, choosing a relationship over career," Tori said. "I let a great opportunity to travel around Europe pass me by, for a guy."

Cleo piped up, "And I've never had to choose either, so... winning!"

Tori's expression turned serious. "When you asked the other day if things were okay with me and Ted...they're not. He's just not into me, we all know that. Maybe it's time I put me first. Kate, you were smart to decide not to go with Greg."

"Except I've been wondering if that was the wrong choice," Kate said. "Imagine how interesting my life might be right now if I'd gone with him?"

Tori smiled. "Your life is interesting. You do the coolest things. I see your Insta, girl."

"It's all a façade. Come spend the day with me, see for yourself. We'll hobnob with all the DC bigwigs, go to fancy salons, shop in expensive stores. We'll get dolled up and attend galas and sip champagne with our pinkies out. But at the end of the day, we'll go back to an empty apartment and wish we had someone special there with us."

"When should I show up?" Cleo joked.

"I know what you're saying, but relationships aren't everything," Delaney said.

"Except when you don't have one," Kate added. Against her better judgment, she blurted her secret. "Greg was going to propose to me!"

"What?" Delaney scrambled to sit up. "How do you know this?"

Kate left the room and returned with a seashell.

"I found this in the sweatshirt he left behind, the one he last wore when he told me he was moving and asked me to go with him. He must have changed his mind after our ugly fight."

"Come here," Delaney said, pulling Kate into a hug. "I'm sorry, li'l sis. I had no idea."

"Yeah, that sucks," Tori said, rubbing Kate's back.

"What am I missing?" Cleo asked from the phone screen.

Kate held up the shell for her.

"Oh, snap!" Cleo exclaimed. "Bullet dodged, girl. And one less bridesmaid dress for me."

"I'd give anything to have what you have," Kate told her sister. "Don't postpone the wedding and live in different worlds. Dalton is crazy about you. He's a good guy, and from my perspective, there aren't too many of them out here."

"Preach," Cleo said. Then quickly added, "Not that I'd know."

Kate was right. She and Dalton had a good thing. She couldn't imagine not having him to talk with at the end of the day, not having his strong arms wrapped around her at night. No matter where life took them, she wanted to be by his side—here in the States, or across the pond in merry old England.

An idea began to form. It was a long shot, but one worth trying.

Marley

WHEN MARLEY ARRIVED AT THE OFFICE ON TUESDAY, she found a bouquet of carnations from Rick on her desk. The card read: *Sorry for being such a jerk. You ARE worth it.*

She'd called him after Sam left the night before, and they had a long talk—both acknowledging their argument wasn't about a vacation, but something deeper. He insisted he was stressed from work, but promised he'd start looking into travel deals so they could plan a trip to an island for their honeymoon.

Marley admitted to feeling insecure over his recent inattentiveness. She'd fallen in love with Rick for many reasons beyond showy gestures of romance, and it wasn't fair of her to expect them now, at his most stressful time.

She was relieved after their talk. Neither she nor Rick were fighters, and having pent-up tension between them wasn't good.

And yay! A tropical honeymoon awaited. Someday.

Work was boring without Sam, but his absence made for

a productive day and gave her the opportunity to lunch with someone other than her sidekick.

Marley arrived at the Clink and scanned the room for Gwen. Instead, her eyes landed on someone else. Two someones.

Sam and Jenna. In a booth. In *their* booth. The one they'd sat in That Night.

Marley's stomach dropped. Had he already put OGG into play, or was this just a warm-up? She wanted to duck and hide but couldn't stop staring.

Jenna leaned across the table and stroked Sam's forearm. He leaned back and flashed his cute, crooked smile. He looked—happy. Like he did in her dream.

Marley glanced away before he could see her gawking.

Too late. He sat up, motioning her to come over. She reluctantly made her way toward their table.

"Can you tell me what the special is today?" he joked.

"I'm sorry, I'm not your waitress," Marley said. "I'm FBI. I need you to come with me for questioning. Something about rat torture?"

Sam laughed out loud. She loved the sound when he did that, pure music.

"Can I see your badge first?" he asked.

"Of course," Marley said. She slowly raised her middle finger.

More cacophony from Sam as Jenna's eyes darted between them.

"Rat torture?" Jenna asked, looking like she wanted to be in on the joke.

Sam ignored her and spoke to Marley. "I thought you were banned from this place?" He raised an eyebrow and sipped his drink.

"It's amazing what a blow job will get you."

Sam did a spit take, spewing water down his shirt.

"That's exactly how I do it too."

Marley raised her eyebrow and turned, stone-faced, before giving herself a victory pump.

She found Gwen at the hostess stand. They were about to be seated when someone squeezed her elbow from behind. His warm cheek slid across hers, his breath tickled her ear. The scent of his aftershave reached her before his words did.

"That was a lot to swallow," Sam whispered.

Marley tossed her head back and laughed, as she and Sam shared a look.

"See you in the torture chamber." He winked and held the door open for Jenna.

Moments later, after Marley and Gwen were seated, her phone buzzed with a text from him.

> Nice comedy routine.

> Tx. I'll be here all week.

> I hope so. Dad's firm is boring.

> Sorry to ruin your very important date. And your shirt.

> You didn't. But Jenna thought you were serious about BJs :D

> Who says I wasn't?

"All right, I'm just gonna come out and ask," Gwen said as Marley put her phone down. "Is something going on with you and Sam?"

"Yeah. It's called a friendship."

Gwen narrowed her eyes and tipped her head. "You sure?"

Marley gave a half smile. "I'm sure."

"I saw the look he gave you when he left," she pressed on.

"What you saw was him on a lunch date with Jenna. He's got it bad for her."

"How does Rick feel about you guys spending time to-gether? I'd think most boyfriends would be insecure."

"Nah, Rick's pretty secure," Marley said. At least she hoped, but memories of Penn's Landing brought a wave of guilt. Maybe she should tell Rick what really happened That Night. *And* the Sunday night sequel.

She pushed it out of her mind. She and Rick had made up, and Sam just had a date with Jenna. As if Penn's Landing never happened.

Marley and Gwen had a leisurely lunch before they parted ways. On her way back to the office, her phone rang.

"What's up?" Sam asked.

"Um, you called me?"

"Oh, yeah. Nice suit. Is it new?"

"Yes," she said.

"I like the tailored look on you. The lavender compliments your green eyes."

"Thanks." Marley was pretty sure he didn't call to discuss fashion. "How'd it go?" she asked.

"How did what go?"

"The last game of the World Series. What do you think? Your date with Jenna."

"Oh," he said.

"Did you profess your undying love?"

"I was about to, before I was accosted by the feds."

"Oh, no!" she said. "Did they take you down?"

"No, but a felon can only hope. I must threaten rat torture more often."

"You gotta watch it, they know everything you're doing."

"I hope not, given the afternoon delight I just enjoyed. Woo-wee!"

Marley made a gagging sound. In jest, but also not. She didn't want to know what went on between him and Jenna. That anything went on between them.

"Just kidding," he said. "Seeing if I could get a rise outta you."

"You got a rise, all right," she said, relieved. "Of bile. You sure it wasn't afternoon de-*fright*?"

Sam laughed, inspiring Marley to go on.

"I don't know how anyone would be into you, the way you just drooled all over yourself."

"Couldn't help it. I've just never heard you utter those two words, much less indicate you know what they mean. I'm impressed."

"You should see what else I know," she teased.

"I've got all day." A click sounded on his end of the line.

Wait. Did he just close a door?

A smile crept across her face. They were supposed to be working, but knowing he was safely down the street in another building—behind a closed door, no less—emboldened her. It was as if their cozy proximity and near-kiss at Penn's Landing had added another layer to their friendship.

She shouldn't be doing this but didn't want to stop.

"You may not know this, but I'm also with the FBI," Sam said, his voice softening. "Penn's Landing Division."

Oh, boy. Here we go.

"It wasn't me," Marley said, breathless with the thrill of his game.

"I have someone here who says it was. And he knows because..."

"Because why?"

A beat. "Because he can't stop thinking about it."

Just then, Rick's number scrolled across her screen. She was tempted to ignore it and continue on this slippery slope with Sam, but it wasn't right. Rick's call was the reality check she needed.

"I'm sorry, Sam," Marley said, her words a machete slicing the sexual tension wafting around her, fogging her better judgment. "I gotta go, Rick's calling. I should take this."

Sam was silent.

"He's coming on Thursday. Probably calling about his flight."

"Oh, that's right," Sam said, sarcasm flooding his tone. "Your big exotic getaway to South Jersey."

"What's that for?" she asked, her guard coming up.

"Nothing," Sam said, sighing. "I just got tagged for a staff meeting. Smell you later."

Marley went full-bore fifth grader. "Not if I smell you first." But he'd already hung up.

Kate

A FULL TWENTY-FOUR HOURS HAD PASSED BEFORE KATE finally heard from Greg.

> Kate! Good to hear from you. How's things?

He hadn't taken her bait on her new beginnings line. She'd have to try again.

> Great! Never better. The roses were really cool. To new beginnings!

> Ha!

"Ha?" Kate asked herself, aloud. What did that even mean? He was always a bit dense. She should clarify.

> Would love to explore new beginnings...

Kate waited for the bubble with the dots to appear. She waited, waited, and then—finally—they appeared. The dots danced around in the bubble for a brief eternity, until his message finally came through.

> I'm sorry, Kate. I just got back together with my girlfriend.

Not the response she was expecting. Humiliation coursed through her. Did she misread this, somehow? But then she thought back to the flowers, to the comment about new beginnings. Meanwhile, all along, he'd had a girlfriend.

Finally, humiliation gave way to anger, then sadness. He'd truly moved on.

Maybe it was time for her to do so too.

Cleo

CLEO RETURNED TO GUS'S ROOM AFTER HER FACETIME call with the girls.

"Why didn't you tell me you have cancer?" she asked, her voice cracking.

"That look right there," he said. "I don't need your pity."

"I don't pity you!" Cleo said. "Maybe I'd want to know so I could help you, old fool."

"So you're an oncologist now?"

"What kind of cancer?" She held her breath, hoping it wasn't one of the more fatal types.

"Personality cancer. Turns out, I'm a jerk."

Cleo smiled through her fear. "And you're just learning this now?"

She tried to keep her voice steady to mask her concern. Gus used humor to get through rough discussions, so she let him set the course until he was ready to talk seriously.

The old man closed his eyes and groaned. She waited for him to fill in the details, but he remained silent.

"Gotta rest now," he said, his eyes still closed.

"Be my guest, grumpy old troll," Cleo whispered in his ear as she patted his arm, "but I'm gonna be here when you wake up. Don't think this is the end of it."

"Can't you take a hint, girl?"

"You think cancer's hard to get rid of? Wait'll you get a load of me."

The corner of Gus's mouth curved into a half smile. Cleo was grateful his eyes were closed so he couldn't see the tears in hers.

She settled into the chair next to his bed, dozing off for what felt like hours. She awakened famished, and was making her way to the door to go find grub when she heard him.

"I'm not dying, you know."

She turned back, her heart in her throat, hoping he was right. "No one said you were."

Many people get cancer and survive. When he was ready to talk, she'd ask more questions. Which reminded her—

"What'd you do before you retired?" she asked.

"Robbed banks."

"That explains the wad of cash. What about your spare time?"

"Pole dancing," he deadpanned.

"Seriously."

"I was a tenured professor of psychology at UPenn."

"Ooh-kay," she said. "This has been fun, but Imma go now so you can get your beauty rest."

Gus started coughing. She returned to his bedside and handed him the cup of melting ice. He gulped it down before collapsing back on the bed.

"Do me a favor," he said, his voice barely a whisper.

"What?"

"Go find him."

"Find who?" she asked, panic setting in. "A doctor?"

"He doesn't have to be a doctor. Just someone who treats you well."

"Oh, for the love of Pete. You're a pain in my keister."

"And you're lovable, Cleo Jane," he said. "Don't forget that."

A nurse entered the room then, bustling Cleo toward the door. "Sorry, hon, you'll have to go. We're taking him for tests."

No need to tell her twice. She'd been in this house of horror all day. She had to get out of here, get away from the putrid hospital smell that brought back memories of her grandmother's last days. The raw emotions burned a hole in her stomach which, combined with the queasiness from her displaced hangover, made her want to puke.

She beat feet to her car. The moment she closed the door behind her, she sobbed, unable to hold it in any longer. The wounds from her grandmother's ordeal with cancer, and her death, were still oozing. Now she had to face it all over again with Gus.

She turned on the car, but instead of heading toward the bridge to New Jersey, she drove in the opposite direction. Toward Center City. Toward the one person she needed the most.

She just hoped it wasn't too late.

Cleo was lucky to find a parking space not far from the Clink. She picked up her pace as she hurried down the sidewalk, hoping he'd be there.

She needed to tell Wells about her change of heart.

The place was unusually crowded for a Tuesday night. Cleo glanced around and spotted him right away, standing at the bar where he usually sat.

She sidestepped through a slew of bodies to get to him, but Wells turned away before she got close. He had two drinks in his hands as he made his way through the crowd in the opposite direction, toward the dining room and its packed tables. It didn't look as if he'd seen her.

Two drinks meant he was here with someone, unless he'd taken up extreme drinking to drown his Cleo-less sorrows. Her eyes scanned the tables to see if she recognized any of his friends or coworkers, but didn't see anyone—

Oh. Seated at a table by herself was a woman in red. A woman she recognized.

"Please don't let him go to that table," Cleo muttered to herself. "Please don't let him—"

Shhhiiit.

"Freaking Sabrina," Cleo hissed.

Freaking Sabrina, or Sabrina, as she was known to everyone else, was Delaney's law school friend who Cleo had met several times. She was a five-foot, nine-inch redheaded bombshell, who looked more like she belonged on the cover of *Cosmo* than in a courtroom. But that was sexist. Sabrina was smart and funny, and Cleo liked her. Just not right now.

Jealousy bubbled from the pit of her stomach.

Her inner adult told her to leave, respect that Wells was here with someone else. Her inner child told her to stay and spy.

Her inner child won out.

She slunk off to the far end of the bar, where she'd be able to see them, but they couldn't see her. She ordered a drink and peered through the pack of bodies surrounding the bar, trying to keep tabs on them.

"Thought you were on vacay?" came a voice from behind her.

It was the new bartender she'd trained last week. He followed her line of vision. "Oh, yeah. That."

She ignored him and tried to discern whether Wells and Sabrina were on a date or whether this was some sort of business tête-a-tête.

Wells reached across the table and held Sabrina's hand.

Cleo sighed. "Damn."

"Yeah, I was a little worried when I saw him come in with Jessica Rabbit," the bartender said. "I figured you and he were—you know—"

Cleo snickered. "Whatever it is you thought, we weren't. He's a complete asshole."

"Right. The biggest. What's she got over you, anyway?"

"About seven inches, red hair down to her waist, big eyes, huge boobs, a law degree and apparently him...shall I continue?"

"Nope, got it," the bartender chuckled and walked away. He returned a minute later with two shots of Jägermeister, slid one toward Cleo and raised his glass. "To assholes."

Cleo threw back the drink. She glanced back over to see a waiter appear at their table with the tableside Caesar salad cart.

"Oh, fuck me," she proclaimed. The only thing Wells ever ate at the bar was beer nuts, but here he was making a table-side Caesar scene. Shit was getting serious at table ten, which could only mean one thing.

It was a legit date.

Cleo sucked on her next drink, watching through the crowd as Wells and Sabrina chatted over their Caesars. She hoped he'd choke on a crouton. Better yet—she'd get a hunk of lettuce stuck on her front tooth and he'd be too embarrassed to tell her. She'd say something tongue-twisty, and the lettuce hunk would fly from her mouth and onto his hand. No—his face.

Cleo chuckled to herself, wishing she'd been kinder to destiny so she could call for some backup.

She couldn't tear her eyes away as the couple finished their salads, their entrées, and a second bottle of wine, until she couldn't bear to look anymore.

The rumbling in her belly reminded her she hadn't eaten all day. She slid off her barstool and crept along the back wall toward the kitchen, hoping to find something to soak up the alcohol and bile sloshing around in her empty stomach. She scarfed a piece of bread and hobnobbed with the kitchen staff as the rumbling in her belly continued.

Suddenly, she realized she had to pee. Possibly puke.

She'd just locked herself into a stall in the ladies' room when she heard a voice in the next stall.

"Oh my god, *so* hot," the woman was saying. "I just can't believe he's single. At the same time I am. *Fi*-nally."

Cleo recognized the voice. It was Sabrina.

"Yes, believe it or not," she said. "He and his girlfriend just broke up."

Girlfriend?

"I have no idea who she is, but she must be batshit bonkers to let him go," Sabrina said, then laughed at whatever the person on the other line said. "I'll say. Apparently, she broke his heart, but I'm here for the rebound!"

Broke his heart? That couldn't have been her. Did Wells have another—

Cue the puke.

"Ew, hold on. Someone's ralphing next to me," Sabrina whispered. Then she called out, "Hey, you good?"

Cleo wiped her mouth with the back of her hand and muttered a "yep" before flushing the toilet and rushing to the sink to wash up. She had to get out of here before Sabrina saw her. She quick-dried her hands on her leggings, flung open the door and—

Stepped into the chest of an oncoming man.

"Whoa!" He grabbed her elbows.

Ta-da! Wells, himself.

"Cleo!" he exclaimed, eyes wide with surprise. "What're you doing here? I thought you were on vacation."

"My friend's in the hospital. I came back to see him." Cleo's voice wavered with emotion.

"I'm sorry," Wells said, giving her a hug as his ocean-y aftershave wafted into her nostrils like a charmed snake.

She was dying to tell him about her change of heart. That, after her shitty day, he was the only one she wanted to talk to.

Instead, she stood there like an idiot.

"I hope everything's okay," he continued. "Do you need me to do anything?"

End your date with Sabrina and take me back.

She was about to open her mouth to say something along those lines when Sabrina emerged from the ladies' room.

"Cleo! OMG. Nice to see you!" Sabrina gave her a perfunctory hug.

"Yeah, nice seeing you," Wells said, his voice suddenly formal. "We have a show to get to, so..."

"See you at the wedding," Sabrina added as they turned to leave.

Shit. Sabrina was Delaney's friend too. Of course she'd be at the wedding. Hopefully not with Wells.

He turned and guided Sabrina down the hall like she was a prized heifer at a farm show (or so Cleo wished).

But really...tableside Caesar *and* a show?

Fuck me twice.

Marley

MARLEY WAS LOOKING FORWARD TO A COZY NIGHT BY herself. She changed into her couch-fit, made popcorn, and queued up Netflix when the *Rocky* theme blared from her phone.

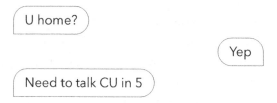

Sam's knock sounded in less than five.

"Hey." He leaned against the door frame, shirtsleeves folded to the elbow, tie undone, jacket slung over his shoulder.

Marley waved him in and grabbed two beers from the fridge.

Sam picked up the remote and turned off her TV.

"Hey, I was watch—"

His eyes were shrouded in seriousness like she'd never seen before. She handed him a beer and sat down, tucking one leg tucked under the other. "What's up?"

Sam told her about his day, how he was helping with trial prep on a business case with huge criminal implications. "It's a real mess," he explained. "They need my help."

"Cool."

Sam was silent.

"Not cool?"

"I wasn't brought into the firm today just for the case. The meeting I was called into wasn't a staff meeting. It was a seduction, to get me to join the firm. A first-year slot opened in the contract division, and they want me to start there until they open a criminal division in a couple years."

"But you said no, right? Our case, the firm—"

Sam exhaled through pouted lips, an indication he was considering it. "I'll be back on Friday to finish helping with the case. But you know my dad's been on me to join his firm. It's something I need to consider."

"Why?"

"Mar, the money is two times what this firm offers. I can't pass it up."

She didn't buy it. The man was raised in a Main Line mansion, silver spoon shoved up his ass, the product of old money. He was set for life even if he chose to dabble in fast food. It wasn't about the pay.

"This is about Jenna, isn't it?" she demanded. "Because criminal law's 'gross' and 'there's no money in it.'" She emphasized with air quotes.

"No." Sam shook his head, looking her dead in the eyes. Just like a liar would.

"I suppose a future with her means money has to come first, regardless of your interests." Marley was surprised at the vitriol in her voice.

"That's not fair."

"No?" Marley got up and paced as the possibility of Sam leaving their firm sank in. He watched her with sad eyes.

"Contracts, really?" She threw her hands up. "You practically failed contracts, you hated it so much. You've always said you wanted to practice criminal law!"

"I enjoy criminal law. But I only got involved with all this because of you. Your interest is infectious. You have a spark whenever you discuss it."

"You do too!" Marley retorted, pointing at him.

"But it's your thing, not necessarily mine. I only got involved with it because of—all that." He waved in her general direction.

"All what?"

"Your passion." He paused, then added, "For criminal law."

"Passion's important, Sam," she said softly. "Without passion for what you do, how do you thrive? Without passion, what inspires you to get out of bed and do good every day? To learn and grow? Didn't you get a law degree to make a difference?"

"I got a law degree because it was expected of me," he said, his voice flat.

"And joining your dad's firm is yet another expectation."

She sat next to him and looked at him pleadingly. Sam remained silent, jaw tensing as he avoided her gaze.

"I think you'd be making a mistake. Even as you're talking about the future with your dad's firm, I don't see any kind of spark."

"I'll learn to like it." Sam's tone was unconvinced as he gave her a half smile. "Sparks take time to develop. Right? Before long, I'll be sparking so much over contracts, I'll light them on fire."

Marley was silent.

"What about you? Aren't you heading to Ohio after graduation, anyway?" he asked.

She didn't answer.

He continued. "The future's up in the air, for us both. We don't know what's gonna happen. But, as my dad likes to point out, I have to think about it now. Soon we'll be taking the bar, and I want to know I have a job. We don't even know for sure this firm will hire us."

"So you're gonna bail, just like that? For your dad."

"Not my dad. I need to do this for myself right now." He stood up and made his way to the door. Without turning back, he added, "It's what's best for me right now."

She waited until he was almost at the door before throwing her final dagger.

"It's what's *safe* for you." Marley hurled the word at his back.

She knew it would sting. She intended it to. Sam was adventurous, daring in nearly all he did. He prided himself on never taking the safe route on anything.

Sam spun around, his expression flipping from sadness to anger. "What's that supposed to mean?"

Marley began ticking points off on her fingers. "It's safe to fall back on a job created for you at birth. To go after money, the hell with making a difference. To listen to what others tell you to do, rather than decide for yourself. To fall for one person and never give anyone else a chance."

Ooh.

Marley instantly wished she could retract that last statement. But it was out there. She'd lobbed the ball over the net and now it was his turn to smash it back.

But he didn't, at least not right away. Marley could see the vein in his right temple throb as it did whenever he was angry.

"I could say the same about you, you know."

"How so?" Marley challenged as she rose from the couch.

He came toward her and stopped mere inches away. He looked down at her, blue eyes ablaze.

"You say passion's important—and, yes, I see it when you talk about criminal law." He cocked his head. "So, then, tell me—why don't I ever see it when you talk about Rick?"

"Rick has nothing to do with—"

"He has *everything* to do with it. He can't even take a week out of his precious time for you, and you're good with that? Is that all you're worth, all you want for yourself? I know he's a nice guy, as you always say, but where's the passion?"

He paused, then delivered the final blow. "Talk about taking the *safe way out.*"

He strode toward the door, looking back as he let himself out. "Don't be a hypocrite. Don't preach about passion if you don't live it where it matters the most."

He slammed the door behind him.

Marley picked up the nearest object she could find—her beer—and hurled it at the closed door. Glass shattered and a tsunami of beer surged to the floor.

Tears stung her eyes. She couldn't decide what emotion should win out. Anger? Sadness? A burning desire to clean up this mess?

Before she could decide, the door flung open. Sam strode

to her, crunching and sloshing through glass and beer.

"I'm sorry for what I'm about to do," he said, as his gaze bore into hers.

He flung his jacket down, grabbed her face with both hands and smashed his lips down on hers. Closed, so it was more forceful than passionate, but he made his point.

Her eyes bugged out, her heart thudded, and her knees went weak.

Sam stepped back as if he was going to leave when he suddenly pivoted, wrapped his arm around her waist, and pulled her into him. Hard. He let out a grunt as raked his fingers up the back of her head and, grabbing a fistful of hair, pulled back, causing her mouth to fall open. His engorged lips parted, kissing her more tenderly this time, his tongue playfully teasing hers.

Both moaned as the kiss deepened, intensified.

It lasted a minute, maybe an hour. Time didn't matter. All that mattered was they were doing this. Finally. After years of teasing and temptation, they were finally doing this.

No one had ever kissed her with such hunger before.

He abruptly stopped.

"Sorry again, Rick," he said, leaning over to pick up his jacket, "but that was a long time coming."

He blew out a breath. Then, "I'm gone now."

He let himself out without looking back, leaving Marley with her mouth hanging wide open. All she could think was...

Who's Rick?

Wednesday, June 14

COUNTDOWN
TO WEDDING
3 DAYS

Delaney

DELANEY AND DALTON SAT ON THE JETTY AT THE EDGE of the churning ocean. It was the first they'd seen of each other since yesterday morning, after agreeing to take some time to consider their options.

Delaney needed facts if she was to make an informed decision about the future of her marriage and career. After having a night to sleep on it, her brain went into fact-gathering mode.

She asked pointed questions about the timing of the move, when he'd start the job, and where they'd live. Dalton told her it wouldn't be until fall, and that they might be able to shorten their stay if everything went smoothly. His firm would put them up in a flat near the new office.

Like a seasoned litigator, Delaney kept the emotion from her direct examination, seeking only information at this time. She still wasn't sure what she'd be able to do with an American law degree in London, if anything. She'd cross that bridge after she had all the facts.

Delaney knew she had the power to decide whether they went or not, but that didn't make it any easier. Especially when she was trying to tame her inner control freak.

"Look, we don't have to do this, Laney," Dalton said. "It wasn't fair for me to spring it on you right before the wedding. Although, if this storm forces us to postpone—"

"Is that what you want?" Delaney interrupted him, keeping her voice even. "Answer like I'm a stranger asking the question. Storm or no storm, do you think we should put off the wedding so you can go to London?"

"No."

He clenched his jaw and stared at the ocean, as if he were gazing pensively toward Mother England.

But then he turned to her. Tears flooded his eyes.

"You are the best thing to ever happen to me and no fucking job is going to come between us."

"I couldn't agree more," Delaney said. "Which means I have some research to do."

Marley

MARLEY GLANCED AT HER PHONE FOR THE FIFTIETH TIME as she prepared to leave the office.

Twenty-two hours since she'd last seen or heard from Sam, his parting words still echoing in her mind.

I'm gone now.

Could this mean he was backing out of her life completely?

Marley had kept herself busy at work to keep her mind off Sam. When she finally pushed open the heavy glass door of her office building, she was met with an unseasonably cool breeze—a perfect night to walk home.

She waited amid a throng of pedestrians to cross the street. In her periphery was the building where Sam's father's firm was located. The doors of the building swung open, and a group of people emerged—probably lawyers, the smart way they were dressed. The group headed toward the same intersection and gathered on the other side.

Among them, a familiar figure.

He looked like an Armani model in a slim navy suit, white shirt, and pink tie, standing at the curb, right hand in his pocket. His hair was combed into what he called his "professional do." He was talking with two middle-aged women, both sporting crisp suits and sharp hairstyles.

Someone joined him.

Jenna leaned up and gave Sam a kiss on the cheek. He put his hand on the small of her back and both masses of humanity merged as they crossed the street.

Marley tried to duck behind a large woman in a burka so they wouldn't see her.

Too late. Sam's eyes met hers.

He gave her a subtle wave at hip level as he passed, expressionless.

Marley, stunned, stopped dead in her tracks as he kept going.

Tears streamed down her face as she navigated her way home, devastated by his dismissiveness. The kiss had betrayed their friendship—exactly as she predicted would happen if she ever let herself get tangled up with a player like Sam.

Felix greeted her with a look of sympathy when she arrived home, as if he knew.

"You okay, Miss Marley?" he asked. "You got boyfriend problems?"

"Something like that, Felix," she gave him a small smile and stepped inside.

"He's lucky guy," Felix called out. "I tell him next time I see him. Boy in red Jeep."

Kate

KATE LEFT HER FAMILY'S HOUSE ON WEDNESDAY EVENING and headed to Avalon, where she'd be staying with her friends for two nights. She was anxious for a break from wedding central—especially given Greg's news.

She couldn't believe he'd sent her roses and referenced new beginnings when he had a girlfriend. What kind of an idiot does that?

Good riddance—for real this time. He could take his award-winning surfboards and shove 'em where the California sun doesn't shine.

She waded through the crowd at Princeton Bar and Grill, where she was meeting her friends, finding them at a high-top table in the back.

"I got you a prosecco," Laura said as she handed her a drink.

Kate took a long sip. The fizzy chill calmed her nerves and helped to wash away the humiliation still haunting her after misreading Greg's intentions.

"She's at it already," Laura said, interrupting Kate's thoughts as she cocked her head toward Bianca. "Her sights are set on the blonde one, don't get any ideas."

"No worries. I'm not here to fend off drunks," Kate said. She wouldn't so much as smile at someone in case they took it as an invitation. "I'm so over the bar scene. And men."

"You're still on that?" Laura asked as she clucked her tongue. "Time to get back in the saddle, old girl."

"Not this old girl. At least not tonight."

Even if she was game, Kate would never trust a guy she met in a bar. Having an older sister who worked in criminal justice had long ago cured her of that.

Looking around, she was shocked at how young everyone looked and wondered if she'd ever babysat any of them.

"The dark-haired one's pretty cute," Laura whispered, nodding to a group of guys.

Out of sheer curiosity, Kate followed her gaze. Laura was right, objectively speaking. He had the perfect combination of dark hair and blue eyes Kate was drawn to. Bonus: he didn't look as if he was still in college. Something about him was intriguing, but she was over men and not about to break her cardinal rule against picking up guys in bars.

Yet, as disinterested as she was, she couldn't look away.

Their eyes met. He nodded and raised his glass. Classy. A

fluttering feeling took her by surprise. Except, it wasn't her heart—it was her phone vibrating from inside her purse, signaling an incoming text.

Greg.

We should talk. Gotta minute?

Kate rolled her eyes. Her ex, the king of bad timing, was probably feeling badly for turning her down and wanted to make sure she was okay. If the intended purpose of "talking" was to assuage his guilt for rejecting her, no thanks. Although a call could provide much-needed closure. But the dark-haired guy was smiling at her, and the prosecco was starting to wash away her inhibitions. She'd better decide soon because he looked like he was about to come over.

She thumbed a text to Greg, telling him she was busy, but her phone screen went black before it sent.

"Damn!"

"What's wrong?" Laura asked.

"My cell died."

"Probably from lugging around that bulky man cover," she joked, nodding at Kate's OtterBox.

She ignored Laura who, like all their friends, often teased Kate about her sturdy, practical, non-aesthetic phone cover.

She tried turning the phone back on with no luck. Never without a charged phone, Kate was rendered powerless against her growing speculation over Greg's comment.

Had he reconsidered her blatant come-on?

No, he was back with a girlfriend. What was there to talk about?

"It's just a dead phone, you can charge it later," Laura said.

"You don't understand."

Laura *wouldn't* understand. Kate purposely hadn't told her about finding the shell. Or that she'd reached out to Greg.

"Here," Laura said, taking the phone from Kate and setting it on the table among a panoply of glasses, bottles, and other phones. "Let's live in the moment. Starting with *that*."

Kate looked in the direction Laura gestured and her eyes locked with the dark-haired guy's. Everyone else seemed to dissipate into thin air, including all thoughts of Greg. Suddenly, living in the moment became infinitely more interesting.

There was something about him that made her forget her resolve to be done with men. He didn't approach her. It was refreshing to make eye contact with someone and not have to fend them off. The longer it continued, the more her interest piqued.

In that moment, Kate realized what she needed, more than a second chance with Greg. To feel chosen. For someone to gaze at her the way this guy was.

For the first time ever, Kate Ross smiled at a stranger in a bar.

She garnered the nerve to go introduce herself, but a friend had just joined him. He set his drink on the table next to his phone and man-hugged the new arrival. Soon after, he began making his way over to Kate. He'd almost reached her when a loud crash came from behind.

Two men tumbled toward them. Kate jumped out of the way as the men smashed into tables, sending everything flying. Onlookers jumped into the fray to pull the fighting men apart before two massive bouncers cut through the flailing sea of arms and legs and ejected the brawling bros from the bar. Patrons righted chairs and tables in the aftermath and picked up their scattered belongings.

Kate searched frantically for her phone and found it on the floor in a puddle of spilled drinks. She hastily wiped it on her jeans, hoping it wasn't destroyed. It was dark in the bar and hard to see, so she ran her finger over the screen. Not cracked, thanks to the bulky-yet-practical phone cover with its ninja-like protection.

"Darn it," Laura pouted after she inspected her phone. "My screen cracked!"

"That's why you need a sturdy 'man cover,' " Kate scolded.

She looked around for the handsome stranger, but he was nowhere to be seen.

"I've had enough for one night," Laura sighed. "Let's get out of here."

Kate was disappointed she didn't get to meet the dark-haired guy, but she was tired from a long day and ready for sleep. So much for feeling chosen by someone, given how he absconded like a Ten Most Wanted Fugitive.

Back at Laura's house, Kate plugged in her phone and, exhausted, crawled into bed. She wanted to respond to Greg, but sleep claimed her before the phone came back to life.

Cleo

WEDNESDAY PROVED NOT TO BE A BEACH DAY, THANKS to shitty weather. Cleo was lying in bed, scrolling through social media accounts, when her phone rang.

She recognized the number right away.

"Hey," Wells said.

She scrambled to sit up. "Hey, yourself. What's up?"

"How's your friend?"

What friend—oh. That's right, she'd told him about Gus.

"Good, I think," she said. "I just heard from Murph, owner of the tavern, who said he was released last night."

"I'm glad to hear it."

Cleo wrapped a short strand of hair around her finger as silence filled the miles between them.

He spoke first. "I, uh, want to apologize for the way I acted last night. I just—wasn't expecting to see you. With your vacation. And...everything."

Cleo wasn't sure if, by *everything*, he meant her bolting from his condo in the middle of the night, or that he'd been on a date when they ran into each other at the Clink.

Might as well cut right to the chase.

"I'm sorry for leaving in the middle of the night," Cleo blurted out.

"Yeah, why did you do that?" Wells asked, his voice softening.

"I don't know."

Wells was quiet. "Was it something—"

"I know why, actually," she amended. "I heard what you said to me."

"That I was falling for you?" Wells whispered.

"Yes."

"And that made you leave?" he asked, confusion flooding his voice.

"As I said in my text, I can't do relationships. I was afraid we were on a slippery slope toward one."

Wells sighed. "I thought we were already in a relationship, Cleo. But I guess it wasn't serious for you?"

Ah, the question she'd been grappling with since it happened. Expose yourself with truth, or protect yourself with lies? She chose the familiar low road.

"No. I'm sorry. I was just in it for fun."

Okay, maybe both the truth and a lie. Either way, she wasn't about to admit the feelings she'd been trying to squelch, especially after seeing him with someone else.

"I guess that's what I needed to hear," he said after a moment of silence. "Thanks for being honest."

"That's me," she said, grimacing, glad he couldn't see her expression. "George Dubs incarnate." Then, added, "Washington, not Bush."

"Thanks for the clarification," he said, chuckling. "I

guess that means you won't mind if I'm Sabrina's date for the wedding? She just asked me; apparently her other date fell through."

"Why would I mind?" Cleo asked, before she had a chance to turn the question inward.

Would she mind? Of course she would. He should be so heartbroken, he couldn't bear to move on, but the fact that he was with Sabrina meant he already had. Something told her to let it go.

"No," she said. "I wouldn't mind."

After their call, Cleo went out to the deck, where the wind whipped furiously, ushering news of the impending storm. As it whirled around her, the feels came too, as she suspected they would. Wells had moved on, and she had no one to blame but herself for shoving him away.

Still, how could someone who was "falling for her" catch himself so easily, and topple so quickly toward someone else? Was she that forgettable? Or just not worth the fight?

She didn't have to ask. She knew.

Cleo gazed at the horizon, but instead of seeing a wind-swept beach and stormy sea, she saw a tempest of indigo, ecru, slate—and an opportunity to create another masterpiece.

To paint away the pain.

She trudged through thick sand and struggled against the wind to keep her art supplies from being ripped from her hands. Digging deep holes for the legs of her easel, she affixed the canvas to its frame with heavy-duty clips to keep her workstation from blowing out to sea. She added several dabs of paint to her palette.

Everything else faded away as she entered her creative zone. Her mind became a blank canvas as she blended, swooshed, and dabbed, covering all thoughts of Wells and Sabrina with layers of acrylic swirls.

Soon her sweeping brush whispered a sound.

New York. New York. New York.

The rhythm of the words brought glimpses of her future, as colors and venues called to her. The greens of Central Park. The browns of Brooklyn Bridge. The steel-gray skyline. Words conducting a symphony of possibilities until it began sounding like something else.

Nigel, Nigel, Nigel.

Of course her brain would venture to thoughts of the hot bartender. Funny, though—in all that time, her thoughts never ventured to the hot attorney.

Painting had a way of bringing things into focus. She thought back to Gus's warning about not confusing lust with love. Maybe that's why she'd been missing Wells so much—not because she loved him, but because of the tingling, heady feeling of lust he gave her. As if he were an addiction, someone she craved for a purely physical connection that somehow filled the empty void of emotion. It would stand to reason that she'd have a propensity toward addictive behavior, given her family background. She was lucky, so far, not to have turned to substances like her parents did, but maybe there was something about being wanted by someone that drove her to seek out men like Wells. Men who would connect with her physically, to give her a false sense of being loved while not having to love back, thereby risking loss in return.

Did she love Wells? Maybe as a friend, but nothing more. The biggest clue: the fact that her mind kept going to Nigel, someone who she'd only met once but who was intriguing for reasons beyond a physical attraction. Even if he was Tori's find.

Hours passed before Cleo was finally clear of mind and satisfied with her work. She packed up her supplies and held the canvas away from the blowing sand, but a walloping gust ripped it from her hand and deposited it on the beach, face down.

"Son of a bitch!"

She dropped everything and snatched it up. Sand stuck to the fresh paint, along with a few tiny shells. Disgusted with herself, she picked up the rest of her supplies and stormed back to the condo.

"Hey, I was wondering where you were," Tori said. Her eyes were red, as if she'd been crying.

"You okay?" Cleo asked.

Tori nodded and pointed to the painting. "Lemme see."

She took the painting from Cleo's hands, held it up, and gasped.

"I dropped it in the sand, like an idiot."

"This wasn't on purpose?" Tori asked in amazement. "Cleo, it's amazing!"

She turned it around to show Cleo. Tori was right—the sand gave the abstract painting a feeling of realism.

"Wow," Cleo whispered as she took it in. "I thought it was ruined."

"I think you may have found a new medium," Tori said.

"Canvas tossing?" Cleo joked wryly.

"Something like that. It's pure serendipity, a fortunate accident. Also known as—"

"Don't tell me. Destiny."

When the painting was finally dry, Cleo ran her fingers over it. This is what she was meant to do with her life—sling canvas, not drinks. Reticence over the move and fear of change gave way to a burst of inspiration. She was going to make this damn dream of hers a reality if it killed her.

Cleo opened her laptop and began doing the research she'd been putting off for too long.

Fuck bartending. Her art degree entitled her to seek a real job, in a gallery.

Time to raise the bar, not work in one.

Thursday, June 15

COUNTDOWN
TO WEDDING
2 DAYS

NATIONAL HURRICANE CENTER
MIAMI, FLORIDA

HURRICANE INEZ HAS BEEN DOWNGRADED TO A TROPICAL STORM, MOVING NORTH-NORTHEASTWARD AWAY FROM THE EASTERN UNITED STATES COASTLINE. LANDFALL NOT EXPECTED AT THIS TIME. THE POSSIBILITY OF DANGEROUS RIP CURRENTS STILL EXISTS.

Delaney

DELANEY BLINKED AND READ THE MESSAGE A FEW TIMES before it sank in.

The hurricane was no longer a threat to her wedding. There'd be no need to postpone—for the storm or otherwise.

Delaney had spent Wednesday night researching how American lawyers can qualify to practice law in London. She'd have to study British law and sit for an exam, as she would if she wanted to practice in another state. It also required having two years of qualified work experience, which Delaney had more than surpassed. That was it. A passing grade on an exam was all she'd need.

Next on her to-do list was to talk to Jim, her main ally at the firm. As a senior partner, he'd let her know if a leave of absence from the firm was possible. She'd been dreading making the call but figured she needed all the facts to make an informed decision, including any partner track–suspending ramifications.

Her hands trembled as she searched for his number, fearful the call could effectively taint her reputation and standing in the firm if her news wasn't well-received.

Jim laughed when she told him.

"What's so funny?" she asked.

"For a second there, I thought you said London. As in fish and chips and double-decker buses."

"I did say London."

"United Kingdom London?" he clarified.

"The same."

"Oh."

Delaney waited for him to explode, to tell her she was fired and had forty-eight hours to remove her belongings.

"I'm only seeking options," she assured him.

Jim told her his cousin was a solicitor in London, and they'd often considered joining forces for an international law practice.

Delaney was floored when Jim went on to discuss various options, all of which entailed her keeping her position—either on loan to his cousin's London firm or opening a UK branch of their own firm.

She couldn't wait to tell Dalton in person when they met later that afternoon.

Marley

THREE A.M.

Marley lay on her side, staring at her phone. Dying to text Sam, desperately needing reassurance. She should be angry at him for the words he said in her apartment. For kissing her like he meant it, then blowing her off.

Instead, she was terrified about what it all meant for their friendship.

She typed out a text but quickly erased it. She wasn't going to grovel when he so rudely ignored her.

Her phone lit up in call mode. Shit! She must have called him by accident when she erased her text. She hung up immediately.

A second later, it rang with an incoming call.

"Hey," Sam said. Casual, as if nothing had happened.

"Hey." She matched his tone.

"Why'd you hang up?"

"I didn't mean to call you," she explained. "I dialed you by accident."

"Well, I dialed you on purpose," he said. "That's how phones work."

"Thanks for the tutorial, Verizon."

She was so relieved to hear his voice. Hopefully this meant their friendship wasn't over.

"What are you doing up so late?" he asked, sounding sleepy.

"My house was just raided by the FBI," she joked.

"Yours too? What do they want you for?"

"For caring about your happiness, despite your cruel and unusual treatment. You?"

"For being cruel and unusual," he said. "Guilty on the first count, but not the second."

"They got you dead to rights on unusual, friend."

Sam was silent for a moment. "I'm sorry. Not for what I said, just the way I said it. And—you know..."

The kiss, Sam. Say it. You regret kissing me.

He didn't have to. He showed it when he blew right by her in the intersection with Jenna.

"You deserve the world, you know," he said.

"You too."

"As your friend, I wanna make sure you're not settling for less than you deserve."

"Right back at you," she said.

A beat. Then, "Touché."

His voice was soft. She could tell from his tone he was smiling.

"So have you done it yet?" Marley asked, dying to know if he'd made it official with Jenna. At the same time, not.

"Done what?"

"Auditioned for *Kinky Boots*. What do you think?"

Sam chuckled.

"Won her heart," Marley clarified.

"Not yet."

"When?"

"I dunno," he said. "Maybe Friday."

"Well, good luck. Doesn't look like you'll need it, though."

After they ended their call, Marley drifted off to sleep, awakening hours later to an incoming text.

A selfie of Rick, standing in the airport.

> Got through security but
> six-hour delay

He looked sad, despite his forced smile. Vulnerable, almost. She instantly felt guilty for all the Sam stuff. Compassion tugged at her heart, taking over where uncertainty had earlier dwelled. She had to make the most of this visit and get them back on track. Their relationship, not to mention her friendship with Sam, depended on it.

She and Rick had been dating for three years—too much time to just throw it away over a few disagreements. They were just going through a rough patch, but they'd get beyond it.

Sam was wrong about them not having passion. People just had different ways of expressing it. Some were showy, some were steadfast. Some had standards so high, they overlooked you. Some stood in crowded airports, waiting six hours to board a plane when they could (and probably should) be at work.

Rick finally arrived that afternoon, looking tired but relieved to be there. After a long, comforting hug, he kissed her with more urgency than he'd ever kissed her before. She felt the familiar stirrings she used to feel in his embrace. His timing couldn't be better; it went a long way in reminding her of what they had together.

She put on some music and they danced around the kitchen, laughing as they prepared dinner, sneaking kisses now and then. Their proximity melted the tension and reset them to normal. It's what they needed. To be together.

Perhaps this is what Delaney was alluding to when she said long distance relationships were hard. It was difficult to maintain intimacy from hundreds of miles away, especially when the demands of their immediate surroundings pulled them apart.

It was time to move forward, toward each other, mend the broken miles between them.

She was finally ready for the talk she'd been putting off.

When dinner was ready, Marley lit candles. Realizing she'd forgotten butter, she went back to the kitchen to grab it. As she turned away from the fridge, she almost tripped over Rick.

Who was down on one knee, ring box held high.

Kate

A HORRIFIC SOUND WOKE KATE ON THURSDAY MORN-
ing—a siren of some sort coming from her nightstand. Her
phone, to be exact.

Weird. She hadn't changed her alarm tone recently, unless
by accident.

She reached over, eyes still closed, and poked the screen
until the sound disappeared.

Ten minutes later, it sounded again. She tipped the phone
toward her, opened one eye, and checked the time.

Eight o'clock. She didn't recall setting an alarm the night
before, but then it all came back to her. The phone had been
dead when she'd fallen asleep.

She scrolled through text previews from names she didn't
recognize. She rubbed her eyes and looked closer.

The first was from someone named The Hand.

> Dude coming for you at 8

The Hand? She tried to remember if she'd met someone
whose number she'd saved in her phone under that name, but
nothing came to her. Confused, she read the next preview,
from Forkface. What the hell?

> Looking forward to golfing with
> you dicks

Then another message from The Hand.

> Brady wake up, dude

Someone must've accidentally given out her number.

She entered her Touch ID code so she could fully open the texts, but her login failed. She tried again. Fail. She stopped before she did it a third time, afraid it would lock her out.

And that's when it dawned on her.

"Oh, my God!" Kate yelled as she sprang up. "This isn't my phone."

It had the same OtterBox case; but now, in daylight, Kate could tell it didn't contain her phone.

The biggest clue of all—the lock screen showed a picture of a thirtysomething-looking guy holding a baby girl.

The events of last night came flooding back: Laura setting her phone down, the bar fight, the knocked-over table. She obviously grabbed the wrong phone in the darkened bar, which meant someone else had picked up hers.

"Oh, no," Laura said, coming over to inspect the phone. "Do you know a Brady?"

"No!"

Kate began to panic. Laura pulled out her own phone and dialed Kate's number.

"It's ringing."

Kate looked at Laura expectantly, hoping this Brady would answer.

Laura's hopeful expression shifted. "He's not answering, but your voice mail's coming on." She held up a finger. "Hello, Brady? If you're getting this message, then you have my friend's phone, and she has yours. Please call your phone so you guys can meet up and switch back. Thanks, bye."

"Will he be able to listen to the voice mail message if he doesn't have my passcode?"

"I'm not sure," Laura said. "Let's text him too."

Laura picked up her own phone again and sent a text to Kate's.

HAVE YOUR PHONE PLS CALL

"Hopefully he'll see the text preview and realize it's not his phone."

"In all caps too, so he knows I mean it," Kate joked.

"You should check with the Princeton when it opens to see if anyone found yours."

Good idea. Delaney would be picking her up soon to run last-minute wedding errands together. Hopefully her sister wouldn't mind stopping by the bar.

She'd never answered Greg's request for a chat. She didn't want to leave him hanging or give him the impression she didn't want to talk, even if his only goal was to let her down easy. He owed her that much after getting her hopes up for "new beginnings."

She and Delaney dropped in at the Princeton, where they inquired if anyone had found her phone. No luck.

Kate kept a watchful eye on the stranger's phone throughout the morning to make sure she didn't miss him. Noon came and went, still with no word. What kind of person goes all morning without checking their phone? She treated hers like an appendage.

She still hadn't heard from the phone's owner when they joined the bridesmaids at the nail salon later that afternoon. Convinced her phone was lost forever, she resigned herself to the fact she'd have to buy a new one.

At four o'clock, the phone finally rang.

"Hi, I think I have your phone," a man said.

"Yes!" she said, relieved. "I've been trying to reach you all day."

"I'm sorry," he said. "I forgot to charge my—I mean, your—phone last night. It was dead this morning, and I was rushing to a golf outing, so I left it to charge. I didn't realize it wasn't my phone until I got back and saw your messages."

Kate was annoyed but he sounded kind. She softened her tone.

"I guess our phones got switched in the bar fight last night," he said. "What are the odds, right? Same phone, same case."

He said he left immediately after the fight and didn't bother to look at his phone or he may have realized the mistake. He suggested they meet up somewhere to exchange the devices.

"I'm tied up in Cape May for a couple hours," Kate said. "Where are you?"

"I'm in AC."

Bummer. Atlantic City was about an hour away.

"Would later tonight work?" she asked.

"Sure, as long as I can borrow a car."

"Oh, no worries," Kate said. "I can come to you if you don't own a car."

Brady laughed. "I own a car; I just don't have it with me. I'm on vacation. But no worries, I can meet you where you are, whenever it's convenient for you."

She wouldn't be free until later that night. The pedicures had just started, followed by manicures, then a family dinner. They agreed to meet at the Princeton at ten.

Deciding it would sound too desperate to ask him if Greg had texted her phone, Kate suggested they exchange passcodes so they could open messages in case something important came up.

He agreed, but added, "I'm pretty sure there'll be nothing earth-shattering on my end."

No shit, if text previews from The Hand, Forkface, and Dingy Dan were any indication. Except—

"Someone named Stephanie has been texting, wondering where you are. Is there something you'd like me to tell her?"

"No, it's all good."

She was probably his wife, which meant she'd already be aware of the situation.

They exchanged passcodes and hung up. Several minutes passed. Kate couldn't wait any longer to know what Greg wanted to talk about, so she went full desperado.

> Hey, I'm expecting an important text. Have I received any?

> Sorry, no texts or calls

> K, thanks

Kate's stomach dropped. Brady texted back.

> Did I receive any?

Kate scrolled through his messages, then responded.

> You're more popular than I am. There's two each from The Hand, Forkface, and Dingy Dan. One each from Crowman and Rob. Interesting names, would love to know how Rob got his. Should I forward any?

He responded with three laughing emojis.

> No, delete them all.

His phone dinged in rapid succession, so she texted him again.

> Three more just came in from Stephanie. Your wife?

He sent more laughing emojis.

> Not married. She's my ex.

The phone vibrated with an incoming call. Kate's number flashed across the screen.

"Hey," Brady said. "I thought it was easier to call and explain this Stephanie thing."

"You don't need to explain anything to me," Kate said, surprised he'd think so. She looked wide-eyed at the other bridesmaids, who were now watching her.

Delaney must have filled them in on the phone-switch situation.

"I feel like I do, since you're having to field all these texts," Brady said.

Before Kate could tell him she didn't mind, he jumped in with the story.

"Stephanie and I broke up a while back. I've moved on, but she wants to keep things going between us. I've tried to be direct but don't want to be hurtful. If you have any advice, feel free to Cyrano de Bergerac the situation."

Kate chuckled. "If I had advice to give, I'd be taking it myself."

"You're dealing with an ex too? I bet yours isn't begging you to see a psychic."

"You'd be right about that," Kate said. "Why a psychic?"

"Can I trust you with the weirdness of my truth?"

"Absolutely." Bring it on. Anything to keep from thinking about her own weird truth.

"I can't believe I'm about to tell you this," he said. "She went to a psychic who insists we're going to end up together. And how would she know this? Chicken bones. You know, you toss bones on a table and your future is determined by how they land. Now she wants me to go, get my own chicken bones read. I kid you not."

"Wow."

"Right? What am I supposed to do with that? We'd only been dating a few months."

"Oh, geez." Kate didn't know what else to say. She couldn't believe she and this Brady had gone from complete strangers to confidants in a matter of minutes.

"Yeah, so it's a bit—"

"No, I get it," Kate said. She wasn't sure who she was more embarrassed for—herself for probing in the first place, Brady for spilling this tea, or Stephanie for grasping at straws (bones?) over a relationship that had apparently run its course.

Perhaps the most embarrassing thing was being able to relate to the latter. Minus the bones, of course.

They reiterated plans to meet later, where he promised to share more of the story. She could hardly wait. Finally, someone else's drama to focus on instead of her own.

Kate ended the call and found the women staring at her.

"Was that Phone Guy?" Cleo asked.

"Yeah."

"Are you getting together to exchange phones?" Delaney asked.

Kate smiled. "Later."

"Look at her, she's blushing!" Cleo exclaimed. "Is he single?"

"I think so, but he has a kid," Kate said.

"What does he look like?" Tori asked.

She held up the photo of the man holding a baby on the home screen, and the women cooed, deciding both he *and* the baby were cute. They tried to convince her to look through his phone and learn more about him, but that would be an invasion of his privacy.

"Here, give it to me. I'll do it." Cleo reached out.

"No." Kate pulled it away.

Another text came in.

> You got a text from Greg.

> Can you forward it, please?

Kate waited, watching the bubble with the bouncing dots. It took forever. Finally, Greg's message came through.

> Can't stop thinking about you. We
> need to talk.

Kate's eyes grew wide as she reread his message. Greg couldn't stop thinking about her! Her heart started fluttering but her brain told it to calm down. Dude has a girlfriend.

Brady texted again.

> I have the name of a good psychic if
> you need it!

Kate laughed out loud, remotely aware the chattering around her had ceased.

Still, this could be the door of opportunity she'd been looking for. Should she encourage more discussion, or leave it in the past?

Another text from Brady came through.

> Cyrano de Bergerac, at your service if
> you need me.

Kate smiled. She was digging this guy's humor; he made her feel oddly at ease. She didn't want to leave Greg hanging, but to respond meant dictating a message to Brady, which would be awkward at best, desperate at worst.

"You look like you just won the lottery," Delaney teased.

Kate looked up. Delaney and the women stared at her again. "Oh, just a funny meme."

She'd have to get back to Greg later tonight, after she got her phone back and had a chance to think about how she wanted to respond.

She turned off Brady's phone so she wouldn't be further distracted. She shifted her attention to her sister and the bridesmaids, just as Delaney's phone rang.

"Hey, Mom," she answered.

Within seconds, the color drained from Delaney's face and her expression grew grim.

"Oh God, we'll be right there!"

She scrambled to get up. "We gotta go!"

"What's going on?" Kate demanded.

"Dad had a heart attack."

Cleo

CLEO PEELED UP ONTO THE SIDEWALK IN FRONT OF THE salon like a getaway driver in a major heist. Delaney and Kate jumped in, and she raced to Cape Regional Medical Center, thankful the cops were too Dunkin'ed up to bother with Mach-ten speeders such as herself. She couldn't afford the extra points but would have gladly taken them, if it meant getting her sisters-from-another-mister to their dad.

In reality, Joe Ross felt like as much of a father to Cleo as he was to Delaney and Kate. The Ross family, who she'd known since she was seven, treated her like one of their own. Joe had accompanied Cleo to her middle school's father-daughter dance when her own father was locked up. He took Cleo and Delaney to see Destiny's Child, their first concert, and spent hours calling the local radio station to win Justin Timberlake meet and greets. He worked a lot, but what little free time he had he devoted to his kids and Cleo.

The last thing she wanted to do was spend more time in a godforsaken hospital, but it's what you do for fam. Blood related or not.

Kate was already heaving full-body sobs when they arrived and joined the rest of the family in the waiting room. Delaney, always stoic for the sake of others, gathered facts about what had happened. They learned their brother, JJ, had been home when their dad announced he wasn't feeling well and passed out. JJ, an Eagle Scout, performed CPR.

"Thank God for your quick thinking," Delaney said to her brother. "You probably saved his life."

Dalton arrived then. Cleo mouthed a thank-you to him as he ushered Delaney to the hallway so she could feel the feels away from her mom and younger siblings.

Cleo tried to comfort Kate but couldn't find the right words. Being in a hospital twice in a week was more than she was ready to deal with herself, especially when the two men who'd been the closest to her throughout her life had been hit with serious, life-threatening conditions within the same week.

She felt it. Loss was creeping in.

Again.

JUST THE SIGHT OF DALTON, HIS SILENT STRENGTH AS HE walked in the room, and Delaney was ready to lose it. Being strong for her family was exhausting. It was still too early to know if her dad was going to be okay, but Dalton's presence calmed her. He wrapped a protective arm around her and led her to the hallway, enveloping her in his arms.

"He's gonna be okay," he said, rubbing her back.

"You don't know that."

"You're right. I don't know anything," he said. "Except, I love you."

Three simple words, but it somehow made the nightmare more bearable. She was fortunate to be loved by Dalton. And her dad. Two great men she couldn't afford to lose.

"I love you too, but you know I can't do this wedding ceremony without him," she said in a feeble voice.

"I know," Dalton said. "And we won't."

She recalled her dad's words about never knowing how much time one has on this earth. Terrifying, to think her dad's time could be coming to an end.

"I thought everything would be smooth sailing after the storm dissipated," she scoffed as tears streamed down her face. "A hurricane feels like nothing compared to this."

Delaney broke down and Dalton held her. He didn't say anything or try to convince her it was okay.

"Hey, guys."

It was her mom, bearing a faint smile.

"The doctor said it wasn't a heart attack. He had blockage. They're putting in a stent."

Relief coursed through Delaney's veins as she pulled her mom into a hug, along with a feeling of gratitude for a new chance at life. Both her dad's and hers.

As they awaited news the procedure was completed, Delaney thought of the many things she was going to do differently. Be more present. Enjoy the little moments. Practice gratitude for what and who she had in her life, knowing it could be taken away in a heartbeat, or lack thereof.

When the doctor confirmed the procedure was successful, Delaney asked if they could see him. The doctor suggested only one family member at a time.

Her mom simply nodded and said, "You go, my dear."

Delaney's dad was asleep when she entered his room. She pulled a chair next to his bed and took his hand. He'd always been the rock of their family, but seeing him looking so helpless, lying in a hospital bed, was a reminder of human vulnerability.

"Oh, Dad," she sighed, as tears began flowing again. "I love you. I promise I'll take more time to be in the moment, and celebrate life, like you told me to."

His eyelids began to flutter.

"Hey," she whispered, taking his hand. She wasn't sure how much her dad knew about what he'd been through. "You're going to be okay."

"That's what they say," he said through a smile, his voice weak. "And they better be right. My daughter's getting married this weekend."

"We can postpone—"

"Over my dead body," he said, wincing. "Maybe it's too soon to joke about that. But I'll be there even if they have to wheel this bed onto the beach."

"So you can upstage me?" she held up a corner of the white sheet. "Only the bride is supposed to wear white, remember?"

Her dad smiled. "You've waited long enough to spend your life together, and I've waited long enough to get rid of you. That's a moment I won't miss for the world."

Delaney squeezed his hand. Other family members were waiting to see him, so she gave him a kiss before she stepped out.

In the parking lot, Delaney exhaled the breath she'd been holding since her mom called hours ago.

"You good?" Dalton asked as he wrapped his arms around her.

"Better than good."

Her dad was going to be okay, and now the idea of postponing the wedding seemed ludicrous.

Life was precious, fleeting for some. She needed to spend every moment she had left with Dalton. There was nothing they couldn't get through as long as they were together.

For better *and* worse.

Here or London.

"Now I see why people elope," she joked. "What do you say? I can't take any more surprises."

"Vegas it is!" Dalton said. "But hey, honeymoon issue: resolved. Hurricane: thwarted. Dad's heart: repaired. And job opportunity: pass. Can we get married as planned? I can't wait any longer to start my life with you."

"Job opportunity, pass? What do you mean?"

"It means I pass," he said, matter-of-factly. "If this night has taught me anything, it's you don't take life for granted. You make my life complete, Delaney Ross. You love your job, you need to be here to do it, and I need to be where you are. So, I pass on London. There'll be other opportunities."

"Not so fast," Delaney said, smiling in anticipation of the good news she was about to deliver. "I did some research and spoke to Jim. It turns out I can work in London. The firm has some connections over there. It'll just take some planning."

"No more planning," Dalton said. "I just want to live our lives. Here, where we belong." He gave Delaney a long kiss. "Shall I point this car toward Vegas?"

"Pass," Delaney said. She, too, was tired of planning.

She was finally ready to embrace the fact that life happens. No matter how much you prepare for something, things can change. Careers shift, weather looms, people get sick, partnerships evolve. The mark of a good relationship isn't when everything runs smoothly, it's when the couple learns to pivot and change, compromise and adjust. Where they expect the unexpected and find joy in the chaos. Where they have faith in themselves as individuals, in each other as partners, and the union as a whole. Faith things will work out, even in the face of impending disaster.

Thank goodness she'd explored the unexpected opportunity to practice law in London—she may yet need it one day, to support Dalton in the fulfillment of his goals, as he'd supported hers.

Until then, they'd stay right where they were. And she'd enjoy every second of it.

"Forget Vegas," Delaney said. "Show me the way to Cape May."

Marley

"**D**ON'T PANIC, IT'S NOT WHAT YOU THINK IT IS," RICK said, still on his knee. "It's just a promise ring."

"Why would you scare me like that?" she blurted out. "A promise of what?"

Rick stood and took the ring from the box.

"The future. I know we have a lot to sort out, but I'm serious about spending my life with you and want you to consider it."

"Aw, Rick," Marley sighed, putting her hand to her chest. It was the sweetest thing he'd ever done.

"So, will you consider marrying me? Someday?"

"Yes, I will consider it." Marley giggled as she regarded the ring, a pear-shaped opal.

"Opal's your birthstone, right?"

It wasn't...but the gesture counted.

Rick slid the ring on her finger. It got stuck on her knuckle.

"Oh, no—" she said.

"Let me just—"

Rick held her hand and pushed the ring with more force.

"Ouch!"

"Sorry. We'll just—"

"—get it adjusted."

Marley stared at the ring, her hand trembling with the promise of its significance. Being someone's wife. Loving them unconditionally. Forever.

Was she ready for the promise?

Rick looked at her with his molten chocolate eyes, the look

she'd been missing, and it reminded her how lucky she was. She had the love of a good man who cherished her and made her feel safe. Chosen. Worthy.

After dinner, he picked her up and carried her to the bedroom.

"I can't wait to do this with you every night..."

Sex between them felt slightly awkward, but Marley chalked it up to the fact they hadn't been together for months. Afterward, she lay in bed toying with the ring, trying to get it beyond her knuckle. It wouldn't budge.

A sign?

She took deep breaths to calm the panic rising within her.

When sleep finally came, she found herself on a beach again. Sam was in the water, playing with the kids. He turned to the woman in the hat with the same look of hunger, longing.

He came closer, pulled her in. He lifted her chin.

Suddenly, Marley was transposed into the very woman Sam was embracing.

She was filled with indescribable joy as he gazed at her, like the night at Penn's Landing.

My God.

And then she felt his lips on hers as he kissed her. Like the night in her apartment, only deeper.

Holy shit.

They lay on the beach and Sam moved over her, pressing their bodies together, not taking his eyes off her.

I'm the woman in the dream.

He kissed her again, teasingly at first, then whispered in her ear. "This is what passion feels like."

"Oh, Sam," Marley said, moaning. "I love you."

He asked her to repeat it.

"I love you. I've always loved you, Sam."

"Are you *fucking* kidding me?"

It was—wait—Rick's voice?

Marley jolted awake, blinking herself back to reality.

Across the room, her future fiancé was jamming things into his duffel bag.

" 'I love you—*Sam?*' " he yelled. "I just gave you a ring and you dream about *Sam?*"

"No, Rick—that's not—"

"I fucking *knew* it!" he yelled, thrusting his finger into the air between them. "You *liar!*"

"Wait, Rick it was just a dream—"

"Was it, Marley? Or just wishful thinking?"

She looked down at the ring, still stuck on her knuckle, its weight now almost unbearable. It hadn't felt right since he tried to slide it on.

She slid it off.

"Wishful thinking," she whispered as she handed it to him, unable to look into his eyes.

"I'm sorry."

She knew, before she heard the door slam—it would be the last time she'd ever see Rick.

KATE HAD LOST ALL SENSE OF TIME SITTING IN THE HOSPItal waiting room. She was surprised when she glanced at the old clock on the wall to see it was ten thirty. No wonder she was tired—they'd been at the hospital huddled in a constant state of fear for six hours. Her eyes were beginning to close again when she bolted upright.

Ten thirty!

Shit. She was supposed to meet Brady at the Princeton at ten. She pulled his phone from her purse and turned it back on to find several texts and a missed call from her number.

"Hey, Kathryn," Brady's voice mail message began. Kate liked the way he said her full name. "Bloomingdale's texted, and they referred to you as Kathryn, so that's how I know your name. Perhaps my phone died, or you got sick of Stephanie and her texts and you've thrown it into the ocean. Oh wait, you're probably at a psychic having your bones read."

A smile tugged at Kate's mouth, for the first time in hours.

"Anyway, I hope you're okay. I haven't heard from you, so I'm wondering if you still want to meet tonight. If you can't, that's fine. I'm heading to Cape May tomorrow morning and can catch up with you along the way. Just let me know. All right. Bye, Kathryn."

Kate sought privacy on a bench in the hallway and returned Brady's call. He answered on the first ring.

"Kathryn," he said in a sleepy voice, sounding relieved. "Is everything okay?"

Hours of anxiety, fear, and exhaustion came tumbling out as Kate explained what had happened.

"I'm sorry to hear that," Brady said, sounding sincere. "How's he doing?"

She nodded before the words could come. A tear rolled down her cheek. She took a breath and waited until her voice steadied. "They think he's going to be okay. It was a shock, the timing especially."

"I know what you're going through," he said. "The same thing happened to my dad, and he's good now. Think good thoughts."

Kate was impressed how quickly he jumped in and offered personal information to make her feel better.

As it turned out, Brady was right. Her dad's procedure had been successful.

Hours later, Kate returned to Laura's house. She was exhausted and ready to escape the chaos of the day, but sleep eluded her. She rolled over and fluffed her pillow when the phone rang.

"I took a chance you'd still be awake," Brady said, as soon as she answered. "How's your dad doing?"

"He's going to be okay," she said, sighing with relief upon hearing her own words.

"That's great news, Kathryn."

She should probably tell him he could call her Kate, but there was just something sexy about the way he said her full name. He continued to assure her the procedure works, and his dad was back to his old self after going through the same thing. She was thankful for his support.

He didn't seem to be in a rush to get off the phone and she wasn't either. It was nice to have a late-night phone chat again, something she and Greg used to do.

"So, is this Greg your boyfriend, or your ex?"

"Ex-boyfriend. We broke up two years ago, but he's reappeared."

Kate gave him the SparkNotes version of their relationship, and the fact they'd just communicated this week for the first time.

"What made you guys reconnect?" he asked.

She told him about the article hailing Greg's success, and the random reminders that had popped up ever since.

"Ah, and you're wondering if you made a mistake breaking up?" he asked.

"Exactly."

Then she found herself peeling back another layer of their relationship for this total stranger. After all, he'd been transparent about his situation. For some reason, the anonymity of a phone call provided a cloak of protection.

"The real reason we broke up was because he chose to leave me to pursue his dream. Which I get, but I wanted to feel chosen.

"Completely understandable," he said. "A lot of us feel that way."

"But now, I wonder if I'm second-guessing the breakup because of his success?"

"That, too, would be completely natural. I think we'd all do the same."

"Thanks for saying that," she said. "My friends and family are acting like I'm looking for a sugar daddy."

"Are you?"

"No. But I will need to see your financials before we go any further."

Brady laughed before sobering a little. "It sounds from his text he's not over you."

"There's more to the story than what I've shared. But I've taken up enough of your time."

"No, you haven't. If there's more tea to spill, I'm here for it."

His gossip-girl enthusiasm made Kate smile. She proceeded to disclose the entire truth, down to the discovered seashell.

"Wow. I wonder what made him change his mind?"

"That's the million-dollar question. It could have had something to do with the fact that I freaked out when he told me his plans."

"No wonder, you were settled in your career," he said. "But he could have stayed and tried to work it out, rather than taken off."

"Yeah, that would have helped."

"It sounds like you guys do need to talk."

Kate agreed, feeling an instant friend-connection to this guy. "Enough about me. The baby on your phone is really cute. Your daughter?"

"My niece, Bella. She's put herself in charge of picking my phone screens."

"Pretty advanced for an infant," Kate joked.

Brady laughed. "She's fourteen. She put it on there a couple months ago, so I'd remember her upcoming birthday."

"Did you?"

"Of course! I just forgot to change the photo."

Kate was becoming more intrigued by the second. No kid, never been married, just a cool uncle who lets his niece change his phone settings. Fueled with this new information, she probed for more intel.

"Why did you and Stephanie break up?"

"She was ready for marriage, but I wasn't."

"Because you didn't want to settle down?" she hedged.

"No, because she wasn't the one. She keeps texting, to see if we can make it work. It's not her fault—there's nothing there to fix. The connection was just never there."

"I think I can relate," Kate said.

"I liked what you said about feeling chosen, earlier," he continued. "I just think marriage was her primary goal, it almost didn't matter with whom. That's not what I want in a life partner."

"Oh my gosh, I'm Stephanie!" Kate blurted out.

"You're no Stephanie, trust me."

"No, seriously. If I'm honest, the thing with Greg was always off, I just blamed it on him wanting to avoid adulthood. I only chose him as a potential spouse because we'd been dating for a long time, and it was the next step."

Greg must have sensed it. Because instead of dropping the shell in the sand for her to find, he'd kept it tucked in his pocket—as if he knew, long before she did, they weren't meant to be. And good for him, because if they'd gotten engaged, she would've insisted he stay and he wouldn't have fulfilled his dream.

"It's clear to me now," she said. "I was too focused on having a fairy-tale ending to realize it wasn't supposed to be with him."

"Maybe you'll still get your fairy-tale ending," Brady said, his voice softening. "You deserve someone who treats you like gold. You're beautiful."

She was about to thank him when—

"Wait. How do you know what I look like?"

"Your phone screen photo."

Ah, of course. Kate recalled the photo, a selfie she'd taken on the beach at sunset last week.

"I was hoping you were the one in the bar last night—"

What?

"Oh my God, are you the guy? The guy who—"

"I was about to introduce myself when—"

"The fight broke out. I'm guessing that's—"

"How our phones got switched," they both said at the same time.

"Oh. My. Gosh. I just assumed—the baby, the guy—I just figured this phone belonged to the guy in the picture, the one holding the baby."

"No, that's my niece's dad holding her, my brother-in-law."

"Wow," Kate exhaled. "But why did you take off so fast? Is there a warrant out for your arrest or something?"

He laughed. "One of our buddies likes to involve himself in other people's fights, so we hustled him outta there before he jumped into the fray."

They were silent for a minute. Kate let the whole thing sink in.

"So, hi, beautiful girl in the bar," he whispered.

"Hi, handsome dark-haired guy," Kate said softly, her heart beating so loud she feared he'd hear it through the phone.

"I was bummed I didn't get to talk to you," he said. "But I'm thrilled I grabbed the wrong phone. Best mistake I ever made. It's like—"

"Destiny," they both said at the same time.

The sky was beginning to lighten through the blinds and Kate had a long day ahead of her. She asked when they could meet to exchange phones.

"Do we have to? I kinda like this," Brady said.

He told her he was going on a fishing trip in Cape May in the morning but would be back in town after lunch. They agreed to meet in the lobby of Congress Hall at two o'clock.

Kate could hardly wait to meet him, this beautiful stranger who'd been placed in her path by none other than destiny herself.

Cleo

DELANEY'S FATHER'S SCARE LEFT CLEO WORRYING ABOUT Gus. She called Murph to check in and get an update. He picked up on the second ring.

"How is he?" she asked.

"Why don't you ask him yourself?" Murph said. After some ruffling in the background, she heard her old friend's voice.

"Murphy's Whorehouse," he answered.

"Gus?"

"Who wants to know?"

"You know damn well who this is," Cleo scolded, although she was relieved to hear him joking around. "What are you doing in a bar? Shouldn't you be home, resting?"

"I am home," he said.

True. Gus spent much of his time at the tavern. It was probably better for him, being surrounded by drinking buddies than being alone in his empty apartment. But—

"Do you really think you should be drinking?"

"I'm having a Shirley Temple," he said.

"I don't believe you. Tell Murph to send a picture," she instructed.

"Okay, Mom," Gus said.

More ruffling sounds in the background. Cleo waited until her phone dinged. She looked at the texted photo and damn if Gus wasn't telling the truth.

"Here, take another," someone in the background said.

The familiar voice was followed by men's laughter. She braced herself, half-expecting a dick pic or something equally crass from one of the regulars.

Another picture of Gus holding up his Shirley Temple, this time toasting a guy holding a Miller Lite. The guy had his arm wrapped around Gus's shoulder like they were best buds. He was wearing a UPenn sweatshirt, a baseball hat on backward, and a sexy smattering of stubble, and she almost didn't recognize him. Until she did.

Wells.

Cleo's temples throbbed. What was Wells doing in the tavern? He'd never been there before, as far as she knew. The tiny tavern was a dilapidated hole in the wall, tucked into the middle of a residential neighborhood in Northeast Philly, undiscoverable even through Google Maps.

She began to feel light-headed as her two worlds collided: the one with Wells, the Clink, and its shiny patrons; and the one with Gus, the tavern, and its bevy of drunks.

"What the fuck is he doing there?" she hissed into her phone.

"He came here looking for you. Hold on, he wants to say hi," Gus said, and before she could object, Wells came on the line.

"Hey, girl," he said. "How's vacation?"

"Um, fine. What are you doing at the Tavern?"

"Looking for you," he said. She could tell he was pretty lit and wondered how many Thursday-night-special one-dollar Miller Lites he'd had. "I totally forgot you were on vacation."

"Forgot?" she asked.

"Well, that and my buddies and I were looking for a cheap place to drink. I remembered you telling me about Murphy's Thursday specials."

The contradiction made her head spin. Was he looking for her, or just cheap drinks?

His voice dropped to a near whisper. "I miss you."

Cleo's heart picked up its pace. She paused before answering, not sure if she should admit her truth.

"Me too," she finally said.

Did she really miss him, or just the fun they used to have?

"Can we talk sometime?" he asked. "After the wedding?"

"Sure," she said, hoping she didn't sound too eager.

She heard more ruffling sounds, then Gus's voice.

"Of course you can talk. He's a fine lad," Gus said. "Just lemme know when you get back together so I can clear my schedule for your wedding."

Humiliation coursed through Cleo's veins. The last thing she needed was for Wells to know she'd told Gus about him, that he mattered beyond a little romp in Egyptian cotton. How dare Gus blow her laissez-faire cover, suggesting they had any kind of future together? It was out of character for the old man—the seizure must have landed him right on his fool head. It certainly wasn't the Shirley Temple talking.

"If cancer doesn't kill me before then," Gus added, as if he knew he'd crossed the line and was seeking mercy.

"Oh, you don't have to worry about that," Cleo said. "Because I'm gonna kill you first."

After she ended the call, she couldn't stop thinking about the fact that Wells missed her enough to try to hunt her down at the sleaziest bar in Philly.

Dollar brews or not, it had to count for something. The way her heart pounded told her maybe she was wrong about him just being a friend. Was this love? Or lust?

Maybe he'd decided to fight for her, in which case she just may have to give him a chance to—as Gus put it—"love" her.

Friday, June 16

COUNTDOWN
TO WEDDING
1 DAY

BYRON JAMES
ABC METEOROLOGIST

"Hey, all you beachgoers, Byron James here, and I've got some great news for you! Remember Inez, that spunky gal who went from tropical storm to hurricane, only to be downgraded again? Well, she won't be a threat to your weekend plans, thanks to wind shear and an upper-level trough that worked in tandem to send her reeling to her final destination in the northeastern Atlantic. Now, instead of being forced to shutter your windows and evacuate the coast, you'll be treated to a picture-perfect weekend. You can expect a high in the low to mid-eighties on Saturday and much of the same on Sunday, with a southeasterly breeze and zero—hear me out on this—zero percent chance of precipitation. We'll bring you the latest on what you can expect for the weekend ahead."

Delaney

DELANEY AND DALTON MET AT THE JETTY ON FRIDAY morning to exchange wedding gifts. They'd agreed not to do anything too expensive or elaborate, just something of sentimental value.

Dalton was already there when she arrived. He handed her a large gift bag. Inside was a sandcastle-making kit.

"I've included instructions," he said, pointing to a laminated card.

How to build the perfect sandcastle:

1. Learn how to make drippies with your hands
2. Make the drippies
3. Marvel at your work
4. Watch the meanie-bo-beanie knock it over
5. Chase him to the water and threaten to steal his heart
6. Steal his heart
7. Say yes when he gets down on one knee
8. Agree to a cheesesteak bar (or not...your choice)
9. Get married
10. Build a sandcastle together

"Aw, Dalton," Delaney said, laughing through happy tears. "This is so cute, and so appropriate."

"There's more," he said, handing her a scroll of paper. On it was a picture of a real-life ornate castle which looked, remarkably, like the one she'd been aiming to recreate when she was seven.

"I tried to find one just like yours, but it turns out none are made that well. Who knew?"

"Of course not," Delaney said. "Mine was engineered with precision."

"Which is why this is long overdue. I booked us two nights in this castle during our honeymoon, right outside London. I hope it makes up for destroying yours."

"Oh my gosh," she said, sighing as she peered up at him. How did she ever get so lucky to find such a romantic, sentimental guy?

"It looks beautiful," Delaney said. Then she noticed something stapled to the bottom of the picture—a realtor's business card. "What's this?"

"That's for when we decide to put down permanent roots. A beach house of our own, where we can raise our babies. We can take our time looking, but I wanted to get us lined up with a realtor now, for when we're ready.

"So that makes something old," he said, pointing to the castle picture. Then he pointed to the card. "And something new."

"Dalton. That's—amazing. I'm speechless. I had no idea you even knew about the whole 'something old, something new' thing."

"It's what I do. I read *Brides* magazine, and I know things."

Delaney laughed again through tears of joy. She hugged her sweet Groomzilla and gave him a kiss before handing him his gift—custom-made gold cuff links in the shape of sandcastles.

"Oh my God," he whispered. "Look at this. Both of us with sandcastle gifts. Like we're reading each other's thoughts."

"But these aren't just any cuff links," Delaney said, trying to keep her voice steady. "Your mom gave me your grandmother's engagement and wedding rings and told me to do something special with them. I consulted her first, and she loved the idea. The castles are made from the bands. And this?" She pointed to the two tiny blue gems—hearts—set in the middle of each sandcastle. "These are the blue topaz stones from her engagement ring."

"So..."

They both spoke at the same time. "Something borrowed, something blue."

They hadn't planned it that way. But that's what happens when you're destined to spend a lifetime with someone.

Marley

MARLEY NEEDED SPACE. AWAY FROM THE CITY, AWAY from work, but mostly away from Sam. Today was the day he'd take out his scribbled napkin notes and win back the woman of his dreams.

Strathmere provided the perfect escape. Her housemates weren't expected until Saturday, giving her time to process everything that had happened before she had to sit at a wedding table, empty spot next to her, facing Sam and Jenna.

She made her way to the beach and had just settled in her chair when the *Rocky* theme jingled with Sam's incoming text.

> Where are you????

She pictured him, back in their office after the gig at his dad's firm.

She snapped a photo of the ocean and sent it to him before turning off her phone, not ready to deal with him just now.

She closed her eyes and drifted off, awakening hours later to the sound of a hovering seagull's fluttering wings. She shooed it away and turned on her phone, where seventeen texts from Sam awaited.

> Mar

> MarDog

> MarleyMcMarley

Variations of her name continued over the course of several texts. He asked why she didn't tell him she was going to the shore. He would've joined her.

Marley texted back

> That's exactly why

Her phone rang.

"The shore, huh?" Sam asked. "What's up?"

She hadn't told anyone yet, but she'd better get used to

saying the words. "Rick and I broke up."

"Wow," Sam whispered after a long silence. "I'm sorry, Mar. You okay? Do you want me to come down and lend you my shoulder? Fly to Columbus and slash his tires? Hire Professor Plum to kill him with a candlestick in the study?"

Marley chuckled. "Nope, I'm good. It needed to happen. I'm...fine."

"Well, I'm happy to go break his kneecaps if you want. You coming home tonight?"

"Nah, I'm down for the weekend. Is Operation Get the Girl still on?" she asked. "I'm a phone call away if you need me."

"You just broke up with your boyfriend and you're offering me support?" Sam asked.

"Yep. You got this."

It was the ultimate act of love. Marley couldn't bear to lose his friendship, even if he was dating someone else and leaving their firm. Relationships evolve and change, especially when both parties are at a crossroads in their lives. She'd better get accustomed to it because there was no way she was living her life without Sam in it. In whatever capacity.

"Do you have the tulips?" she asked. She liked her tulip idea.

"I'll buy them on my way."

"Sam!" Marley exclaimed. "Tulips aren't in season now. They're hard to find."

"Does the corner market sell them?"

"I don't know but leave enough time to find them in case they don't. And—" She took a breath. "Good luck."

Marley exhaled after their call, cleansing herself of emotion, bringing herself to the present, taking in the beauty around her. The late-afternoon sun danced on the waves of the Atlantic, shimmering in peridot green and tumbling white sea-foam. She envisioned the crashing waves washing away all the emotions from the week, receding into calm; the soft sea breeze swooshing away her sadness.

Despite all that had happened, she felt at peace. As hard as it was to close a three-year chapter of her life, it had been the right thing to do. She just wished she hadn't hurt Rick—he didn't deserve it. Maybe someday she'd get the chance to apologize to him.

Still, the heart wants what it wants.

The weight of indecision about her future had finally lifted. Soon, she'd be studying for the bar, hopefully with a tentative job offer under her belt. Most importantly, she didn't have to leave the city she loved to live out her dream of being a lawyer.

Or the person she loved. Even if he belonged to someone else.

It was close to dinnertime and other beachgoers began packing up their gear. In the distance, a seagull sang. Children's laughter drifted from the dunes, and a breeze carried the chatter of happy hour revelers from a nearby deck. It was her favorite time of day on the beach, but the distant sound of clinking glasses reminded her that happy hour also had a certain allure.

She went to her house, returned with a bottle of wine, and poured it into a Solo cup.

"To truth," she said, as she raised her cup to the sea.

Breaking away from Rick had allowed Marley to discover her truth. And her true north.

It wasn't found in another person, but within her. It was her life and everything she loved about it. Living in Philly, being close to family. Interning for a firm she loved, in a field she was passionate about. Hope for her future and the love of good friends. These were the things she turned to when the world spun off its axis.

Her true north once included Rick, but only temporarily. A life partner shouldn't be a crutch, a consolation prize for what you really want. A future with Rick would've required her to readjust her compass away from her true north. And the truth about her feelings for someone else.

2

Before this week, Marley had viewed marriage like a business partnership—a solid union based on congeniality, commonality, and trust. It's what her parents, still together after thirty years, had modeled for her.

But Sam ignited a passion she didn't know existed, a desire for more than she ever thought possible.

She didn't want to slide into a marriage as a logical next step. She wanted to dive headfirst into one. She wanted toe-curling, world-rocking passion, years of lustful glances across crowded rooms, the kind of love that burns throughout the years.

Rick wasn't the person to give her that.

After Sam's kiss—my God, *that kiss*—Marley vowed nothing short of her wildest expectations would do. It wouldn't be with Sam, who was about to confess his love for someone else. He was just an example of the kind of person she hoped to someday find, who'd give her all the passion and pizzazz she longed for.

Nothing less.

Kate

KATE PACKED UP HER CAR ON FRIDAY MORNING, SAID goodbye to her friends, and headed to Congress Hall, where the rehearsal and wedding would take place. She couldn't wait to meet Brady in person and find out if he was as cute in daylight as she remembered him being that night.

Too bad for Dalton's cousin, her intended blind date, but he'd be no more than a one-shot deal. There was no messing with destiny.

A meet-cute. That's what she and Brady had—when two fictional characters meet each other in an unlikely yet romantic way. In their case, two people in a bar, obviously interested in each other, about to meet when an intervening bar fight impeded their connection. But thanks to a phone switch, they were brought back together.

What a great rom-com movie their story would make.

After checking into the hotel and unpacking, she perched on the wide window seat overlooking the beach where, tomorrow, her sister would marry the love of her life. The couple had gone through a lot to get to this day. Despite the challenges, their love for one another never faltered. They were getting their fairy-tale ending.

Kate wondered if this could be the beginning of hers.

Finally, it was go-time. She shimmied into her pink strapless Trina Turk dress and finger-fluffed her flaxen locks until they fell just right at her shoulders. She applied one final coat of mascara which, in concert with her Bali tan, gave her brown eyes a golden glow.

She made her way to the grand staircase leading to the lobby, already buzzing with friends and family members of the Ross and Brooks families, arriving for the big event.

There he was. Leaning up against a wall, a certain dark-haired guy. Kate's breath caught as their eyes met, the look on his face reflecting exactly how she felt—hopeful, happy.

"It's nice to finally meet you. I'm Kathryn," she said when they reached each other. It felt strange to introduce herself by her full name when hardly anyone called her that, but that's how he knew her, so it seemed to be the right thing to do in the moment. "You must be Brady."

"Charmed," he said, taking her hand and kissing it. "Actually—"

His introduction was interrupted by a high-pitched shrill as her boisterous aunt Kim heralded the entrance of the royal couple themselves.

The room erupted in applause as Delaney and Dalton made

their way through the crowd. Kate gave a little clap when Delaney began heading toward them.

"That's my sister," she told Brady. "She's getting married tomorrow."

"You mean Delaney?"

Kate shot him a look. "Wait, you know her?"

Delaney hugged Kate as Dalton pulled Brady into a man hug.

"Hey, cuz," Dalton said, then he turned to Kate. "I guess you guys have met."

"Actually," Kate said, hoping to set the confusion straight, "this is—"

"Ryan," Delaney said, as if it was obvious. "Your blind date."

Cleo

"OI, MY TWO FAVORITE PATRONS!" NIGEL EXCLAIMED AS Cleo and Tori found barstools at the Point.

"And our favorite bartender," Tori said, giving Nigel a fist-bump.

Cleo gave her an odd look. Pretty chummy for Tori, given she'd only met Nigel once and found fist-bumping barbaric and germ-laden.

The women ordered cosmos to celebrate the beginning of wedding weekend, one quick drink before they headed to Cape May to join the rehearsal.

"Have you told her?" Nigel asked as he handed them drinks.

"No, I was waiting for the right time to celebrate." Tori and Nigel shared a look before she held up her drink to Cleo.

"A toast," Tori said, "to my newfound singlehood. Thanks to Nigel, I'm no longer dating Ted the Turd."

"Really?" Cleo's mouth flew open and she shot a look at Nigel. "What happened?"

Besides meeting Nigel, obviously. She couldn't blame her friend for knowing a good thing when she saw it.

"He made me see the light," Tori said. "Ted was holding me back, and I couldn't be my best self in a relationship with him."

"No shit, Sherlock. I've been telling you this for years."

"I know," her friend said. "But sometimes you need to hear it from a stranger."

"Wait, when did you—have you guys been talking?"

Tori nodded, a huge smile on her face. "We went out for brunch on Wednesday while you were sleeping. I came right home afterward and called Ted to tell him it was over."

That would explain why Tori had looked as if she'd been crying that afternoon.

"Why didn't you tell me sooner?" Cleo asked.

"There was so much going on, with Gus and Joe...I didn't want to burden you with my emotional baggage too."

That was Tori, always putting others first.

Cleo turned to Nigel. "What did you say to make her pull the plug?"

"She deserves a guy who lets her be herself," he said. "Life's too short to twist yourself into someone else's version of you."

Yep, exactly what Cleo had been saying.

"At this stage of life, we should be exploring our interests, our goals," Nigel continued. "We're just starting to figure out who we are. How can we do that with someone holding us back?"

Then he said something else that grabbed her attention.

"I'm not against relationships, just relationships with the wrong people. Are we really ready to judge that for ourselves in our twenties?"

Cleo could only answer for herself. Her answer, apparently, was no.

Nigel sauntered off to wait on newly arrived patrons.

"There's more!" Tori whispered, leaning forward with excitement. She squealed and clapped her hands. "I'm taking that trip. I'm finally doing it."

Cleo gave her a congratulatory hug and demanded details.

"I leave on Monday," Tori said.

"This coming Monday?" Cleo asked, shocked.

Tori nodded. "I don't want to waste any time. I'm heading to London."

"Because of Nigel?"

Tori giggled. "No. But he's a hottie, isn't he?"

"Meh, if you're into that sort of look," Cleo said, glancing at their bartender. The one whose look she was definitely into.

Wow. Within the next forty-eight hours, her two closest friends would be cementing their Adult Life Plans—Delaney with marriage and Tori, the adventure of a lifetime. Cleo reminded herself she, too, was forging ahead with her own plans. She hadn't yet found an art gallery that was hiring but did have some promising leads on bartending jobs until a gallery job opened up.

While sliding whiskeys into the mouths of slobbering drunks wasn't as glamorous as her friends' plans, it was a means to an end, her ultimate goal. When she wasn't working, she'd have a world of artistic opportunities at her paint-stained fingertips.

Hopefully Nigel was still planning to go to New York, unless he'd changed his mind and would be heading back to the motherland along with Tori.

Cleo's phone signaled a notification—a new post from Sabrina's Instagram. For some sick reason, she'd followed her account after seeing her with Wells that night.

A picture appeared on her screen: Sabrina and Wells on the beach with the caption, "Spending the weekend with this hunk before our friend's wedding."

A bitch slap of epic proportions. Their wedding date was now a weekend thing.

Let's talk, my ass. Wells could fuck right off with that.

Cleo suddenly had the clarity she needed. She wasn't meant to be with someone like Wells, who could so easily move on to someone else. Cleo didn't doubt he cared for her, but she'd need more than that to slide out of the friends-with-benefits zone and into the L-trap.

"What's wrong, love?" Nigel asked upon seeing her expression.

"I hope that's not about Gus," Tori said.

"No. It's—nothing." She tossed her phone onto the bar. The app was still open to the picture of Wells and Sabrina.

"Oh, honey," Tori said, as she grabbed Cleo's phone and looked up at her with sad puppy eyes. "What's he doing with her?"

"What's who doing with who?" she asked, as if she didn't know exactly who Tori was talking about.

"I know about you and Wells," Tori said.

"What do you know?" Cleo demanded, ready to deflect any relationship accusations.

"You've been acting differently lately, like happier or something, and I figured it had to do with a guy."

"Probably me," Nigel offered.

"Dream on," Cleo teased.

"You acted goofy when Delaney said Wells had asked about you," Tori continued. "I figured it was him."

Cleo recalled Tori's glass-smashing intervention at the bar Sunday night.

"Did someone break your heart?" Nigel asked.

Cleo sighed, tired of the lies. She was ready to admit she needed the advice of her friends.

"All right, here's the deal. Wells and I have been hanging out, nothing serious. Until he told me he was falling for me. And I put the kibosh on it."

Tori clasped her chest, gasping, "Oh my gosh! How romantic!"

"Except no, Tori, it's not," Cleo said. "I wasn't looking for anything serious."

"But you found it!"

"Doesn't matter, if she didn't want it. Right, Cleo?" Nigel offered.

"Right," she said, turning to Tori. "You know I don't do relationships."

"I know that's your narrative, but maybe you can start a new one."

"So he can hurt me? No thanks."

"She thinks everyone's gonna hurt her," Tori explained to Nigel. "Her parents were neglectful."

"No need to sugarcoat it, Tor. You can go ahead and say it—they were abusive. To each other, and indirectly to me."

"Kids with past trauma often develop an internal alarm system as a protective mechanism to warn them of danger," Nigel said.

Panic attacks. Fear of intimacy. Bolting the second Wells went soft on her. It made sense.

Cleo nodded. "I'm damaged goods."

"No, not damaged," he said, placing his hand on hers. "Just informed. Your innate sense of self-protection tells you when a situation isn't to be trusted."

"She does it all the time with relationships," Tori said.

Nigel shrugged. "You just haven't met the right guy yet. You'll know it when you do. When you don't feel the need to shut down."

Cleo stared at Nigel in amazement. Was he some sort of shrink?

"How in the fuck could you know all this?"

"Did you have a similar upbringing, Nigel?" Tori asked, her eyes welling like the sympathy emoji.

Nigel smiled. "Nope, only child of two doting parents.

Mum still makes me text every night to let her know I got home. I'm almost thirty."

"But how—"

"I just read a lot." He turned to Cleo. "I can give Mum your number so she can text you in all caps every night, demanding to know if you're home."

Cleo laughed. "That sounds lovely."

"You're asking for it. She'll mother you to death."

When he turned to wait on a group of women who'd just arrived, Cleo drained her drink.

"We should probably get going," she said. "Almost time for the rehearsal."

"Okay, but first I need to know more about this Wells thing."

"Nothing to know. It's over," Cleo said. "Fun while it lasted, though."

She told Tori about seeing Wells with Sabrina on a date, and now the Instagram photo. Despite how it weighed on her, she also felt some relief in confiding to Tori. It was good to talk to a girlfriend about it, and not just a grumpy old man.

"I was right to bounce," she concluded. "How much could he have cared if he's already on to someone new, right?"

"Hmm," Tori said. "I'm not sure what to say."

"What's weird is, when I called the Tavern last night, he was there. With Gus. He told me he misses me and wants to talk. Almost fell for it, but no thanks, after he's shacking up with her all weekend."

Tori sighed. "Maybe you just need to—"

"Give a guy a chance," said a deeper voice.

Cleo's head shot up. Gus's words, coming from Nigel, across the bar.

"I'm working as fast as I can, ladies!" Nigel said to the group of middle-aged women flocking around him as he quickly poured shots, his words obviously meant for them.

"What are we celebrating?" he asked as they raised their drinks.

"To love!" one said.

"To Becks finding her soulmate!" yelled another.

"Congrats, Becks!" Nigel said as he raised his glass of water. "Who's the lucky man?"

"A guy she met in a bar. Can you believe it?"

"She had to kiss a lot of frogs before she found him," another explained.

"There's a lid for every pot," Nigel said, taking Cleo's breath away. "Congrats on finding yours. In a bar, no less!"

Kate

KATE'S MOUTH HUNG OPEN AS SHE STARED AT BRADY. Ryan. Whoever he was.

"I thought your name was Brady?" she stammered.

"Brady's my last name. First name, Ryan. So, you're—"

"Kate," she said. "Short for Kathryn."

"My friends and I never call each other by our actual names, as you could see from my texts. I guess I got off easy, only being called by my last name."

The whole thing almost toppled her out of her high strappy sandals. It wasn't just a meet-cute; it was a meet-cute with a twist. A twist of fate. Destiny doubled.

"How did you guys find each other?" Delaney asked, looking from Kate to Ryan. She must have noticed her sister's stunned expression because her eyes widened. "Oh, my God, Ryan! Are you Phone Guy?"

Kate and Ryan just smiled at each other.

"It looks that way," he said. "Speaking of which..." Ryan handed Kate her phone, and she reciprocated.

Dalton asked who Phone Guy was, and they filled him in on the story.

261

"I'm glad you finally met," Delaney said. "We figured you'd hit it off with so much in common, both working in politics and living within a few minutes of each other. If anything, we thought you'd become friends. But—maybe more."

Kate couldn't seem to take her eyes off Ryan. She hoped he was thinking the same thing she was.

News of Kate and Ryan's meet-cute spread like wildfire throughout the bridesmaids' camp. Once everyone arrived, they gathered on the lawn for the wedding rehearsal, buzzing around her to hear the details. They audibly swooned as Ryan emerged from the hotel and walked toward them, flanking Dalton on one side as Alex took up the other.

He came straight to Kate and kissed her hand.

Even Cleo, the world's biggest relationship cynic, seemed swept away. She threw her phone on the ground and cried, "Oh no, I dropped my phone! Has anyone seen it?"

Ryan wrapped his arm around Kate's waist. "Sorry, but I've already had my meet-cute for the weekend."

Delaney

DELANEY COULDN'T STOP STARING AT KATE AND RYAN AS they made their way to the beach, where the rehearsal would soon take place.

"Look at them," she whispered to Dalton. "It's like they were meant to be together."

"I can't believe we didn't think of this sooner," he said.

"Except I don't think we can take credit for it. The universe found a way to bring them together without our help."

"Now you're really sounding like Kate."

Delaney chuckled. "She may be on to something. Destiny

works in mysterious ways."

"Kind of like us."

Delaney smiled up at her handsome groom.

And then they went and practiced how to get married, even though they didn't need to.

On some level, they'd been married all along.

Marley

THE SUN SANK TOWARD THE HORIZON, CASTING THE SKY in hues of orange and purple. From its angle, Marley guessed it was around eight o'clock. By now, Sam and Jenna would be seated at a romantic restaurant, planning a future together.

Maarrlleeyy! the breeze seemed to whisper her name.

Or was it the wine? She'd only had one cup, maybe three, but certainly not enough to hear voices.

Until she heard it again.

She put her book down and sat up in her chair, preparing to run if necessary. Working in criminal justice had taught her to be on high alert and ready to defend personal safety at all times. Thank God too, because now here she was, alone on a beach, with nothing between her and the safety of her house but a potential killer.

She looked wildly around for a weapon and grabbed her (more than) half-empty bottle. She rose and turned slowly, hoping to see no one there but the ghost of wine bottle past.

Instead, a man in a suit sauntered across the sand—pants rolled to mid-calf, tie loosened, a pair of Gucci shoes in his left hand.

And in his right, tulips.

Marley laughed at the unexpected sight of Sam.

"You must be lost. Philly's that way," she joked, pointing north.

"Thanks for the directions, Google Maps," Sam answered. He continued to walk toward her with a lopsided smile, his gaze steady.

Marley's brain scrambled to make sense of what was happening. Was he here just to console her over her breakup?

He handed her the tulips. "For you."

Sam was here. With tulips. For her.

He reached into his pocket to retrieve something.

A napkin.

Their napkin—the one from the market on which he'd written notes on how to win someone's heart.

"I'm here to 'just be honest,' " Sam read, making air quotes with his free hand. "The time I had with you last week was the 'best time I've had in a long time.' "

He looked up and scowled. "Not really, the last two days were kinda brutal. But I digress."

Marley gasped and covered her mouth to keep from giggling. Sam continued to scan his notes. "Let's see, dated a lot of women, never found someone who makes you feel the way she does. I mean, you do...Oh, fuck it." He sighed and gazed at her the way he did at Penn's Landing. The way he did before he kissed her in her apartment. In her dream.

And now, standing before her. Crumpled napkin—and heart—in hand.

"I don't need a napkin or tulips to tell you how I feel, Marley May. Which, by the way, you were right—tulips are friggin' hard to find! I had to go to five florists. They're your favorite, right?"

The breath had been sucked out of her and she could only nod in utter shock.

He laced his fingers with hers and pulled her in. "You're incredibly hot in that bikini, you know." His voice was husky and low.

"Thanks. It's new," she said, finally finding her voice.

"I can tell."

Sam let go of her hand and pulled off the price tag dangling from her hip.

Whoops. She'd missed that.

He looped his fingers into the sides of her bikini bottom and gave her a shy smile. "Please tell me you haven't gotten back together with Rick in the last hour."

"Who's Rick?" Marley teased.

"Come here." He tugged her closer. "There's something I need to tell you. I love criminal law and I'm passionate about the pursuit of justice, and all that happy horseshit. But you, Marley Maguire, you're what I'm most passionate about. As if I didn't know it a long time ago, that kiss Tuesday night—*whew*. That sealed it for me. You give me the craziest butterflies."

Marley's heart pounded; her knees went weak.

"Someone far wiser than me once said, 'If you care about someone, let them know.' So, here's me, letting you know..." He inhaled as his ice-blue eyes melted into hers. "I am so crazy in love with you, Marley."

The world swirled around her, a mix of sand, sea, and sky. The only clear thing was Sam.

"Me too," she breathed.

"Oh my God." He hugged her hard, enveloped her, almost toppling over as they laughed. He pulled back and cupped her face with his hands. "You mean it?"

"Yes," Marley said, laughter bubbling from her as tears streamed down her face. "I love you, Sam. I've always loved you."

"She loves me!" Sam shouted as he gave a whoop. He picked her up and spun her around, then slid her down slowly in front of him.

"I don't believe this is happening," he whispered. "I've wanted to do this for so long."

She was afraid to ask but felt compelled to. "What about—?"

"Jenna?" he guessed. "This was never about her. This was always about you."

"But I thought Operation Get the Girl was to—"

"Get the girl. I asked you how to win someone's heart. I just withheld one tiny little detail—it was you. For six freaking years, it's been you."

She looked up at him, breathless once again.

"Jenna's been nothing more than a friend. Although, she did kinda come on to me that weekend, but I told her my heart belonged to someone else. She guessed it was you, and that I had it bad. Smart girl, just nothing compared to you."

Marley's heart swooned.

"Marley, Marley," Sam whispered, his arms wrapped tightly around her waist. "You've been it for me from the moment you saved my ass freshman year."

"Not your best moment," Marley said.

"Nah, but definitely yours. You were so serious, so smart. You saw right through my bullshit, and I loved that about you. I was instantly drawn to you. You and those big green eyes, and this crazy hair."

He wrapped a curl around his finger, his hungry eyes sweeping the length of her as his teeth grazed his lower lip.

"You're so freaking hot. How could you ever think I'd have eyes for anyone but you?"

She was overwhelmed by Sam's admission and swept away by the tsunami of desire rushing through her as she realized Sam was her destiny. On some level, she'd always known that—they just had to navigate their way through a beautiful friendship and around their own insecurities to find each other's hearts.

She thought back to that pivotal moment in time when destiny brought them together for a chance at friendship. Thank God she'd made the choice to join him that night when it all began—the study session for two. It was just as Kate described during the conversation at Delaney's bachelorette party: where choice meets chance, there lies destiny. Their happily ever after.

"You're not as transparent as you think," Marley said as she smiled up at him. "I'm just glad I agreed to join you for a study group."

"Yeah, about that." Sam chuckled. "There was no group."

"So *that's* why nobody showed up."

"Sorry for that, but I didn't want to let another dude get to know you the way I hoped to." He chuckled. "And then... That Night. Girl, you have no idea how hard it was to turn you down."

Marley smiled. "Not *my* best moment."

"I disagree. You could've done that striptease to circus music, riding a unicycle, eating a corn dog. I still would've been massively turned on, as I was that night."

"You're in luck, Barnum and Bailey. The show's about to begin."

"I hope so," Sam said. "All I could think about that summer was you. I was gonna tell you how I felt when I got home, ask you on a real date, but you'd just started dating Rick. You seemed totally into him, and I wanted to respect that. Nice guy and all, but not for you. I tried to tell you, that night I met him."

"When I asked what my type was, and you doused me with beer?"

"I worked on that move for a while. Really wanted the moment to be right."

So she hadn't imagined it.

"For years, I've tried to be your Mr. Right. Being your friend, getting you coffee, carrying your bags. Holding your hair back when you puked. Hanging out with you and your *boy*friend. Waiting, hoping you'd realize I was the one who was madly, deeply, ridiculously in love with you."

"Oh, Sam..." His words shot straight to her heart.

He cupped her face with his hands and whispered, "I want to kiss you so badly. But I don't want to be your rebound guy."

"Rick was my rebound guy," she said, her voice husky. "Rick happened because I didn't think you felt the same."

"Maybe this will convince you." Sam lowered his mouth to hers, lingering before gently brushing her lips with his.

He kissed her softly, lightly. But soon his mouth's caresses intensified, moaning as lips parted, tongues probed.

A jolt of electricity shot through her, a hundred times stronger than the night at Penn's Landing. And this kiss, oh this kiss *right here*, was a thousand times better than the one in her apartment. Because this one was for real, the culmination of a mutual and unspoken attraction sizzling below the surface for years, all while being brushed off, excused away, rationalized, ignored.

Now it lay bare, uncovered. Honest. True.

The sun discreetly tucked itself below the horizon and the moon took its place, basking them in the soft glow of dusk.

"Hey, friend," he whispered between kisses. "I have a question for you."

"Yes?"

"There's this wedding coming up, not sure if you know about it. Will you be my plus-one?"

"Yes," Marley said, giggling. "I'll be your plus-one for Delaney's wedding."

"And every wedding thereafter," he whispered.

Kate

KATE AND RYAN COULDN'T STOP STEALING GLANCES AT each other during the beach rehearsal as the sun set behind them. Afterward, as the group made their way into the hotel for dinner, Delaney pulled Kate aside.

"What do you think?" she asked. "Pretty awesome, isn't he?"

"He's dreamy," Kate said. "I just can't get over the fact he was the guy in the bar, then Phone Guy, and now my blind date. How you can you possibly say destiny isn't a thing?"

"You may have changed my mind about that," Delaney said. "I guess we aren't always in total control of our future. I'm learning it's important to let some magic in, once in a while."

"I knew you'd come around," she said, giving Delaney a hug.

Kate was excited about the wedding and couldn't wait to get to know Ryan better. She said a silent prayer, thanking God for her older sister, who seemed to know better what Kate wanted than she, herself, knew.

Cleo

AFTER THE REHEARSAL DINNER WAS OVER, CLEO WENT TO her room to retrieve Delaney and Dalton's wedding gift.

"Hey, guys," she said as she approached their table. "I hope you don't mind, but I'd like to give you my wedding present tonight. It requires an explanation."

"Of course!" Delaney exclaimed, her eyes lighting up when Cleo lifted the large, rectangular, wrapped gift, obviously a framed painting. "An original?"

"Kinda," Cleo said.

Delaney and Dalton gingerly unwrapped the gift and gasped.

"Oh my!" Delaney exclaimed, clasping her hand to her mouth, tears flooding her eyes.

"Cleo," Dalton said, his eyes watering too. "How did you—"

"It's from a picture my grandmother took," Cleo told them. "I found it when I was cleaning out her stuff."

The second she saw the tattered photo, she knew she'd have to paint it for their wedding gift. It was of Delaney and Dalton, age eight, building a sandcastle together. Significant, because the pair had met over Delaney's destroyed sandcastle. The following year, when the picture was taken, the two were starting to become friends. Now, here they were, about to build a life together.

"This is the summer you all had chicken pox, wasn't it?" Delaney asked.

Cleo nodded.

Delaney bumped her shoulder against Dalton. "Remember? We were the only ones untouched, and you were the only kid I had to play with. This was the day we became friends."

"I do remember," Dalton whispered. He wiped his tears and stood up.

"Come here, sweetie," he said as he wrapped Cleo in an embrace. "This means so much to me."

"To us both," Delaney said as she joined in the hug. "I feel like Grandma's still with us."

"It's a gift from her as well," Cleo added, choking up. "She knew she wasn't going to be here for your big day, so I showed it to her before she died. She included a special note for you."

Cleo pulled an envelope she'd affixed to the back and handed it to Delaney. She looked on as the couple read her grandmother's note. Cleo had helped her write it and knew the general sentiment behind it. Grandma had watched them grow up together, fall in love, lose and find each other again. She was even there when they got engaged, as the families gathered on the Rosses' deck to watch Dalton's beach proposal.

Delaney held the note to her chest when they finished reading it, and the three of them wiped away more tears. Then she picked up the painting again and gazed at it.

"This is, and will always be, a most treasured gift," she said. "Like your friendship."

Dalton offered to take the painting to their room for safekeeping, and Delaney was pulled away by the wedding coordinator to go over last-minute details.

As her friends walked away, Cleo thought about the one small detail of the photo she'd kept from them. She, too, had been in the photograph, standing to the side, watching. Furloughed from chicken pox prison to get some fresh air, she'd begged to join her friends in building the castle, but her grandmother made her keep her distance. She had Cleo smile for the camera as her friends played behind her.

For obvious reasons, Cleo had chosen not to capture that part of the scene in her painting—the little girl on the sideline, whose fake smile couldn't hide the loneliness in her eyes. The one who didn't belong. Either on the beach that day while her friends built the sandcastle, or at home with her parents, or in a loving adult relationship now.

Didn't belong anywhere, it seemed.

The DJ started playing music and couples flooded the dance floor. Nigel swooped Tori into an embrace. Wells twirled Sabrina. Delaney and Dalton eventually joined them, looking more in love than ever.

Once again, Cleo watched from the sidelines.

Still holding her grandmother's letter, she opened the envelope and reread it.

I hope you realize you're surrounded by all the people who love you. As long as you remember that, you'll never be alone. May love be all around you—this day, and forever.

She sighed when she got to the last line.

Love was all around, for certain. Just not for her.

271

Saturday, June 17

WEDDING DAY

Delaney

SUNBEAMS DANCED ACROSS DELANEY'S CRISP WHITE bedspread and burst into a spectrum of sparkling color reflecting off the ring on her left hand. Exactly how a bride should awaken on her wedding day—to a spectacular diamond light show.

She threw back her covers and leaped to her feet, excited to get the day started. Her bridesmaids would be there soon, along with the stylists she'd hired to help the bridal party get ready.

A knock came at the door. "Room service."

Delaney opened the door to a Disney parade of hotel workers, wheeling in carts of silver cloches covering hot breakfast items. A beverage cart was next, boasting silver urns of coffee and hot water for tea. Still more staff poured into the room, setting up bar tables and snapping on linen tablecloths while others arranged baskets of assorted pastries, fruit, and other goodies. Still more with trays of plates, coffee mugs, and water glasses.

And then, just as quickly as they came, the staff disappeared. The door was closing as a man's hand reached out to hold it open.

"Father-daughter time!" he cried out.

"Daddy!" Delaney rushed to greet her father, hugging him with careful yet exuberant enthusiasm. It was the first time she'd seen him since he was released from the hospital.

"Sorry I wasn't here for the rehearsal last night, but I had a good excuse."

"I'm gonna have to see a doctor's note."

It looked as if he was hiding something behind his back.

"I wanted to pop over and give you a special gift before the party begins."

From behind his back, he pulled a gift wrapped in turquoise paper and tied with a tangerine bow.

"My wedding colors!" she exclaimed.

"Your mom's doing."

He explained the gift was from her grandmother. Delaney's eyes filled with tears. So thoughtful of both Cleo and her dad to give her gifts originating from their beloved grandmothers, who were like second moms to both girls growing up. Neither would be there today to share in her joy but, as she unwrapped the gift, she could feel their presence.

"She asked me to give this to you on your wedding day if she wasn't here to do it herself," her dad said, choking up.

It was a journal, filled with her grandmother's neat handwriting.

"She started writing in it the day we brought you home. She knew you'd be curious about where you came from. She wanted to capture every little thing she could about you, to make up for missing pieces."

Delaney was overwhelmed. "Oh my God..."

"She wrote down everything you said and did. Your first words, funny sayings, memories of the special times you spent together. She even did some research. Here."

He flipped to the back of the book, where her grandmother had written the few details they knew about Delaney's adoption, such as the hospital where she was born and the name of the adoption agency.

"You were born before the internet was really developed, so we didn't have much to go on, even after we got a computer. And it turns out Pennsylvania adoption records are sealed. I'm sorry there's not more we can tell you. But like I said, they do have those DNA test kits now, in case you ever want to learn more."

THE WAY TO CAPE MAY

Delaney thanked her father and hugged him. "I don't care what happened before you guys. You gave me life."

"And you gave us ours."

Kate

THE BRIDESMAIDS WERE DRESSED IN MATCHING TURquoise silk robes, sipping champagne, as stylists flitted about the room doing their hair and makeup.

"Hey, sis," Kate said, coming up behind Delaney after their hair and makeup were done. She snapped a selfie of the two of them..

Delaney turned her head to kiss Kate on the cheek.

"That's for being the best sister and maid of honor a bride could ask for."

"The pleasure's all mine," Kate said, giving her a kiss in return.

"Oh wait—cute sister moment!" Cleo exclaimed as she snapped a photo of them.

"Send that to me, please," Kate said.

The familiar ding of an incoming text was a welcome sound. It was good to have her own phone back, not to mention the bonus that came with it—a very cute, very available blind date who was beginning to rock her world.

But the text wasn't from Cleo, as expected. It was from Greg, asking if she'd received his previous text.

"Shit," she mumbled.

She'd never responded to his text from two days ago. She started typing.

> Hey! Sorry I haven't responded.
> Today's Delaney's wedding day! Talk
> next week?

> Awesome! Tell them I said congrats!
> Congress Hall, still?

> Of course!

Greg had still been in the picture when Delaney and Dalton got engaged, and her sister's heart had been set on Congress Hall as their venue from the start.

A chorus of oohs and aahs sang out as Delaney slipped into her gown. She was stunning.

Kate released a flood of tears, more excited about the wedding than anticipated. Her sister was marrying someone she'd loved for years, and Kate was about to walk down the aisle with someone who had captured her own heart.

Bonus: he'd be wearing a tux—perhaps a preview of things to come.

Cleo

IT WAS ALMOST GO-TIME FOR THE BRIDE AND HER ENTOU-rage. Cleo sucked back the last of her champagne, marveling at the magic the stylists had worked, transitioning her from edgy to sophisticated.

The photographer directed Delaney and her mom to the mirror to affix her veil. Cleo looked on, knowing this was something she and her own mom would never share, but she took joy in witnessing her friend's tender moment.

Her eyes met Delaney's in the reflection, and it took her back to Halloween, circa age nine, when Delaney had dressed as a bride and tried to convince Cleo to be her groom.

"I'm not going as a boy," Cleo had said defiantly as she lay upside down on Delaney's bed, head hanging off the side.

She was already planning to dress as a farmer (a boy), she just didn't want to wear a tux. A flannel shirt and bandana were as far as she was willing to stray into men's fashion.

"But I need a groom!" Delaney cried, making a veil from a pillowcase.

"Get a boy to do it," Cleo said. "Besides, my mom says no woman needs a man."

"Some women do. My mom needs my dad."

"My mom doesn't, and I won't either. Men are just gross grown-up boys."

"You'll change your mind someday," Delaney predicted with the wisdom of a woman four times her age.

"Why don't you get Dalton to be your groom?" Cleo taunted, knowing the reaction she'd draw. She rolled onto her stomach to watch.

"Gross!" Delaney yelled, throwing a stuffed animal at Cleo. "Dalton is a gross boy with gross boy cooties!"

"Delaney and Dalton, sitting in a tree, K-I-S-S-I-N-G," Cleo had teased. "First comes...COOTIES!"

Delaney shrieked and ran across the room. She clamped her hand over Cleo's mouth and wrestled her to the floor. Cleo continued singing through Delaney's hand until they were breathless from laughter.

The tears stinging Cleo's eyes brought her back to the present. Now it was real. Her oldest and dearest friend was about to marry the love of her life, who'd proven not to be a gross boy with gross boy cooties. Or so Cleo hoped—otherwise, she'd just wasted a shit ton of money on a bridesmaid dress she'd never wear again.

"Delaney and Dalton, sitting in a tree..." Cleo sang softly to Delaney's reflection.

"Oh my gosh, Cleo!" Her friend's eyes welled with tears, and she waved her hands in front of her face. "Stop. My mascara!"

"Love you, Laney," she said softly, her heart swelling as she blew her friend a kiss.

"Love you too, Cleo."

It was at that moment Cleo finally understood what all the hype was about.

Love came in all forms, and was something to cherish, not fear. She felt fortunate for the love of her besties, and Gus, and her surrogate family. As for the romantic kind, Nigel was correct in his psychoanalysis—she just hadn't found the right person yet to share it with. But she knew it was out there.

Love was waiting in the wings, to take away her loss.

Marley

MARLEY AND SAM HELD HANDS AS THEY MADE THEIR way toward the beach, no longer attempting to hide their feelings from themselves or the world. When they approached the end of the beach path, Sam pulled her in for a slow, purposeful kiss.

"You have no idea how many times I've imagined doing that in public," he said. "And how many times I almost did."

"Me too."

"And everything else," he said, giving her a lustful grin. He let out a soft whimper as he pulled her closer. "Girl, you rock my world. I can't wait for tonight. Get ready for me to ravish you again.

"Mmm," Marley moaned into his kiss.

Did they really have to go to this wedding?

For the past twenty-four hours, they'd explored every square inch of each other's bodies. Marley was finally able to touch him in all the places she'd either gawked at or dreamed of for the past six years. The feel of his strong arms around her as he carried her to the bed, their legs entwining as they kissed, their naked bodies pressed together. The way he entered her as if they were made for each other, succumbing to one explosive orgasm after another, laying her head on his chest when they were spent. His touch was like nothing she could have ever imagined. Just when she thought they had nothing left, they'd be at it again. She, too could hardly wait for tonight, their first hotel stay together as a couple.

"Delaney's gonna lose her shit when she finds out about this," he said.

"In a good or bad way?"

"Good, of course."

"I hope you're right. I'd hate to jeopardize my career for a one-night stand."

"Those days are over," he said.

"I was talking about me."

Sam laughed and kissed her again. "Let's go witness this sensational wedding."

"Okay, *People* magazine. Lead the way."

A string quartet played aside a simple white arch, the soft music setting the tone for an elegant ceremony. As they took their seats, she caught a glimpse of Delaney and the bridesmaids gathering at the end of the aisle. Even from where she sat, Marley could see the joy radiating from her as she prepared to marry her best friend.

Maybe one day she'd be so lucky too. As she turned back to face the altar, Sam caught her lips in a quick kiss, the look in his eyes conveying his thoughts.

Someday.

He put his arm around her and wrapped a curl around his finger. Bringing it to his lips, he kissed it and whispered in her ear.

"Mine."

Delaney

DELANEY TOOK A DEEP BREATH AS EACH OF HER BRIDES-maids walked down the aisle in turn. Her dad kissed her on the cheek, and then it happened: the moment she'd been waiting for, the one that almost didn't.

As the familiar strains of the processional began, Delaney and her father stepped off the wooden pathway and started the long walk toward her new life.

This was the part of the day she'd been most nervous about, having hundreds of eyes upon her as she hoped against a flip-flop blowout or a wind-sailing veil. While she was comfortable being center stage in a courtroom, she avoided it at all costs in her personal life. But with her dad by her side, now healthy and strong, she felt balanced and protected.

She kept her eyes focused on her handsome, sobbing groom waiting for her at the end of the aisle. By the time they made it to the altar, Delaney's dad was ugly crying too.

The couple had written their own vows and Dalton was to go first. He bit his lip as he prepared to speak.

Instead, he belted out the first line from the song "On the Way to Cape May." Their song, the same one her bridesmaids sang the night of her bachelorette party.

Delaney chuckled nervously, waiting for him to say he was messing around. It wasn't completely out of character for him to break out in song, but she assumed, today of all days, he'd be as nervous as she was.

But then best man Alex popped out from behind Dalton and sang the second line, followed by her dad, who stood up and belted out the third as guests kept time finger-snapping.

Delaney looked around in utter shocked delight.

The rest of the groomsmen jumped in, swaying back and forth as they sang, followed by the bridesmaids with the same choreographed moves. One by one, guests stood and sang their lines until she heard a chorus of voices behind her. She spun around to find a large crowd of beachgoers who'd also joined in the singing, with the same choreographed moves. Delaney took it all in, this joyful, unexpected serenade.

In his final act as Groomzilla, Dalton had planned one last surprise: a singing flash mob.

The chorus gave way to a singular voice—Dalton's—who sang the last line of their song, asking her to be his spouse.

"I know I promised no more surprises," Dalton whispered in her ear as their guests cheered. "I hope you'll forgive me this last one."

Delaney gazed up at Dalton, tears streaming down her face. "I more than forgive you. Please don't ever stop surprising me."

Cleo

CLEO LOOPED HER ARM WITH HER BRIDAL PARTY PARTNER to begin the recessional, when something dark and curly caught her eye. It was the tousled mop of a certain Englishman, sitting by himself in the second to last row. The Baron of Beautiful British Bartenders.

He waved at Cleo as she passed, and her heart leaped.

Down, girl—he was here as Tori's date.

After the wedding party photo session, Cleo and Tori hightailed it to the cocktail party on the lawn. High-top tables were adorned with linens, billowing in the soft sea breeze.

Guests mingled at the tables while others sat in Adirondack chairs overlooking the ocean.

It looked like a scene from a movie—all these beautiful people sipping seaside like Gatsby guests while the sun slid beneath the horizon. Polite waitstaff in crisp white shirts and black vests butlered hors d'oeuvres while a jazz quintet played softly in the background.

It was almost too perfect.

Cleo hoped something amusing would happen, like a dog would come out of nowhere and leap from table to table. Or a waiter would fall in the pool with a tray full of drinks. Not her drink, of course, but others'.

That would be hilarious.

"I spy, with my little eye, a certain hot bartender," Tori announced.

Nigel appeared to be juggling something to the amusement of a small child. Puff pastries, it turned out, most likely borrowed from the tastefully decorated tower of treats topping one of the tables.

Now, this was amusing.

Nigel caught each pastry successively. "Okay, Eli, your turn. Remember what I said, start with one, then add another when your timing's down."

Cleo was instantly charmed. Not only by Nigel's easygoing attitude and kid-friendliness, but his stellar juggling talent. He was checking off boxes Cleo didn't even know she had. He'd spent the last hour at a cocktail party where he knew nobody, but he'd made a friend and taught someone to juggle hors d'oeuvres in the process. What more could you want in a man?

Nigel encouraged Eli as he started his practice, and then walked over to the women, hugging Tori, then Cleo. "Wow. You clean up good."

"Thanks. Not so bad yourself, for a barkeep," Cleo said,

trying to avoid eye contact. He was Tori's date, and not hers for visual consumption. "I need a drink."

"What do you ladies fancy? I'll get it."

Cleo minded herself for once and refrained from answering his question with "you" again. After all, he was here with her friend, and Cleo was dressed like a lady-who-lunches. She should probably act the part—even if she was the furthest thing from a lady, and rarely awake before lunch.

She tried extra hard not to watch Nigel as he swaggered away. Epic fail—she was only human.

When he returned with their drinks, Tori offered a toast.

"To new friendships and new beginnings."

Cleo caught the look passing between Tori and Nigel as they clinked glasses. Knowing when to take a cue, she left the googly-eyed couple and went in search of her own date. She found Kirk in a sea of other gamers, talking—what else—video games. She checked in with him to see if he needed anything—a drink, a Happy Meal, some Bitcoin—but he was fine. She wasn't even sure why she brought him.

Oh, that's right. He understood the most important etiquette required of a wedding date: the art of getting lost.

Kate

KATE AND RYAN STOOD AT A HIGH-TOP TABLE ENJOYING Delaney and Dalton's signature drink, aptly named Tangerine Sunset. Other guests mingled around them, but they could've been naked as far as Kate was concerned. She could only see Ryan.

"You look beautiful," he said for the fifth time since they first linked arms during the recessional. She hadn't been able to stop stealing glances at him during the wedding—she'd never seen a guy wear a tux so well.

"Thank you," she said, blushing. "I'm excited to get to know more about you." They'd been tied up with rehearsal activities the previous evening and hadn't had much time to talk.

"I know a lot about you," Ryan said, smiling. "I asked a million questions before agreeing to be your date."

"What do you know?"

"You live in Alexandria. And you're a successful environmental lobbyist."

"I try," Kate said. "Here's what I know about you..."

Hmm. What had Delaney told her about Ryan? She came up with nothing. She must have blocked it out due to disinterest.

"You nailed it," he said, when she didn't go on.

"No, it's coming to me. You live in..."

"Georgetown," he said. "Not far from you."

"You're—something to do with politics?"

"Wow, Delaney gave away all my secrets. Political analyst."

They launched into a discussion of their favorite hangouts, discovering they had several in common.

"Do you think we ever saw each other out before?" Kate mused.

"Not in DC. Trust me, I'd remember. But we have met before."

He must have her confused with someone else. She would have remembered meeting someone so fine.

"I believe we were five," he said. "My family was visiting Dalton's shore house. You and I were partnered up for a three-legged race, and we won. We even beat the teens."

"Wait, that was you?" Kate vaguely recalled the race but didn't realize it was Ryan. Both families had a gaggle of relatives cycling through their summer homes, and it was hard to keep everyone straight. "Did you visit often?"

"Only when we were little," he said. "My family moved

overseas when I was in second grade, so I never spent summers in the US as a teen. Shame too. We coulda had a shot at the Olympics."

"Do you still dabble in three-leg, or have you retired?"

"Heck no. There's too much race left in me. I'm ready to challenge anyone who wants to take on the dream team. How 'bout them?" He nodded toward an octogenarian couple.

"Dude, they're the reigning Russian champs," she joked. "I thought you knew this sport?"

Ryan laughed out loud. "I had no idea a blind date could be so fun," he said, brushing a strand of hair from her forehead. "I've never felt such—I dunno, is this what chemistry feels like?"

"I think so," she said, breathless. She'd never felt it, either. Not with Greg, definitely not with Shoe Fetish guy, not with anyone.

As the sun made its graceful dive toward the horizon, Ryan leaned in closer, his indigo eyes reflecting the same passion stirring within her.

"Is it okay if I kiss you?" he asked in a husky whisper.

She nodded, gazing up at him, as his lips found hers. For a moment she wondered vaguely if Delaney and Dalton had requested fireworks for their wedding, but then she realized it was just the best kiss of her life.

She had no idea if the other guests were still milling around, if they were staring, ignoring them, or doing the hokeypokey. She didn't give Two Shits about what was going on beyond them. Soon it would be time to go inside for the wedding party introductions, but she couldn't think of a place she'd rather be.

Here on the grand lawn of Congress Hall, kissing the hell out of Ryan Brady.

The blind date that almost wasn't.

Cleo

HOURS LATER, THE RECEPTION WELL UNDERWAY, CLEO had just finished talking with Delaney's parents when she went to search for her friends. They were all on the dance floor, once again coupled up.

Nigel pulled Tori in close. He whispered in her ear and Tori threw her head back in laughter. A tiny stab of jealousy was soothed by happiness for her friend. Tori had found a keeper, for sure. Nigel was an absolute gem, and Cleo couldn't remember the last time her friend had laughed so heartily.

Next to them, Wells and Sabrina glided around the floor like they were final contestants on *Dancing with the Stars*. Cleo had to admit, they looked like they belonged together: two beautiful people who had everything going for them. Including law degrees, which meant they could sue the fuck out of anyone who wronged them. *(Note to self: don't wrong them.)*

The observation made her realize: Wells wasn't her person. Not when he so easily glided out of her life into the arms of another, with whom he appeared to fit so well.

Cleo's eyes shifted to Delaney and Dalton, who looked as if they were in another world, foreheads touching, talking to one another as they swayed to the music. Another couple who belonged together.

Cleo stood there, waiting for the feels to come. She listened for the old mantra to begin playing in her head, always there to remind her of how alone in the world she was. Unlovable. Unworthy. She expected to feel the same way she felt as a child on the beach that day—in the scene, but not a part of it.

Yet as she stood on the edge of the party, looking in, something had changed.

Perhaps it was Gus's constant banging of the "you're lovable" drum. Or the fact that Wells had once made her feel that way. Maybe Nigel's recent psychoanalysis played a role, or she was just seeing the world through rosé-colored glasses after having a few. Whatever it was, she was no longer the misfit, the third wheel, the child nobody wanted, the adult no one could love. It was her right to take up space and belong, wherever she was. She was going to be okay.

Better than okay.

Watching her friends having fun, Cleo realized her grandmother's words to Delaney and Dalton had been written just as much for her as for the newlyweds. Love was all around her—from her surrogate family to friends, new and old—it was just a different kind of love. As long as she remembered that, she'd never be alone.

Cleo smiled as a couples switch appeared to occur on the dance floor. Dalton slid over to Tori and took her from Nigel's arms, as Delaney pulled Wells into an embrace. Sabrina waltzed over to Nigel. The three couples laughed as they switched partners again, men with men, women with women.

Suddenly, Wells broke away and danced over to Cleo.

"May I have this dance, my lady?" He bent at the waist in a formal bow.

"Who you callin' a lady?" she joked.

Cleo took his offered hand. He whisked her to the dance floor and twirled her around. Fuck law, this man should seriously consider a career in ballroom dance. As the song ended, he dipped her. She grabbed onto his shoulders for dear life, afraid he'd drop her.

"Don't worry, friend," he said as he smiled down at her. "I got you."

He pulled her back up and whispered, "Can we go have that talk now?"

Delaney

"**H**EY, BRIDE," DALTON SAID.

He wrapped his arm around her waist and pulled her in close as the band began playing their favorite song from high school.

"That's wife to you," Delaney joked.

"Hi, wife," he said, smiling down at her. "That's going to take some getting used to."

"I hear ya, hubs. Wow, what a nice ring."

"Not as nice as this one." He raised his left hand and admired the new wedding band that had replaced his engagement placeholder.

"I can't believe we did it," she said.

"We did. And—"

"Wait!" Delaney stopped dancing and pivoted Dalton around. "Please tell me I'm seeing what I think I'm seeing?"

Dalton followed her gaze. "A girl and guy kissing? Oh wait, that's not just any girl. It's Marley, right?"

Delaney nodded, her mouth hanging open.

"Must be her boyfriend, or—holy shit! Is that Sam?" Dalton spun back around to look at Delaney. "When did *that* happen?"

"I don't know," she said, "but it's about fucking time!"

Marley

MARLEY MELTED INTO SAM AS THEY SWAYED TO THE music.

"We fit perfectly together, Marley May," Sam said, his voice husky. "And just so you know, now that I gotcha, I'm never letting you go."

"You better not," she said.

He leaned down and kissed her, urgently, passionately. She wondered if she would ever get used to how good it felt to be kissed by him.

After the song, he took her hand and they walked to the beach. Climbing into a lifeguard stand away from the glare of lights, they looked up at the star-studded sky.

"There's one," Marley said, pointing at a shooting star falling from the night sky.

"Our shooting star," Sam said. "We shall name it..."

"Moist Styrofoam Chicken Strip."

Sam chuckled. "Look at you, being all romantic and shit. Oh, wait." He pointed beyond her to where the wedding arch still stood. "Come on!"

He jumped off the stand and helped her down. Scooping her up, he carried her across the sand.

She laughed and snuggled his neck. "You're crazy."

"Love makes you do weird things," he said.

He set her down a few feet from the arch, standing behind her as he wrapped his arms around her waist.

"I predict you and I are gonna stand under an arch like that someday," he whispered as he kissed her neck.

"You think?" she asked.

"I know."

"Okay, Nostradamus. Whatever you say."

He turned her around, cupping her face in his hands, his gaze intense. "And then...I'm gonna marry the hell out of you."

Once again, Sam Adams made Marley Maguire's heart burst. She'd loved him for so long but never in a million years dreamed she'd be standing here, his arms wrapped around her, talking about spending their lives together.

She looked up at him with a teasing smile. "But first, you have to win my heart."

"I've had six years of practice, but I'm just getting started."

Kate

RYAN TOOK KATE'S HAND AND LED HER TO THE DANCE floor.

He wrapped his arm around her and pulled her in close, whispering in her ear. "Kate, I don't know what it is about you—about us—but I've never felt like this before."

"Me either," Kate said.

She finally understood what people meant when they said they had an instant connection with someone. It was too soon to even think it, but perhaps this is what love at first sight felt like.

"Delaney and Dalton were spot-on when they decided to fix us up," he said. "I've never loved my cousin more than I do right now."

"I feel the same about my sister. Sometimes your family knows what's good for you, even when you don't."

"We should have our first official date at the Princeton," Ryan joked. "Finish what I tried to start before the bar fight. Maybe we can find those dueling dudes and thank them."

"Let's not forget to acknowledge the starring role OtterBoxes played in this story, causing us to grab the wrong phones."

"Except you're forgetting we would have met each other the next night at the rehearsal, anyway," Ryan said.

"True, but I'd already decided I wasn't going to like you. Especially after I'd gone and met the coolest guy on my own, not knowing he was the same guy Delaney had been trying to push on me."

"Push on you?" Ryan chuckled, his eyebrows raised.

"Relentlessly. She couldn't stop saying what a great guy you are."

"Maybe I'm with the wrong sister," he teased.

"Too late, friend. Her ship's already sailed."

"Look at them."

Kate followed his gaze. The newlyweds were dancing, deep in conversation and looking so in love it was palpable from across the room. They truly made the perfect couple.

"That's what being with the right person looks like," Kate said.

She looked up to find Ryan staring at her.

"And so is this," he said as he kissed her.

"Hey, guys, I hate to interrupt..." Tori was standing next to them, waving. "I'm heading out early. I have a lot of packing to do."

"I'm so excited for your trip!" Kate exclaimed as she gave her a hug. She asked questions about her travel plans and Tori filled her in on the details.

The song ended, and Delaney and Cleo joined them, offering to walk Tori out while she awaited her ride. Kate excused herself from Ryan to join them.

Outside, a thin veil of fog had rolled in from the ocean. Tori's ride arrived and after one last goodbye, the women turned to go back inside. At the last minute, Tori grabbed Kate's hand.

"He seems like a sweetheart," Tori said when the others were out of earshot.

"He does, doesn't he? I'm kinda blown away."

"I heard you when you said you're lonely. I know how that feels. I hope he's a good one and makes you happy."

Kate thanked her and made her promise to send pictures

of her travel adventures. Tori climbed into her Uber and Kate waved as the car pulled away.

Across the street, a figure emerged from the fog.

The shape of his body, the stride in his step as he walked toward her, were all too familiar.

"Kate," he said as he stepped up onto the curb.

It was Greg.

Cleo

WELLS TOOK HER HAND—IN FRONT OF EVERYONE—BUT this time, Cleo didn't mind. He led her to the beach, where they sat on a bench.

"So," he said, taking a deep breath. "I know I suggested talking after wedding, but what I have to say is important and can't wait."

"Look, Wells, I don't think—"

"It's gonna work?" he said. "I know."

"You and Sabrina—"

"This isn't about Sabrina," Wells said. "It's about you and me."

Cleo took his hands, facing him. "I owe you a huge apology for everything, mostly telling you I didn't do relationships when, you're right, we were already in one. At the time, I couldn't risk you finding out I wasn't worth it."

"First, you are worth it. And second, I knew that's what you were doing."

Wells brushed a wayward bang from her forehead. "We spent a lot of time together, Clee. Whether you realize it or not, I'm a pretty good judge of character. I sensed your fear but thought I could be the guy who'd help you conquer it."

"In a way, you did," Cleo said. "You never once made me feel unworthy of a relationship—I did that all myself. But if

I'm being honest, I was falling for you too. Just too stubborn to admit it."

"It's probably for the best, right?" Wells asked. His eyes searched hers, as if he sought affirmation. "Gus told me you're moving to New York to pursue an art career. I think that's awesome. You're so talented, you need to give it a shot."

"Thanks, Wells."

"And I have a career here that I love. Not the right time or place for either of us."

Cleo put her head on his shoulder. As much as she cared for Wells, he wasn't her person. In Nigel's words, if he was, she wouldn't have felt the need to bolt.

"You changed my whole outlook on relationships, Cleo," Wells said. "I wasn't looking for one, but hanging out with you was so fun, so easy. I was insanely attracted to you even though you're the opposite of what I usually go for."

Cleo couldn't help the laugh that bubbled out of her. "Me too."

"The whole thing crept up on me. I didn't see it coming," he continued. He took her hand and met her eyes. "And that's because you gave me the space to be me, without pressure for more."

"You did the same for me."

He gave a soft chuckle as he shook his head. "Girl, you're unlike anyone I've ever known. Exciting. Sexy. Brilliant. You keep me on my toes. You make me laugh like nobody else ever has."

Everything he said translated to one word in Gus-speak: lovable.

"To be honest, I wasn't just falling for you," he said. "I'd already fallen. Hard."

"I'm curious, though. Why didn't you fight for me?" Cleo asked. "Try to talk sense into me? I think that's what I was waiting for. Hoping for."

Wells was silent for a moment, then lifted her chin and looked at her.

"'That's what I'm doing now," he whispered. "Fighting for you. The only way I know how. By letting you go, not forcing you into something you don't want."

There was a vulnerability in his eyes that told her he still had feelings for her.

"Go pursue your dreams. I'll always be here, your biggest fan. I can't wait to come visit you in your gallery."

"I love you, Wells," she said as she kissed him. This time, just a peck on the cheek.

The kind you give a good friend.

Kate

GREG SAUNTERED OVER TO KATE, A SHEEPISH SMILE ON his face. He pulled her into a long, tight hug as if no time had passed between them. His embrace instantly transported her to the past, and all her feelings came rushing back, a force of habit.

"You look amazing," he said, pulling back to gaze at her.

She was stunned silent, mouth agape, heart threatening to flop onto the sidewalk.

Greg Fallon, CEO of the Sea, had surfed back into her life.

"I hope you don't mind me crashing the party." He gave a nervous chuckle as he ran a hand through his sun-streaked hair. It flopped obediently back over his one eye, as one would expect from the locks of a legit surfer.

"I thought you were in California." Kate swallowed, her mouth dry. She had no idea why she felt nervous, other than the fact that her glamorous ex-boyfriend was standing in front of her, looking so fine.

"I flew in to spend the week with friends before the reunion. My buddies and I were doing a pub crawl, and I broke away to see you."

It felt good to see him. He looked relaxed and happy (Successful! Rich!). And damn, the magazine photos did zero justice in showing just how toned, tan, and ten (plus) he was.

But this wasn't the place—certainly not the time—for the reunion she'd been hoping for all week. Although, shout-out to destiny for making this happen at a time when her hair was done and her makeup fierce. Squeezed into flattering, form-fitting formalwear instead of being poured half-assed into the sloppy, coffee-stained sweats she'd otherwise be donning on a Saturday night.

"It's great seeing you, Greg. I'm glad you stopped by, but I should—" She waved toward the hotel. "You know, the wedding—and stuff. Maybe we can talk next week?"

She wasn't sure why she was inviting further discussion, especially now that Ryan was in the picture. Perhaps she needed that closure she'd been seeking, although if her racing heart was any indication, something remained unresolved between them.

"Of course. I just wanted to peek in, give my best to Delaney and Dalton and be on my merry way. Actually—" He put his hands on her waist and pulled her close. "I just wanted to see you."

Kate's heart skipped a beat, until she remembered his text. "I thought you were back with your girlfriend?"

"No. Well, yes. Kinda. It's—complicated."

Kate flinched. "Is it? You're either back with her or you're not. Right?"

"I don't know what's going on. I only know I can't stop thinking about you. I've never been able to stop. Can we give it another shot?"

It's exactly what Kate had hoped to hear from him all week.

She inhaled to stop the words from tumbling out. Words that were about to agree to another chance. All thoughts of moving on from him disappeared as he wrapped himself around her. He felt like home, like a worn pair of comfortable pajamas.

He started lowering his lips to hers just as a figure appeared in her periphery.

Ryan.

She pulled back in haste.

"Hey," she called out to Ryan.

"Everything okay?" he asked as he looked from Kate, to Greg, and back.

"Yeah, all good," she said.

"Delaney was just looking for you." Ryan pointed back to the hotel. "I'll tell her you're busy."

"Is that—wait, do you have a boyfriend?" Greg asked.

Kate knew the next word to come out of her mouth would alter the course of her life.

Say yes, and the thing with Greg would likely not be revisited. She'd be making her choice. It would be Ryan, or some other future guy, but it wouldn't be Greg.

Say no, and the thing with Ryan, if it were to become a thing, would start off on the wrong foot. Despite it being the truth, she'd only be saying it to hold open the door of possibility with Greg.

Is that what she wanted?

She stood on the threshold of the past with Greg and the future with Ryan, and realized right here, right now, was her moment of truth. Would she choose Greg? Or Ryan?

She chose herself.

"He's—just a friend."

It was the truth. She'd only known Ryan for a little more than forty-eight hours. But she'd never felt such hope and promise as she had with him in these past two days.

She could tell Ryan heard her, from the look on his face. He turned without another word and went inside.

Kate's heart lurched, and suddenly she had all the clarity she needed. Wherever these feelings about Greg came from, they evaporated as soon as she watched her person walking away.

"He's not my boyfriend yet," she offered more truth. "But I'm hoping he will be. Someday."

Greg looked disappointed.

"I'm sorry," she whispered.

"No, I get it. I should have done this a long time ago."

Kate's eyes pooled with tears as she prepared to say goodbye to her past.

But first...

"I found the shell," she admitted. "In your hoodie pocket."

"What shell?" he looked confused, but then it dawned on him. "Oh. I wondered where that went."

"I just have to know. Why didn't you go through with it?"

Greg sighed. "I knew I was going to California, one way or another. I wanted to gauge your reaction first. I didn't want to trick you into an engagement knowing I was leaving."

At least he'd been honest. He'd done the right thing.

"I'm sorry for my reaction," she said. "I wanted to spend my life with you, and it felt like a major rejection, you choosing something else over me."

"It wasn't a matter of either-or, Kate. You'd already created the life you wanted, but I hadn't. I needed to give it a shot, or I'd have regretted it, and resented you in the process. No way to start a life together. I just hoped, once you knew my plans, you'd go along with it."

Delaney's words rang in her ear: know what you want for yourself before you can find the right person.

But wait...hadn't she known all along what she wanted? In choosing not to go to California with Greg, she'd chosen herself and her DC life. And she'd continued putting her needs first, by refusing to settle for one of the loser-ish guys she'd dated in the aftermath of their breakup.

She didn't need to figure out what she wanted in a relationship—she already knew. She wanted someone who'd slide easily into her world, the life she loved, without forcing her to change a thing. About her life, herself, or her geography. Someone who wanted her, as she was, where she was.

Someone like Ryan.

Kate finally had the closure she'd needed. Greg hadn't chosen something else over her, he'd chosen something else *for* her. The life she was already living, untethered by someone's conflicting goals.

"It certainly turned out to be the right decision for you," Kate said, smiling up at him. "Look at what you've made of your life."

"And you too. You gave me the inspiration to do something amazing. I had to, in order to make leaving you worth it."

"I guess this is where our story ends." She took his hands in hers, went up on her tippy toes and gave him a kiss on the cheek.

He gave her a final hug. "Not the ending I wanted, but I hope you know you'll always have my heart."

It meant a lot to hear that. But right now, there was someone else who had hers.

They parted ways and Kate headed back to the reception, toward her future. She was excited to tell Ryan how she and Greg found the closure they'd needed. She just hoped he hadn't walked away for good after seeing her with Greg.

The party was winding down, and the crowd had thinned. Kate made a few passes around the room, searching for him, with no luck. She asked the remaining wedding party members if they'd seen him, and nobody had. Fear that he'd already moved on began to mount.

Kate had left her phone in her room for the reception, as

she didn't want the repeat performance of a lost communication device. She went upstairs to get her phone, hoping to track Ryan down with a text or a call.

She kicked off her shoes and perched on the edge of her bed as she typed out her text, telling him she was looking for him. She waited for his response, but none came. When she still didn't hear from him, she called him.

His phone rang several times before going to voice mail. Kate's heart sank, knowing he had his phone with him. She knew from personal experience it was set to a fairly obnoxious notification sound, not easily missed. Was he ignoring her?

Perhaps. After what he'd just witnessed.

Or—maybe he'd silenced the phone for the ceremony and forgot to turn it on.

She hung up and called again, this time letting his voice mail play out so she could leave a message.

"Hey, Ryan, it's me, Kate. I've been looking for you. Give me a call, okay?"

She lay back on the bed, waiting. The longer she didn't hear from him, the more concerned she became. She should probably go back downstairs to search for him again, but she was exhausted from the day and needed to rest for a moment.

She lay there, phone in hand, watching the screen. When her eyelids became too heavy to keep open, she rested them, awaiting his call.

It never came.

Cleo

CLEO SAT ON THE BENCH FOR A LONG TIME AFTER WELLS left, thinking about the relationship she'd ended. She'd done the right thing. She loved Wells as a friend, but he wasn't for her. They were just too different. Gus and Nigel were right—there was a lid for every pot; she just hadn't found hers. Wells had come close, but something told her it wasn't meant to be. She had to trust her instincts.

Thanks to Nigel's therapy session, Cleo came to see her internal alarm system as a strength, not a weakness. She was a survivor, a warrior—strong and complete, just as she was. When she did find someone who didn't give her pause, she'd give him a chance. Until then, she shouldn't force a relationship she knew, on some level, wasn't right for her.

Cleo gazed at the ominous night ocean with its churning black waves. It looked a lot like her future—vast, uncertain, scary. Her whole life was about to drastically change before her eyes.

On the horizon, a distant light bobbed, reminding her that good things lay ahead. She was at peace with her life—where it was now, and where it was going.

Cleo was finally ready for the ride.

She headed back to the hotel and was startled to see a dark figure standing next to the bushes, lit cigarette in hand.

"I've been looking for you," Nigel said, flicking the ashes.

Without asking, Cleo took the cigarette from his hand and took a drag. It had been four years since she quit, but she still missed it. She let the hot smoke fill her lungs before violently expelling it.

Nope, not worth it.

"I saw you guys take off for the beach," he said. "Everything okay?"

"I'm fine," she said, "thanks to our talk the other night. It helped me process some things."

"That's nice to hear, but I'm sure I didn't tell you anything you didn't already know."

"I guess on some level I did. But sometimes it's good to

hear it from someone else. You're a lot more observant than you look."

"Comes with the job," Nigel said. "You know that."

"Someone said there's an open bar around here?"

Nigel smiled. "That's what they say. And for once, we're not serving."

They headed for the bar when the first strains of Journey's "Don't Stop Believin' " began.

"Come 'ere, small-town girl."

Nigel led her to the dance floor and serenaded her with lyrics that perfectly summed up her current stage of life.

Before this week, she hadn't believed in much, but that had all changed.

"Question for you," he said as they danced.

Of course, here it comes. "Yes, Nigel. I'm pretty sure she's into you."

"Who are you talking about?"

"Your date? Tori? I've never seen her happier."

Nigel laughed. "You're a daft old bird, aren't you? I'm not here for Tori. I'm here for you."

Cleo jerked her head back. Only a desperate fool would choose her over Tori.

"I'd love to hang out in New York sometime," he said. "I think you're kinda cool."

While she loved flirting with this man, there was no way she'd step on Tori's toes.

"Look, I'm highly flattered, but Tori—"

"Why don't we ask her?" he said, pulling out his phone.

Cleo, mortified, sputtered for him to stop, but the call was already ringing on speaker.

"What did she say?" Tori asked as soon as she picked up.

"She'd like your permission," Nigel said.

Cleo stared at the phone, confused. "What's going on?"

"Nigel only agreed to be my date because he 'fancies' you,"

Tori said on the line. "And I think you'd be great together—for what it's worth."

"So, I'll ask again," Nigel said. "Can we keep in touch, grab a drink, have dinner or something? As friends. Not a date, of course."

Cleo laughed. "Of course not."

"We're too young for that shit," Nigel said.

"No need to be tied down."

Gus's words rang in her mind. *Give some guy a chance.*

"But then," Nigel hedged, "maybe—"

"A shag?" Cleo said. "Oh wait, did I say that out loud?"

"You did. But I thought it first."

Cleo looked up at him, afraid to open her mouth for fear her fluttering, hope-filled heart would splat all over his wing-tipped shoes.

He spoke first. "Just give me a chance."

Sunday, June 18

THE DAY AFTER

Kate

KATE AWAKENED WITH A START, HER PHONE STILL IN hand.

The events of last night flashed through her mind. Greg appearing, Ryan disappearing, falling asleep before she found him.

She scrolled through her texts to see if he'd responded. Nothing. No calls, either.

Kate was simultaneously furious and worried—furious she'd sent Ryan off so rudely; worried he was blowing her off. She needed to make it right.

As she rose from the bed, something on the floor caught her eye. An envelope. Someone must have slipped it under the door. It was addressed to "Kathryn," in the neatest handwriting.

She tore at the envelope and flipped open the card.

My dearest Kathryn,

I realize this is so 1880 of me, but I couldn't let Congress Hall's beautiful stationery go to waste. I'm penning you a note instead of texting because it's early and I didn't want to wake you. Sorry for not responding last night, I was asleep. It was great getting to know you. I've never met anyone who stole my heart until I saw you in the bar that night. Our phone switch was an absolute stroke of luck, destiny's finest work. I was happy to find out the person who had my phone was the girl I'd been looking for. You've got it all (brains, looks, three-legged race chops, and the handsomest phone cover ever). Greg's a lucky guy! Now that we're somewhat related by marriage, I know our paths will cross again. Until then, I wish you the best of luck. I, and the planet, thank you for all you do to make this a better place. Yours truly, Ryan Brady.

Kate had barely finished reading the note when she tossed it aside, threw open the door and raced down the grand staircase, almost taking out an entire family as she jockeyed past them.

"What room is Ryan Brady in?" she demanded when she reached the desk. "It's an emergency."

A lie, yes. But letting someone like Ryan walk out of her life would be an emergency of epic proportions. A tragedy.

"Sorry ma'am. He's already checked out," the clerk said.

Kate's eyes watered. She tapped her hand on the desk, trying to think.

The clerk leaned forward and whispered, "I believe he took the shuttle to the ferry. You may be able to catch him."

Kate tore out of the lobby and ran to the shuttle stop. The bus was there, empty, except for the driver.

"Was a man just on this shuttle?" she demanded. "Dark hair, tall—"

"Yeah. Just dropped him off at the ferry."

"Take me there!" Kate jumped on board, begging the driver to go quickly.

She plopped into a seat, ruing her decisions of the night before. Talking to Greg, hugging him, letting Ryan walk away before she could explain the situation.

"Fool!" she muttered.

"Come again?" the shuttle driver snapped, casting a confrontational glare in the rearview mirror.

"Sorry, that was directed at myself," she explained. Then, never knowing what's too much to share, she added, "I'm a fool because I just let the best guy get away."

"Why didn't you say so?"

The driver floored it, and Kate flung backward in her seat.

"The ferry leaves in three minutes, but Imma get you there," she assured Kate. "What's one more speeding ticket?"

They peeled into the parking lot like a race car pulling in for a pit stop. Just as the ferry was loading.

"Thanks," Kate called out as she leaped from the shuttle. "I owe you one."

"Just make sure you invite me to the wedding!"

Kate ran toward the ferry, scanning the faces of passengers gathered on the deck. It blasted an obnoxious toot as it began to pull away, almost knocking her off her feet.

And that's when she spotted him.

She called his name, but he didn't seem to hear her. She called it again.

This time, it worked. His eyes softened as they found hers.

"Are you here to steal my phone again?" he called.

"No," she called back, "just your heart."

A slow smile spread across his face. "I think it's fair to say you already have it."

"I hope so." She walked along the wooden walkway flanking the canal, keeping pace with the ferry as it slowly drifted toward the bay. "I got your note. Very Victorian of you!"

He nodded. "Love the dress. And they say you'll never wear them again!"

Kate looked down, horrified to discover she was still wearing her bridesmaid dress. "Someone had to prove them wrong! This isn't a walk of shame, by the way."

The ferry began picking up speed. She hiked up her dress and jogged alongside.

"You mean, the run of shame?" he yelled, then *ba-dum-bump*'ed his hands on the railing.

"No shame at all." She had to shout louder now over the ferry's revving engine. "Greg and I are done. It was goodbye, not hello."

"Really?" He looked happy. Hopeful.

"I'm sorry you had to see that," she cried out. "Can I have a do-over?"

The ferry pulled out of the canal just as Kate reached the end of the walkway. Ryan held up his phone and pointed to it. She threw her hands up to let him know she didn't have her phone.

"I'll call you!" he shouted. "Let me take you to dinner tomorrow night!"

She gave him a thumbs-up, then bent over to catch her breath as the ferry turned toward the bay.

"Hey Kate," he yelled once more, pointing to the back of the ship. "Looks like you may get that 'ferry-tail ending' after all!"

Kate laughed as tears flowed down her face.

As he drifted toward the horizon, he cupped his hands around his mouth.

"I just hope it's with me!"

And then he raised his hands and held them above his head in the shape of a heart.

Delaney

DELANEY AND DALTON WERE STATIONED IN THE LOBBY, bidding farewell to their remaining guests. They made plans to visit Cleo once she got settled in New York. Delaney was happy to learn Nigel was heading there too. Cleo insisted they were just friends, but Delaney wouldn't be surprised if it developed into something more. They seemed right for each other.

"Hey guys, we're taking off," Sam said as he and Marley hugged the newlyweds. "Great wedding. We had a blast."

"I'm so happy about this," Delaney said, her eyes twinkling as she pointed back and forth between them. "It's about time. Thanks for handling the case until I'm back."

"What case?" Sam asked.

Marley punched him in the arm. "Don't worry, it's in good hands."

When they were certain their guests had all left, the couple sent for their car and prepared for the drive back to Philly to drop off their wedding gifts. Their flight to London left that night.

"It's just us, now," she said to Dalton. "I guess you're stuck with me."

"There's no one else I'd rather be stuck with," Dalton said, giving her a kiss. "Let's go start our life together."

Epilogue

DELANEY AND DALTON WERE RUNNING LATE FOR KATE'S birthday party, but they had a good excuse. It was their six-month anniversary, and they'd rushed home from work to celebrate in their own intimate way before joining the family for dinner.

When they finally arrived at the Clink, flushed and breathless, the owner greeted them at the door. "Ah, your family awaits. Let me show you to the party."

He led them through the restaurant to a back room. When they stepped inside, they were greeted with thunderous applause.

"Surprise!"

Delaney clutched her chest. Dalton laughed out loud.

The room was adorned with balloons featuring Union Jack flags. Several round banquet tables, dressed in white linen, displayed crown centerpieces. A large banner on the wall read Bon Voyage!

Kate and Ryan were the first to greet them with hugs.

"Welcome to my fake birthday party," Kate said. "Also known as your going away party."

After months of planning, negotiating, visa-securing, and flat hunting, the newlyweds were pursuing an opportunity to move to London. Dalton had accepted the promotion, and Delaney was on loan to the London firm of Jim's cousin, a precursor to a possible trans-Atlantic merger. They were set to leave right after the holidays.

"Sorry we lied about leaving work early today," Marley said when she and Sam greeted them.

"We were in charge of decorating. What do you think?" Sam asked. "We do good?"

"Brilliant!" Delaney said in her best British accent.

"Okay, Martha Stewart," Marley said, linking her arm with Sam's. "Let them greet their guests."

Delaney was amazed to see all who were there—members of both of their families, close friends, work acquaintances from both their offices.

"I can't believe you guys pulled this off," Delaney said.

"It was all Kate." Ryan beamed as he put his arm around his girlfriend. "I know I don't have to tell you this, but she's amazing."

"I'm just glad you like surprises now," Kate said to her sister as she looked beyond her. "Because there's another..."

Someone tugged at Delaney's sleeve. She pivoted to find Cleo and Nigel standing there.

"Oh my god!" she cried out, bursting into tears. She hadn't seen Cleo since she left for New York in August.

"Look at you," Delaney said as she stroked a strand of Cleo's hair, now in a chin-length bob that made her look sophisticated. Grown-up, almost. "You went back to red!"

"I was gonna Union Jack this bitch, but my British boyfriend said it would be too much."

"I love her natural color," Nigel said, wrapping his arms around her waist. "Go 'head, tell her the other reason."

Cleo beamed. "You're looking at the new creative assistant for ImagineArt Gallery. I just found out this morning."

"Cleo, that's amazing!" she exclaimed. "Congratulations!"

"It's a start," Cleo said. "I'm also volunteering with the Home for Arts program, to help homeless youth find a creative outlet. I gotta look like and act a grown-ass adult now."

Delaney was proud of her friend. Once she'd made up her

mind, there was no stopping Cleo from finding success in New York. Success as she defined it.

Nigel stopped a waiter carrying a tray of champagne. He passed flutes around and they toasted to Cleo's success.

"To Nigel too," Cleo added. "He's looking into culinary arts school. Someone has to cook for me, once I have my own gallery."

"At your service, my lady," Nigel said, bowing before her. "Always."

Later, as Delaney worked the room and greeted guests, she found Marley and Sam at a table by themselves, heads together, talking. His arm was wrapped around her, his hand resting on her hip. The vision of young love, at its finest, between two best friends.

"Hey, guys," she said, approaching them. "I don't know how much I'll see you with the holidays and our departure coming up, but want to thank you for all you've done these past few months."

Delaney was indebted to her interns after they'd worked tirelessly to help her win the case. Rupert James had been exonerated, and was now a free man.

"I can't believe you kept this party a secret, working together as much as we have."

"I can't tell you how many times I almost gave it away," Sam said, exhaling in relief.

"Like the other day," Marley said, putting her right hand to her forehead. On her finger was a ring Delaney hadn't seen before.

"What in the Sam Hill is that?" Cleo exclaimed, brushing by Delaney on approach to the table. She yanked Marley's hand toward her. "My God, it's blinding!"

Marley smiled. "Early Christmas gift from Sam. My birthstone."

"Is it a real?"

"Cleo!" Delaney exclaimed.

"It's real," Sam assured Cleo. "To match her gorgeous eyes. I couldn't wait until Christmas to put a ring on it."

"Is this—"

"No!" Sam said, as if he knew what she was about to ask. He gave Marley a shy look. "Not yet at least. Still trying to win her heart."

Delaney took Marley's hand and gawked at her glowing emerald. "Simply beautiful. I had no idea you were such a romantic, Sam."

"I did." Cleo boasted. "I could tell you had it bad for her, the way you used to look at her in the Clink. I wanted to smack you and tell you to go for it. Just glad I didn't have to resort to physical combat."

"Me too," Sam said, ducking.

"Are you guys doing anything special for the holidays?" Delaney asked.

"Christmas eve with my family, Christmas day with hers. And then we're off to the Mal-*deevs*."

"Another Christmas gift," Marley said, looking embarrassed. "He's too much."

"Never too much," Sam said, enveloping her in an embrace. "You're worth it."

Dalton waved to Delaney from across the room. She excused herself and joined him and Ryan.

"Hey, Laney," Ryan said when she approached. "I'd like a word with both of you."

"Yes, you can marry my sister," Delaney joked. "Just kidding. What's up?"

"Well..." Ryan said, his eyes twinkling.

"I was only joking," Delaney said, mouth open in disbelief.

The look on Ryan's face told her he wasn't.

"Dude, are you serious?" Dalton clasped Ryan's hand and pulled him in for a man hug.

"Oh my God, Ryan," Delaney said, bracing herself for what she knew—hoped—was coming.

"I knew from the moment I met Kate. She's it for me. Crazy to think it's only been six months when it feels like I've known her forever, but I can't imagine my life without her. It won't be right away, but soon. That being said—is it okay with you if I ask Kate to marry me?"

"Yes," Delaney said, laughing as she wiped her flowing tears. "Of course! Who am I to mess with destiny?"

Acknowledgments

THEY SAY IT TAKES A VILLAGE TO RAISE A CHILD, AND WRITING a book is no different. When I started out on this venture, I knew very little about the process but there were so many people, both named and unnamed, who helped me along the way. I'll do my best with this shout-out.

First and foremost, my editor, Emily Ohanjanians, is nothing short of an angel on earth. You gave me so much more than editing advice, you gave me hope. Your kind first notes about my writing style and your LOL comments made me believe I was on the right track to be writing a book. Your input has been amazing, your advice spot on. You've helped inspire me to put this little story of mine, that I'd been dreaming of for years, out into the world. This is just the beginning of our literary adventures together.

To Jessica Kleinman, my amazing cover art and book designer, it's been an absolute joy working with you. You were so patient with my many book cover ideas, striving for something "Cape May-ish", and you nailed it. The fact that you're a fellow Philly girl was one of the reasons I chose you, but your experience, guidance and design flair is what made me enjoy working with you. I'm happy geography brought us together! Can't wait for the next project.

I found both Emily and Jessica on Reedsy, a clearinghouse for all things booksy. The incredible organization not only linked this newbie writer to seasoned professionals, but it's filled the universe with gobs of book-writing advice and resources. I highly encourage anyone who wishes to write a book to reach out and utilize their services.

That brings me to the writing community itself, the many individuals behind the organizations, websites, conferences, and more who have dedicated their talents and passion to assisting would-be authors. Special shout out to Alexa Bigwarfe, CEO and founder of Write|Publish|Sell and host of the Women in Publishing Summit. Your story and generosity have been so inspiring to many of us, and WIP School and the Summit have been invaluable resources.

Now, the personal stuff. My team, the first people who laid eyes on this story, gave me invaluable feedback and support. Michelle, Kara, Pat, Nancy, Julia, Stacie, Lynn—you're not only the most voracious readers I know, but you are important women in my life. You didn't sugar coat your feedback but gave it to me straight. You told me what worked and what didn't. I love you for your honest feedback and your desire to see me succeed with this little project of mine.

To my Mom and Dad, I thank you from the bottom of my heart for telling me I could do anything in this world I put my mind to, and giving me everything I've needed to soar. You've been great partners—sitting with me in Wegman's over coffee, on the phone, or at the dinner table, going over every excruciating detail of my plot, and giving me advice on all the other aspects of launching a writing career. Oh, and for instilling in me my love for the southern Jersey shore!

To my daughter, Julia, you have and always will be my biggest inspiration. I hope you always reach for the stars and know there's no limit to what you can do. You're an amazing person and were integral to the development of my storyline and characters. I love you for your insight, kindness, and beauty. Raising and discovering who you are has been the greatest joy of my life.

To my hubs, Dan, I can't thank you enough for your support and for not mocking me too much when I said I was gonna write a book. I did it! Your humor is most appreciated, and I'm grateful for this laugh-filled life of ours. Thanks also to my loving in-laws for raising a great man.

Lastly, but certainly not least, I want to thank the readers who I hope to keep connecting with as I continue my writing journey. If you're reading this, it means you cared enough to find out who was behind this book. Please stay in touch with me through my website, kimberlybrighton.com, and share your stories as inspiration for future novels. Who knows—your love story could be my next book. Go forth with love in your hearts, and be kind to one another!

Reader's Guide

ABOUT THIS BOOK
BOOK CLUB QUESTIONS
PLAYLISTS FROM THE BOOK

About This Book

INSPIRATION

Like many authors, both published and not, I spent a lifetime dreaming of someday writing a book. It started when I was five, when my dad helped me write and publish my first book using hand-drawn illustrations, cardboard and yarn. Upon graduation from high school, my goal was to become a writer for Saturday Night Live. I started out with the best of intentions, pursuing a degree in a highly reputable Journalism school. Until I got lost in the City of Philadelphia, turned the wrong way down a one-way street, and earned myself a ticket. I knew the street wasn't marked, so I decided to fight it. That unexpected detour through the streets of Philly became symbolic of my life, as I steered away from 30Rock and found myself veering into law school, marriage and motherhood. When my only child went off to college, I was given a great piece of advice: Start writing your new chapter.

So, I did—both literally and figuratively. Beginning with the words, "Chapter One", I renewed my writing goals and sat down to write a book. Despite my age (possibly, because of it), I somehow managed to reinvent myself as an author—my lifelong dream, finally realized. So let that be a lesson to all: it's never too late to pursue your dreams!

This book is my love letter to the southern Jersey shore, where I've spent much of my life. It was inspired by the Jersey-famous song, "On the Way to Cape May", written in 1960 by Maurice "Bud" Nugent, who ad-libbed lyrics to entertain his family as they traveled to Cape May. The lyrics are protected by copyright, so I wasn't able to capture them here in this book. If you haven't heard the song, all you need to do is go into any southern Jersey shore bar with a cover band on a summer night, and you'll likely hear it. I originally envisioned this book to be a series of short stories, each one taking place in the eight coastal towns along the Cape. But then, while watching the movie, *Love Actually*, I re-envisioned it as a multi-character story featuring interrelated characters, all on their way to a Cape May wedding. And, of course, their own happily ever after. The result: my debut novel, *The Way to Cape May*.

SETTINGS

Here's a little bit about the towns and places appearing in this book.

Philadelphia

Philadelphia, or "Philly" as locals call it, is known as the "City of Brotherly Love" and is located along the Delaware River, across from New Jersey. Many people flee the city in summer to go "down the shore", as they say in this region. Home to Super Bowl Champs, the Philadelphia Eagles, Philly's also well known for its cheesesteaks. But its biggest claim to fame is being "the birthplace of America", home to William Penn and Ben Franklin, among other founding fathers. It was here the Declaration of Independence was signed, and where the Liberty Bell still stands.

Reading Terminal Market

The Reading Terminal Market was one of the original farmers' markets in Philly, created in 1893. Today, this ridiculously popular market features literally anything you could want, from fresh produce to international cuisine, baked goods to housewares, vintage clothing to souvenirs. It's a popular lunch and dinner venue for locals, and a must-visit for tourists.

Ocean City

Ocean City is known as "America's Greatest Family Resort". It boasts of a 2.5-mile boardwalk filled with rides, shops, and dining establishments. This fun-filled town has been the recipient of many "Best Beach" awards from National Geographic Traveler, The Travel Channel, and others. Coastal Living Magazine once named Ocean City "The Best Beach Town in America".

The Ocean City Boardwalk

The Ocean City Boardwalk is considered one of the top ten boardwalks in America by The Travel Channel and others. The boardwalk, first built in 1880, offers shopping, dining and amusement rides in addition to being a great place to walk, run, bike, or simply sit and enjoy a Kohr Brothers Frozen Custard while people watching. And if you're looking for a great lunch venue, Delaney and her dad suggest The Hula Grill (official name Hula Restaurant). Their Hawaiian Chicken is to die for!

Strathmere

Strathmere is a sleepy residential community situated on Ludlam Island, between Ocean City to the north and Sea Isle to the south. It's the home of a couple restaurants and offers expansive white-sand beaches, no beach tag required.

Deauville Inn

The Deauville Inn is a popular bar and restaurant nestled on the shore of Corson's Bay in Strathmere. Built in the 1800s, the Deauville Inn is rumored to have been a speakeasy during Prohibition, a rum-running station, and a gambling casino during the '20s and '30s. Today, it stands as a beacon for fine dining, cocktails, and live entertainment with a great beach bar area where boaters can dock, and kids can play, while adults sip cocktails and watch the sun set.

Sea Isle City

This bustling seaside town shares Ludlam Island with Strathmere to the north, and Townsends Inlet to the south. It features a 1.5-mile-long paved promenade which runs along the beach, making it the perfect place for walking, running, or biking. The town offers shopping, dining and plenty of activities, including water sports, playgrounds and much more.

The Point

The Point is located along the beach in Sea Isle, where the popular Springfield Inn and its outdoor counterpart, the Carousel Bar, once stood. I spent much of my twenties there and couldn't write a book about the shore without paying due respects. During the writing of this book, the Springfield Inn was sold, and the building and gazebo bar were demolished. In its place, grew this beautiful tropical beach bar where I now hang out with my twenty-something daughter. Full Circle.

Avalon

Avalon is known for its maritime forest and wild dunes lining the beach, the largest of their kind on the southern Jersey Cape. Avalon shares its barrier island home with Stone Harbor to the south. This swanky seaside town has a small shopping district and offers excellent dining opportunities, as well as a non-commercialized boardwalk, perfect for walking, running, or biking.

The Princeton Bar and Grill

This popular bar and restaurant is located in the center of Avalon. In addition to a spacious bar, cozy dining area and outdoor patio, the Princeton features three night clubs under one roof. With live music throughout the summer, the Princeton is popular with both locals and tourists.

Cape May

Known as "America's Oldest Seaside Resort", Cape May is the southernmost New Jersey town, located on the tip of the Cape. The town is best known for its beautiful Victorian architecture, bed and breakfast establishments, and lighthouse. It features several shopping districts such as the "Washington Street Mall", and a wide variety of dining options. Cape May offers year-round activities and events for all ages.

Congress Hall Resort

Established in 1816, Congress Hall is considered the oldest seaside resort hotel in America. Its grand presence along the beach in Cape May offers luxurious and fun experiences for visitors and is a major destination for couples seeking a romantic beach wedding.

For more information about these awesome places or others along the southern Jersey shore, please check out my website, *The Shore Blog* (theshoreblog.com)

Book Club Questions

This book tells the stories of four characters and their quest for love. My intention in creating these specific characters was to enable readers to identify with similar challenges they may face in their own lives. But, also, to learn more about their own beliefs, choices and chances as they navigate the often pothole-riddled road to romance. Let's face it—finding and keeping love is one of the most challenging aspects of life. That's why "happily ever after" books draw readers in by the millions.

Like our characters, each of us has likely faced (or will face) a moment when re-examination of our chosen actions was (or will be) necessary in order to find (or keep) love. For some, it may involve reflection upon values, rectifying the past, overcoming doubts, or adjusting our paths. It may require identifying and redesigning outdated and unnecessary self-beliefs which can impede the quality of our relationships with ourselves and with others.

This reader's guide is meant to promote discussion and self-reflection. I hope some of these questions inspire robust conversation among your book club peeps or fellow readers, as well as a discovery of something about yourself or your relationship that's helpful. There are no right or wrong answers here, just yours, and all thoughts are welcome and appreciated.

1. Each of our characters began their story with a self-belief impacting their ability to reach their full potential. What would you say was each characters' unproductive belief, and how did it limit their chances to achieve

their individual dreams and goals, or at least hinder their process?

2. How did each of our characters' beliefs about themselves and/or relationships in general impact their ability to find and keep love?

3. At the bachelorette party, our characters discussed the concept of destiny. Delaney believes we choose our own future, while Kate seems to believe it's more about chance. Marley suggested it could be a little of both. What do you believe?

4. Delaney likes to be in control and doesn't like surprises. She was frustrated with Dalton over some decisions he made about their wedding, including changing their honeymoon. Do you believe Dalton was unresponsive to Delaney's needs, or was he trying to help her find joy in the unexpected? How, if at all, did his actions change her view about control?

5. At one point, Kate questions whether she knows what she wants in a guy, after Delaney suggested she'd never taken time outside a relationship to get to know herself. What do you think—was Kate really that confused, or had she known all along and just hadn't yet met the right guy? Did you want to see her get back together with Greg, or take a chance with Ryan?

6. What do you believe held Marley back from being honest about her feelings for Sam? What about Rick kept Marley in that relationship, instead of pursuing one with her hot bestie?

7. Cleo's story began with her in a steamy, surface-level relationship with Wells. Did you root for them to get

together, or did you want to see her with Nigel? How do you think the characters' similarities and differences would impact the success of their relationship if Cleo ended up with Wells? With Nigel?

8. Which character do you most closely associate with in terms of personality and outlook? Head on over to Spotify to see the character's playlists and see whose song choices speak to you (search under "Profile" for "The Way to Cape May")

9. Did any of the characters' self-beliefs or challenges speak to you on a personal level? Is there anything you would do or view differently in your own life, in achieving your goals or finding love, after reading this book?

10. What would you like to see happen for each of our characters in a sequel? (This is where I'd love to hear your feedback—please head on over to KimberlyBrighton. com to share!

Playlists from This Book

(Available on Spotify. Search "Profile", then "The Way to Cape May)

On the Way to Cape May Playlist

On the Way to Cape May – *Al Alberts*
Wildwood Days – *Bobby Rydell*
Under the Boardwalk – *The Drifters*
Knee Deep – *Zac Brown Band*
Vacation – Go-Go's
Life's a Beach – *Heymous Molly*
Beyond the Sea – *Bobby Darin*
All Summer Long – *The Beach Boys*
Island Song – *Zac Brown Band*
Sweet Caroline – *Neil Diamond*
Summer Breeze – *Seals and Crofts*
Island In The sun – *Weezer*

Sam's Roar to the Shore Playlist

Surfin' USA – *Beach Boys*
Classic – *MKTO*
Opus 17 (Don't You Worry) - *Franki Valli & The Four Seasons*

Just Like Heaven – *The Cure*
The Best in Me – *Sherwood*
Soul Sister – *Train*
Love You Inside Out – *Bee Gees*
The Ghost in You – *The Psychedelic Furs*
Don't Forget About Me – *Glass Tiger*
If This is It - *Huey Lewis & the News*
Waiting in Vain – *Bob Marley & the Wailers*
Can't Fight This Feeling – *REO Speedwagon*
Butterflies – *MAX, Ali Gatie*

Marley's Beach Playlist

You Belong With Me – *Taylor Swift*
Why Can't I – *Liz Phair*
Falling in Love at a Coffee Shop – *Landon Pigg*
Only Wanna Be With You – *Hootie and the Blowfish*
Fallin' For You – *Colbie Caillat*
Cruel Summer – *Taylor Swift*
Tempted - *Squeeze*
This Kiss – *Carly Rae Jepsen*
Waterloo – *ABBA*
Somebody's Got To – *The Band McMillan*
Turn Me On – *Norah Jones*
At Last – *Etta James*

Delaney's Wedding Playlist

Chapel of Love – *The Dixie Cups*
Marry Me – *Train*
Third Finger Left Hand – *Martha Reeves & The Vandellas*
I'm Yours – *Jason Mraz*
I Choose You – *Sara Bareilles*
Speechless - *Dan + Shay*
I Do, I Do, I Do – *ABBA*
Lucky – *Jason Mraz, Colbie Caillat*
This Will Be (An Everlasting Love) – *Natalie Cole*
Love Like This – *Natasha Bedingfield*
Sandcastles – *Skye Peterson*

Kate's Summer Playlist

Brown Eyed Girl – *Van Morrison*
Summer Feelings - *Lennon Stella & Charlie Puth*
Single Ladies – *Beyonce*
Put Your Records On – *Corinne Baily Rae*
A Simple Twist of Fate – *Sarah Jarosz*
Blank Space – *Taylor Swift*
Gold Digger – *Kanye West*
Magic – *Olivia Newton John*
Brighter Than the Sun – *Colbie Caillat*
(I Can't Help) Falling in Love – *UB40*
Bubbly – *Colbie Caillat*
Butterflies – *Kacey Musgrave*

Cleo's Starving Artist Playlist

All I Wanna Do – *Sheryl Crow*
Red Red Wine – *UB40*
Hit Me With Your Best Shot – *Pat Benatar*
Hippiechick - *Soho*
Different Drum – *The Stone Poneys*
You Oughta Know – *Melissa Etheridge*
Just A Fool – *Christina Aguilera & Blake Shelton*
Damn I Wish I Was Your Lover – *Sophie B. Hawkins*
I Hate Myself for Loving You – *Joan Jett & the Blackhearts*
I'm the Only One - *Melissa Etheridge*
Don't Stop Believin' – *Journey*
The Best – *Tina Turner*

READ ON FOR
AN EXCERPT FROM

A Cape May
Kind of Love

BOOK TWO IN THE
CAPE MAY SERIES

MARLEY MAGUIRE RUSHED HOME AFTER AN EXHAUSTING day at her law firm internship, anxious for the night to begin. She looked forward to a relaxing evening and indulging in her favorite guilty pleasure.

After changing into her comfy clothes—leggings and an oversized Eagles' sweatshirt—she settled into her plush couch, waiting for her best friend to join her. The best friend who, as destiny would have it, was also now her boyfriend.

Sam sauntered across the room in rhythm to the soft music playing in the background, wearing a sultry smile. He gave a little salsa shuffle before handing her a frosty bottle of Dock Street beer. Plunking himself down on the couch, he slung his arm around Marley's shoulders and clinked his bottle against hers.

"Cheers to a new season," he said, as he propped his feet on the coffee table. "Bring on *The Bachelorette*."

Watching reality TV dating shows was their mutual obsession, something they'd started back when they were "just friends". Not only did it provide a perfect escape from the harsh rigors of law school, it also gave them an excuse to get to know each other better. As they dissected the stars' love lives, they shared their own thoughts about dating and relationships, unaware they were also planting seeds where feelings for one another would secretly begin to grow.

"I'm hoping for some juicy drama this season," Marley said with a lascivious grin as she snuggled up to Sam.

"I'm with you, *National Enquirer*. Bring on the tears and sob stories." He smiled down at her, then added, "theirs, not ours."

"No drama here," she said, as she sipped her beer and laid

her head on his shoulder.

He kissed her forehead. "Not in a million years."

The show began with its typical teaser as the host promised this season would be "the most dramatic *ever*, in the *entire* Bachelor Nation history."

Marley giggled. It was something the host was compelled to say every season, but for some reason she still believed the hype.

A few minutes into the show, Sam hopped up from the couch.

"Forgot the grub," he said. "Keep it running, be right back."

As he salsaed his way to the kitchen, Marley's eyes were drawn to his swaying hips, moving in sync with his broad shoulders and tight glutes. His perfect physique and sexy dance moves were just two of the many reasons she'd fallen so hard for him. Boy was *Hot* with a Capital H.

On screen, a limo had pulled up, signaling the arrival of the contestants. Man after gorgeous man stepped from the limo as the camera trained on expensive shoes before panning up to reveal a designer suit, buff body, gleaming smile, and perfectly styled hair. Each man was more stunning than the last.

But none more stunning than her real-life bachelor, still in the kitchen, now rifling through a potato chip bag and singing a Taylor Swift song in pitch-perfect falsetto.

What on earth was taking him so long?

She was about to pause the show when the final contestant's limo pulled up and his foot emerged onto the gravel path.

Marley gasped.

She'd know those shiny red Nikes with orange laces anywhere. Even on the screen of her television. Even if it made no sense how they ended up there, of all places—outside the L.A.-based mansion, attached to a hopeful bachelor.

The camera slowly swept higher, revealing the next dead giveaway: his cringe-worthy outfit. He was clad in tan khakis and a blue blazer, in stark contrast to the other men's stylish garb. No slim fitting, designer suit for this man. He owned one, that wasn't the issue, but he claimed the suit pants made a tent in his crotch when he sat down, raising eyebrows and suspicions and (in some cases), hope. Not one to lead others on, he paired the jacket with better-fitting khakis instead. Assuming "paired" would be the correct word.

For most occasions, his version of "dressed up" was—*meh*, okay. He worked in IT, so his lack of fashion sense was not only excusable, but expected. However, if he hoped to win the heart of a gorgeous social media star on international TV, he should have gone with the jacket-matching, crotch-tenting suit pants for the sake of style—with the added bonus of optical illusion for as long as he could get away with it.

The camera hadn't quite made it to his face when the sound of his voice eradicated any lingering doubt in Marley's mind. The last time she'd heard it was the night they broke up.

Marley sat there, mouth agape, unable to speak.

Sam returned with a bag of chips. Flopping down next to her, he offered up the bag. When she didn't accept it, he shot her a glance. "What's wrong?"

He took a swig of beer as Marley pointed at the TV, speechless.

Sam erupted, spewing beer all over her brand-new Ikea coffee table. "Is that—"

"Ergh," Marley gurgled her disbelief.

"No. Fucking. *Way!*" Sam exclaimed.

"Hello Brie," the man on the screen cooed as he bowed his head to kiss the cheek of the flaxen-haired, sequin-clad bachelorette. "It's a pleasure to meet you. I'm Richard Alabaster Smith the Third. But you can call me—"

"Rick?" Sam yelled, laughing as he wiped the dripping beer from his chin. "On the fucking *Bachelorette*? Are you *serious* right now?"

Yes, it seemed—as serious as reality TV could be. Richard Alabaster Smith—*aka* Rick, *aka* Marley's former farm-bred, socially awkward ex-boyfriend—was on the fucking *Bachelorette*.

Rick. The guy who became tongue-tied around anyone outside his circle. The guy who hid behind thick, wire-rimmed glasses and avoided social interaction at all costs. Yeah, *that* guy. Yet despite all that, he'd somehow managed to put together an audition tape and beat out thousands of handsome, muscle-bound, Pinterest-worthy hunks to be selected as a contestant on the wildly popular, world-televised dating show.

This had to be a joke.

"Good God," Marley whispered.

"Oh, I am so *here* for this!" Sam yelled again, punching the air.

He gave a hearty laugh and spun to Marley, who continued to sit there, mouth hanging open. "Marley! Rick's on *The Bachelorette*!"

"No shit, Sherlock. I can see that."

"Those damn sneaks of his." Sam shook his head and laughed. His face bore a combined expression of admiration and astonishment, as if Rick had just ripped a loud fart on national TV. "You *go*, dawg."

Marley blinked, wondering if she was imagining this. Was it possible to get drunk on a sip of beer? Because this couldn't be real. Rick would be the last person to put himself out there like this.

On the screen, Brie tipped her head and smiled. "Hello Rick, the pleasure is all mine."

Rick pulled a sock from the breast pocket of his jacket. "I'm here to sock it to you," he said, straight-faced, as the lovely Bachelorette doubled over in a fake TV laugh.

"That was darn good," Brie quipped.

Sam laughed out loud. Marley groaned. There was no way

Brie the Bachelorette was keeping Rick the Corny Jokester past the first episode.

"What a dork," Marley muttered.

"Oh Mar," Sam said, aqua eyes wide with revelation. "I heard chicks dig dorks now. It's a whole new thing."

"Thanks, *Glamour* magazine, but I'm pretty sure dorks have always been in."

"Am I a dork?" Sam asked, eager eyebrows raised.

Marley chuckled. Sam was anything but a dork, although the fact he'd asked the question got him a little closer.

"The dorkiest."

"Good.

As the premiere progressed, Brie met with each of the men and got to know them. Marley's shock soon turned to dread when it was Rick's turn to chat with her in the garden.

"So, have you had many girlfriends?" Brie asked him.

"Just one," Rick said, giving her a shy half-smile. "And she broke my heart. Shattered, more like it."

"Oh, please," Marley whimpered, stiffening, her fists clenching the couch cushions. "Please don't go there."

Her heart pounded. Marley had been Rick's only girlfriend. She was terrified he'd tell their story and tarnish her name in the process. But Rick flipped the script and began asking Brie about her past. She, too, had suffered a broken heart—*de rigueur* for the formulaic show.

Marley's relief was only temporary as Brie excused herself from Rick and picked up a rose.

"Oh God," Marley mumbled, hoping against hope Rick wasn't the intended recipient of the first impression rose. Receiving the rose meant he wouldn't be sent home that night, which also meant he'd be on the show for another week. "This can't be happening."

"Oh, it's happening, Mar!" Sam exclaimed, as he stood up and did the cabbage patch dance. "Go Riiick! Go Riiick! Go Riiick!"

Marley, dumbfounded, watched as her current boyfriend cheered on her ex.

"Do you really want him to continue on? And have to see him on our TV another week?"

"Of course!"

"I thought you hated Rick?"

"Only because he was dating you," Sam said, plopping back down on the couch and clasping her knee. "Now that I got you, I'm rooting for the dude to find love."

Marley raised an eyebrow.

"Come on, Look at him!" Sam said, pleading his case. "Poor guy's not gonna find it, otherwise."

Sure enough, Brie handed the rose to Rick. "You made the best first impression on me. You seem so genuine, and that's exactly what I'm looking for."

The only thing Marley was looking just then for was a barf bag.

Better yet, the remote.

She grabbed for it, but Sam yanked it away. "Oh no. We're doing this."

Marley slunk back on the couch and covered her face with a throw pillow. She hadn't spoken to Rick since the night of their breakup. She cringed, remembering how he'd surprised her with a promise ring on his last visit to Philly, and she thanked him by crying out Sam's name in the middle of a steamy dream, professing her love for him.

Already suspicious of the besties' close friendship (which they'd tried hard to convince themselves and the world was strictly platonic), Rick woke her up and confronted her before storming out, never to be heard from again.

It was a dramatic ending for their otherwise drama-free relationship. Rick had been her rock, and despite his understandable ire that night, he was a truly decent guy. Brie was spot on, sensing his genuine nature within seconds of meeting him. Still, if someone had offered her a bet, Marley would have wagered all ten of her toes (with a couple fingers thrown in) there was no chance Richard Alabaster Smith would end up on a dating show.

She likely would have stayed with Rick forever, if her feelings for Sam hadn't toppled over the dam she'd so carefully built against them. Despite valiant efforts, she was incapable of denying the best friend crush that had been slowly burning for six years. After all, the heart wants what it wants. And what her heart wanted—had always wanted—was Sam.

Who could blame her? Her best friend since their freshman year of college, Sam was the most fascinating person she'd ever known. He had a great propensity for goofiness, and an uncanny ability to make her laugh, even in the direst of situations. Sweet, yet strong, with an amazing legal brain and sexy AF. He consumed every one of her senses. He was beautiful, with tousled, sun-kissed hair and eyes the color of the Caribbean Sea. His deep voice and hearty laughter were music. Her skin tingled every time he touched her. His kisses tasted like honey, and he smelled like a sunny day at the beach.

She'd never loved anyone like she loved Sam.

Looking at him now, slunk back on the couch in his faded Sea Isle tee shirt and sweatpants, she felt her heart skip. She took in his perfect profile, the long sweep of his lashes, the way he bit his lower lip whenever he was sleepy, aroused or deep in thought.

He rubbed her back with one hand as he held the neck of his beer between two fingers with the other and took a sip like a badass. No matter what he did, what he wore, what he said, he just oozed sexiness and Marley was grateful she no longer had to hide her feelings for him.

"I know what you're doing, Mar," he said, not taking his eyes off the TV as it went to commercial.

"Oh yeah?" She curled her legs under her and teased her

338

fingers through his hair. "What am I doing?"

"Undressing me with your eyes. I feel like a cheap piece of meat."

"Busted," Marley said. "Well played, Perdue."

Sam set his beer down, hit the pause button on the remote and pushed her into the plush cushions, emitting a lustful growl as he grasped her bottom and slid his leg between hers.

"Please don't ever stop looking at me that way," he whispered, as his lips brushed against hers. He kissed her lightly, grazing his teeth against her lower lip and playfully biting it, releasing a soft whimper as his teasing tongue probed deeper.

She rolled them over and straddled him. Her auburn waves fell around his face as she took her turn teasing his sensuous lips.

This is exactly what she left Rick for. The wild, untamed, full-throttled passion she felt for this man, who gazed up at her, helpless against her intentions.

He slid his hands inside the back of her leggings, his warm fingers clasping her cheeks. She slowly, seductively, undulated against his rigid hardness straining to be released. His head thrust back into the cushions and he gazed at her with sheer rapture.

"God, Marley," he moaned, "look what you do to me."

Marley pulled the waistband of his sweatpants aside, her fingers frantic to find her prize.

Sam let out a low grunt as she clasped his hot, throbbing member, fondling it before he flipped her on her back, hovered above her, teasing her lips with his.

He ran his fingers, light as a feather, down her navel and slid them into her leggings, past her soaked panties, until he found her sweet spot, satiny with anticipation.

"I'm about to rock your world," he whispered in her ear as his fingers swirled their magic.

"Oh, God," Marley moaned, back arching, not able to take any more.

They tore at their clothing and gave in to raw desire. The air between them practically combusted. Working each other to a frenzy, their passion erupted as they came together. As always.

"World...rocked..." Marley panted afterward, fully sated.

It had been a year, almost to the day, since Sam had confessed his love for Marley—when they scrambled out of the friend zone and dove into the relationship they'd been denying for years. It felt as if they'd made love a million times since then, yet each time was better than the one before, each encounter thrusting her further and further into an other-worldly dimension. Just what a simmering, sizzling, slow burn will do to friends destined to be more.

"God, I love you," he whispered as he fell against her, spent, chest heaving.

Her head spun and dopamine coursed through every inch of her being, rendering her powerless against movement.

His raspy words asked the question she pondered every time. "How does this keep getting better?"

"I don't know," she said, finally finding her voice, looking up at him. "It just does."

He clasped her hand in his, squeezing hard as he gazed at her. "You are the love of my life," he whispered. "Can I please marry the hell outta you now?"

She kissed the tip of his nose. "You know my answer. Not until we pass the bar."

They'd only just graduated from law school, and the monumental bar exam loomed a month ahead. She didn't want to make any major life changes until she found out she'd passed.

"What if you meet someone else before then?" he whined with a sad face.

She gave him a teasing glance. "I guess that's a chance you gotta take."

"Alright." He sighed. "Just be warned. If you ditch me, mine will be the next shattered heart stepping out of a limo on *The Bachelorette*. Only with better footwear."

She swatted him with a couch cushion, and he laughed. He may have been joking, but they both knew the truth.

Marley and Sam were in it for the long haul. Nothing would ever come between them.

About the Author

KIMBERLY BRIGHTON IS A FORMER CRIMINAL LAWYER, incidental humorist, and asparagus enthusiast from the Philadelphia area. She studied satirical writing and screen-writing at The Second City and is the author of *The Shore Blog*, a travel website, and *BlaBlaBlog*, a humor website. *The Way to Cape May* is her debut novel. When not dreaming up swoony romance plots, she spends her time searching for food expiration labels and sitting at red lights. Married for 25 laugh-filled years, she's discovered the key to a lasting marriage: takeout.

To stay in touch and learn about upcoming releases, sign up for her newsletter at KimberlyBrighton.com

Made in United States
North Haven, CT
27 August 2023

40818112R00211